Triplet Trouble For My Father's Best Friend

An Age Gap Surprise Pregnancy Romance
Claire Kirby

Contents

Chapter One

Emma

"Clark Stone was loved by his friends, family, and community alike. Many of you may know him as the owner operator of The Signature on Main, right here in Santa Fe, the stylish speakeasy-styled hotel that exploded in popularity after he and his late wife bought and remodeled it in celebration of the turn of a new century. The hotel was his..."

I zone out as the officiant continues to tell the crowd of people about my father's accomplishments.

Twirling a lock of strawberry blond hair around my finger, I take a peek at the group of people standing around the burial site.

Most of them are, in fact, community members; people my father dealt business with or employees at the hotel.

Everyone really did love him, and how could they not? Dad was the kind of person that people gravitated toward: charismatic, funny and sharp as a tack.

I glance slyly beside me—a frown mars my stepmother's perfectly curated appearance, a down-turned smear of pink against her pale skin.

Every now and again she sniffs dramatically and dabs her eyes with a suspiciously dry tissue. My step-sister Jackie stands beside her, sobbing loudly, a stark contrast from her mother.

I resist the urge to roll my eyes at her theatrics. It's really not fair; Jackie and I may not get along all that well, but I know that she really did love my dad.

"Now we will have a few members of the family say a few words for Clark. First up is his daughter, Emma." I look up at the officiant, who smiles at me warmly.

I swallow and offer the crowd a weak smile as I make my way to a spot next to the officiant. A tear makes its way down my cheek as I turn and face the crowd.

"Hi, I'm Emma. Clark was my dad." I croak, staring out at the crowd dumbly. How is my throat so dry when my eyes have been constantly leaking ever since the moment my dad took his last breath?

"I had a whole speech prepared but, um, it seems that I've forgotten it. Now that I'm standing here looking at everyone."

My stepmother clears her throat and arches a shaped brow. Her disapproval of this amount of honesty is written all over her face. The most important thing about this funeral for her is her image, as it is with everything.

Looking and being perfect is Frances' entire purpose in life. Which must be why she hates me so much—I'm an ever constant reminder of the fact that things in her life aren't perfect.

"Anyway... My dad is—was—a great person, but also a great father. He taught me so many things. Normal everyday things, like how to ride a bike, but he taught me other things, too. Like kindness, empathy, and compassion. He taught me humility, and to never take anything for granted."

I take a shaky breath and look out at the encouraging smiles of the crowd. My stepmother's face is the only stony one in the crowd.

"When I was six years old, my dad started taking me to the community kitchen every week. We would prepare food and spend time helping the people who came through. We always signed up under assumed names, because he didn't want it to be made into a big deal that he was there. He wanted it to be about helping people, and I think that really speaks to his character as a person. He would probably hate that I'm telling this to such a large group of people now, actually."

I chuckle and the crowd chuckles with me.

"We volunteered at that community kitchen every week up until his death. He was incredibly caring and dedicated, and has made lifelong friends because of his character. These are all things I admire a lot about my dad but, if I'm honest, the things that I will miss the most about my dad are the things that simply belonged to the two of us. Waking up to burnt pancakes every Sunday morning, because he was too impatient to let them cook over a low heat. Watching him sitting on the back patio with a pair of binoculars, as he observed the birds at his feeder. The way he would come into my room before bed and say— "

Tears stream down my cheeks as I take a deep, shaky breath. I'm almost done, and I can do this. "He would say, 'Tell me about your day, Emmybear. You know it's my favorite part of the day.'

My dad was a truly magnificent person, one who made the world so much better just by being here. I will miss him so much."

I wipe the tears streaming down my face and keep my face down as I walk back toward my stepmother. I step into place and her hand immediately grips around my arm. In a gesture that might look comforting to an onlooker, but the way that her nails are digging into my flesh stings, showing exactly how displeased she is.

"We worked on a speech for you, and it didn't include telling a crowd of people about how your father burned pancakes. Honestly, Emma, don't you have any class?" she hissed under her breath.

"That was a beautiful speech, Emma. Next I'll ask Frances to come up, Clark's wife for nearly eight years."

My stepmother smiles at the crowd and pats my arm before going to the officiant's side, leaving me and Jackie standing side-by-side. I stare at my stepmother, tuning out her speech and watching her face as she speaks the words she spent hours rehearsing in front of the mirror.

When I was a teenager, I was convinced that Frances was an alien, the way she would spend hours sitting in front of the mirror practicing facial expressions, or repeating phrases before events.

As time went on, though, and as I matured, I realized she was just obsessed with what people thought of her—all the time. It's all she's ever thought about.

I never have, and never will, understand what my dad saw in her, but I know he must have seen something. I just wish I knew what. I believe he must have just been so very lonely after Mom died.

Jackie throws an arm around me and sobs, bringing me back to the present moment. The gesture of affection takes me by surprise, and the only response I can muster is a gentle patting of her arm.

"The way he took Jackie in and treated her as his own speaks to what a truly incredible man Clark was. Jackie is his daughter as much as Emma is, and he never made her feel less than."

Frances smiles at the crowd and Jackie sobs even more. It's a good thing I don't like this dress, because I think it's toast with all the snot and tears soaking the sleeve.

***

"That was a beautiful service. I think everyone loved it."

Frances takes a mirror out of her purse and checks her reflection. She loves looking at herself. "Thank goodness for waterproof mascara, right girls?"

I don't mention how Frances didn't shed a single tear, but instead look over at Jackie, who is an irrefutable mess. The foundation she had immaculately applied this morning is patchy across her cheeks, baby pink lipstick smeared at the corner of her mouth. Her mascara is still undeniably intact, though. I'm sure I don't look much better.

"Wait, where are we going?" I ask as the car passes the entrance to our neighborhood.

"Oh, did I forget to tell you? We're hosting a repast at the hotel for some of your father's friends and business partners. He would have wanted that." She gives me an empty smile.

I'm sure my father would have wanted that, but it's not like she knows for certain. It's not like he had a will. My dad was only forty-five, and no one expected him to die so young.

In a car accident, no less. Truly, my stepmother's perfect makeup is a miracle considering the amount of bruising she still has on her face after hitting the dashboard in the accident.

"Mom, I don't think I can socialize. I just want to go home," Jackie says, frowning.

"This is a great way to honor your father's memory, dear. He would be so happy to see us celebrating him with some of his closest friends, don't you think?"

"I guess so." Jackie sighs heavily.

I almost feel bad for her. We've never gotten along, mostly because Frances discourages us spending time together. Jackie is a mean girl—not as mean as Frances, but she's played her own role in making my life miserable ever since the two of them arrived in our home.

Despite that, she loved spending time with my dad, more than with her own father, who sends a card once a year for Christmas, which is the extent of his involvement in her life. I don't think he even remembers her birthday. I pat her arm gently and she shrugs me off.

"Ugh, don't touch me. Your hands are all clammy and gross."

I roll my eyes and turn away. So much for the closeness displayed at the funeral.

The car pulls up in front of the hotel and we all get out.

I look out at the magnificent building wedged between a coffee shop and a historic bookstore. When my mom and dad bought the hotel originally, it was in bad shape.

An old saloon that had been left to the elements after prohibition ended, they decided to run with that theme and brought the hotel back to its former glory, all gorgeous wood floors and restored antique furniture filling its thirty rooms.

It even has a secret speakeasy in the basement, which is immensely popular with hotel guests and town locals alike.

As soon as we step through the front doors, Frances makes a beeline for the conference room, Jackie trailing behind her.

The smell of food prepared by our excellent chef permeates the room and, despite my growling stomach, I slink away behind the front desk and into my dad's office.

It's the one place that Frances hasn't changed—at least not yet.

The back wall is lined with bookshelves, filled with tons of books on business or classic novels that my dad loved.

A giant oak desk picked out by my mother sits in the center of the room, topped with pictures of me as a kid and sheaths of paper. I plop down in the comfy office chair and let out a huge sigh.

What happens now?

There's no will, and because of that, Frances gets the hotel. She knows nothing about the hotel business, and mostly keeps her nose out of it, beyond demanding an offending picture be removed or a certain alcohol be added in the bar.

Is she going to run the business my parents created together into the ground?

I open the top left hand drawer of the desk and pick up a picture of my mom and dad that he's kept there. It's a wedding photo, my mom smiling radiantly in a lacy white gown next to my dad. I can't help but smile.

Jackie would never have allowed him to keep the photo on display but there wasn't much she could do about it as long as it was out of her sight.

"You are the spitting image of your mom," my dad would always tell me.

It's true, too. I inherited her wavy red hair, millions of freckles and wide, round eyes. The only thing I got from my dad is my eye color, which my dad always called a 'radiant amber' while my stepmother has always likened them to pools of mud.

Opposite sides of the same coin, I suppose.

Three sharp raps at the door cause me to jump.

"Yes?" I say hesitantly. The door opens and the front desk girl, Lily, pokes her head in.

"Emma, I hate to bother you, I'm sure you're busy, but your stepmother is looking for you. She seems, um, pretty upset that you're not socializing with the guests."

Lily smiles at me wanly. None of the staff are fans of Frances, and they'll do anything to avoid her wrath. It's a miracle that we still have staff, honestly, although we have lost a couple of long term maids after Frances berated them about the way towels were folded in the linen closet.

"Okay, I'll be out in a second." I wave her away and she closes the door. I look at the photo one last time and sigh.

"I don't know what's going to happen to the hotel, guys, but I promise I'm going to do my best to make sure it doesn't go under."

I put the picture down and stand up, smoothing my dress. There are some unsightly stains on the shoulder as a result of Jackie's crying fit at the funeral, but there's nothing I can do about that at this point, really.

After taking a deep breath, I grab the door handle and brace myself for whatever is going to happen next.

Chapter Two

Lucas

I turn the page to take a look at the next property. When I talked about acquiring another property, my assistant delivered an entire folder of hotels currently on the market.

Some of them are good contenders, like the small boutique hotel, The Bryant, in New York City that features a rooftop garden. It is gorgeous, but I try to stay away from New York if I can.

It's not the competition—I know how to make a hotel stand out compared to a Marriott or a Hilton—it's just the sheer amount of people. I'm not anti-social, but there is never a quiet moment in New York. For some people, that's the appeal.

To me, that's my own version of hell. I thrive on quiet, little moments of refuge and escape amongst the chaos.

Still, if there are no other suitable options, The Bryant will present a good challenge for me. I sigh and put it in the maybe pile before taking a look at the next hotel.

The bold letters at the top of the page jump out at me and I sit up a little straighter. The Signature on Main.

I know this hotel. I've stayed in it many times, and quite frankly, I'm surprised to see it sitting in this pile of potential acquisitions.

Clark is thinking about selling?

I rub my chin, memories running through my mind. I remember when Clark and Ginny, his late wife, bought the property twenty-five years ago. Ginny was pregnant, and nervous about such a large under-taking.

I assured them both that I would assist them along the way. I installed many of the light fixtures myself, helped Clark restore furniture and Ginny figure out the logistics of insurance and policy.

Their acquisition of The Signature on Main is what kick started my own interest in the hotel game.

After helping them get their boutique hotel on the map, I was hungry for more. There was something exhilarating about taking something that wasn't doing well and turning it into a successful business. I don't specialize in renovating older buildings into hotels, though.

No, my business is more focused on acquiring failing hotels and then making them profitable again.

I love giving hotels new life, at least as it relates to their business potential and profitability. It's not that I mind rolling up my sleeves and doing the dirty work of painting walls and installing flooring, which I did plenty of in the early days; I just prefer the numbers.

Seeing the P&L numbers a hotel starts with when I acquire it, and then watching those numbers move into positive territory just gives me a thrill that can't be replicated in any other area of my life.

Not that I haven't tried.

Many of my personal relationships have been what Ginny had called fixer-uppers. I never thought of them that way—I've never gone into a relationship trying to change someone.

But if I really reflect, and am honest with myself, I guess I do have a habit of wanting to play the hero, of making someone else's life better, of rescuing a woman who I think needs to be rescued. The whole 'damsel in distress' thing, I suppose.

The problem is that the other person has to want to be rescued, too. And, as I've learned through hard experience, a lot of women don't.

I'm not sure if I'm reading the signals incorrectly or if they truly don't need to be rescued at all.

"Mr. Bennett?"

My assistant, Royce, knocks and then opens the door. I resist the urge to sigh heavily. Royce has been with me for almost a year and a half, and no matter how many times I ask, he just will not wait for a response before opening the door. It's not like I'm doing anything here that necessitates privacy, I just prefer it. For some reason, Royce doesn't seem to get that.

"Yes?"

"Elaine Griggs is on the phone for you, she really wants to schedule that interview."

Royce smiles, and I resist the urge to grimace. Elaine Griggs, a local reporter, has been a thorn in my side trying to get an interview for a feature piece on me. I think she's less interested in me from a work standpoint than she is from a personal one, but I have no interest in Elaine, so I've been dodging her for well over a month.

"I'm going over potential acquisitions right now. Tell her to send me an email, please."

Royce nods before closing the door. It's the same thing I say every time she calls, and she never emails. I shake my head and turn back to the paper in my hands. It lists the hotel's assets—thirty gorgeously designed rooms, full service, and a luxurious speakeasy located in the basement. It doesn't list the perfectly curated garden space located in the back of the hotel that I'm familiar with, which might be why it's only valued at nineteen million dollars.

I frown. Clark selling is unexpected—this place is as much his baby as his daughter Emma is, and his selling is out of character to an absurd degree.

I open my laptop and type his name into the search bar—I've had a very limited social media presence, preferring my privacy, but I know Clark will always be on it as a community staple.

The first thing that comes up isn't a profile from any social sites, but instead an obituary. I'm stunned, unable to move for a second before I click on the link.

Clark Stone, 45, of Santa Fe, New Mexico, passed away in a car accident on March 8th. A beloved member of the community and owner of The Signature on Main...

I skip past the background information that I already know by heart—the story of The Signature on Main that proudly hangs on the main wall in an article done by The Santa Fe Times, featuring a picture of him, Ginny, and a young Emma standing in front of the hotel.

Clark Stone is preceded in death by his parents, Margaret and Giles Stone, and his first wife, Virginia Stone. He is survived by his wife, Frances Stone, and two daughters, Jacqueline and Emma Stone.

I blink, unable to process the news before me. Clark is dead. How could I not know? He died almost a month ago, and not a single word from Frances.

Not that it's surprising, I suppose. A memory from their reception seven years ago surrounds me.

***

"Isn't she beautiful?" Clark asks, walking up to me and smiling proudly. My eyes shoot to where Frances is standing, talking to another wedding guest. Her long dress is tight fitted, with a veil that stretches long past her heels and trails behind her.

"She looks lovely. I'm very happy for you," I say, a smile lighting up my face. I hate to admit this, but I've always been a good liar, which is why he had no inkling that I was skeptical of Frances from the beginning.

She presents perfectly—polite, civil, and smart. There's just something under the surface that always gives me pause, as if everything she puts out in the world is an act and she's on stage.

"Is Emma excited?" I ask him.

"She misses her mom," Clark responds, his smile dropping a little.

I feel Frances' eyes slip to us despite not facing us.

"It was hard for her when Ginny died. Well, hard for both of us. It's been just the two of us for quite a while now. I certainly think it will be an adjustment... but she gets along with Jackie, and the two girls spend a lot of time together. I think it will be good."

I nod and take a sip of my drink. I won't tell him about what I witnessed earlier when passing by the bridal room.

Jackie and Frances both insisted that Emma wear a different dress than the one she had chosen for herself, telling her she was looking 'a little pudgy' in it.

I had easily picked up on the tone beneath her words, of the disdain Frances had while telling Emma that she would look much better in the plainer dress that she chose for her. It's better to not ruin his happiness.

"That's good. With time, I'm sure you will all come together." We both turn to look at Frances, who is staring at the two of us like a hawk.

"She looks a little concerned."

"Ah. She gets a little nervous... just because of everything with Ginny. I assure her that I love her, and that Ginny is my past while she is my future. Still, she is a little insecure about it."

"What does that have to do with me?"

"Well, you knew Ginny, we were all close. I think she gets anxious about people from my past reminding me of Ginny." Clark's eyes are filled with sincerity but I can't help the grimace that slides over my face.

"You're allowed to remember her."

"Of course, but I can imagine that it's hard to feel that you're constantly in the shadow of someone else. Not that she is, but if Ginny were still alive, I wouldn't be marrying Frances, and I think she knows that."

We both look at each other before I sigh.

"We won't be seeing much of each other from now on, will we?"

Clark's eyes cast downward as he pats my shoulder.

"You'll always be my dearest friend, Lucas. You know you always have a place here, a place in my family."

"But?"

"I want Frances to be happy."

I nod, swallowing.

"I understand," I say. And I do—we might send an email every now and again, but it's clear that there won't be any more long vacations visiting each other.

"You'll always have me, too. You've been my best friend since high school, and always will be. I know Frances' happiness is important to you."

Clark smiles and wraps me in a hug.

"Thank you. You're the best friend I could ask for."

***

I wipe away a tear as I'm brought back to my office and the present day.

If I had known then what I know now, that Clark would die without me even being able to say goodbye, would I have accepted our drifting apart so easily?

I should have reached out more. We sent Christmas cards, emails, presents, but when was the last time we had an extended conversation?

Honestly, it was at the wedding. I can't believe I let this happen.

Even more, I can't believe I let Frances get in the way of our friendship because of her own insecurities. I didn't like the woman before, but now?

There's a rage burning inside of me at the rift that she caused between the two of us. Before Frances, Clark and I would talk every single day, even after I moved to Edgewood.

When he was with Ginny, she fostered our friendship even more, becoming more like another best friend rather than my friend's wife.

The fact that the hotel is for sale tells me two things—one, Frances has no respect for Clark's memory and simply wants to monetize it. If she ever loved Clark, she would know how important the hotel was to him. So perhaps she didn't love him.

The second thing it tells me is that Clark didn't have a will, because if he did, he would have left the hotel to Emma. He told me that he wanted Emma to have the hotel one day. There's no way in hell he would have let it be sold or turned it over to Frances to run.

I stand up and stretch before grabbing my suit jacket off the back of my chair. It's one of those lumbar support chairs, something that Clark introduced me to and that I've continued to use ever since.

Royce looks up in surprise when I open my office door. I don't usually leave before five, even taking lunch in my office most days.

"Mr. Bennett?"

"Royce, I need you to reschedule all my appointments for the next two weeks, and book me a suite at The Signature on Main in Santa Fe. I have some business to attend to there."

"Ah, I knew that one would catch your eye. I remember you grew up there."

Royce smiles and taps his temple, as if remembering where I grew up is some obscure trivia that he tucked away to whip out at the perfect moment.

"Thank you. Book yourself a room, too. I get the feeling I'll need assistance while there." I give him a smile before heading to the elevator. The truth is that I don't trust Royce to mess up a million little things while I'm away—he's best kept under a watchful eye. I've considered letting him go, but there is potential there. I just have to develop it.

"Certainly, Mr. Bennett."

Chapter Three

Emma

"Come on!" I groan as I struggle to get my hands out of the fluffy blue comforter. I finally pull a hand free and slap my alarm clock off my nightstand.

Most people set their alarms on their phones these days; unfortunately, I have a tendency to sleep right through those, which is why I have a traditional style alarm clock, complete with two dinging bells on the top.

I'm not ready to get up.

A groan sounds from the spot next to me as Jackson, my twelve year old golden retriever, stretches as he wakes up. Jackson was technically my mom's dog—she adopted him from the local shelter when he was a puppy and he was five when she died.

The runt of his litter, he was expected to have health problems for life, which deterred any would-be adopters.

My mom, though, saw the potential in Jackson, and saved him from "death row" as she called it. My mom always loved potential in unusual places. It's the same reason that she and my dad created The Signature on Main.

Jackson sits up and blinks slowly. Gray fur marks his face, but despite his age he still has puppy energy a lot of the time. He does nap a lot more, though.

"I guess we have to start the day sometime, don't we?" I say. Jackson lets out a long doggy sigh before lying down.

Oh, well. It seems like I'm the only one who has to start the day.

Stretching, I climb out of bed before heading into my en suite bathroom to take a shower. The bathroom is more like an extension of my room, decorated in the same cool blue tones with plants covering most every surface.

The skylight in the ceiling allows the filtered light in, to keep the plants happy.

I soak in the hot water as it runs over me from above. A few years ago, my dad helped me install a rainwater showerhead in the bathroom. He is everywhere, a part of every aspect of my life in ways that most people can't even imagine.

It's been almost a month since I lost him and it's still hard. Today is burnt pancake day, but as I get dressed and head downstairs, there's no sweet smell wafting through the house.

Despite the wax warmers filled with scents of lilies and begonias set all over the home, courtesy of Frances, there's no warmth here. It's almost sterile, now lacking my dad's strong and loving presence.

When I step into the kitchen, Jackie is sitting at the counter on her laptop.

"Hey," she mutters without looking up. Although it seems cold, it's actually more than I usually get from Jackie.

"Hey. What are you up to today?" I ask as I pull a bottle of orange juice from the fridge and pop some toast in the toaster.

"Looking at wallpapers. There's these cute floral ones, kinda moody. I think they'll be pretty." Her voice is flat, almost monotone.

"Oh, are you redecorating your room?

Jackie's brows fly to her forehead as she looks up at me.

"Wait, has mom not talked to you?" This time there's expression in her voice—surprise. My brows knit together.

"About what?"

"Oh, um. You know what, I have to get to yoga. I'm meeting Delilah." Jackie closes her laptop and scurries from the room.

That was weird.

I finish my breakfast and load the dishwasher before heading into the living room. If Dad was alive, we'd be heading to the community kitchen in an hour. I haven't been back since he died, though.

And I know that's wrong. Dad would be disappointed in me.

It just feels empty without him. I can't muster the same enthusiasm, and I don't want to feel like I'm doing a chore going there. It never felt like a chore when I was there with him.

"Oh, Emma, I'm glad you're here," my stepmother's voice rings into the empty living room, taking me by surprise.

I'm pretty sure she's never said those words to me before.

"You are?"

"Yes, I need to talk to you about something."

She briskly walks across the room, sitting down next to me. Her white dress is immaculate, a thin gold belt accentuating her waist. Her makeup is perfect, like always, as her blue eyes stare into me.

There's nothing but coldness behind them, and not for the first time, I wonder what my dad saw behind her pretty exterior.

"Jackie and I were talking, and we really think it would be a wonderful idea to do some renovations."

"What kind of renovations?" I ask. Jackie putting wallpaper up is more in the realm of remodeling in my opinion, but I guess it could be considered a renovation.

"Well, you know Jackie's room is really quite small, considering that it used to be your mother's office. I just think she could really do with more room, and she agrees. So we're going to be knocking the wall down between your rooms."

I freeze. Knocking the wall down? Jackie doesn't have her own en suite bathroom, which I know bothers her, but how is sharing a bathroom with me going to be better?

"I don't really want to share a room with Jackie."

Frances barks out a laugh and smoothes her skirt.

"Oh, no, of course not. That would be silly, you're both adults." Frances gives me a toothy smile. It's more akin to a dog baring its teeth.

"You'll be moving to the basement."

I blink.

"That's been my room since I was born."

My parents specifically decorated the nursery before I was born. I grew up in that room. It is filled with memories from my life. My mom and I painted it together when I was in middle school. She can't possibly be serious.

"I know, and don't you think it's time for a change? I mean the basement is finished. It has its own bathroom and its own kitchen! I think it will really be great for you to branch out."

Frances shimmies her hands with excitement but I sit up straighter, now on edge.

"No, I don't think it's time for a change. That's my room, and I don't want to give it to Jackie."

The fake smile Frances dons flattens, her lips pressing together.

"Emma, I'm not asking you. This is my house, and I'm telling you that we are knocking the wall down between the two rooms. It will be Jackie's room. The way I see it, you have two options: you can move down to the basement, and live rent-free due to my generosity. Or you can find your own place in town.

"Now I know what I'd rather do, but I can't stop you from moving out if that's your choice."

Frances fluffs her hair and gives me a forced smile. "I'll need you to move your things out of the room by next weekend so that we can start the renovations right away."

"I work all week." As the manager of the hotel, the work isn't physically grueling, but there is a lot to do and I like to rest after work. Like a normal person.

"I guess you better get started then!"

Frances claps her hands together and stands up.

"I have a meeting with the contractor. I didn't have any time to get moving boxes, so you might want to head out as soon as you can and start packing. Anything left after a week I'll just have to get rid of."

I watch as she leaves the room, anger running through my veins. It's not enough for my dad to die, she apparently wants me totally miserable. I take a deep breath and blink away the tears. If I cry, then she wins, and I'm not going to let her control me like that.

Sighing, I stand up to grab my keys. Looks like I'm taking a trip to grab some boxes.

***

Monday's are always filled with paperwork, numbers reports and the weekly staff meeting.

When I was a teenager and started showing interest in the hotel, my dad would schedule the meetings after school so that I could attend. There was always coffee and bagels from the little shop next door, and it was clear how much respect he had for the staff.

There was clear communication about everything going on in the hotel. My dad made sure to recognize a member of staff every week, mentioning that Sandra had received compliments for her turn-down service or Carter had glowing reviews from guests.

Since his death, she insisted on being involved and running the meetings, despite having no interest in running a hotel.

We still served coffee and bagels, but there was no further staff recognition, and it became very much about increasing numbers, making profits. There was little heart left in the meetings after Frances took them over.

Dad always seemed happy when Frances showed any kind of interest in the hotel, not seeming to notice the way everything she touched turned shortly to shit once she got involved.

It's as if she has the Midas touch in reverse.

"Is everyone here?" Frances asks, smiling at us as we sit at the tables in the conference room. About half of the faces in the room are brand new, starting within the last two months.

Before Frances took over from Dad, our staff hadn't turned over in years, but she started driving them away too, and we've lost several long term employees recently.

Jackie glides in, late as always, and grabs a bagel before slinking to the back of the room.

"Wonderful. This week's meeting is going to be a little different than usual."

"Miss Frances," Jonas, the head of the maintenance crew chirps up, "there is something important about the new showerheads that I... "

"Jonathon, are you interrupting me right now?" Frances asks, scoffing as she shakes her head.

"I apologize," Jonas shifts uncomfortably, not bothering to correct her. It would be futile—she knows what his name is.

"Of course you do. As we know, things are a little different here now without the presence of my beloved husband."

She clutches her chest before letting out a big sniff and dramatically wiping away an invisible tear.

"We are all devastated by the loss. To be frank with all of you, despite my best efforts, I know very little about the hotel game. It's not easy for me to admit this fault of mine to you all, but I truly think that the hotel would do much better in the hands of someone else. With a heavy heart, I have to tell you all that I have listed the hotel for sale."

"What?" I shoot up. "You can't sell the hotel!"

"Emma, please, I am not done." Frances smiles tightly before continuing, but I'm not listening anymore.

This is where I grew up. My father's heart and soul is poured into this business, and she cannot do this. I sit numbly, blocking out her words until the meeting ends. Her heels click as she leaves the room and I follow after her.

"Frances," I say loudly, but she pretends not to hear me. "Frances! I'm talking to you."

She whips her head around, seemingly surprised by my boldness. It almost surprises me a little, too.

"You don't need to yell at me, dear."

"You can't sell the hotel."

"Oh, Emma, I know it's hard to hear, but this place... it's just too much for me. I have my hands full."

She pastes on a look of faux sympathy, one that I've seen her practice in the mirror many times.

"It's not too much for me! I can handle the hotel. I know what I'm doing." I look at her with determination. "Just let me have it."

Frances smiles at me before patting my shoulder.

"Honey, I would love to do that. Unfortunately, I'm not sure you're ready, and who's around to make sure it goes smoothly? I've already talked to a few lawyers, and selling is truly the best option."

"I'll buy it from you."

Frances laughs.

"With what money? This hotel is valued at nineteen million dollars, which is sure to go up after a couple of renovations."

"I—" I lick my lips. I have some money saved up, but I definitely don't have nineteen million dollars. I didn't inherit anything from my dad, since he didn't have a will. "Please, Frances. Don't do this."

A sickly sweet smile spreads across her face.

"I'll tell you what, Emma. If you can come up with the money in... say, six months? You can have the hotel. I know you think I'm being mean, but this is truly for the best."

She smoothes her hair. "Oh, I'll also need you to get your father's personal effects out of his office. It needs updating."

She spins on her heel and clicks away. Tears prick at my eyes as I look down at my feet. There's no way I can come up with nineteen million dollars in six months.

"Miss Emma?" Joe, the old doorman who has worked here since the hotel opened, touches my arm. "Anything I can do for you?"

I smile at him and shake my head as a tear falls down my cheek.

"Thank you, Joe, but I don't think so. I'll be in the office if anyone needs me."

As soon as I'm at the office door, I slide down the wall and let the tears flow freely.

Chapter Four

Lucas

I stare up at the face of the hotel that I helped build with my best friend.

Clean black bricks frame the original big leaded glass windows that allow a peek into the gorgeous lobby, plants picked out by Ginny hanging and still going strong in the windows after all these years.

The golden letters naming the hotel still gleam brilliantly, almost as shiny as the day we put them up so long ago.

"Wow, this place is beautiful," Royce says as he comes up beside me with two cups of coffee. "Here's your coffee."

I smile tightly and take the cup from him. Sending him to grab a cup of coffee was truly just my way of getting away from him for a short period of time.

The car ride from Edgewood to Santa Fe is only an hour, but with Royce chattering incessantly the whole time, it felt like it lasted ten years.

"Thank you, Royce." I take a sip before heading inside, not listening to what he says as he follows behind me.

Stepping into the lobby is like taking a step back into the past. I remember putting up the gold chandelier that is the lobby's centerpiece, emerald colored crystals hanging from the lights.

The walnut check-in desk is exactly the same, sepia colored prohibition-era photos hanging behind it. Still, there are differences.

The ruby red couches that used to occupy the corner by the elevators have been replaced by sleek, cream colored couches, and a large picture of Frances and Clark hangs beside the elevator. I immediately notice the slight off-centeredness of it.

"Welcome to The Signature on Main! Checking in?" The girl behind the counter chirps, a customer service smile lighting her face.

"Yes, we have two reservations. One for Mr. Lucas Bennett and another for Royce Johnson. That's me. Thank you...Lily," Royce chimes in, giving her a boyish smile as he reads her nametag.

I resist the urge to groan. Royce tries his best to be charming, but between the messy mop of brown curls on his head and the slightly too large dress shirt, he is more reminiscent of a kid playing businessman.

"For you, Mr. Johnson," she says a moment later, handing Royce his room key. She looks up at me through her lashes. "And for you, Mr. Bennett."

"Thanks," I spit out gruffly. Lily blushes and I have to look away.

I'm aware of the effect I have on women—I'd have to be blind not to be. It doesn't make it any less uncomfortable for me, though. I can turn up the charm when I need to, but I don't feel the need to flirt with every woman who crosses my path. "When did they change the couches?"

Lily looks over to the sitting area and blinks.

"Oh, have you stayed with us before? Honestly, I'm not quite sure when the couches were changed, they've been the white ones since I started here almost eight months ago." She shrugs.

The door behind the check-in desk opens and my heart speeds up, almost expecting Clark to be walking out of the office. That's impossible though. Dead people don't appear out of offices.

The woman that steps out instead, though, definitely has my attention.

She's tall, despite wearing flats and it's easy to see how shapely her long legs are with black pants so tight, they could be painted on. The deep green blouse she's sporting is unbuttoned at the top, leaving only an idea of the cleavage underneath.

Long red waves fall down her shoulders, and freckles cover her face. If I didn't know any better, I'd think Ginny was walking out of that office.

"Hey, Lily, I'm going out to grab some lunch. Do you want me to bring anything back?" When she looks up, my eyes meet her warm green ones, and it immediately clicks who I'm looking at.

"Emma?" I can't hide the surprise that is infused in my voice. The last time I saw Emma, she was a gangly, awkward teenager sporting braces and thick bangs. This isn't an awkward teenager standing before me, though.

No, this is a woman in front of me.

Her forehead crinkles, as if trying to place me for a moment before recognition lights her eyes.

"Clark Bennett?" There's hesitation in her voice, as if worried about a case of mistaken identity. I laugh.

"Yes, that's correct. It's been a while since we've last seen each other—I think it was at your father's wedding."

Her lips flatten as she nods.

"Right. Of course, I remember." Emma clears her throat. "Well, um, I'm sorry. I don't know if you've heard. My father passed away about a month ago now."

I nod and tuck my hands into my pockets.

"Yes, I heard. That's why I'm here, actually. I wanted to give my condolences in person. I'm sorry I couldn't make it to the funeral."

I don't know why I'm apologizing. I didn't even know the funeral was happening, and it aggravates me that Frances couldn't even be bothered to tell Clark's best friend that he passed away. I'll never forgive her for having to find out via Google.

Emma nods, but says nothing. What is there to say to that? I guess I wouldn't know, either.

"You said you're going to lunch? Let me treat. I'd love to catch up and learn more about what's going on in your life," I say, and I can't ignore the hope rising in my chest with the question.

Lunch with a beautiful woman was definitely not something that I had anticipated when arriving in Santa Fe.

No, I shouldn't think like that. This is lunch with my late best friend's daughter. That's all it is.

"Oh, sure! I was thinking of going to La Bouchon? I don't know if you care for French food."

"I know a great Italian place on the other side of town if you're interested? It's never let me down," I tell her.

I raise a brow. Emma's face flushes, and she looks down, letting her red hair fall over her face in an attempt to hide her blushing cheeks.

"Yeah, that sounds good, let me just finish up in the office. I'll meet you here in fifteen minutes?"

"Fifteen minutes then." I nod and head toward the elevators as she slinks back into the office. Royce follows, shuffling the room keys in his hands.

"Want me to make a reservation for three?" He pulls out his phone and looks at me expectantly as we step into the elevator.

"Actually, Royce, this is more of a personal lunch. Catching up and talking about her father. It would probably be best for you to stay behind this time." I do my best to let him down gently, but it doesn't stop him from deflating.

"Oh, right, of course." He presses the button and stands beside me silently for a moment. "That Emma sure is gorgeous."

I don't say anything, shifting to look at the watch on my wrist.

"Do you think she's single?" Royce asks. I turn to look at him.

"I'm not sure, but I don't think it's a good idea for you to get interested in a woman who lives an hour away."

"Yeah, maybe not," he responds glumly.

The doors open and I let out a breath. I let Royce lead the way, and try to ignore the fact that I've been wondering if Emma is single since I laid eyes on her.

***

"Oh, wow, this place is beautiful," Emma says as we're seated at a table in Bella Napoli. The table I requested—the one that I always used to sit at when I came here with Clark—has a view of the city with the mountains in the background. It truly is a marvel.

"I think so, too. The food is great as well."

"Thanks for bringing me here."

Emma opens the menu. I observe her as I pretend to look at my own. Full lashes flutter against her deliciously blushed cheeks, a strand of hair falling over her shoulder and gracing the table with its presence. Her pink, heart shaped lips part slightly as she reads the menu silently to herself.

"Of course. This was one of your father's favorite places to host business lunches."

I shift uncomfortably at the mention of Clark. I shouldn't be looking at the lips of my best friend's daughter.

"I was very surprised to learn of your father's passing. I only learned through reading his obituary."

"Frances didn't inform you?" Her eyes dart up to me, annoyance evident in her tone. She shakes her head. "No, of course she didn't."

"You don't get along with Frances?"

"We get along fine." Her tone is curt, warning that this particular conversation topic was off limits. "How is business?"

The server interrupts, and we order two glasses of wine before I get to answer her.

"Business is good. I don't know how much you remember about what I do... "

"I know you're also in the hotel business. Dad always talked about how you helped him build this hotel."

"Yes, I own a series of hotels, most of them quite similar to The Signature on Main."

Emma stares at me, suspicion marring her features. Clearly I've said something wrong here.

"Are you trying to buy the hotel?" she asks, the words leaving her with such venom that it catches me off guard. The server drops our wine at the table before scurrying off, sensing the tension.

"I haven't thought about acquiring the hotel, yet. I was so surprised by the news of your father's death that purchasing the hotel wasn't at the front of my mind."

I take a sip of my wine and Emma mirrors me. "I have to admit, though, I was surprised to see it in my pile of possible acquisitions. I never imagined your father would sell. In fact, I always thought he would leave the hotel to you."

Emma sighs as she stares out of the window.

"He wanted to. He would tell me all the time, 'This place is yours. Yours to do whatever you want with.' But he didn't have a will when he died. Why would he? He was only forty-five. That's not old enough to think about dying."

I chuckle.

"I have to agree with you there. I don't think forty-five is old at all." I shrug a shoulder and smile at her. She raises her brows in surprise before letting out a giggle and looking down.

"Of course," she sighs. "I'm sorry if I seem combative. I don't… I don't want to sell the hotel. Frances technically owns it, though, and she just doesn't care about it one way or the other. She can't wait to cash it in, if I'm honest."

"I got that sense when I knew her back then."

Emma studies me, searching for some unknown thing in my face.

"You were my dad's best friend."

"Yeah."

"Why'd you stop visiting? Where have you been all these years?"

My brows shoot up my forehead. I wasn't expecting this bold line of questioning, but I suppose I should have been.

Her mother was a spitfire, something Clark always loved about her. It makes sense that Emma would have inherited that temperament.

"Ah, well. It wasn't by choice. Frances didn't seem to approve of our friendship very much. Your father and I had a conversation about it. We both knew that we would see little of each other after they got married, but please understand that it doesn't mean he wasn't my best friend. Clark was and always will be my best friend."

"Of course it was Frances," Emma mutters. A pensive look strikes her face as the server puts our plates in front of us.

"I do regret it. I don't want you to think I stayed away to avoid her—I just didn't want to make your dad's life any harder. He deserved to have an easier life, so I was trying to make that possible." I swallow. "Your father was a very good man."

"Yeah. He was." Emma looks out the window, the food in front of her seemingly forgotten.

This certainly isn't the catch-up lunch I was expecting.

Chapter Five

Emma

When Lucas and I return from lunch, my mood is still sour. I almost feel bad for him—I know I wasn't the best lunch company.

I shouldn't have even agreed to lunch with him considering the way I was feeling.

There was just something about that moment, with a handsome man asking me to lunch, that compelled me to say yes.

And he is handsome.

It would be an understatement to say that I was shocked when I heard him call my name. He's taller than I am, which is saying a lot considering that I tower over most people. His hazel eyes are piercing, his jaw strong, and his smile enough to melt any girl's heart.

I felt like he was staring right through me all during lunch. Not that it was a bad thing. His hair is longer than you'd expect, but styled immaculately, dark, peppered with streaks of gray.

Honestly, he's gorgeous. Easily the most handsome man I've ever laid eyes on, but he's also twenty years my senior. Not to mention he was my dad's best friend, which adds another layer of impropriety to it.

Surely he has his pick of gorgeous, age appropriate women lining up for him. I know he's not married, since he doesn't wear a ring.

Not that I was looking for a ring exactly. I just happened to notice when he was sipping his wine, and when I Googled him later—just out of curiosity and to see which hotels he owned—I confirmed his bachelor status.

"Lucas Bennett?" I hear a familiar grating voice chirp as Lucas and I step into the lobby of the hotel. I resist the urge to roll my eyes as Frances steps up to us, her clicking heels echoing across the lobby.

Before Frances, we had a cozy runner lining the hall for noise reduction. When she started to complain about the runner giving her allergies, she convinced Dad to get rid of it.

"Hello, Frances," Lucas responds as she wraps him in a hug and kisses his cheek. I gag silently, and only when Lucas laughs do I realize that he saw the gesture.

"How are you? I'm so sorry to hear about Clark. I read about his obituary online."

Frances pulls away quickly and gapes, panic coloring her eyes. I turn away so that I can smile. He's bold, I'll give him that. He's not afraid to make Frances squirm.

"Oh goodness, yes, it was so sudden. Please forgive me for not telling you, it was just such a trying time, you know. It's never easy when the person we love passes."

Frances places her hand over her heart and frowns. It would appear genuine to someone who doesn't know her, or see through her act.

"Of course," Lucas says curtly. He's not buying any of the bull she's selling today. "I wanted to offer my condolences in person. I'm sure that you could use some help managing the hotel during this time."

Frances gets a mischievous glint in her eye.

"You know, I could use assistance. I'm actually selling the hotel." She feigns regret. "I don't want to, but without Clark here, I'm up to my ears in paperwork and renovations, not to mention the staffing issues we've been dealing with over the past few years. From what I remember, you own quite a few hotels. I'd love to pick your brain about how best to go about this."

Frances steps up and places a hand on his arm. If I didn't know any better, I'd think she was flirting with him. Instead of gagging again, I retreat to the office in hopes of having some solace. I can only handle so much of watching Frances try to manipulate people in one day.

***

"All right, Jackson, it's time to get some moving done," I mutter as I take the elastic around my wrist and throw my hair in a sloppy bun. Jackson whines, laying his head down on my soft comforter.

I'm not sure how to move out my bed. It's an enormous, comfortable king. I spent a ton of time finding the perfect mattress topper, and covered it with two duvets and a comforter. Not to mention all the pillows. All of this will be hard to fit into the basement space.

A problem for future Emma to handle, though. I guess I'll have to call some movers and just squeeze it in somehow. For now, the boxes of memories and clothes are a good start. I still can't believe she's forcing me out of my own room. Frances really is evil incarnate.

I hoist a box of clothes on my hip and stumble. Damn, I almost threw my back out.

"I'm going to have to be more careful. Hard to take you on walks if I'm on bed rest for weeks." I look over at Jackson. "Are you coming with me?"

He whines and snuggles deeper into the blanket. I sigh. That's what I get for making my bed so comfortable: a traitorous dog.

I take the stairs carefully one by one, ensuring that I'm holding the banister with my free hand. When I reach the ground floor the front door swings open, nearly knocking me over. I steady myself as three people step into the home.

"We're looking at doing some renovations to the house as well—things that Clark and I had talked about before he passed. There's nothing like death that makes you feel like you need to start doing the things you planned."

Frances' shrill voice assaults my ears as she steps through the front door with Lucas and Jackie in tow.

"I'd love to know more about the hotel business. I've really always had such an interest in it, and, while there's a lot I learned from Dad, I know it's not everything there is to learn," Jackie is chirping as she follows along. I roll my eyes.

Jackie has never taken an interest in the hotel. She'll hang around for the free food or have drinks at the speakeasy, but she's never once paid attention in a meeting and never asked my dad about anything to do with the business. She must have gotten her lying abilities from her mom.

"Hello, Emma." Lucas' eyes find mine immediately in the dim hallway, and my cheeks heat up immediately.

I'm more than a little embarrassed by my appearance at this moment.

If I'd known that the hottest man I've ever laid eyes on would be walking through my door, I'd be wearing something better than my ratty cloud pajama pants and a grey tank top. I move a self conscious hand to my face—I already took off all my makeup, and the circles under my eyes are distinctly reminiscent of a raccoon.

"Hi."

"Oh, hello, Emma. I didn't see you," Frances says coolly. "I invited Lucas to dinner to talk business."

"Are you eating with us?" Jackie asks, although she doesn't seem particularly interested in whether I am or not judging by how quickly she whips out her phone.

"Judging by the box in her arms, Emma is a little busy moving. Perhaps next time?" my stepmother answers for me.

She starts toward the dining room. Lucas doesn't move and Jackie looks between the two of them, seemingly unsure if she should follow or stick around.

"You're moving out?" An eyebrow shoots up.

A shudder goes through me—the way he looks at me is tantalizing, as if he can see right into the depths of my soul and know everything.

"Under, actually. I'm being relegated to the basement."

"Emma!" I whip my head around to see Frances standing down the hall, her face contorted with anger. I've never seen her show outward anger in front of another person before, much less because of me.

She must catch onto the fact that she just lost control in front of her guest, because she blinks before letting out a chuckle. "That is such an inappropriate joke. We're simply doing renovations."

She looks at Lucas, who looks between the two of us before nodding.

I continue outside to the exterior entrance to the basement in the midst of the awkward situation, but I feel eyes on my back as I leave. I just can't tell if it's Frances' daggers or Lucas' smolder.

***

Jackson whines at me as I'm about to head out the door with another box.

"I told you that you could come with me, you don't have to stay in here the whole time," I say out loud. Even though he's a dog, I do think he understands most of what I'm saying, which is why I engage in conversation with him way more often than I really should.

He barks and jumps off the bed, wagging his tail.

"Oh, I get it. You have to do business."

I look around the room. There's still a lot to move, and I don't have to get it all done today, but I definitely prefer to have it done sooner rather than later. A break would be nice, though.

"Okay, let's go on a run." Jackson barks again. "Shhh, you're gonna rile up the wicked witch."

I pad quietly down the stairs in my running clothes with Jackson so as not to disturb anyone.

Then I round the corner to where his leash is hanging up, being cautious not to make too much noise.

Just to be courteous, of course. It's definitely not so I can eavesdrop.

"...and you know, I'm just not sure if it's sale ready yet," Frances' voice floats from the dining room.

"I think nineteen million is rather low for the property, personally," Lucas responds.

I grip the leash a little harder. I don't know Lucas, not really, but it somehow still feels like a betrayal to hear him talking about the sale of the hotel I practically grew up in.

"That's what I thought, but I don't know anything about hotels. The appraiser said that there isn't a cohesive look to the hotel."

"Have you been updating the rooms? My room looks like the original one that Clark and I designed, but my assistant's room is... newer."

My breath catches in my throat. Frances has been on an updating spree. The updated rooms are more 'modern', with stark white furniture and marble finishes. It doesn't match the themes of the prohibition room, and the changes were not something my father really approved of.

"Yes, I convinced Clark that it was time to give the hotel a more modern appeal. The prohibition theme is so... tacky."

"Personally—and I'm saying this as a potential buyer, not as someone who helped design the hotel—the prohibition theme is going to sell. It's not tacky. It's not cowboy paraphernalia covering the walls and horseshoes hanging in the bathrooms. The furniture pieces are quality antiques, the color themes specifically chosen to be reminiscent of the period without being gaudy.

"The juxtaposition of modern in some places with historical in others gives the hotel an identity crisis. And with the speakeasy in the basement of the hotel, it would be more beneficial to stick with the prohibition era theme if you want to maximize the valuation."

"We can't just turn the speakeasy into a regular hotel bar?"

"You could, but to be frank with you, it would be a stupid business decision. The speakeasy brings people in and makes them feel like they're experiencing something, not just heading down to the bar for a drink. It's a gimmick, for sure, but that's what makes it work. Without the speakeasy, it's just a hotel with a garden and rooms that cost $400 a night."

Before Frances can respond, Jackson barks, bringing me out of my spell. My eyes widen in panic, and I scurry to the front door, leading Jackson outside before putting his leash on.

"Dude, you blew my cover." Jackson stares at me, his big brown doggy eyes melting my heart. "Okay, fine, I shouldn't have been eavesdropping. Especially when you need to go potty. I'll do better."

Jackson wags his tail and barks before dragging me off the porch with so much force I almost fall over.

Chapter Six

Lucas

"Thank you so much for letting me pick your brain. It was very informative," Frances says as she leads me to the front door.

"Of course. Thank you for dinner, it was delicious." I smile, and she smiles back, one of those false smiles that looks more like a Cheshire cat than anything genuine.

"Yes, Gambino's is the best Italian in town! I'm glad they were able to do a last minute delivery."

It would be an understatement to say I was caught off guard when Frances invited me over for dinner, mostly because I know she doesn't cook.

It's one of the many things Clark told me about her when they officially started dating all those years ago. It had been surprising, because Ginny loved to cook, and was knowledgeable about a variety of different cuisines.

So when Frances invited me, I was curious about what she would cook. Technically Clark never said that she couldn't cook, just that she doesn't. Maybe she's actually a master chef and just hates it. Not that I'll ever know, since dinner was ordered.

"I'll see you tomorrow!" Frances gives a small wave as she shuts the door behind me. I grimace as soon as the door is closed.

Her company is actually intolerable, but if I'm going to restore the hotel to its prohibition era-esque glory, I'm going to have to spend more time around her.

As I make my way to the car, I'm surprised to see Emma struggling her way down the driveway with a box. I hurry over, taking the box easily from her arms.

She looks up at me, her big green eyes filled with surprise.

"Lucas? You don't have to carry that."

"Seriously? You're struggling. Just let me help."

For a moment, there's a fiery look on her face as she looks from the box to my face, and I think she's going to argue. Then she sighs and throws her hands up.

"Fine! I'm sick of carrying all these boxes anyway. It's so stupid."

Emma stomps down the driveway and I follow her.

"Um, I thought you were moving into the basement. Why are you carrying all these boxes outside?"

"The only access to the basement is from the outside. When Frances' tried her hand at being an interior designer, she wanted the basement to be her own space where she saw her interior design clients and wanted it separate from the house. She gave that up a couple years ago, but they never reconnected the basement entrance to the interior of the house."

Emma shrugs as she steps up to the door and lets me in. I set the box down by the others and look around.

The basement is a large, walk-out space, with floor to ceiling windows lining one wall and a view of the backyard. On the opposite wall is an open door, revealing a shower in what is clearly the bathroom. The walls are the same sterile white as the carpet, and pictures of seashells adorn them as if we're in a beach house.

"It's... something. At least you have your own bathroom."

"I had a walk-in rainwater shower in my bathroom upstairs," Emma says wistfully, looking at the ceiling as if she can bring the bathroom to her by sheer willpower.

"Well, it's only until the renovations are done, right? Then you have it all back."

My eyes meet Emma's and she laughs.

"No, I'm never getting it back. The 'renovation,'" Emma makes air quotes with her hands, "is the wall between Jackie's room and my old room being knocked down so that Jackie has one giant room with my bathroom."

"They're kicking you out of your own room?"

My jaw drops, which feels a little silly, but it's actually shocking to me how mean Frances can be. "That's ridiculous. This is your house."

"No, it's not. Frances' name is the one on the deed now that my dad is gone."

I stare at her and Emma shrugs. "No will, remember?"

I sigh, folding my arms over my chest and leaning against the wall behind me.

"Your father would not approve of this."

"He's not here to object to it, unfortunately."

"I am."

"I doubt Frances will listen to you about what goes on in the house. Besides, I'm not going to live here forever. Well, not anymore. I was hoping that I'd get to keep the house and one day pass it to my children but I guess..." Emma trails off.

"Oh, shoot, I need to get that box from my car!"

She zooms out the door, and I consider following her, but before I can make that decision she's back in the door, carrying a considerably smaller box inside. The bottom of the box catches on the door, unbeknownst to Emma.

She continues walking through and the bottom pulls open, the contents of the box spilling all over the floor.

The door closes behind Emma as we both lean down to pick up the contents of the box. We both reach for something, and my hand grazes Emma ever so slightly.

A little zap goes through my fingers, and judging by how quickly Emma pulls her hand back, she feels it, too.

"Sorry, I—" she starts but I pick up a piece of origami and chuckle.

"Is this a paper crane?" I ask, examining it. I'm not sure why I ask, because I'm already well aware of the obsession Clark had with making paper cranes. Maybe I just want to hear Emma's voice some more. It's pretty, velvety and smooth like honey.

"Yeah. Dad had it sticking in one of the picture frames on his desk."

"Your dad was obsessed with making these in college." I turn it over in my hand and glimpse a math problem on the back of the crane. "Actually... this might be one of the ones he made in college. This looks like a math exam."

"Really?" Emma holds her hand out and I pass it to her, my wrist brushing hers as the crane changes hands. "Oh, my gosh, it is. He made them out of math exams?"

I laugh and shake my head.

"He made them out of anything he could find. Event fliers, take out menus, homework. He even ripped a page out of a library book to make one."

"That's terrible! Did he get fined?"

"He never even returned it! Your dad was horrible at returning his library books. I used to do a weekly haul and take them for him. I think it was over spring break one year that he made one, and then he lost the book."

Emma shakes her head.

"Wow, that doesn't sound like my dad at all."

"Well, it was college." I shrug. "The paper cranes were actually part of a larger project."

"Oh?"

"Yeah. On the wall of our apartment, he started taping them up one day. And of course I was like, 'Hey man, what are you doing to our wall?'"

"So what was he doing to the wall?" She leans in, immersed in the story.

"He arranged them to make the shape of a crane on the wall. A hundred little paper cranes, making up a giant crane on the wall. It took him months to finish the project, and when he finally did, he blindfolded me and brought me into the living room. Ripped the blindfold off and said, 'Tada!'"

"What?!"

"Yup. So of course, I was like 'What is this?' And your dad looked at me with the most serious expression, and he said, 'This is art, Lucas.'"

Emma laughs and I'm immediately captivated by the sound. I study her, the way she throws her head back, strands of wild red hair flying out of the bun at the top of her head.

The curve of her neck leading to heavily freckled shoulders. The tank top that's cut a little too low—and as my eyes move lower, it's obvious she's not wearing a bra from the soft peaks of her nipples pulling the fabric.

Emma looks at me and my eyes immediately meet hers. If she's wise to where I was actually looking, she doesn't let on. We're quiet for a moment, and her cheeks pink up.

"Thanks for sharing that. That's actually a really cool thing to learn about my dad."

"Of course. I have a lot of stories, if you're ever interested in hearing more."

Emma sucks in a breath, her soft green eyes pouring into mine. I lean in, and when she doesn't move away, I take a stray piece of hair and tuck it behind her ear. Her face moves into my hand, nuzzling it gently.

We move closer, the space between us nearly closing when a soft whine sounds from the corner.

Emma jumps back and bumps her head against the wall.

"Ouch!" she announces, rubbing the back of her head and glaring at the wall. I resist the urge to chuckle.

"Are you okay?"

She whips around to look at me, and concern spreads across her face.

"Oh gosh, yeah. Um, it's so late. You should probably go." Emma stands up and wipes her hands on her pajama pants. "I think Jackson is getting pretty tired. I should take him back upstairs."

Her eyes move to the corner of the room and I follow, until I spot the aging golden retriever occupying the corner of the room.

"No way. Jackson?" I can't hide the excitement in my voice, and when the dog hops up and gallops over to me, I rub him all over. "Hey boy, how's it going?"

"He likes you."

"Of course he does, I'm his best friend."

"Uh, no, I'm his best friend." I look up, and the look of disgust on Emma's face makes me burst out laughing.

"Okay, fine, but he loves me."

"Clearly."

"You have to let me take him to the dog park sometime."

"Sure, you can join us on Saturday."

I give Jackson one last pat before standing up and meeting her eyes.

"It's a date," I say. Emma's eyes widen in surprise, and this time I can't resist chuckling at her. "That's an expression."

"I know that," she hisses before reaching behind her and opening the door. It knocks aside the items on the floor that we didn't pick up. "Come on, it's late."

I step out of the door and wave before getting into my car and heading back to the hotel.

It's hard to get the picture of Emma laughing out of my head. I know I shouldn't be lusting after my best friend's daughter. But it's hard not to. She's the most beautiful woman I've ever laid my eyes on.

More than that, though, she's smart and determined. I can see it on her face whenever she talks about the hotel, or is talking to her stepmother. It's obvious that she doesn't yet have a plan of what to do about the hotel situation, but I can see the wheels turning behind her eyes whenever it's brought up.

Not to mention her immensely quick wit. She inherited her mother's sarcasm, that's for sure. It's exactly the type of back and forth that I've always enjoyed when talking to women, someone who isn't afraid to give it back to me.

What would Clark think, though? Surely, if he was here and he was alive, he would disapprove, right? I mean, we never talked about anything like this, but why would we? It's not the sort of thing we could ever have imagined back then.

Though, the more I think about it, the more I wonder. I know Clark. Well, I knew him. He would want Emma to be happy, healthy and taken care of.

I can guarantee at least two of those things would be assured if she were with me, and health is something that no partner could promise.

I sigh as I pull up to the parking lot for the hotel. Truthfully, I don't know what to do. It's undeniable that I'm attracted to

Emma, and I'm good enough at reading women that I know she's attracted to me.

I just don't know if pursuing her would be dishonoring Clark's memory or whether we would have his blessing.

<u>Chapter Seven</u>

Emma

Jackson snores beside me, but I can't manage any sleep. Every time I close my eyes, the only thing I can see is Lucas' face and his hazel eyes looking deeply into mine. Moving in closer. Our lips would have met—we would have kissed.

What would it have felt like?

I'm not an idiot. Or a virgin. I've kissed people before. I've had a boyfriend- I had a boyfriend for a year and a half in college.

Clearly, it didn't work out. Partly because he wanted to move to California to go to law school, but also because, if we're being honest, I didn't really like him all that much.

It was obvious that Andy was really into me—he pursued me relentlessly. My friends at the time were very encouraging—telling me to go for it! Lose my virginity!

So I did, but truthfully, it was very unimpressive and underwhelming. It never got better either, and by the time we broke up, we hadn't had sex in months.

I haven't had a relationship since then. Maybe I have unrealistic expectations; watched too many movies or read too many romance novels.

I want something that's passionate, someone I am so attracted to that I can't keep my hands off him.

Which is exactly how I'm feeling about Lucas right now.

I shiver, remembering the way the warmth of his palm felt against my skin. It was electric, surprising but wonderful. These are not feelings I should be having. These are not thoughts I should be thinking. Lucas is forty-five. I mean, he's a hot forty-five and much more desirable that any guys my own age.

He's also successful, building his business from the ground up as soon as he finished college. Success is very attractive, and the idea that someone like him might want someone like me—well, I can't deny that I'm flattered by that.

"Ugh!" I groan and turn over, slamming my face into the pillow. I need to sleep. I have work tomorrow, and I need to be able to focus and function. Although with Lucas in the hotel, I'm not sure that I'll be able to.

Oh, God. I seriously need sleep. The last thing I need is to show up to work with even darker under-eye circles than I'm sporting right now.

I clear my mind, balancing my breathing so that I can calm down.

In no time, I manage to slip into dreamland.

***

In my dream, Lucas knocks on the door again just moments after leaving. I open it, surprise pulsing through me.

"Lucas?"

"Emma, I can't leave here without kissing you."

He rushes in, his hands clasping the side of my face. I suck in a breath as his eyes meet mine.

"Lucas..." I whisper.

"Shh." In a second, his mouth is on mine. His lips are soft, although the kisses are anything but. His lips press against mine with a sense of urgency that is unbelievably foreign to me.

I part my lips, and his tongue slides between them. My tongue meets his, rolling against it as Lucas pushes me further into the room, laying me down on the bed.

"You're so beautiful," he whispers, finally separating our mouths. I bite my lip as my fingers fiddle with the buttons at the top of his shirt. He grabs my hands, trapping them above me on the bed and shakes his head. "No, tonight is for you."

He places his lips on my neck, kissing gently at first, and then nipping at my neck as he moves toward my collar bone. I hiss and push my chest up toward him, hoping—no, praying—that he gets the hint. He chuckles.

"Don't move your hands," he whispers as he grabs the end of my tank top and pushes it up, allowing the cold air in the room to rush over my chest. My nipples harden as he kisses around them, leaving no part of my breasts untouched.

Lucas looks up at me through my lashes before taking one of my breasts in his hand and placing his mouth on the nipple. I arch my back and moan, the feeling of his wet mouth on such a sensitive part of my body immediately sending shocks of pleasure through me.

He flicks his tongue over it one last time before switching to the other breast, not leaving a part of it untouched. He runs his thumb gently over the nipple on my other breast, and I can feel the heat emanating from the spot between my legs.

I shift my hips up to meet him and he laughs.

"You want me down here?" He asks, trailing his fingers down my chest toward the waistband of my pajama pants. I nod, unable to get out any words as he toys with the fabric.

Lucas obliges me, dipping his hands under my pants. He brushes his fingers across my clit over my panties and I shiver. His fingers move slowly over them, teasing me with what I want. I grip his arm, sliding my hand down it until my fingers join his in my pants.

I guide him to the spot where I want his fingers to be touching. I'm done with the games, I want his fingers on me. His thumb moves in a circle, and then he looks up at me, his eyes drinking me in.

Lucas leans in close, opens his mouth, and says...

"EHHHHHHHHHHHHH!"

I shoot up in bed, breathless as I turn to the offending sound.

My alarm. I was asleep. I just had a sex dream about Lucas.

I grab my pillow and scream into it on the bed. What. The. Hell. I don't know what I'm angrier about—the fact that I had a sex dream about him or the fact that I so, so badly wanted the dream to be real.

Jackson barks, causing me to come back to reality. He's standing by the door to my room, wagging his tail.

"You need to go outside, don't you?" I ask, disappointment coloring my tone. Jackson tilts his head and I sigh. "Fine, let's go."

***

I get to work a little earlier than I normally do. I try to convince myself that it's because I want to get a head start on today's tasks, but truthfully I'm hoping that if I get there early enough I'll be able to avoid Frances. She prefers to sleep in when she gets the chance, and if I can slip into the office before she gets here, it will make my life that much easier.

Okay, that's not the whole truth. I'm also hoping to avoid Lucas. Things were going to be awkward enough after the almost kiss last night, but now that I've had a sex dream about him?

Well, I might have to start wearing a lot more blush so that the redness of my cheeks seems normal.

"Good morning, Miss Emma!" Joe smiles at me as I walk in the doors. "It's a beautiful Tuesday, isn't it?"

"It's certainly Tuesday!" I say gamely. Joe laughs before going back to what he was doing. It's a game we play every time it rains, whether it's a light drizzle or torrential downpour, Joe thinks it's beautiful and I loathe the rain with every fiber of my being.

"Hello, Emma," a familiar low voice says. I take in a deep breath before looking up. It takes everything in me not to bite my lip. Lucas looks amazing in a pair of jeans and gray t-shirt that hugs his arm muscles, allowing their perfect definition to shine. He obviously works out.

"Hi, there. Lots to do today?"

"I have a meeting with Frances today, but I was wondering if you wanted to grab a coffee this afternoon?"

Lucas' eyes are hopeful, and I don't miss the rapt attention our conversation is getting from Lily at the front desk.

"It will depend on what my afternoon looks like work-wise. There are a lot of supplies that need to be ordered, and..."

"Oh don't worry about supplies! I actually ordered them yesterday when you left early," Lily chimes in, giving me a wink and a smile.

I don't know if I want to hug her or strangle her.

"Well, in that case, sure, that would be great."

Lucas is about to say something, but before he can get a word out, someone crashes out of the elevator at the end of the hall. We all turn to see a lanky, curly-haired kid shoving papers into a briefcase as he walks our way.

"Mr.Bennett, I found those papers you were asking about! Sorry for getting them to you so late, I thought they were in a different folder and... "

The guy blinks, noticing the attention he has garnered. His gaze stops on me and he gives me a goofy grin. "Ah, hello! You're Emma, right? I'm Royce, Lucas' assistant. Nice to meet you!"

I look over at Lucas, who looks as if he's concocting his own murder plot for his assistant.

"Nice to meet you." I nod before spinning on my heel and heading to the office. I don't want to stick around for whatever dumpster fire of a conversation is about to be had between the two of them.

Lily follows me through the door.

"Oh, my gosh, Lucas Bennett totally just asked you out on a date!"

"What? He didn't!" I say as I plop down in the chair behind the desk. Lily scoffs, sitting on the corner of the desk.

I don't know what she thinks she's doing—she's never once stepped foot in this office, but all of a sudden she's playing wing woman and encroaching on my personal space.

"He totally did, and you were just going to blow him off!" she tucks a strand of shoulder-length blond hair behind her ear. "That guy is super hot, and he's obviously loaded."

"He happens to be my dad's best friend, and he's forty-five years old."

Lily rolls her eyes.

"Oh, my God, who cares how old he is? It's not a big deal. I mean, especially when they're that hot. Who's going to judge you? Not me. And who cares what Frances thinks?" Lily shoots me a look.

"I don't know. You don't think it's weird that he was my dad's best friend?"

"Maybe it would be a little weird if he was, like, a surrogate uncle or something. But you didn't even recognize the guy when he walked through the door yesterday. So, no, I don't think it's weird."

"Wait, you noticed that?"

Lily preens proudly.

"Oh, I notice everything. That's what makes me great at working the front desk." I study her. I've never talked to Lily extensively. She's only been working here for eight months, but she does do a good job. I never have to correct any work she's done.

"So, are you going to go?"

"Yeah. I mean it's just coffee, right?" I ask. Lily shoots me a look and I know it's not just coffee. "Okay, so he's hot. And it's a coffee date."

She squeals and hops up from the desk.

"Give me your phone!"

"What? Why?" I ask, but I'm already pulling my phone from my purse and handing it to her.

"This is my number. I want you to text me later and tell me everything! Also, the dress you're wearing right now is super cute. You made a good choice today."

Lily floats out of the office and I stare after her, dumbfounded.

Being asked for coffee by the hottest man I've ever met was surprising. Making a friend? This is record breaking.

Chapter Eight

Lucas

"Lucas!" Frances' shrill voice rings across the lobby and I wince. I'm glad she wasn't here to witness Royce fumbling his way through the lobby.

After Emma and Lily disappeared into the lobby I sent him to fetch some coffee, which might have been a mistake. Hopefully he doesn't trip through the front doors and drop it everywhere.

"Thanks for meeting me so early. I'm not usually such an early riser, but I'm excited to get started on this project."

"I am as well." I nod toward the door. "I sent my assistant to grab some coffees, he should be back pretty soon."

I follow Frances to the conference room and take a seat at the table across from her. She looks at the door and lowers her voice.

"Listen, I didn't want to mention this out there. I already have an offer on the hotel."

My heart rate quickens but I manage to keep my composure.

"Oh?"

"Yes, from Marshall Bridgers. I'm sure you've heard the name. He's some huge hotel mogul." She waves her hand in the air as if this information is insignificant.

I am familiar with Marshall Bridgers. He loves to take small hotels, remove all the character, and turn them into soulless corporate rooms for rent. I hope this isn't written all over my face.

"He's quite popular in my circles, yeah."

"Well he made an offer for twenty million, for the hotel as-is. Identity crisis and all." She smiles at me smugly. It takes only a second to realize that this is her bragging—her changes to the hotel didn't damage its saleability in her eyes.

"Twenty million is an okay offer. You could definitely get more for it, though." Not to mention that Bridgers would basically gut this place and take away all the personality.

That argument won't work on Frances though. She doesn't place sentimental value on this building; perhaps she doesn't place it on anything. That's why I'm not telling her that I want the place for the memories. That won't move her. It might even make her want to reject my offer, considering how much disdain she seemed to have for Ginny.

"You think so?" Her ears perk at the thought of more money. Cold hard cash, that's her language. I've dealt with many people like her. It's hard to imagine what Clark saw in her. She must have a softer side, some sort of emotion to offer that would have spoken to him.

"Definitely. It won't cost much to make the hotel worth a whole lot more, and in the end you'd get a lot more money."

"Hmm." Frances sits back in her chair and taps her chin thoughtfully.

Then Royce bursts through the door with coffee.

"Hello there, Mrs. Stone! I brought some coffee, creams and sugar. I wasn't sure how you took it."

My eyes roll over Royce and it's clear something happened that caused him to be late, if the giant coffee stain on his sleeve is any indication.

Royce catches me looking at the stain on his sleeve and slides his hand further under the cloth, as if hiding his hand will make the stain disappear.

"Thank you so much, Ryan. That is very thoughtful to think of me on your coffee run," Frances purrs, taking a cup from him.

"Actually, it's Royce," he mumbles under his breath before walking around the table. I almost tell him not to bother correcting her—even if she remembers his name, she'll pretend she won't.

Truth be told, Frances is a very particular kind of person, one that I've come across many times.

The kind of person who thinks they're better than everyone, and will do anything to prove it while trying to appear effortless.

Royce hasn't had enough experience with her type to understand this yet, but with more time under my wing, I'm confident that he'll be navigating the world with ease.

"Oops!" Royce trips over the chair he's trying to sit in. Frances blinks in alarm but doesn't move to help. "Man, that chair came out of nowhere!"

I give a pity chuckle at his lame joke, but Frances doesn't acknowledge it.

Maybe navigating the world with ease is a little generous, but he'll at least be more confident in his own abilities. Sometimes that's the best one can hope for.

"All right, let's get down to business. If Marshall Bridgers has already put an offer on the property, it's only a matter of time before the other fish start biting."

I clear my throat and open the folder of papers in front of me.

"The thing that makes this building unique is its attribution to the history of Santa Fe, and it's not unintentional. Clark knew how much success an idea like this would bring. I understand you've been trying to update it, and that your intentions are good, but you are actively diminishing the sale value of the hotel by doing so."

Frances blinks. My tone isn't confrontational, but she likely isn't used to people being so candid with her. She gives me an uncertain smile and tucks her hair behind her ear before responding.

"I see. I didn't realize how important the saloon theme was for the hotel—"

"It's prohibition themed, actually," Royce chimes in, flipping through the papers in front of him. For all his clumsiness and awkward demeanor, he is efficient. How long did it take him to put together all this information about the hotel's history?

"Right. I didn't realize how important the prohibition theme was for the hotel. Clark never informed me, and quite frankly, I'm an interior designer at heart. I know very little about the hotel business, especially when it comes to boutique hotels, which I know is your specialty. That's why I want to sell it."

Frances lowers her voice as if what she's about to say is a secret. "The Signature on Main was Clark and Ginny's project. I know they put their heart and soul into making this place a success, and I don't want to take that away from them."

"So you're interested in preserving their memory?" I ask, my curiosity piqued. Frances doesn't strike me as particularly sentimental.

"Well, I loved Clark. The only thing he loved more than Emma," Frances gives a small frown, "was this hotel. So, of course, ideally I'd love for the hotel to stay as it is. I think he'd like that. I just also think that a more... modern style hotel would attract more guests and raise profits. I think a hotel should give off a clean, crisp, professional vibe."

She smiles at me, but it's not a genuine smile. It's the smile of someone who definitely does not love the hotel the way it is.

"Respectfully, Frances, you are not the target guest for The Signature on Main. Of course, if you had a two hundred room hotel on your hands, a polished vibe for the regular business man would be exactly what was needed."

I flip through the folder in front of me until I find exactly what I'm looking for—a guest profile write-up that I asked Royce to create.

"The Signature on Main is a thirty room themed boutique hotel. We are not simply selling a room to sleep in while someone is on a business trip. We are selling an experience, a chance to step back in time to the prohibition era and see history. Every piece of furniture in this hotel was handpicked and preserved or restored by Clark and Ginny, the paint on the walls all chosen from a historically-accurate 1920's color palette. The speakeasy downstairs isn't just any hotel bar, it's a moment frozen in time that our guests today get to experience for themselves."

"And it's a stop on four of the six prohibition tours in Santa Fe," Royce chimes in.

I blink, caught off-guard at the statement. Royce really did his research when putting together the file.

"Exactly! Over the past twenty years, The Signature on Main has become a staple in the Santa Fe tourism industry. That is what you are selling, not a hotel. In that framing, you can get much more for the hotel than what most will attempt to offer you."

Frances seems to contemplate this, tapping her manicured nails on the table slowly. Then, she nods.

"I have to admit, I never considered any of those factors when I thought about selling the hotel. How long do you think it will take to reverse the remodeling of the five rooms that have been completely updated?"

"Do you still have the original furniture pieces that were in the rooms?"

"Some. I'd say about half have sold."

"Okay, we will take inventory of what we have left, and then start the process of replacing what we no longer have. Truthfully, we will need to talk to a contractor for pricing the flooring and paint."

I grimace. "If we can find wood floors that match the original flooring. Otherwise we might have to settle for a close match since they aren't common places. We should be able to get by with that."

Frances nods, then her phone beeps.

"Thank you for meeting with me. I'm afraid that is all the time I have today, but I'll look at contacting some contractors so I can get estimates."

"Why don't you let Royce do that? He's excellent at research, and he can have a great list of contractors drawn up for us by the end of the week."

Royce scoffs.

"End of the week? I can have it by tomorrow."

I shrug.

"All right, tomorrow then. What do you say?" I raise an eyebrow at Frances. She gives me a tight smile as she stands up.

"That sounds like more off my plate. How can I say no?"

"Great, we will get to work."

"Thank you. I'll get in contact with you later."

Frances shakes our hands before leaving. I let out a heavy sigh before taking a sip of my now cold coffee.

"Mr.Bennett?" Royce's tone is uncertain, as if he's unsure about what he's about to ask.

"Yes?"

"I thought you wanted to buy the hotel. Why are we helping her renovate it just to sell it to someone else?"

"We're not. I'm going to buy it."

"I don't understand."

"Frances does not like me. Don't get me wrong, she'd sell to me, but she's just petty enough to take a lower offer just to spite me." I tap my fingers on the table. "If I help her, and she sees the results of what I'm saying are accurate, she'll be more inclined to sell to me. Especially when she sees that my offer is better than everyone else's."

"Wait, she doesn't like you? She's so nice!" I turn to look at Royce. He's being completely genuine. I sigh and shake my head.

"You've got a lot to learn about people, Royce. Frances acts nice because it's benefiting her. If I don't serve a purpose, then she has no reason to be nice to me. That's why she isn't nice to you."

"She isn't?"

"Royce, she doesn't even bother to remember your name."

"Maybe she's forgetful."

I laugh and shake my head. Royce chuckles along, but it's obvious that he doesn't understand what exactly about this conversation is funny.

"I really appreciate your optimism about people. It's refreshing to see in this line of work."

And it is. Most of the people I interact with are shrewd and cutthroat, like lions lying in wait for an antelope at the watering hole. It's interesting, and also concerning, that Royce is more of an antelope than a lion.

It won't make him successful, but it does make him likeable.

"Thanks, Mr.Bennett." Royce beams before standing up. "Do you want me to start on the list of contractors?"

"Nah, why don't you take a break and do some sightseeing or something? I have to get ready for coffee with Emma."

Royce gives me a nod before shuffling off. A paper flies out of his briefcase as he zips out the door.

Chapter Nine

Emma

Why did I agree to this? Yes, Lucas is hot, but I'm a disaster.

At least that's how I feel looking into the mirror in the lobby bathroom. Stepping out into the garden for a morning break was not the move. Despite the normally dry heat of the Santa Fe desert, the morning storm had left the air feeling stickier and more humid than normal.

Which is why the hair I spent an hour curling has strands of frizz poking up from it. My mascara is smeared under my eyes, and there's a distinct shiny sheen on my forehead. I sigh.

"Great," I mutter to myself. I don't bring any makeup or hairspray with me to work—why would I? It's not like I'm trying to impress anyone.

Well, not usually.

I smooth my hair down, but it does little to tame the offending fly-aways. I sigh before reaching into my bag and digging around for a scrunchy for my hair with. I manage to arrange my hair into a fluffy side braid when my phone alerts with a text from Lucas.

I take one last look in the mirror before releasing a deep breath and stepping out of the bathroom. Lucas is standing in the lobby, and when the door shuts behind me he looks up, giving me an easy smile.

"Hey, you. Ready to go?"

He shoves his hands in his pockets and offers me his arm. I resist the urge to chuckle at the gesture—it's old-fashioned, but endearing. I slide my arm in his and we stroll out the front door.

"Oh! I thought we were getting coffee?" I ask as he steers me in the opposite direction of the coffee shop.

"We are, but we're going to my favorite coffee shop. I discovered it when I was in high school and went every morning until I moved."

"Every morning?"

"Like clockwork." He nods.

"Wow. I bet your picture's on the wall and everything," I say, resisting the urge to chuckle. Lucas throws his head back and laughs.

"You definitely got your wit from your mother."

"Dad always said I was just like her."

"He was right." Lucas clears his throat and adjusts his tie. "Seriously, though. You're going to love the coffee. One sip and you'll be a total convert."

"We'll see about that."

***

"Okay, this might be the best coffee I've ever had," I say as I sip my latte and smile over the rim of the cup. "Something about the flavor. I don't know, it's different."

"That's because they make all their own syrups." Lucas winks before taking a sip of his own drink.

"Impressive."

"I think so." He waits a second and then smiles. "So how's the moving going?"

I run my finger around the rim of my cup and sigh.

"Good, for the most part. The only thing is that I don't know how to get my bed downstairs."

"Wait, there's already a bed in there, though," Lucas points out. Our gazes meet, and even though it happens in less than a second, I don't miss the way his eyes flash down to my lips. Then he looks away.

"Yeah, but it's not my bed."

"The distinction is important?"

"Um, duh." I give him an incredulous look. "The bed in the basement is just whatever Frances found at Mattress Town and threw down there to be a guest bed. My bed is a perfectly curated Sleeptopia, complete with mattress covers, and more pillows than can be counted."

"It sounds... Do you sleep with all the pillows?"

"Of course not. I have a chest at the foot of my bed that the pillows go in at night."

"Hmm." Lucas shifts in his seat. "I could help you."

"Move my bed?" I blink in surprise.

"Of course. I'm strong and capable. I'm sure we can handle getting a mattress and some pillows down the stairs between the two of us. And I can always draft Royce in to help if necessary."

"Well, that's very kind of you. I might have to take you up on that offer."

I smile at him and he smiles in response. One corner of his mouth lifts higher than the other, and his teeth are white and straight, but not like they've been created by a dentist. It's a nice, natural smile, and I can't ignore the butterflies working up in my stomach.

A comfortable silence fills the space around us, mirroring the comfort I feel around him. I'm very used to silences—having no friends and living with a stepmother and stepsister who hate me has taken care of that.

The silences I'm used to, though, are typically tense, filled to the brim with animosity.

I want to enjoy this silence with him, soak up this moment where things are quiet because words don't have to be spoken to bond. Unfortunately, my curiosity gets the better of me.

"So, how did the meeting go with Frances?"

He chuckles and puts down his mug.

"I was wondering how long it would take you to ask me that."

He raises an eyebrow when I don't say anything back. I make a noise of exasperation and sit up straighter.

"Well, are you going to tell me?" I can feel my eyes going wide with curiosity, which makes me self conscious, but I can't stop my feelings from being written all over my face.

"It went well. She's agreed to revert the hotel back to the prohibition theme."

"Is that it?" I ask after a couple of seconds go by.

"Well, yeah."

I can't help the sound of disgust that leaves me.

"Are you serious? How does that stop her from selling the hotel?"

"The plan was never to stop her from selling it, it was—"

"I thought we were on the same page about this!" I cut him off and stand up."You're supposed to be helping me."

"I am helping you! When the renovated rooms are returned to their former state, and the prohibition theme is once again consistent throughout the hotel, she's going to list it for a higher price. At that point, I'll make an offer she can't resist."

"Wait." I pause as I process the information. "You want to buy the hotel? You said you didn't want to buy it."

"Excuse me, is this seat taken?" A coffee shop patron points to my chair.

"Yes, sorry." I sit back down and Lucas shakes his head.

"No, I said I hadn't thought about buying it."

He smiles sadly. "The truth is, Signature on Main isn't my typical hotel. I like fixer-uppers, a project. We're renovating some of these hotel rooms, but the rest of the hotel is fine. It would sell for millions even if we left the updated rooms alone. Signature on Main is personal for me. Maybe because I was there at the beginning, maybe because..."

Lucas trails off. I tap his foot with mine and smile to encourage him.

"Truthfully, it feels like a piece of Clark. He was my best friend, and I didn't get to talk to him for years due to Frances' influence. I know it might seem hard to understand given that you don't know me very well, but Clark and Ginny were the closest thing I had to family for a long time."

"Your parents?"

"Passed away twenty years ago."

I nod slowly.

"Okay, I get it. I understand why you want the hotel."

"Thank you for understanding." He clears his throat, but before he can continue, my phone alarm goes off.

"Shoot, we have to start getting back." I stand up, gathering my bag. It's a shame I didn't get to finish my latte, but I'll definitely be back.

"Hey, Emma?" Lucas says earnestly from across the table.

I look up at him. "I promise I would never leave you in the dust. I know the hotel is important to you, very possibly more important to you than it is to me."

"Thanks, Lucas."

The ride back to the hotel is filled with more comfortable silence. I can't help sneaking peeks at Lucas every few minutes.

His jaw is strong and sharp, which looks intense on most people. Despite the serious expression on his face, he exudes a genuine kindness that I haven't seen from anyone else.

Before I can ask him what he's thinking about, Lucas pulls up to the curb and hands the keys to the valet.

"So I'll see you tonight?" he asks as we walk into the lobby of the hotel.

"Tonight?"

"Yeah, to move the bed."

"Oh!" My brain freezes immediately.

It really isn't a big deal—he's just offering to move some furniture. Still, the idea of having someone like Lucas in my room feels so private, so intimate that it makes me unsure of myself.

"Actually, I can't tonight. Maybe tomorrow?"

I can't read the expression on his face, but he nods and gives me a pleasant smile regardless.

"Sure, just let me know."

I nod and give him an awkward smile before scurrying back into the office and dropping heavily into Dad's comfy office chair.

I count my lucky stars that Lily isn't at her desk—I'm not prepared to answer a million questions about what was decidedly not a date. Nothing happened. Unless I count when he looked at my lips.

If I'm honest with myself, being alone with Lucas makes me uncomfortable, especially after the dream I had. I don't know if I can trust myself to not start something that is ultimately a bad idea.

He wants to buy the hotel, and that's great.

I don't know him very well—honestly, my memory of him even before Dad married Frances is fuzzy. He came around every once in a while, but he was always traveling and buying hotels. Fixing them up, Dad would say, whenever he talked about Lucas.

It almost feels like I didn't know him at all before he showed up at our hotel door, which makes me both hopeful and cautious.

Hopeful, because any idea of romance with him doesn't really feel like I'm thinking about fucking my Dad's best friend. I'm not sure if he feels the same way—he almost certainly remembers things about me from past years that I don't recall. He might not even think of me as a grown woman.

But he sure is a grown man...

But I also feel hesitant, because even though something about Lucas is familiar, it's also true that I don't really know this man. He's had the benefit of my trust because he knew my Dad, but maybe I shouldn't be so quick to accept him into my life.

I gently kick off the edge of the desk so the chair spins slowly, the background of bookcases and wooden walls blurring in my vision.

"Emma!" Frances' voice shrieks through the office door. "Are you back from lunch? The toilet in Room 8 is overflowing, and I can't find Jonas anywhere."

Frances opens the door, annoyance coloring her features.

"It's his day off. Why didn't you call a plumber?"

She sighs heavily.

"Really, Emma. As the GM, it's your responsibility to take care of these things."

The smile on her face drips with malice. With the way the light is filtering in from the small window on the wall, she almost looks like a villain on a movie poster.

"Fine. I'll call an emergency plumber to get right over here and put in an ASAP order for someone from housekeeping to clean up the mess."

I roll my eyes but don't turn around. I don't need to see her to know exactly which smirk she's sporting.

Chapter Ten

Lucas

Being back in Santa Fe is weird, especially without Clark.

It feels like coming home, except it doesn't. I sold my parents' house when they died—it wasn't a decision I came to lightly.

The house I grew up in was special to me, but the memories of being in my parents' home were painful without them there.

It was eerie sitting at the kitchen table in the months after they had passed, sipping coffee in silence. I was used to the sound of my father's bare feet shuffling across the wooden floors, or my mother tut-tutting quietly at the soap operas she watched on TV. Without them there, the house had no life, so I made the difficult choice to put it on the market.

It was the practical thing to do, anyway, I'd told myself. I hardly ever visited Santa Fe, not since moving to Edgewood where my business really took off. Hotels kept me busy and, after losing my parents, throwing myself into a project was easier than going to therapy.

Not that I was opposed to going to therapy. I just didn't have time for it back then.

"Can I help you find something?" The shopkeeper asks from behind the counter. Creases appear on her face when she smiles at me, the marks of someone who has spent more of her life smiling than frowning.

"I'm looking for some floral pieces to put on some graves," I respond, turning back to the overwhelming displays of flowers.

She steps out from behind the counter, picking up an apron and slipping it over her head. It shakes some silver strands loose from the low bun behind her head, the strands glowing in the light filtering in from the shop's window.

"I'm sorry for your loss," she says, smiling sadly.

There's a genuine warmth to her voice that catches me off guard. It's not the rehearsed sympathy that I grew accustomed to after each of my parents died, but I guess you'd expect some true empathy from a woman who sells flowers for a living and probably deals with grieving relatives a great deal.

"Thank you, that means a lot."

She beckons me to follow her. She navigates around the shop with ease, the way she's probably done a million times before stopping in front of a row of arrangements.

"Traditional funeral flowers are lilies—although gravesite adornments don't have to strictly follow funereal tradition. I usually suggest arrangements that combine lilies with the deceased's favorite flowers."

"My mother's favorite flowers were lilies, actually. And I'm not sure my father had a favorite."

I tap my leg as I think about Clark. He loved flowers—he was incredibly sentimental. I used to tease him about it in high school. Then one day, in college, he explained to me why he loved them.

"Flowers have meaning, dude. They're symbolic," he'd said enthusiastically as we stepped into the flower shop.

I snorted.

"Meaning? Come on, Clark. That's cheesy."

"They do! Haven't you ever read the Farmer's Almanac?"

"Why would I ever have read the Farmer's Almanac?"

"It has a lot of useful information. And more importantly, flower meanings."

We had been out that afternoon looking for the perfect bouquet of flowers to get Ginny for their first date.

Well, Clark was looking, and I was tagging along to give him opinions. Not that I needed to tag along; we did everything together. Practically inseparable, as my mother said.

Clark had walked up to a large bouquet of red roses, picked them up and held them out to me with such a grandiosity that I couldn't help but laugh.

"Red roses, for instance, say 'I love you.'"

"Coming on a little strong for a first date, isn't it?" I'd cocked an eyebrow, expecting push back. Instead, he pointed at me and nodded.

"Exactly! Which is why I'm having a bouquet custom-made for her."

"A custom bouquet for a first date? Don't you think that's a little intense?"

Clark shook his head and started for the counter, knowing I'd follow.

"Maybe, but I have a very specific vision in my head. Besides, Ginny is worth the effort." He smiled at me, but it was clear his mind was off in dreamland by that point. "I'm going to marry her one day."

"You haven't even been on the first date yet. What if it goes terribly?"

"It won't."

Even then, Clark's confidence was something to be admired. I'd never met anyone as sure of themselves as my best friend, and I'd aspired to be like him.

The first date had gone massively well, of course, given they ended up getting married and having Emma.

Truthfully, I wasn't sold on the importance of flowers until after Clark reported back on their date, declaring it a total success.

Back then, I'd only viewed them as a waste. Why would I willingly spend money on something that would only die a week later?

It wasn't until I gave my mom her first bouquet of lilies that I'd realized the importance of them. The value in flowers isn't the amount that is spent on them—it's the way someone's face lights up when they get them

Or how they smile every time they pass them after putting them in a vase, reminding them that someone cared enough about them to gift them flowers.

"I'll take two bouquets of lilies," I say finally.

Those will do for my parents' graves—I'm not certain my father would have cared if I put a pile of herbs on his headstone, but my mom would have appreciated the lilies a lot.

"And one of red roses."

Some people might think it's weird to put a bouquet of red roses on my best friend's grave, but Clark would love it, and that's all that really matters. I know he'd instantly get the reference to the flower shop memory.

The woman nods and grabs two, handing them to me as she leads me up to the counter.

As she taps buttons on the screen, I can't help but wonder what Emma's favorite flower is.

Guilt fills me as I leave the shop, though. I look down at the bouquet of red roses in my arms—what would Clark think of me pursuing Emma? If he was here, I wouldn't even dream of such a thing. It would be sacrilege in my mind.

Does it make me a bad person that I consider it now that he's gone?

I like to think that Clark would simply want us both to be happy, and if we happened to find that happiness in each other, he would be fine with it.

The unfortunate truth is that I just don't know.

Emma didn't date much in high school—from what I remember of her back then, she was shy and awkward, with unruly hair and a little too skinny in the way only kids can be.

Clark never talked about her dating, beyond a boy she was with in college. As far as I know, that never went anywhere, and even if it had, it obviously didn't last.

I wish I could just ask Clark. Talking to the dead is impossible, but even something as simple as a sign would be great.

I shake my head. What am I talking about? I'm not the kind of person who believes in signs from those who are gone.

Not anymore. I spent enough time after my parents passed, hoping for something from them and never received it.

Of course I didn't. Ghosts don't exist.

The symbolism behind gifting flowers, though? That's definitely something I can get behind.

***

As soon as I step through the front doors of the lobby, a most unpleasant scent hits me. I can't stop my nose from wrinkling at the offending scent—it's like a toilet that hasn't been flushed for days.

The door behind the check-in desk clicks softly, and I turn, fluttering in my chest at the anticipation of seeing Emma. Instead, Frances steps through, her nails tapping loudly on her phone screen.

"Frances," I say, and she looks up, pasting a forced smile on her face.

"Oh, hello, Lucas. How are you?"

"I'm fine, but what is that smell?"

Frances sighs before waving dismissively.

"Oh, someone overflowed a toilet. We're working on it right now, but the smell is taking longer to get rid of than I'd hoped. Emma's called the plumber and is getting odor eliminators and room fresheners, so hopefully that will help take care of it.

"How is Jackie? I feel like we've been talking so much about hotel business that we haven't really had much time to catch up."

Frances blinks, and for the first time ever, a genuine smile crosses her face.

"That is true. Jackie is wonderful—she's still figuring things out of course, but she honestly is my pride and joy. It's a mystery to me how I managed to raise such a wonderful daughter."

"I'm certain she is wonderful," I say placatingly, but I don't really know. It's clear that Jackie is her soft spot, though.

It's good to know she has one. For a while I was beginning to wonder if she was a robot.

"Ew, mom, it stinks in here," Jackie's voice rings out as she comes through the lobby doors. "Why does it smell like that?"

"Jackie, not in front of a guest!" Frances chastises, but it's half-hearted at best.

I nod at Jackie as she passes by, and she smiles back.

"That's all right, I'm going to head up to my room for the night anyway. It was lovely seeing the both of you."

Their voices echo each other as they wish me goodnight.

Once I get in my room, though, I don't know what to do. I don't have the usual distractions I have at home—none of my books or any place to make food.

It's a little lonely, actually. It's not often that I'm confronted with both the fact that I have nothing to do and no one to do anything with.

After a hot shower, I climb into the plush bed and look around the room. A painting in a stunning deep green shade hangs above the television, matching the thick curtain hanging over the window. It really is a beautiful hotel, and I'm grateful to have been a part of making the vision happen.

My phone buzzes, drawing my attention away from any potentially surfacing memories.

Help me move my bed tomorrow? A text from Emma pops across the screen.

Please. Another comes through before I can respond.

Of course. I take payment in the form of pizza.

Three dots appear on the screen, and I can't help but be aware of the way my heart twitches in anticipation.

Pizza? Your payment is the pleasure of my company.

I chuckle.

All right, fair enough. I guess it wouldn't be very nice to charge someone who needs my help. I add a wink, then delete it. It feels too forward.

Three dots, and then they disappear. I stare at the screen for a few more minutes before deciding to put it away. It's not particularly late, but staring at the screen and waiting for a response feels a little too intense for how early on in the... whatever this is.

I grab the remote and turn on the TV, flipping to a station with some late night comedy special playing for background noise. At home I have a sound machine that plays melodic tunes of ocean waves and cracking thunder, but at the hotel there is no such device.

When I was young, I could only sleep when it was completely silent and exceptionally dark. Now I struggle without some sort of background noise. Maybe it's a side effect of the uncomfortable, empty silence I endured in my parents' house after they passed.

Perhaps because when it's silent, the sound of my thoughts become ridiculously loud.

My phone buzzes, and even though I don't normally pick it up after I've turned on my background noise, but the thought that it could be Emma makes me throw out habit.

I'm asking for your help, and I do appreciate it. Just so you know.

I chuckle and roll my eyes at her insistence. Then I turn over and fall asleep before I can think about anything.

<u>Chapter Eleven</u>

Emma

I desperately need his help.

When I came home, I was determined to get my bed moved to the basement.

Well, after I had a shower that is. The toilet in Room 8 was backed up, and sewage gunk was pouring out of it.

My dress did end up getting messy, and though I could have tried to wash it, I don't think I'll ever be able to get the smell out of my mind, let alone my dress. So I wrapped it in three trash bags after getting out of the shower and walked it straight to the outside garbage.

My determination to move my bed put me into action right after getting clean, though. I spent an embarrassing amount of time in the garage, where my dad kept an assortment of tools for whatever needed doing around the house.

I wouldn't say Dad was particularly handy, but he knew how to do the basic stuff, and anything he didn't know how to do, he knew who to hire to do it.

Moving the bed definitely would have fallen under the 'knew how to do it' category.

Without Dad, and with the right tools, I got to work taking apart my bed frame, which was easy enough. What I didn't account for was how ridiculously heavy a solid oak king-size bed frame would be.

Which is why I'm currently trapped underneath it on the floor of my room.

Okay, trapped is maybe a bit theatrical. I'm definitely capable of getting out from under the headboard. Unfortunately, disappointment in how much harder this is than I expected it to be is preventing me from moving at all.

Well, except to text Lucas, of course.

My phone is still resting in my hand, although it's been twenty minutes and he still hasn't responded to the last text I sent, so he must be asleep. It's only 9:30, but he clearly wakes up early, given how perky he is when I show up for work in the morning.

I sigh. I probably need to be getting to bed soon, anyway. I sit up and push the headboard off of me. Jackson trots over from the corner of the room where he watched the whole ridiculous event unfold, and licks me on the cheek.

"All right, all right. Let's go to bed." I look around my room before putting Jackson's leash on him and walking him out the front door.

I'm still upset about not having my room, but the idea of being so removed from Frances and Jackie is starting to become appealing to me. Not having to see them every morning before work, or running into them when I want to grab a bottle of water from the fridge in the middle of the night is a dream.

Jackson does his business, and then we trudge to the basement door. I unlock it and let us both inside.

Jackson immediately runs for the bed and hops on, indicating that he's ready for sleep. I laugh and roll my eyes. Then I grab my favorite pair of pajamas and climb into bed.

Sleep evades me, though. It always does when I'm stressed.

I've tried every tactic in the book in an attempt to curb my sleep problems: white noise, melatonin, meditating, shutting off my phone an hour before bed.

So far, only one thing has ever worked. Which is why I get out of bed and stroll over to a box. I dig inside until I find what I'm looking for—a poorly made stuffed red colored bear, with huge eyes and a heart-shaped nose.

I'm not sure where Mom got it—Dad's story always changed. He won it for her at a carnival, or skillfully extracted it from a claw machine at a Mexican restaurant. Or when I was younger, stole it from a pirate's treasure chest. I'd bet money even he didn't remember.

Truthfully, it doesn't matter where he got it. He gave it to mom early when they were dating, before I was even born.

I'd been having nightmares for weeks before Mom gave it to me. I don't remember what the nightmares were about—I was so young then—but I would wake up bawling my eyes out every single night.

Then one day Mom brought me the bear, affectionately named Snuggles, and told me it wasn't just any bear. Snuggles, you see, was a warrior, a fighter of bad dreams. Sleep with Snuggles, she said, and you'll never have bad dreams.

It's funny to think about, but I didn't have nightmares after that. Of course it's all psychological, but Snuggles still brings me comfort when I need him.

After Mom died, I started talking to her through Snuggles. I'm not certain she can hear me, but I hope that she can.

"All right, Mom, I guess a lot is going on," I whisper as I climb into bed. "Frances is trying to sell the hotel. I want the hotel, but Dad didn't leave a will. By the way, if you run into Dad up there, tell him I miss him and also I'm kind of mad at him for leaving me all alone with Frances."

I try to smile at my lame joke, but my heart isn't in it. It's still too fresh.

"Okay, sorry, that wasn't funny. But seriously, it sucks without you guys. It was hard enough when you left. Now I'm really alone."

A tear bubbles in my eye. I sniff and wipe it away once it rolls down my cheek.

"Well, not totally alone. I have Lucas. I'm sure you remember him. Dad's best friend." I hesitate before continuing. "I actually have a little bit of a crush on him. That sounds so childish, but it's true. He's smart and super hot."

I look at the bear. It says nothing, but there's a twinkle in his round eyes.

"We almost kissed. The other day, when he was helping me with some boxes. I'm not sure what to do about it. It's like... obviously I'm attracted to him. I barely know him, though. And he was Dad's best friend. Is it weird that he's so much older than me?"

Jackson whines and stretches, crawling over to the other side of the bed. Not that he can get very far—this bed is no match for my king.

"It's even weirder because I kind of had a...," I lower my voice, "a sex dream about him. It was so shocking, but the dream was nice. And he is really dreamy. He's going to help me move my bed tomorrow night, and I don't know what I'm going to do. Like... What if he kisses me? What if we go further than that? I'm nervous."

I am nervous. It's not like I'm a virgin. I mean, I've only had sex with one person. My college boyfriend, Jake. We dated for six months, and only had sex a few times before I broke up with him.

The sex wasn't very exciting, but that isn't why I broke up with him. He was just boring. There was very little chemistry between us. He also didn't understand why I disliked Frances so much—he totally bought into her fake nice act, and I just can't be with someone who doesn't understand the dynamic between me and my stepmother.

I blink as tiredness begins to overwhelm me. I hug the bear and turn on my side.

"Goodnight, Mom." I kiss the bear and close my eyes. Sleep catches me sooner than I expect.

***

"Oh, my God! I have a feeling tonight's the night. You guys are actually going to hook up!" Lily squeals and gives my shoulder a gentle shove. I brush her off and roll my eyes, but I can feel my cheeks heating up.

"We are not! He's just helping me move my bed, that's all."

"Yeah, I'm sure he will help you move your bed." She winks and rocks her hips, causing the entire desk to tremble. I sigh and shake my head.

"Ugh, are you always like this?" I ask, and Lily only laughs in response.

"I'm just teasing you, Emma. You're so serious all the time. By the way, how did coffee go?" She reaches into the bag of chips we're sharing and pops some in her mouth.

I shrug.

"It was fine, I guess. We mostly just talked about the hotel."

"What about it?"

"He wants to buy it. Don't tell Frances, please," I plead, my eyes wide as I take her in.

"I don't talk to Frances. Personally, she's kind of a jerk. I mean, we all have our moments, but some people just seem to permanently have a stick up their ass and she's one of them."

Relief floods through me—another person who sees through Frances' act is always a plus in my book.

"She's always been like that. At least for as long as I've known her."

"Cudos to you for keeping your cool with her. I would have exploded at her by now."

"I'm just not that kind of person, I guess." I tap my fingers on the desk before turning to her. "Okay, so suppose I do have sex with Lucas. What then? Does it become awkward?"

Lily looks at me, her mouth dropping open.

"Emma, are you a virgin?"

"What? No!" I sigh. "I'm not a virgin, but I've only had sex a few times. And never with someone experienced. What if I suck?"

"Do you want tips?"

I shudder at the idea of Lily telling me what to do during my most intimate moments.

"Uh, no thanks." Lily passes me a chip. I pop it in my mouth and finish chewing before a thought pops into my head. "Why were you so surprised at the idea that I could be a virgin?"

Lily scoffs as if the answer should be obvious to me.

"You're super hot and wicked smart."

"You think I'm hot?" I ask. I know I'm focusing on the wrong thing, but the idea is completely foreign to me.

"Are you kidding? You got that long red hair and a rocking body. Anyone with eyes would think you're hot."

I look down at my outfit today—a pair of fitted jeans, with heels and a snug red blouse. Not groundbreaking, nice enough for work, but not overdressed.

"Thanks, Lily. That means a lot. You're very attractive, too, you know." I smile at her and she rolls her eyes playfully.

"Gosh, if you want to date me, just say so." She hops off the desk and wipes her hands together, ridding them of any potential chip crumbs. "I really need to get back to the desk. That's the only problem I have with making friends at work—I'd much rather chat than get any actual work done."

I laugh and shake my head. But my heart swells at the thought that I've made a friend—something that I was pretty sure would never happen.

"You're great at your job. We're very lucky to have you on the team," I say, wiping my own hands.

"Thanks, Em. I hope all this praise comes with a pay upgrade."

She winks and I can't help but laugh again. "Seriously, though, I want you to text me an update as soon as he leaves tonight. Don't forget like you did with the coffee date."

"I didn't forget! There just wasn't anything to tell you about."

It's only a half-lie. I definitely forgot, but nothing newsworthy happened. Unless you count looking at my lips, which I don't.

"Yeah, yeah, whatever. Catch you later!" She gives a little wave before stepping out of the office door. I stretch my arms before leaning over the computer. There's payroll to do.

Chapter Twelve

Lucas

When I pull into the driveway, the sun is in the process of going down, illuminating the house against the darkening sky. It's gorgeous, the way the sunlight glints off the windows.

The beautiful sight does nothing to quell my nerves, though. I don't know why I'm so nervous—I'm just helping Emma move her bed. It's not like that means anything.

That's a lie. I know it means something that she's accepting my help. Especially since she seemed to be a little wary of me at first. It's clear, though, that she's warming up to me.

I haven't been nervous around a woman in a long time. In fact, I think the last time I felt this way before going on a date was when I finally asked out my high school crush. She was pretty, and I was heads over heels for her.

I scan the property, looking for a sign that anyone besides Emma is home. There's no cars parked in the driveway, but that doesn't mean anything since the cars could well be in the garage.

Sighing, I hop out of my car and head up the front steps. If I run into Frances, I run into her. There's not much I can do about it. Besides, I'm here for Emma.

I ring the doorbell and wait a moment. It doesn't take long until it's swinging open and Emma is standing before me.

She looks stunning.

Her long, red hair is pulled up into a strategically messy bun, strands falling out and framing her face. Warmth radiates from her eyes as a smile lights up her face. It's difficult to resist the urge to drop my eyes lower—her top is low cut, revealing her cleavage. Is it intentional?

"Hi! I'm so glad you're here," Emma says. Then she steps aside and lets me in.

"Me, too." I playfully sniff at the air. "Weird, I don't smell any pizza?"

Emma bumps my hip playfully and, for a moment, I enjoyed the feeling of her body against mine, even if only for a split second.

"I told you, no pizza. But maybe we could order Chinese after we move the bed."

She leads me up the stairs, and I'm suddenly aware that there is something intimate about being led to a woman's bedroom.

"What do you have against pizza?" I shoot back playfully, instilling effort to keep my nerves from showing in my voice.

"I don't have anything against pizza; I was just in the mood for Chinese. But if pizza is the price I need to pay for your help, so be it," she says, a shyness taking over her as she steps onto the second floor landing.

"I appreciate that."

She looks past me before her eyes meet mine again. "My room's this way."

I follow her down the hall. I can't help but notice the way her hips gently sway—the leggings she's wearing leave little to the imagination, not that I'm complaining.

The house is quiet, and Emma seems to be the only one home

Emma pushes open a door and gestures me inside.

"This is the place. Home sweet home. Or, it was."

The bedroom is surprisingly neat considering Emma is in the middle of a move. There are a few boxes stacked in one corner, and there are faint outlines on the wall where things clearly once hung, but there are no dirty clothes on the floor or clutter on the dresser like I would have expected.

The mattress is on the floor in the middle of the room, while the bed frame sits in disassembled pieces in the back corner. The solid wood headboard lays flat next to it.

"Looks like you've been busy," I say after scanning the room. "I'm impressed with how organized this is. Not what I expected."

Emma shrugs, but a glint of pride sparkles in her eyes.

"I've never really moved, except home from college, I guess, but I hate mess. Keeping things organized makes everything less stressful for me."

I walk over to examine the bed frame, running my hand over the smooth wood of the headboard. It's solid oak, heavy and well-crafted.

"This is a nice piece. Is it an antique?"

"My mom picked it out. You know how she always had an eye for that kind of thing."

A small smile lights up her face. "It's actually a part of a matching set—includes a dresser that was my mom's and the desk in my dad's office. She thought it was sweet for us all to have a piece of a matching set."

"That sounds like your mom," I confirm. Ginny always had a streak of sentimentality running through her. That's what made her and Clark so good together. Two lovey-dovey saps who were crazy about one another.

I lean toward the headboard for a closer look.

"I'll take good care of it, I promise."

When I look up, Emma is watching me with an intensity that makes my stomach flip. Our eyes lock, and for a moment, it's like there's an electricity between us, something both alarming and exciting.

"So, um, I figured we'd take the mattress down first so it's not in the way, then the headboard. Save the frame pieces for last."

"Sounds like a plan. Lead the way."

We position ourselves on either side of the mattress. As we lift, our eyes meet over the top of it, and I can't help but think about how this is the mattress where she sleeps every night. Where she lays her head down and dreams. I lick my lips and push the thought away. It's important to focus while lifting heavy things.

"Ready?" I wince at my tone—it's raspy, deeper than I intended.

She nods, and we begin our awkward shuffle toward the door, her in the lead. The mattress is heavy and solid but we manage to get it through the door with relative ease. It's the stairs that pose the real challenge.

"Let me take that side." I offer as we stop at the staircase to readjust.

"Why? Want to show off your tough guy muscles?" she teases, but she leans the mattress against the wall and shuffles toward me anyway.

I roll my eyes.

"The leading end of the mattress going down is the heavy part. I'm just trying to avoid you falling down the stairs and ending up with a mattress on top of you. I don't think that would make for a very productive evening."

Emma lets out a laugh, and I can tell it's a real one from how voraciously it erupts from her. It's full and warm, and it's a laugh I want to hear again and again.

When she stops, she cocks an eyebrow at me.

"Sorry, I'll get out of the way so you can grab my end."

"Your end?"

I roll my eyes and she chuckles. I grab the other end of the mattress and carefully maneuver it down the stairs, me walking backward and Emma guiding from above. I'm acutely aware of every step, knowing one misstep could result in a bad fall.

"So," Emma says, breaking my concentration, "what kind of food do you like? Besides pizza."

"Hmm." I haven't been asked this question in such a long time, that I'm not even fully sure how to answer it.

"I'm a sucker for a good burger. Especially smash burgers, the kind with the onions in the beef. Or Korean food. Honestly, I'm not very picky—unless it has peanut butter."

The mattress halts.

"You don't like peanut butter?"

I have to laugh at the incredulousness in Emma's tone.

"I absolutely can't stand it." I shudder dramatically. "The smell, the texture... none of it works for me. Honestly, just peanuts in general."

We reach the bottom step and then approach the front door.

"What?" Emma asks when I don't immediately open the door.

"We should have wrapped the mattress."

"Wrapped it? In what?"

"Protective covering. So it doesn't get dirty as we drag it outside."

Emma scoffs and throws her hands in the air.

"Oh, for goodness sake. I've never moved before! I don't know any of this stuff."

"Hey, it's okay. We can use garbage bags."

"Okay, I'll be right back."

Emma retrieves a box of trash bags and duct tape. We get to work ripping bags and taping them up into a makeshift mattress cover before finishing the journey from the front door to the basement.

"Where do you want it?" I ask.

"Just put it against that wall for now."

I go in the direction she indicates. We lean it up against the wall.

***

By the time we've brought the rest of the frame and headboard down, only an hour has passed.

I look around after we're finished.

"Seriously, thank you so much. You have no idea how much harder this would have been without you," Emma says, stepping closer to me.

"Of course, anytime." I look over at the bed in the corner of the room. "So what are we doing with the old bed?"

Emma stares at me blankly.

"Shit."

"You don't have a plan for it?"

"Honestly, I wasn't thinking past getting my own bed down here."

I laugh and shake my head.

"Hey, no worries. Want me to have someone haul it out of here this weekend?"

"Oh, my God, would you? I would owe you forever." My eyes meet Emma's, and I immediately feel a little overwhelmed by her presence. My body is acutely aware of the proximity to hers, how only one movement would put my lips on hers.

"You don't have to owe me. I'll do it regardless."

Emma looks up in surprise, her eyes lingering on mine a beat longer than necessary. Does she feel it, too? The almost magnetic pull between us.

"Well, I'd still like to thank you properly," she responds.

I raise my brows and she blushes. "Chinese food, remember? I know just the place."

She pulls out her phone and waves it, the tension between us breaking. I chuckle, mentally kicking myself.

"Chinese food sounds perfect."

She walks toward the bed in the corner and takes a seat, then looks at me expectantly. I follow and sit beside her.

"So this is going to be your new space, huh?" I ask, looking around.

Emma nods while scrolling through the menu.

"Yeah. It's actually growing on me. I have my own space, and I won't have to deal with Frances and Jackie all the time. More privacy."

She lifts her shoulder casually.

"Privacy is good."

Emma looks at me from the corner of her eye, and I have to look away.

I wasn't trying to be suggestive, but it's obvious why she might have taken it that way.

Still, she doesn't move away. In fact, she leans closer, tilting her phone screen in my direction.

The faint scent of vanilla and musk wafts over to me, and I resist the urge to deeply inhale the scent. It's intoxicating

"So I was thinking some dumplings, egg rolls, a load of fried rice, and maybe some General Tso's?" Emma looks at me expectantly and I just hold my hands up.

"Hey, I trust your judgment. Just no—"

"Peanuts, yup, I got it."

Emma puts the order in.

"We should probably head upstairs. They'll definitely go to the front door."

"Will it be awkward when Frances and Jackie get home?"

Emma blushes.

"Frances and Jackie are staying at Frances' sister's tonight."

I raise my brows.

"So we have the whole place to ourselves?"

"The whole place," Emma responds bashfully.

I suck in a breath as I follow her to the door.

This is definitely trouble.

Chapter Thirteen

Emma

I can't ignore the suggestive nature of having the whole place to ourselves.

In truth, it's all I've been thinking about since Lucas showed up to help. I've been trying to distract myself by chattering to him about random stuff, but for some reason my mind keeps coming back to that little fact.

I set out plates, glasses and silverware on the table with a few napkins, and take Lucas' drink order.

"Ice water is good for me," he says.

"Wow, it smells amazing," Lucas says as I rip open the bag and set the boxes around the table. We each grab a plate and fork and start serving up the food.

"Tastes even better."

"Best Chinese place in town." I smile thinking about it. It's the same place my dad used to order for us- always on the last day of the month.

"Well, I'm starving. Thank you so much for ordering."

"Uh, thank you so much for helping me move that bed!" I blush. "I actually have a confession to make."

"OK. I can't wait."

"So, last night, I tried to move the bed on my own. Well, not the whole bed. I knew I couldn't move a king sized mattress on my own, but thought I could probably get the frame and headboard down there."

"You tried to move the solid oak headboard by yourself?"

The look of shock on Lucas' face makes the whole confession worth it. It's absolutely comedic the way he's looking at me.

"Yeah, emphasis on 'tried.' It was super heavy, and fell to the floor. Just moving the mattress to lean against the wall was too much for me. I ended up underneath it for a time until I made my way out from under."

Lucas laughs and I can't help but join in. Our laughter quiets, though, as we dig into the food, savoring the flavors.

After we've finished eating, I clean up and walk Lucas outside.

"Thank you again for all your help."

Lucas turns around, standing directly in front of me. His eyes stare deeply into mine and my heart quickens with the intensity building in the air between us.

"Wait, do you think I'm leaving?" Lucas asks.

My heart skips a beat. Is he suggesting staying the night?

It's forward, but honestly, with how close he is to me, I would immediately fold and say yes.

"Um..."

I take a shaky breath.

"Your bed is in shambles on the floor. I'm not going to leave you to put it together yourself." Lucas shakes his head.

I lick my lips and look at my feet. How embarrassing—I hope he can't read my mind.

"Oh, right." I shake my head before turning swiftly, starting a jaunty jog to the basement. "Last one there's a rotten egg."

I make it to the door first, and as we step into the basement, I playfully wave the air in front of my face.

"Whew, smell that? Stinks like rotten eggs." I roll my eyes. Lucas closes the door behind us. "Pee-YOU!"

I plug my nose, keeping my eyes open so I can watch Lucas throw his head back in laughter. Then he gently takes my hand, and I let him remove it from my nose. His skin is warm against mine.

"Hey, now," he says, his voice soft and low.

It rumbles through me so much that I'm almost trembling. Or maybe I am trembling.

"I think you'll find that I smell very pleasant."

My eyes don't leave his as I lean in close, and take a soft breath. He smells incredible—like evergreen and nutmeg. Without thinking, I breathe in again, deeply so that I can bask in his scent.

I can practically feel my face turning red with heat—we're so close that I'm practically drinking in his scent, and the warmth radiating from his body makes me dizzy with anticipation.

"You do smell nice." My voice is barely above a whisper. "Better than rotten eggs, at least."

Lucas chuckles, then his hand trails up my bare shoulder, brushing so gently that it makes my hair stand on end. I suck in a breath. His eyes look down at my lips, just like they did the other day.

"We should probably start putting that bed together," he says after what feels like a long time.

"We probably should." I hate how ragged my breath sounds. He's so calm about being so close to me, and I'm falling apart at the seams because he's touching my arm.

He leans in closer and it's like time slows down. My heart is beating so thunderously loud that Lucas can probably hear it.

"Emma," he whispers. His voice catches, betraying his cool and collected facade. He's nervous, too.

I lean in and close the distance between us, surprising even myself with the bold move.

The kiss is gentle at first, hesitation evident from both of us. Then Lucas tugs me forward, wrapping his other arm around me.

His tongue flicks into my mouth and I can't help the moan that escapes me. My hands find the thick muscles of his arms and continue until they're running through Lucas's thick hair.

Our mouths come apart but our hands don't leave each other. He pulls me closer and tips his forehead against mine.

"I've been wanting to do that since I walked through the front door."

He brings up a hand and brushes my cheek gently, then runs his thumb over my bottom lip. "You have perfect lips."

"Just since then?" I ask, teasing. "I've been thinking about it since you helped me carry my boxes the other day."

He rolls his eyes and chuckles.

"Not everything is a competition, you know."

"All the fun things are."

He shakes his head and leans down again.

This time when we kiss, there's nothing tentative about it. His hands roam my back, pulling me impossibly closer as I melt against him. We stumble backward until I feel the wall behind me, cool against my heated skin.

His lips move further down my neck, kissing until they reach my pulse point. When he sucks gently on it, I gasp.

I feel him smile against my neck and that only turns me on more.

He plays with the hem of my shirt before lifting it over my head, revealing the bra underneath.

It's not frilly or lacy, but it is black.

Lucas' eyes roll over me, and when I bite my lip he sucks in a breath before reaching around and deftly unsnapping my bra with one easy swipe.

My skin prickles and my nipples harden at the feeling of the cool basement air against my skin.

Lucas' eyes darken as he takes me in.

"You're beautiful," he says, his voice quiet but direct.

I don't say anything as I take his own shirt and lift it over his head. It's my turn to look at him, but I can't stop with just my eyes.

I run my hands over his sculpted chest, soaking in the way curls of hair erupt from it.

The area between my legs pulses with desire. I don't want this to stop.

As if reading my mind, Lucas cups my breasts in his hand, giving a gentle squeeze before taking a nipple in his mouth. I shiver at the feeling of his tongue brushing over it, the combination of his wet mouth and soft touch making me throb.

He turns his attention to the other one, brushing his thumb over my wet nipple as he repeats his actions on the other.

Then Lucas grips my waist and pushes me toward the bed in the corner of the basement— the old one that's already assembled.

I thought I'd be more nervous when the time came, but instead I'm eagerly anticipating Lucas fucking me.

My legs hit the bed, and Lucas gently pushes me backward onto it.

His fingers find their way to the waistband of my leggings as he kisses me again. He pulls back and looks into my eyes.

"Is this okay?" he asks.

His voice is low and rough, and I can feel the vibration of it against my skin.

He kisses me, his fingers brushing the damp heat between my legs, and I whimper.

"Oh, God, yes" I gasp, the words a plea.

Then he stops, hesitates.

"Don't stop," I plead.

He groans, his fingers skimming over my flesh, his mouth claiming mine.

He kisses me until I can't breathe, until the world starts to spin.

And then, just when I think I can't take any more, his mouth moves lower. His lips trail along the sensitive skin of my neck, his teeth scraping lightly.

He sucks a spot just below my ear, and I moan, my hips bucking.

He moves lower, his tongue sliding over the curve of my collarbone, the hollow of my throat.

"You have no idea how hard I am right now," he whispers.

"Show me."

I expect him to take me up on the offer, but instead, his fingers trail down my spine, tracing the curve of my ass, the back of my thigh.

His mouth follows, his tongue tracing a path down the center of my chest.

My hands fist in his shirt and I work to take it off of him.

But, instead, he moves lower, his lips brushing the underside of my breast, his fingers tracing the curve of my hip. He hooks a hand behind my knee, pulling my leg over his shoulder, and then he's there.

Right there. At the hot, wet entrance to my pussy.

His breath is warm, his tongue soft and insistent.

"Oh, my God."

He licks a line across the top of my inner thigh, and I shiver.

My hands tangle in his hair, and he groans, his mouth finding the tender skin at the juncture of my hip.

He sucks gently, and I moan, my hips bucking.

His fingers tighten, holding me in place as his tongue traces the line of my thigh.

"Lucas," I whisper.

I can feel the heat of him, the warmth of his breath.

I ache for him, ache for more.

"Please."

The word comes out a whimper, and he groans, his tongue stroking a lazy line up the center of my pussy.

"Don't stop."

He licks the sensitive bud, and I cry out, my fingers digging into his shoulders.

His tongue swirls around my clit, his fingers digging into my thighs, his breath hot and ragged against me.

I arch into him, my body aching for more.

He looks up, his eyes dark and hungry, and then he's back, his tongue moving over me in long, slow strokes.

"Oh, God."

My head falls back, and his fingers tighten on my thighs, pulling me closer, his tongue moving faster, in and out of my cunt, his breath hot and heavy against me.

I can feel the pleasure building, my body tensing as I move my legs even farther apart to allow him the fullest possible access as I feel my wetness begin to drip from my pussy into his waiting mouth.

"Fuck, Lucas. Don't stop. Please."

I can hear the desperation in my voice, but I don't care. Not when he's licking me, sucking me, driving me wild.

I can feel the pressure building, the need for release almost unbearable.

"Please," I beg.

He groans, his tongue circling the swollen bud, his fingers digging into my hips.

"Cum for me, Emma," he whispers.

He doesn't stop, his tongue relentless, his fingers tightening on my hips, pulling me closer, and suddenly, like a floodgate, the pressure breaks.

The orgasm rips through me, making me cry out, and he doesn't stop.

He licks me through the aftershocks, his mouth soft and gentle, his fingers stroking my hips.

This.

This is what I've been missing, I think dully.

My mind is a muddle of scattered thoughts and my pounding pulse. Sex was never like this with Jake. Sex with Jake and what's happening now are two very, very different things.

When I finally catch my breath, he presses one last kiss to my thigh and begins to move up my body.

I can feel the hard length of him against me, and I grind against him, desperate for release.

He groans, his fingers digging into my hips. His voice is rough, strained, and I can tell he's struggling to hold back.

But I don't want him to.

I reach between us, fumbling with the zipper of his jeans, and then I'm gripping him, my hand wrapping around his shaft.

I may not have much experience, but I refuse to let that stop me. I feel a surge of pride at pleasing him when he drops his forehead to mine and groans in pleasure.

I stroke him slowly, reveling in the way he reacts to every little touch.

He's hot and hard, and I can't get enough of him. I run my thumb over the tip of his cock, and he hisses, his hips jerking forward toward me.

My head falls back, and he moves between my legs, his lips brushing the soft skin behind my ear.

"I'm going to fuck you now," he says gruffly. "Tell me you're ready for me."

My pulse races, and I can't seem to find any words until finally, "Please, Lucas. Fuck me now. Hard. Fast."

I wrap my arms around his neck and pull him close, kissing him until I can't breathe.

He shifts his weight, pressing against me, his cock teasing my entrance.

He kisses me again, hard and hungry, and then he thrusts into me, his huge cock filling me completely.

"Oh, God," I moan, arching into him.

His fingers dig into my hips, holding me steady as he withdraws and thrusts again, slowly moving in and out and I can hear the wetness of my pussy as he slides back and forth.

He's big, and I can feel every inch of him, but the slight stretch of my pussy only makes it better.

I'm stretched, filled, and it feels so damn good.

My head falls back, and he buries his face in the curve of my neck, his breathing ragged, his body tense.

"You feel so fucking good," he murmurs, his lips brushing the shell of my ear.

I'm overwhelmed by the sensation of him, the feel of him.

It's as if I'm desperate for him; as if I've waited too long for this. He growls, burying his face in the space between my neck and my shoulder.

His skin is warm, his body hard and unforgiving. He's incredible, and I can't get enough. I'm wet and I'm tight and stretched to my fullest for him.

"You're so fucking perfect," he tells me.

I know I'm not going to last much longer, but I don't want this to be over, so I try to slow it down.

Lucas must feel the same, because he slows his thrusts, making me moan in protest, but he just continues his gentle in and out motion as I struggle to hold on until he's ready.

Finally, I can't stand it any longer. I cry out and arch into him, teetering over the edge into the abyss of orgasm.

"Fuck, Emma," he says, his voice hoarse.

He thrusts into me one last time, then yet again, hard and strong and deep, and I feel him fill me with his cum.

I grit my teeth, letting the orgasm take me, every nerve ending crying for release. My body shudders, then begins to relax, my breathing slowly returning to normal.

"I love all your freckles. They're so sexy."

He kisses me and then slides onto the bed next to me, gathering me into his arms.

"There aren't any words to describe how you make me feel, Emma. That was absolutely amazing," Lucas murmurs. I kiss him on the forehead and smile slyly.

"You can enjoy it more next time," I say teasingly. He smirks as he eyes me.

"So we both agree: there will definitely be a next time?"

I smile and study him.

He's playing it off like he's being flirty, but it's clear that the question is genuine. I nod and hug him closer.

"There will definitely be a next time."

"You know, I'm actually still kind of hungry." Lucas looks at me and I can't help but laugh.

"Seriously? You just fucked me silly."

"What? I didn't realize until just now. My mind was elsewhere."

His eyes roam me suggestively. I just shake my head, but I can't stop the grin that is spreading across my face.

"Okay, you get a pass. Let's grab some more food and maybe we can watch a movie."

"What about the bed?"

"We can put it together tomorrow."

It almost feels overly-confident to assume he'll stay the night and help me again tomorrow.

But mostly it just feels right.

Chapter Fourteen

Lucas

When I wake up the next morning, it takes a second for me to remember where I am.

I don't even remember falling asleep last night.

After our second dinner, Emma and I retreated to the living room to watch some sort of comedy she picked out. She started dozing off during it, though. So I woke her and we both went to the basement.

I was almost dreading climbing into her bed, considering how many sleep issues I've been having. There's no white noise machine, no television in her room to provide any sound.

Only the ambient noises of the basement echoing against each other, a creak from upstairs here, the wind against the door there.

Surprisingly, though, I was only listening to them for a few minutes before I was out cold. I even dreamed, though the memories of it faded before I was even fully conscious.

"Morning sleepyhead," Emma says from beside me, setting her phone at her side.

"Have you been awake long?" I ask, pulling her in to kiss her forehead. She smiles and shakes her head.

"Nah, just about fifteen minutes. What do you think about coffee?"

"It's delicious."

She huffs and rolls her eyes. She's adorable when she's annoyed.

"I'm game for some, yes."

"Perfect. I was thinking the place we went for lunch the other day? You were right; it really was amazing."

I study her before nodding.

It is delicious coffee, but I know the reason she wants to go ten minutes out of the way for coffee is because she doesn't want to be confronted by anyone we know.

"You don't have to work today?"

"No, I'm off on weekends. One of the perks of being the manager."

"That is quite the perk."

I pull her in and nuzzle her ear. She giggles and swats me away.

"I have to get Jackson and let him outside first. Come on, we have a lot to do today. Let's get started."

***

An hour and two cups of coffee later, we're both sitting on the floor putting the bed frame together.

"Okay, I need a screwdriver." I turn and Emma digs around in the toolbox. "A Phillips."

Emma nods and then digs around before handing me a screwdriver.

"This is a flathead."

"Well." Emma throws her hands up in exasperation. "I couldn't find one that said Phillip's on it!"

I laugh and shake my head.

"Didn't your dad teach you anything at all about tools?"

"Of course not! He was the only one who used them."

"And yet you thought you could put this bed together by yourself? Amazing. A flathead is just one line at the tip. A Phillips head looks almost like a star."

Emma stares at me before nodding and going back to look again.

The morning had gone much like this, making it obvious that Emma knew nothing about finding her way around a toolbox.

And I'm loving every minute of it. It's natural, sitting here with her and putting a bed frame together. As if this was what I was always supposed to be doing in the first place.

"Found it," Emma says, triumphantly holding up a Phillips screwdriver. She waves her hand under it as if presenting a trophy. "I think. Does this look star-ish to you?"

I chuckle, then take it from her and nod.

"Perfect. You're a natural."

"Oh, stop, you're going to make me blush." she says, but I can see the pleased smile on her face.

"That's supposed to deter me? You're pretty cute when you blush"

"Oh yeah?" She scoots closer. "Am I cute even when I do this?"

Emma crosses her eyes and sticks out tongue. A smile forms on my face.

"Even cuter."

She bumps my shoulder playfully before settling next to me, sitting cross-legged on the floor. She watches intently as I use the screwdriver to join the two pieces of the bed frame together.

"You know, I could get used to this." Emma says after a while.

"What? Watching me do manual labor while you supervise?"

"Exactly." She leans back on her hands. "It's kind of mesmerizing, watching you work with your hands."

"So it's my hands you like?"

She sucks in a breath as her face lights up red. I smirk and move to the next screw.

"Yeah, your hands are definitely...something," she whispers.

I tighten the last screw and step back to admire my handiwork. The bed frame looks solid enough. My eyes draw to the small bed in the corner of the room.

"Is that where you want this bed to go?" I ask, gesturing to the frame.

"Unfortunately, yes."

"Hey, it's no problem. Let's just take apart the old one and wrap the mattress."

Emma runs to grab more trash bags and duct tape while I get to work dragging the old mattress off the frame and stripping off the sheets and bedding.

"Here we go." Emma says as she walks through the door.

Wrapping the mattress is easy enough, and we prop it against a wall before taking apart the cheap, metal bed frame.

"This is a lot easier than taking apart the wood one."

"Oh, that's right, you did it yourself. I'm surprised you didn't strip the screws, considering you didn't have any idea what you were doing."

Emma scoffs.

"'Some people's talents lay in the creations their hands make, while others lay in the way their minds work.'"

She quotes, then looks at me pointedly. "Guess which category I fall into?"

"What's that quote from?" I ask. It's familiar, but I can't quite place it.

"It's just something Mom used to say. I think she told me it was a quote from Ralph Waldo Emerson."

Emma shrugs.

Ginny is where I heard it too. She said it once in college, when Clark was upset about messing up something at his job. It cheered him up at the time, although Ginny probably could have said anything and it would have put a smile on his face.

Silence fills the space as we both concentrate on dismantling the frame.

Emma stands up to grab something from the toolbox, but trips over one of the loose pieces and falls forward, crashing into me. The frame creaks underneath her and breaks apart.

I pull her off the frame and examine her.

"Are you okay? Anything hurt?"

"Just my pride," she says glumly and I laugh.

"Come on, your fall just saved us from having to finish unscrewing that joint. It's just a crappy metal frame, anyway. Besides, we have your new one ready to go."

"But no one will want it now. It's useless."

"No, it's not. We'll just take it to the thrift store. If Frances really wants it, we'll replace it but I doubt that's going to be a problem," I say.

A shy smile colors Emma's features as her eyes meet mine.

"What?"

"I don't know. It's just cute how you say 'we.' As if we're a team."

"Well, we're both working on it, and I should know better than to be leaving all these pieces of bed frame around the floor. Really, it's my fault that you fell."

My words have the desired effect, and Emma throws her head back in laughter, her red hair shaking over her freckled shoulders.

She really is beautiful.

I help her up, and we stand together for a minute, just absorbing each other's presence. Then I pick up a piece of the metal frame.

"Let's get rid of this so we can set up your real bed."

***

An hour later, Emma's bed is set up. The old mattress still leans against a wall—I don't really know what to do with it. The soonest it can get hauled off is next weekend, and there's not really a place to store it. It will unfortunately have to stay where it is for a while.

I look over at Emma as she admires her bed. She grabs my arm, and when she looks at me, excitement is lit up all over.

"I am so happy to have my king bed. I love all the space."

"I'm glad you're happy."

"We need to celebrate!"

"Yeah? What did you have in mind?"

She makes a noise, as if offended.

"Hey, I planned Chinese, a movie, coffee, and the idea of a celebration. It's your turn to do some legwork here."

I wrap my arms around her and pull her close, pressing my forehead to hers.

"First of all, you didn't plan a movie. That was a last minute decision."

She wrinkles her nose and opens her mouth to protest.

"Second, I am more than happy to come up with a celebration. And I know just the thing."

"Do tell."

"How do you feel about the farmers market?"

Emma's brows shoot to her forehead.

"Oh. I haven't been in a really long time. I do like it, though. I used to go with Mom every Saturday, and she would buy me a pack of honey straws."

"Up for a walk down memory lane?" I tilt my head.

"Can Jackson come?"

"Of course. The more the merrier."

"Okay, I'm officially excited."

She grins and wiggles in my arms. I plant a kiss on her lips before releasing her.

"All right, let's get Jackson and head out."

***

The old golden retriever sniffs at the ground as we pass by the various stalls set up around the farmers market.

His tail wags lazily, occasionally brushing my leg as he walks beside us.

Jackson is a sweet dog, and I remember the puppy pictures Clark sent me when they first got him. He still has some of his old puppy energy, eager to be here, the only sign of his aging the graying surrounding his eyes and snout.

"Honey straws." I point at the jar containing the plastic sticks.

It's hanging dangerously close to the edge of the honey vendor's table. As we approach Emma pushes it further onto the table, careful not to knock anything over.

"We have sample packs for five dollars. Jars are fifteen for a small one and twenty-seven for a large one," the woman says, pointing to each item.

After mulling over the decision, Emma grabs two different sample packs and I hand over the money to the woman. She nods as we walk away.

"I want one right now."

"We can have all of them right now."

Emma looks at me from the corner of her eye and shakes her head.

"We are adults, Lucas. We can't just suck down honey straws without having anything substantial in our systems."

She takes a straw from one of the packets before shoving the rest in her purse. Then she rips off the top with her teeth, and shoves it in her pocket.

"Do you keep the tops?"

"I don't want to litter."

"Give it to me."

I hold my hand out expectantly. She flicks the top into my hand and I throw it away quickly before returning.

Emma presses her thumb into the honey stick and holds it out to me. I suck down a third of the tube before Emma pulls it away.

"What do you think?" she asks.

I lick my lips and smile.

"Delicious."

She nods before sucking down her own portion.

To my surprise, she doesn't take the rest. Instead, she has only a third before kneeling down and offering the rest to Jackson. He laps it up happily as she squeezes it out of the tube.

Emma really loves this dog, and it's the sweetest thing in the world.

When the straw is empty, she holds it out to me to throw in the trash again. Emma kisses Jackson's head before standing in front of me.

"Where to next?"

"This way," I murmur, kissing her forehead and taking her hand before leading her away.

Chapter Fifteen

Emma

Lucas is holding my hand, and in public, no less. I feel like a teenage girl, giddy over her first boyfriend. Not that I had a boyfriend as a teenager—I guess I wouldn't really know what it feels like.

But I imagine that it felt a lot like this.

Lucas points out different stalls as we stroll through them—veggies, knitted items, fresh eggs. He finally stops in front of a stall loaded with flowers.

They're bright and beautiful, the colors so vibrant that for a moment, I wonder if this is all a dream.

"Do you like flowers?" Lucas asks.

"Are there people who don't like flowers?" I snort. His shoulder bumps mine.

"Oh, you'd be surprised, dear."

The woman at the stall studies Lucas before nodding. "Ah, hello there. You were in the shop the other day! How did you like those arrangements?"

I look up at him. He was buying flowers?

"They were beautiful, and they looked great. Thank you for your help." He turns to me. "I bought flowers to put on my parents' graves. And your dad's."

My heart swells with warmth. The more time that I spend with Lucas, the more I become okay with the fact that he was my dad's best friend.

In fact, I find it endearing. Through him I can learn about a whole new side to Dad.

It doesn't bring him back, but it keeps his memory alive.

"That's really sweet of you. What did you end up getting?"

"Lilies, and roses for your dad."

I gasp and smack my forehead.

"Lily!"

"No, lilies-" Lucas starts to correct, but I shake my head.

"I was supposed to text her last night and completely forgot."

Shoot. I am a terrible friend. This is the second time. I pull out my phone and shoot her a quick text—will update later.

She sends only a magnifying glass emoji and nothing else.

"You're good friends?" Lucas asks.

I shrug.

"Actually, we sort of just became friends. And she's my only friend."

Lucas stares at me, which makes me feel compelled to continue.

"I just don't get out much. The only time I'm around people my age is when we check in guests. Everyone else working at the hotel is older. Or I don't click with them."

Not that I've ever tried to click with anyone. Including Lily. It's more like she forced her friendship on me, but I'm glad she did.

It's weird having someone to update about my love life. It's weird that I have a love life to update about at all.

Life has certainly changed these days.

"That's okay. Really you just need a couple of close friends to keep you happy," Lucas says. He's so incredibly kind.

I lick my lips and turn back to the flowers. Every time I think about how nice he is, I think about how great he was last night.

"I like those." I point to a basket of light pink blooms. The petals look so soft, almost like they'd be the texture of worn paper rather than stiff like some flower petals are. "They look so delicate."

"Hollyhocks. Beautiful flowers, some of my favorites as well," the stall owner says. "Said to represent ambition and strength. And fertility."

I blanch, but the woman says it so casually that I feel the need to reign in my reaction.

"We'll take a dozen," Lucas says, seemingly unbothered by the mention of fertility. Maybe I'm reading too much into things. They're just flowers, of course.

Except my dad was really into flower meanings. I didn't memorize them, and I never read the Farmer's Almanac no matter how many times he wanted me to.

"Excellent choice."

She picks the flowers from the basket and begins to wrap them in butcher paper, finishing them off with a string of twine tied around the base. Then she hands me a small packet of powder. "Flower food. Cut the stems at an angle and put them in water. They'll last longer with this packet, too."

I nod as Lucas takes the flowers and I deposit the pouch into my purse. Lucas pays her and we stroll away. Lucas hands them to me and I smile, cradling them in the crook of my elbow.

"Thank you. They're beautiful."

"You do know how to pick them." Lucas winks before looking around the farmers market. "Where to next?"

My stomach growls in response. We both laugh.

"Food. I'm starving."

Lucas nods and leads me away. At the end of the Farmers Market is a circle of food trucks. As we approach, a familiar voice sounds through the crowd.

"Mr.Bennett! Mr.Bennett!"

A gangly college kid emerges from the crowd, curly hair flopping atop his head. He gives us a lopsided smile. "Hey, Emma! Y'all shopping today?"

I blush and look down at the flowers, but Royce seems oblivious. Lucas and I aren't holding hands anymore, but it still feels as though we've been caught doing something.

"Just spending a relaxing weekend out. What are you doing here?" Lucas asks.

"I heard there was going to be an antiques dealer here today, so I thought I'd come check it out! I know we're looking for pieces to revert the rooms."

Royce nods and stands up straighter.

Lucas raises his brows.

"You're working on the weekend?"

Royce looks away and shrugs.

"I wasn't really sure what to do, since I've never been here. And the hotel kind of stinks right now."

This grabs my attention.

"What?" My tone is sharper than I intended, but Royce seems undeterred.

"Yeah, there's some sort of plumbing issue happening on the second floor. Hotel's waiting for a plumber to come out on Monday, the front desk guy said."

He shrugs as if this is unimportant.

I sigh.

"Right. The plumber can't come out to fix it until Monday." I kick at the ground.

"It's no big deal. Not like most people spend their whole day in the hotel, anyway," Royce responds.

Royce's phone blares out a fuzzy show tune. He fumbles in his pockets and digs it out. "Oh, it's my mom! I've got to answer this. See y'all later!"

I almost feel bad for the relief I feel when he leaves.

Apparently, Lucas doesn't.

"Thank goodness. I like the kid but he can be a lot." He shakes his head. "Let's grab some food."

We chose a food truck at random—a barbecue joint. Lucas orders a fried bologna sandwich, while I try my luck at a loaded pulled pork baked potato. We take a seat at one of the picnic tables, and even though I want to devour the food in front of me, I'm more starved for conversation with Lucas.

"Tell me something I don't know about you." I grab my fork and smash around the potato. Lucas chews his food and then shrugs.

"Like what?"

"Like... what's something you're scared of?"

"Butterflies."

I roll my eyes.

"No, really."

"No, yeah. Really."

We look at each other, holding our gaze like it's a challenge. When he doesn't look away, I relent.

"Okay, fine. Let's say I believe you're scared of butterflies. What would be the reason?"

"When I was young, my grandmother had a huge flower garden. My dad's family was from South Carolina, so there were a lot of flowers. Anyway, I went to stay with her one summer, and she would force me to garden. One day, I'm leaning over a plant, helping her water, and I feel this..."

Lucas gags. "This itching sensation on the back of my neck. Turns out it was a spider and my grandmother knocked it off. It was the worst thing I've ever felt in my life."

I smash my lips together, trying to hold in the laughter. When Lucas' earnest eyes meet mine, I'm unable to hold it back anymore.

"Hey! It was a very traumatic experience for me."

"I'm sorry! I couldn't help myself. I'll be good." I nod and straighten up. He shakes his head and looks down at his feet.

Lucas opens his mouth, but before he can say anything, my phone starts blaring. I look at the screen and groan.

"It's Frances."

"Are you going to answer it?"

I click the green button as our eyes meet.

"Frances?"

"Emma, you need to get to the hotel now. It's a mess, the whole place is a mess!" Frances' tone is frantic, unlike anything I've ever heard from her before.

"Whoa, what's going on?"

Lucas' interest increases as he takes a step closer, undoubtedly trying to hear the other end of the conversation.

"There's water EVERYWHERE! It smells horrible. Oh, God, this is a train wreck. Please just get here!"

I hear someone say something to Frances, she snaps at them and then the line goes dead. I look at Lucas and frown.

"We need to go to the hotel. Lunch will have to wait."

***

"This is a disaster!" Frances wails from somewhere beyond as Lucas and I step into the lobby. I take a cursory glance around the lobby—everything looks normal, but there is a distinctive... mildew-like smell permeating the area.

Lucas hangs behind as I follow the sound of expletives being shouted by Frances. As much as I'd love to have his support behind me at this moment, it's smarter if Frances doesn't see us coming in together on my day off.

Not that I think she'd notice; Frances is pacing in the staff kitchen, her usually perfect hair slick and frizzy, as if she's been running her hands through it a lot.

"Frances?" I ask softly, trying not to rattle her.

She whirls, and her eyes widen as she steps forward, grabbing my shoulders with a grip so tight that it makes me wince. Her nails will definitely be leaving marks in my shoulders.

"Emma! Oh, God, Emma, we're doomed! I'm never going to make a penny on this awful hotel."

The slight on my parents' hotel makes me bristle, but Frances is clearly panicked, so I'm choosing to ignore it.

"Okay, let's just take a second and breathe. Tell me what is going on."

Frances nods, stands up straight and breathes as she composes herself. This is probably the nicest interaction the two of us have ever had, but I don't get the chance to savor it as she launches into business mode.

"I'm certain you remember the other day when we had to call the plumber."

She doesn't wait for me to affirm.

"Well, he left on Friday after fixing the clogged toilet, but said that he wanted to check out some other plumbing and pipe related things on Monday, since we hadn't had an inspection for quite a while and our systems and building are quite old. So, I thought sure, fine, whatever, it can't hurt to have the pipes looked at. But I wish he'd done it sooner, because one of the pipes burst this morning and it turns out that most of the second floor pipes are rusted through. It's going to cost a ton of money to replace the galvanized pipes with copper plumbing and we'll also have to repair the affected floors and possibly some of the furniture, depending on the water damage the second floor pieces might have sustained."

I let out a deep breath and shake my head.

"Okay, yeah, that's a problem, all right."

Frances lets out a bitter laugh.

"I'll say it's a problem, Emma. All the guests currently staying on the east end of the second floor? We have to find them new rooms or alternative hotels since those rooms are no longer habitable. Not to mention all the reservations we have to cancel in the coming weeks."

"Wait, we have to cancel reservations?" I respond in surprise.

She rolls her eyes.

"The repairs are estimated to take three weeks. I asked him if he could get it done any faster—I mean, we're trying to run a business here! He said he could get it done faster if I have a magic toolbox stored somewhere."

Frances scoffs. "He has the nerve to be sarcastic with me. And I really do think he might have prevented this had he done routine inspections in an orderly manner. "

We hear a crash of some sort from the lobby. Frances closes her eyes in frustration and then storms out of the kitchen, me following after her.

Chapter Sixteen

Lucas

"For goodness sake, what now?!" Frances yells as she storms across the lobby, Emma behind her.

Jackie sits on one of the lobby couches, wincing at her mother's tone but focusing heavily on her phone, as if trying to avoid the situation completely.

Royce smiles sheepishly from his place on the floor, where he's gathering the bags of noisy trinkets he gathered from the market.

"Sorry, Frances. I grabbed some gifts for my family while I was out today and... well, I'm a little clumsy."

He stands up and brushes off his pants. Frances licks her lips and looks away. Whatever is going on, it clearly has her worried.

"How are things going this morning?" I ask, keeping my tone casual.

I'm not supposed to know there's a situation going on—I can't say for sure how Frances would react knowing that I spent the night, and consequently the morning, with Emma, but I'm certain it would not be a positive reaction.

"Honestly, Lucas, I— "

She waves her hand in the air and shakes her head. "When you and Clark were working on the hotel, did you replace the plumbing?"

I frown. That's not the question I was expecting. I shrug.

"Uh, I couldn't tell you to be honest. A lot of that was stuff Clark and Ginny handled. I don't remember replacing the plumbing, but if you're looking for that sort of information, it should be in Clark's files. He was a phenom for paperwork and recording everything."

"Emma." Frances turns around, narrowing her gaze. "You know where your father keeps his files, correct?"

"Yes, of course."

"Good. I need you to comb through every piece of paperwork on what your parents did to this place. I don't want any more surprises."

Frances turns back to me. "The plumbing on the second floor is worn out. We have to have it all replaced. It's costly and it will take weeks. Given the age of this building, we might have to replace all of the galvanized pipes in the hotel in the coming months."

"My room is on the second floor." I'm suddenly grateful I wasn't here when a pipe burst this morning."

Frances sighs.

"Of course it is. And yours?"

Royce blinks as she looks at him, seemingly surprised that she's addressing him at all.

He shakes his head.

"Nope, third floor."

"Well, you'll be fine, Roy. Unfortunately, Lucas, we're going to have to relocate you. We've already moved a couple of guests to the third floor, and those rooms are full."

I choke back a laugh. Relocate me, like I'm a pesky cat getting under her skin constantly.

Actually, that might be a more apt description than I think even she realizes.

"I can look into other hotels, don't worry about it." I try to sound casual, but I can hear the displeasure on the edge of my tone.

Being further away from the hotel means I won't be able to be as hands on with whatever Frances cooks up.

And fewer chances to see Emma.

If I'm honest, seeing Emma less is more of a motivating reason to try to stay close by.

"You could always room with me, Mr. Bennett. There's only one bed, but I could take the couch."

"Why doesn't he stay with us?" Jackie pipes up from the sofa she's lounging on.

"I'm sorry?" Frances asks, her tone abrupt as she turns to Jackie.

"We have a guest room. He's an old family friend—it only makes sense, right?" Jackie shoots me a smile that makes my stomach drop.

"The guest room," Frances repeats slowly, as if chewing on the thought as she says it out loud.

She glances at Emma, who looks simultaneously thrilled and terrified at the idea of having me so close by. "I suppose that could work."

"That's quite unnecessary. I'd hate to impose on you. There are other hotels."

"Don't be silly!" Jackie squeals, pocketing her phone as she stands up. "It makes perfect sense. Mom, Lucas is helping you with the hotel, so he'll be close by for any paperwork or input. Or other emergencies."

Jackie gives me a flirty glance, and I have to resist the urge to frown. This is not a situation I prefer to be in—now it makes things even more difficult if I want to continue to see Emma.

"I'm sure Lucas would feel much more comfortable in a hotel—-" Emma chimes in, anxiety written all over her face. She's in full-on panic mode.

"Actually, Jackie's right. I think it's a great idea." Frances looks between me and Jackie as a smile crosses her face.

What is she cooking up? Do I even want to know?

"The guest room is lovely, decorated by Clark, which I'm sure you'll appreciate. You'd be doing us a favor, really. With you so close by, we'd be able to confer about decisions more easily. Besides, you're practically family, being his best friend and all."

I glance at Emma, whose cheeks are so pink they're practically glowing as she studies the floor.

When I look back at Frances, she's giving me an expectant grin. I can't refuse now, not after she said I'm practically family.

"That sounds lovely. Thank you Frances."

"Of course. Jackie can help you move your things later."

"That's not necessary, Royce can... "

"Come on now, your assistant doesn't need to go out of his way! Jackie will be heading to the house anyway."

"I can help him," Emma says. Frances rolls her eyes.

"Emma, aren't you supposed to be looking for some files? They aren't going to find themselves," Frances snaps. The looks she gives Emma could wither even the hardiest winter plants.

"Yes, Frances." Emma's eyes meet mine with a knowing glance before she turns on her heel and heads for the office.

"Perhaps I could help? I'm quite familiar with Clark's filing system. It's one I still use to this day."

I choose my tone carefully, one of polite disinterest. As if I couldn't care less about the filing system, but want to be helpful.

"It's the least I could do in return for you offering me your guest room."

"Thank you, I appreciate that. If you don't mind, I have a lot to do."

Frances' heels click away as Jackie approaches me, laying a hand on my shoulder.

"I'll meet you in the lobby at 4:00 and help you move your things to the house."

She bats her lashes, and as much as I want to shove her hand off my shoulder, I instead give her a polite smile and shift as if to walk away.

"Thank you, Jackie. I'm going to go help Emma, now."

***

"This is seriously a mess," Emma says as she flips through another file.

Clark was old fashioned—he had digital copies of everything, but he preferred his paper files over everything.

"This is actually impeccably organized, there is just a lot of information here," I respond, grabbing another file, this one labeled 'March 2001.'

"Not the files, Lucas! This whole situation!"

I grunt.

"By the situation, do you mean the plumbing, or me sleeping only two floors above you?"

I give her a cheeky grin and she rolls her eyes, bumping my shoulder with hers.

"Ha ha, very funny. You know exactly what I mean." She sighs. "They're obviously trying to throw Jackie at you."

"Yeah, that's not going to happen."

"Clearly. How are we supposed to stay away from each other?"

"Who said we have to?"

"Come on. We can't be sneaking around the house trying to avoid Frances like a couple of teenagers!"

"Can't we? I think it might be kind of fun."

Our eyes meet, and I move forward, tucking a strand of her loose red hair behind her ear. She responds immediately, tucking her face against my palm. I take the chance to move forward, gently pressing my lips on hers.

Emma pulls back, the whisper of a smile on her face.

"We really shouldn't do this here."

"Do what? We're just looking at some files."

This time Emma comes to me, wrapping her arms around my neck to pull me in closer. The kisses become more frantic as I pull the rolling chair closer. She giggles as I thumb at the hem of her dress.

I trail my kisses down her neck and move my hand up her skirt, softly tickling at the soft skin of her inner thigh. She moans, pushing closer so I can brush my thumb against the fabric of her underwear.

The door to the office swings open and we spring apart.

"Um, hey, Emma, you never updated me about your date with—Oh! I see it must have gone well," Lily grins as she walks in.

"Oh, this isn't—we're not— " Emma babbles in an attempt to cover up our illicit office activities.

"What Emma means is that we're just going through these old files about the renovation of the hotel." I hold up a file.

Lily rolls her eyes, "Oh, my God, relax, I'm not going to shout it from the rooftops or rat you out to Frances or anything."

I stand up, gathering some files and putting them in my briefcase.

"Maybe I should leave so you two can chat. It's about time for me to meet up with Jackie, anyway," Lucas offers, a small grin forming on his face.

Lily wrinkles her nose and then shoos me away.

"Yes, yes, it's girl time. You go along."

I laugh and kiss Emma on the cheek, then head out the office door. I close it softly behind me and Jackie stands up from her spot on the lobby couch.

"Lucas! Are you ready?"

How can I avoid this?

"Just about," I respond, patting my briefcase. "I just need to grab my things. I travel light for the most part, so it shouldn't take too long."

Jackie twirls a strand of hair around her finger, smiling up at me flirtatiously.

"I'll come with you! Just to make sure you don't forget anything."

Great. Just what I needed.

"That's not necessary, it will only take a few minutes."

"I insist." Jackie heads to the elevator, and I begrudgingly follow, watching as she pushes the number two once we step on. "Did you and Emma find the files you were looking for?"

"We found a lot of files- it will probably take a while to go through everything. I put some files in my briefcase so that I can study and catalogue them later."

"You're such a hard worker. That must be why you're so successful." Jackie beams up at me.

The elevator doors slide open, saving me from a response. From the second floor wafts a damp smell that heralds the presence of water seepage and the beginnings of mildew from the broken water pipe.

"Um, maybe I'll wait in the lobby after all, if that's okay," Jackie pipes up, covering her nose with her shirt.

I nod. As if I hadn't been trying to get her to do that the whole time. I head to my room, noting the slight dampness of the wood beneath my feet.

I quickly gather my suitcase with my things—it's a good thing I make a habit of leaving my suitcase on the dresser instead of the floor, otherwise it would be toast.

After quickly packing my things and making the fastest getaway known to man, I head down to the lobby to meet Jackie.

The drive to the house is fast; Jackie chatters incessantly about how many followers she has on the latest social network, about the sort of clubs she likes to go to with her friends—"You should join us sometime!"—and how much it means to her mother that I came to help with the hotel.

As we pull into the drive, I look up at the house that I had just left this morning. Emma's car is still parked in the driveway. Jackie's brows knit together, but I interrupt before she can make a comment about it.

"Do you drive Jackie?"

"Car's in the shop. Something wrong with the... rotator cuff?"

"I think that's a body part."

She shrugs.

"Whatever. Come on, I'll show you to your room."

Chapter Seventeen

Emma

"Are you gonna spill the details or what?" Lily asks, throwing herself down in the chair.

"Also, when are we going to get rid of that smell? I'm worried it's going to start sticking to my hair and clothes."

I sigh dramatically, but truthfully, I enjoy having Lily to commiserate with. With everything going on, I think I'd explode keeping everything to myself.

"We're having plumbing issues, it's supposed to take a few weeks to get it all fixed. Now that the water has been turned off to that area, I'm going to get a company in with fans and equipment to dry out the area and help clean the air. We need to avoid as much mildew as possible and that should keep the smell down.

"Uh, yeah, cause it's going to drive away guests, too." She leans forward. "But you know that's not what I care about most!"

"I know, I know, you want to hear all about how Lucas helped me move."

"Yeah, I bet that's not all he helped you do." Lily rocks her hips raunchily against the chair. "Come on, did you two get together? Really together?"

I take a deep breath and let out a laugh. This girl is ridiculous.

"Okay, yes, we did. And, it was really good."

"Yes! I knew you weren't a prude."

"Hey!"

"What? I'm just telling you exactly what was going through my brain." Lily squeals and scoots the chair closer. "Tell me everything! Was it sweet and tender? Or did he throw you against the wall? I bet he's actually a total freak underneath all those buttons."

I swat at her but we both crack up anyway.

"It wasn't like either of those things. I don't know how to describe it. We brought down my nightmare of a bed frame—"

"Oh my God, you did it on the dismantled bed frame, didn't you? That's so wild. And dangerous!"

"No!" I throw a pad of sticky notes at her but she catches it easily.

"We were talking about putting the bed frame together and then... I kissed him. It sounds lame but the moment was amazing."

"So you jumped his bones. Nice, I wouldn't have expected you to make the first move!"

I roll my eyes.

"It was a mutual bones jumping, thank you very much." I sigh and look down at my hands. "There's a major problem, though."

"Now you want him all the time," Lily says, leaning back assuredly.

"God, would you get your mind out of the gutter? Not everything is about sex."

She sits up straight and nods, miming straightening a tie.

"You have serious Lily now. Speak away."

"All the rooms on the east end of the second floor are damaged from the busted pipe. Lucas was staying on the second floor, and this morning Jackie had the idea for Lucas to stay in our guest room."

"That's brilliant. What is she now? Your wing-woman?"

"No, I'm pretty sure she has a thing for Lucas." I sigh. "And it's not brilliant because I'm not sure how we're going to maintain a... whatever this is that's going on between us."

"Hmm." Lily taps her chin, thoughtfully. "That is a bit of a pickle. Although maybe sneaking around under Frances' nose could be kind of hot. Like a forbidden romance!"

I groan.

"I cannot handle a forbidden romance along with everything else going on." I drop my voice to a whisper, as if anyone else can hear us through the thick office door. "He's going to be just upstairs. How am I supposed to act normal?"

"Have you guys talked about what happened? Like what happens next?"

"Not really," I say, shrugging. "We went to the Farmers Market this morning, but Frances called with the plumbing emergency and we really didn't get to talk about anything like that."

"All that time in this office and you guys didn't talk about any of this?"

"Okay, I agree. We need to talk, but first we need the opportunity. We were so busy going through files we really just didn't have a chance today. I think he has a sense that I was troubled by things—he could definitely tell that I was freaking out in the lobby this morning."

Lily grabs my hand and gives it a squeeze.

"Girl, you need to talk to him. As soon as possible— like, before he starts moving boxes into your hallway at the house."

"Well, it's not boxes, it's one suitcase. And it's not the hallway, it's the guest room."

Lily shoots me a look and I continue.

"Okay fine, I get your point. But a talk with him before he gets there isn't possible, because he's headed to the house with Jackie right now."

Lily's jaw drops, and I think this is the first time she's been silent in any of the time that I've spent with her.

"So Jackie is seriously trying to throw them together? I thought that was just front desk talk."

"Front desk talk?"

"You know, like stuff people talk about at the front desk when they think I'm not paying attention."

"I definitely didn't know that term, but I guess I'm grateful I know it now?" I shake my head. "We're losing the plot. What did you hear?"

Lily giggles conspiratorially, clapping jovially.

"You're not going to believe this! So the other day, Frances and Jackie were talking near the front desk. Hence, front desk talk. But Frances was telling Jackie about Lucas, and how she finds him insufferable but he's so knowledgeable—and wealthy, too, you know that—and that she can't believe he isn't married after all these years. And Jackie was like, 'what if he married me?' and of course, Frances was appalled at first. I mean, the age difference alone...don't look at me like that. It's true. Frances was in complete shock. I don't think I've ever seen an expression like that on her—"

"Lily? Focus?" I ask, my heart sinking into my stomach.

"Right, sorry. But Jackie and Frances basically concocted this scheme to get Jackie and Lucas together. I was confused, because Frances is Lucas' age. But Frances obviously dislikes him, and I think she knows it would be quite suspicious if she suddenly started to cozy up to him."

"This is appalling!" The shock of the situation shoots me right out of the chair. "What do I do?"

"Um, move in on Lucas first?"

"Why? Do you think Jackie has a chance?" I look at her with wide eyes. "What if Lucas thinks that was just a one night stand? What if he doesn't feel anything more than lust for me?"

Lily stares at me and then bursts out laughing.

"Come on. You guys went to the Farmers Market. That's basically being married for twenty years. You'll be fine, and I can see he really seems to care about you, but it will definitely make things awkward."

"I definitely have to tell Lucas about this."

"I agree. I don't know how you're going to get him alone now, but I think you definitely need to clue him into their plan so he can protect himself."

I look down at my phone.

"Okay, it's a little after 4:00 now. I don't get off until—wait, what am I talking about? This is supposed to be my day off. I don't have to be doing any of this!" I slap the folders into my purse.

"Oh, yes, I love the action." Lily stands up.

I storm for the door before stopping.

"Shit. My car is at the house. Lucas and I carpooled this morning."

"Yeah, cause that isn't suspicious at all. You two are terrible at hiding things."

"Well, excuse me for never having a secret relationship before." I swallow. Is this a relationship? Oh, God, this is a mess. "Do you think you can give me a ride home?"

Lily looks down at her phone.

"Well, I don't get off until 5:00, and I do work today. So you'll have to wait an hour."

I sigh and sit back down.

"Right, okay. Back to work for both of us."

"You got it, boss."

I slump back into the seat to look through more files. Not that I'll be able to focus with all the drama in my life.

***

"Wow, this is nice. Can I spend the night sometime?" Lily asks as we pull into my driveway an hour and some change later.

I look at her in surprise. I've never had a sleepover before—that sounds totally lame, but I've never had many friends.

Even the ones I had in high school were never allowed to sleep over. My dad was fine with it, the problem was Frances. Anytime I asked to have friends stay, there was always something going on, like some special event or she had a headache and didn't want more people in the house.

Surprisingly, there were never any problems when Jackie wanted to have friends over.

"Sure, that would be fun."

Frances can't object if I have my own space where she won't be disturbed. After all, I'm an adult now, not a teenager she can control—well, at least not completely. Right?

"Okay, see you later and don't forget to update me!"

I nod and march my way up to my basement door. Jackson trots toward me, wagging his tail. He enjoyed his time at the market, but also had no complaints when we dropped him back at home. Being older means he loves his nap time.

As I'm walking Jackson around the yard so he can do his business, my phone buzzes.

You just got home? Lucas' message lights up the screen.

Before I can respond, he's calling.

"Hey," I answer. I kick myself- why am I trying to be casual? I need to be more forward.

"I'm happy to hear from you."

"Yeah? I'm just calling to invite you to dinner."

"Where do you want to go?"

"Your dining room in thirty minutes."

I blink.

"You're going to make dinner?"

Lucas laughs. Even through the phone, it sends little shivers down my spine.

"Hardly. Frances wanted to have dinner together—my first night in the house? You'd think I was moving in."

I choke out a laugh, but my throat is drying up.

"Are you sure dinner with them is a good idea? I mean, I don't have a very good poker face."

"I think it's a great idea. You didn't get to join last time, and besides, I don't want to face them on my own. I can, but it would be much more enjoyable with you."

Okay, so he knows how to butter me up.

"All right, fine. I'll see you in thirty minutes."

We hang up, and I bolt back to my room. After taking the quickest shower known to man, I spend a couple minutes trying to find an outfit that's cute, but not too cute, and head upstairs.

When I step into the dining room, Frances is setting plates of food onto the table.

"Oh, Emma! What are you doing here?" She regards me coolly.

"I invited her. I thought since she didn't get to eat dinner with us last time, it would be nice for her to be here, especially since she lives here too. All members of the house should get to enjoy this delicious food from... where did you get it?"

"Hanna's Home Kitchen," Jackie helpfully supplies, looking up at Lucas through her lashes. He doesn't pay her any attention, and she sits down in frustration at the table.

"That's so kind of you, Lucas. Of course, I meant to text you Emma, but it must have slipped my mind."

Frances gives me a tight smile, which I return.

"That's okay. I know it's been a hectic day."

"It certainly has."

"At least Lucas is here, helping us. That's so thoughtful," Jackie chimes in, propping her elbow on the table to lean closer to Lucas.

Lucas leans away so lightly, it's almost instinctual.

We all sit down around the table and look at each other, as if unsure what to do next.

"Well, let's dig in!" Frances announces, passing plates to Jackie and Lucas. "I'm so sorry, Emma, dear. I didn't know you'd be eating with us so I only grabbed three plates."

"No problem." I head into the kitchen to grab a plate and let out a deep breath.

The tension in the dining room is so unbearable, I'm not even sure if I want to go back in.

I take my time choosing a plate before stepping back into the chaos that is sure to last for the next few weeks.

Chapter Eighteen

Lucas

"That was the most awkward dinner I've ever been a part of," I say as I help Emma put leftovers away in the kitchen.

As soon as we finished eating, Frances ordered Emma to clean up and put away the leftover food. Her penance, I suppose, for being bold enough to take me up on my dinner invitation.

"It was certainly tense." Emma shudders. "Jackie is really trying hard with you."

I glance at her—is that jealousy?

It's obvious that Jackie has a crush on me, but I didn't realize it was obvious enough for Emma to pick up on. I don't know why. Emma is smart and extremely perceptive. Of course she'd see it.

"Well, she doesn't have a chance."

"Oh, is that right?"

"One could say I have my eyes on someone else." I brush her hand gently with mine as we put away a container of food. She looks at me and pulls her hand away.

"Lucas! We're in the kitchen."

I sigh.

"Okay, okay, I'll behave."

"Look, we seriously have a lot to talk about. There's stuff you don't know."

Her big, warm green eyes stare into mine, the expression on her face stopping me. She lowers her voice. "Stuff regarding Frances and Jackie. And also with us. Can we talk tonight?"

She's serious, and it's obvious. But she looks so beautiful and focused, all I can think about is the pinkness of her lips.

"You want me to sneak down to your room?" I laugh and she rolls her eyes, but there's a smile spreading across her face.

"We could reasonably do a phone call... but you could sneak down."

Emma licks her lips and I have to look away to avoid kissing her.

"Sounds like a plan to me."

Footsteps in the hallway cause us to spring apart. I rinse off a plate as Jackie stops in the kitchen.

"Oh, hey you guys! I'm just here to grab some juice."

The fridge opens and closes behind me, and then a presence stops at my shoulder. "Lucas, do you like movies? There's a new one coming out, I think it's an action movie. You're into those, right?"

"I've seen a few of them in my time."

"We should go see it. I think the first showing is this weekend."

I turn to her and smile.

"I'll have to check and see if my schedule will allow it. Thank you for the invitation."

Jackie's smile dims but she nods.

"Of course, I'm sure you're super busy. Just let me know. I'm right down the hall."

She gives a flirty finger wave before exiting the kitchen. Emma's eyes meet mine and she shakes her head. We chuckle before going back to washing the dishes.

***

My phone beeps at 1:00 in the morning with a text from Emma. I stretch and slip my house shoes on before slipping out my bedroom door and into the hallway quietly. No sound comes from Jackie's room, and a raucous snoring emits from the direction of where Frances sleeps.

How did Clark sleep in the same room with her?

I step down the stairs, listening quietly in case the snoring stops. It feels silly, a 45 year old sneaking around the house, but it's also sort of thrilling. It reminds me of being a teenager sneaking out to parties.

Emma opens her door before I can knock.

"Thanks for coming."

"Middle of the night visit to you? I can't imagine many would say no."

She rolls her eyes as a blush heats her cheek.

I shut the door behind me. She's really spruced it up in here since I was there this morning—plants line the window in the small kitchen, framed prints of landscapes hang on the wall and a fluffy comforter lays under a dozen pillows on her bed.

"It looks great in here. You've been busy."

"I still have a ton of plants in the corner. I don't know where to put them. In my old room, I had them all in my bathroom, because I had this amazing skylight." Her face lights up.

"Oh, gosh it was beautiful, I wish you could have seen it. There's no skylight in the basement, obviously. It would just be light from the main floor half bath."

I chuckle.

"You're funny. We'll figure out a place for them." I stick my hands in the pockets of my bathrobe.

"So, what do we need to talk about?"

Emma sighs and gestures to me to sit on her bed. I take the spot next to her.

"Frances and Jackie are scheming to marry you off to Jackie."

I burst out laughing, but when I look back at her, it's clear that she's not playing a prank.

"You're serious?"

"Yes. Lily told me she heard them talking at the front desk the other day."

"Quite irresponsible of them."

She shrugs.

"Employees are basically invisible to Frances. They might as well be pieces of furniture to her."

I frown. It's a disgusting attitude to have toward anyone, but especially your own employees.

"That's terrible. Well, I can assure you that Jackie didn't stand a chance before you told me about this, and certainly doesn't now. I only have eyes for one woman in this house."

"Frances?" Emma teases, leaning in to kiss me.

I roll my eyes and she laughs.

Then shakes her head. "I'm getting ahead of myself. We need to talk about us."

"What about us?" I study her face. She looks away and sighs.

"What are we doing? I hope you know that I don't just sleep with random men. So, us sleeping together... it meant something to me. It means something to me."

Surprise courses through me. Did she think I was just using her?

"It means something to me, too. I'm not the kind of person who womanizes or has 'conquests.' I find you absolutely captivating—you're beautiful, smart. Ambitious. I feel this connection with you, drawn to you in a way that I've never felt with any other woman. So please don't think that you're just a notch in the belt. I want to have a real relationship with you."

"How are we supposed to do that with Frances breathing down our necks?"

Emma sighs in exasperation. When she looks at me her eyes are glassy, but no tears fall.

"Once the hotel is sold, we can go public. You won't have to worry about Frances and we can have a shot at a real relationship."

I brush my thumb against her cheek. "I promise that this isn't for nothing."

Emma searches my face and then smiles.

"Okay, I trust you."

"Good. I'm happy to hear that."

Emma intertwines her hands with mine.

"We shouldn't end this night on a sour note."

"What did you have in mind? Maybe a movie?"

Emma shakes her head.

"I was thinking maybe something else..."

She licks her lips and I feel arousal stir within me. I can't get enough of her. She leans in and brushes a feather soft kiss against my lips. I deepen it, leaning into her.

Emma's finger trail across the soft fabric of my shirt, making circles on my chest. I grip her waist and pull her closer. She smells like lilies and vanilla. I want to savor her.

"You're sure? That was an emotional talk we just had," I murmur against her ear, gently nipping it.

Emma looks from under her lashes and bites her lip.

"I'm more than sure. After we were interrupted in the office? I've been wanting you all day."

I kiss her, urgently this time, my hands tangling in the mess of red hair. I give it a gentle tug and Emma gasps before taking a nip at my bottom lip.

I suck in a breath then ease her back onto the comforter, the mass of pillows creating a nest around us.

I take her in. A pair of soft pajama shorts reveal her freckled legs, her nipples poking through the thin fabric of her tank top. The outfit is simple, but sexier than any piece of lingerie I've ever seen on a woman.

Emma pulls my shirt over my head, tossing it to the floor.

Her hands roam my chest as I kiss down her neck. I suckle gently against the pulse point under her chin, enough to elicit a response from her in the form of arching her back, but not hard enough to leave a mark.

I slip a hand under her tank top, taking the time to squeeze each breast, brushing my thumb softly against each nipple.

Emma's soft moans fill the air as her fingernails dig into my chest, making me acutely aware of the growing hardness between us. My heart races as I pull the tank top over her head, revealing her perfectly shaped breasts.

The color of her pert nipples is reminiscent of the shade of red in her hair.

"You're so beautiful," I tell her sincerely, pressing my lips against hers before trailing kisses along her collarbone and eventually reaching the waistband of her pajama shorts.

I tug them down, taking her panties with them. Emma gasps at the sudden exposure, and I can't help but smile at her reaction. "Absolutely beautiful."

I waste no time in lowering myself between her open thighs, my tongue eagerly exploring the warmth and wetness that waits for me there.

As my tongue flattens against her sensitive skin and rises up to tease her clit, Emma's eyes flutter closed, and the soft moan that escapes her encourages me further. She arches her back, the soft peaks of her breath rising.

"Quiet, sound travels," I remind her, aware of how much I can hear echoing against the walls of the room.

Emma sighs and when I take another lap at her, she arches her back and moans louder, smiling.

I grin mischievously, moving up to kiss her deeply while my fingers replace my tongue, circling the entrance to her intoxicating warmth before pushing my fingers inside slowly. Her low groan sends shivers down my spine.

"Please," she whispers, her voice trembling with anticipation.

I pull my fingers out, gently caressing her swollen labia. I push two fingers back into her wetness. She shudders beneath me, showing her approval.

I move slowly at first, letting her adjust to the sensation of my fingers deep inside her. Gradually, I increase my pace, my movements becoming more deliberate and insistent.

Emma's breathing becomes more ragged, each exhale a mix of pleasure and desperation.

She's near climax, so I shift my position so that I can rub circles against her clit with my thumb. I can feel the pressure increase with each passing moment as Emma's pussy muscles tighten around my fingers and her moans becoming insatiable.

"Oh, my God," she gasps against my lips, her eyes wide with ecstasy. Every muscle in her body tenses as waves of pleasure cascade through her.

Her walls clench tightly around my fingers as she reaches the peak of her orgasm. I continue moving slowly within her until her body goes limp and she heaves a satisfied sigh.

I chuckle as Emma reaches and fumbles with my waistband, struggling to push my pants down as her body continues to tremble from her orgasm.

She manages to push them down, revealing my briefs, which cling to me with anticipation. A soft grunt escapes her lips as she slides those down, too, and I'm freed, my hard cock throbbing and pulsing for the warmth of her cunt.

Emma's slender fingers curl around my wrists, guiding me gently to lie back against the bed. She leans over me, our breath mingling together before her lips find mine in a tender kiss, aching for more.

"I want to be on top this time," she whispers, a barely audible plea that fans the flames of desire within me.

I nod eagerly, licking my lips in anticipation as she straddles me, her warm thighs gripping my hips.

Taking hold of my erection, she guides me to her entrance, the heat of her teasing me becoming almost unbearable. Emma lowers herself onto me and I groan at the feeling of her cunt enclosing my hard, fat cock.

She moves her hips tenderly at first, a hesitant rhythm that quickly evolves into a harmonic dance between our bodies.

Pleasure blooms from the point connecting us, radiating outward like flames licking my body. My hands find their way to Emma's waist, digging into her flesh as I match her motions with purposeful upward thrusts.

Emma's head falls back, her red hair cascading down her bare back like a waterfall of flames.

The sight of her above me, skin flushed and eyes closed in ecstasy, is almost enough to send me over the edge. I grip her hips tighter, trying to slow our pace.

"Look at me," I whisper, my voice hoarse with pleasure.

She listens, and the moment her glowing green eyes lock with mine, I twitch inside of her. A small smile plays on her lips as she rolls her hips in a slow, deliberate motion that makes me hold back a moan.

"I love the way you feel inside of me," she says, leaning forward so her breasts brush against my chest. The change in angle makes me gasp, and I feel her warmth tighten around me further, gripping me with her pussy muscles and my cock seems to harden even more.

My hands slide up over her sides, mesmerizing every curve and freckle. When they reach her breasts, I cup them and lean up, flicking my tongue over each nipple. She shivers, her pace slowing.

She leans down so that I can take her nipple into my mouth, sucking delightfully while my cock goes in and out of her, both actions in the same rhythm as she matches me thrust for thrust.

"Keep going," I murmur, my hands finding their way to her hips and guiding her back into tempo. I'm entranced by the way our bodies move together, the sounds she makes when I hit just the right spot.

"I'm close," she whispers, her movements becoming more urgent and less coordinated. "So close..."

I slip a hand between us, finding her sensitive bundle of nerves with my thumb. I circle gently at first, increasing the pressure as her breathing becomes more erratic.

"Let go. I got you," I whisper.

Emma's entire body tenses, and I clamp a hand over her mouth to dampen her cries as she comes undone above me.

Her pulsing cunt pushes me closer to release, and I thrust upward once more before pulling her against my chest and rolling us over in one easy motion.

Now above her, I thrust harder into her, punishing her with my hardness. As I rise to meet my orgasm, I push into her wet pussy one final time.

My release pushes through me and into her like a tidal wave. I push my face into her neck to stifle my groan, breathing in the scent of lilies and desire on her skin.

I fall to her side and I brush her hair gently as we tangle together. My heart pounds against my chest as I pull her into me, cuddling softly as we fall into sleep together.

Chapter Nineteen

Emma

My alarm chirps loudly at 5:00 sharp. I sit up, aware of another body in my bed. I blink and wipe the sleep from my eyes before looking over at Lucas.

Oh, my God. Lucas! I reach over and shake him.

"Huh?" he looks around, his eyes bleary. "What's going on?"

"We fell asleep!"

"Oh, yeah, we did. That was great." Lucas grins at me and there's a tugging at my heart, but I push it away.

"You are supposed to be upstairs in the guest room." I stress each syllable, and only then does Lucas seem to wake up.

"Shit. I have to get upstairs. Are they awake?" His eyes are alert now, anxiety fluttering over his face.

"How am I supposed to know? I just woke up!" I let out a sigh and shake my head.

"Sorry, sorry. I'm cranky. I'll go upstairs and scout it out. Send you a text when the coast is clear."

Lucas nods and lies back down. I hope he doesn't fall back to sleep.

I slip my shoes on and grab Jackson, letting him do his business before heading to the main floor. It's quiet in the house, but that doesn't mean anything—Frances is deceptively quiet in the morning.

I don't even think she's sneaking around, she's just much quieter without those heels she's usually sporting.

I stick my head into the living room— it's clear, and I make my way into the kitchen.

"You're up early," Frances says, eyeing me carefully. She's fully dressed, sporting her signature heels. How early did she wake up?

"Oh, I, uh... haven't had a chance to get groceries yet! Wanted to grab something easy," I mutter, reaching for a cabinet and rummaging around.

"I see. Well, make sure you do that soon. It will make your mornings easier if you don't have to trek up here every day."

Frances glances at me and then gives me a wry smile. Of course it's not genuine concern; she just wants me out of her hair. It's obvious in the way that her smile never reaches her eyes.

"Of course. Sorry to disturb you."

We're both quiet for a few moments until I hear movement from behind me. I pull down a box of granola bars—not my first choice, but good enough for an excuse.

"By the way, have you finished sorting through those files?"

"Not yet, I was planning on having them finished today."

"Hmm." Frances comes up next to me. "You'll likely have a lot of duties today at the hotel. You might not have time to go through the files at work."

"I will do as much as I can."

"Really, I don't want you distracted It might be better for you to go through them once you get home."

I scoff as I turn to her.

"You want me to go to work, do everything there, and then come home, and go through files for hours? What are you even looking for?"

Frances narrows her eyes and cocks her head.

"If you were listening the other day, you would know that we are looking for anything else that could cause problems in selling the building."

"Like what?"

"Like anything that might pose a potential problem in the near future." Frances takes a sip.

"Frankly, Emma, it all sounds like excuses. Just get the work done. I don't see why it's a problem. It's not like you have anything else to do with your time."

Frances' phone beeps. She glances at it and sighs. "I have to go. Don't let me down. I'd hate for you to have to move out of the basement."

She fluffs her hair and clicks out the door, letting it shut silently behind her. She just threatened me. Is this what it will come to? If I don't do anything and everything she wants, suddenly I'm on the verge of being homeless? She's almost laughably evil, more akin to a cartoon villain than a real person.

I pull out a text and send Lucas an all clear text. A few minutes later, he comes through the front door and into the kitchen.

"Granola bars for breakfast?"

"Ugh, no. I needed an excuse."

I shove the box back into the cabinet and turn to him. He swipes a quick kiss and I swat him away. "Hey, none of that in here. Jackie is still home."

"Right, I'll be good." He sticks his hands in his pockets and looks at me earnestly. "What do you say we get some breakfast?"

"Did I hear breakfast?" Jackie sing-songs as she glides into the kitchen. For a split second, I'm worried about what she might have heard, but given the look of surprise on her face at the sight of me in the kitchen, she didn't hear anything.

"Oh, Emma. What are you doing here?"

"I live here. I was grabbing something to eat. Haven't gotten any groceries for my kitchen yet."

"I haven't either," Lucas chimes in, smiling easily. "I was just suggesting to Emma we grab a quick breakfast before work."

I feel my face fall at the addition of the word 'quick' even though I know it's important to keep things under wraps.

"That sounds nice! I'd love to join," Jackie responds as if she were invited.

I resist the urge to roll my eyes, but before I can give an excuse on why she can't come, she continues.

"I have plans with my best friend, though. We're going to check out this new club in the next town over."

"At 5:00 in the morning?" I'm unable to keep the incredulousness from my voice. Jackie scoffs.

"No, Emma, not at 5:00. I have to get ready and look amazing. She knows the owner of the club so we're getting an exclusive tour before it officially opens." She makes a pouty face. "I'd invite you, but I know how busy you are with work. Too bad."

Jackie winks at Lucas before heading back up to her room with a juice bottle.

"Seriously, let's get out of here," I mutter, motioning for Jackson to follow suit.

***

"I found some floors that might match the original ones!" Royce announces as he strolls into the conference room a couple days later.

Lucas and Frances look up at him as he enters. "There's only one problem: they're in Albuquerque."

"Albuquerque?" Frances says incredulously.

"I can rent a truck and go look at them this weekend," I offer.

Appeasing Frances is my number one goal right now. Anything to avoid getting kicked out of my own house.

"That would be very helpful." Not a thank you in sight from her, of course.

"I can go with her," Lucas asks. All eyes in the room whip to him. What is he doing? He's going to out us before I even have a chance to breathe.

"Oh?" Frances inquires with a simple word.

"Well, normally I'd offer that you take Royce. But he's going home this weekend for his mom's birthday."

"Hey, you remembered!" Royce beams. Frances rolls her eyes, but he doesn't seem to notice.

"Of course." Lucas clears his throat. "I'm offering to go because flooring is really quite heavy, especially wood. There might be people to help Emma load, but it's not a chance I'm willing to take. I'd hate to see the trip, gas, and truck rental wasted when she can't get all the flooring in herself."

"That... makes sense, I guess," I concede.

Normally I'd bristle at the implication that I can't do something myself, but I won't complain about getting to spend more time with Lucas.

"We can check out some of the antique stores while we're there, keep an eye out for some furniture."

Frances sits back thoughtfully. I'd give anything to read her mind right now—is she suspicious? Does she know there's an ulterior motive?

Eventually Frances shrugs.

"That sounds fine to me. Takes more off my plate. We'll need to store the floors somewhere until the new pipes are installed."

Frances sighs and rubs her temples. "Oh, I didn't even think about how much we'll need. The entire east side of the second floor will have to be replaced so you'll need to figure out how much we need, Emma. Hopefully they have enough."

"Has the plumber updated you on his time frame?" I ask.

"Ugh, he says it's going well. It's going to take another two weeks, though. Which is shorter than the time frame I originally anticipated, but somehow just as costly. I have half a mind to just sell the hotel as-is."

My eyes meet Lucas' but he shakes his head.

"It was definitely a setback, but it's much better to find this out now than, say, two weeks before we decide to sell. It's truly a blessing that it happened so early on. It's best to keep a positive attitude about this kind of thing. Otherwise, it might have been caught during a buyer's due diligence process and could conceivably cause a deal to fall through."

Frances nods her head and then smiles. It almost looks genuine. Almost.

"Yes, you're right. Thank you, Lucas. I will look into a storage unit, you and Emma will go check out the flooring."

Frances stands up and stretches.

"I'm going to head to lunch, I suggest you two do the same. Emma, make sure to finish those files before you and Lucas go to Albuquerque."

"Oh, I already finished going through them. I'm just working on compiling them into one document so that you don't have to go hunting through them."

"Perfect. Have it to me by Friday." Frances heads out of the conference room and I sigh.

"Boy, she sure is a breezy lady," Royce says, shivering animatedly.

"Thanks for letting me go home this weekend. Do you want me to book some rooms in Albuquerque for you?"

"Actually, just do an Airbnb. I figured we could hit up the hot air balloon festival while we're there," Lucas says, leaning back.

Royce eyes him quizzically but nods instead of asking questions.

"Sounds like a plan. Have you ever been to the hot air balloon festival, Emma?"

I shake my head. It's something Dad talked about taking me to for a long time, but never got around to it.

Every year we would talk about it, and then determine that we could always go next year.

If we had known that there wouldn't be a next year, we might have gone to the last one.

"I think it sounds like fun, though. I'm excited to go. And to do some antiquing!"

My phone beeps. "Oh, that's Lily. We have lunch plans. I'll catch the two of you later."

I stand up and wave to Royce. I give Lucas a shy smile and step out into the lobby. Lily already has her car pulled around. She offered to drive, claiming that my driving gave her motion sickness last time we went to lunch.

"Miss Stone," Joe nods, opening the door for me.

"Thank you, Joe. How's the family doing?"

"Just wonderful! Lacey had her baby yesterday—I'm officially a grandfather." He grins proudly, and I can't help but smile back.

"That's amazing! Congratulations."

"Thank you. My time off starts tomorrow."

He waves me off. When I get into Lily's car she turns to me.

"Ugh, I have to update you about Cody. He is so off the list."
She rolls her eyes. 'The list' refers to Lily's curated catalogue
of men she's dating in an attempt to find the one.

Our friendship is an unlikely one.

Lily and I couldn't be more different. She's bubbly, and loves
to talk about men, celebrities, and things I know nearly
nothing about.

She teases me about being painfully pop culture averse and
gives me advice about situations with Lucas and Frances.

She also vowed to give Frances death glares every time her
back is turned, which I told her wasn't necessary, but she still
does anyway.

Lily pulls away from the curb as she tells me about why Cody
is now off the list and Ryan is so totally on it.

Chapter Twenty

Lucas

"How are things going, Royce?" I ask over the salads we're having at the deli nearby.

"Good. Busy." Royce sighs as he pushes a cherry tomato around his plate. "Honestly, my mom's birthday is turning into a much bigger production than I anticipated."

I raise my brows and he continues.

"She's turning fifty, which is a pretty big deal. I mean, generally, I know fifty is a big deal, but in my family it turns into this whole shindig. It's like a family reunion, birthday party and bar mitzvah all in one.

"I want my mom's fiftieth birthday to be awesome—she's the greatest mom in the world. She's always there for me, and did all she could for me. So I want to give back. But my sister sort of pushed her way into the planning. It was supposed to be something at the house, but now it's at a rented venue and there's sixty people on the guest list. Shannon is always trying to show me up."

"You're not close with your sister?"

I admittedly don't know much about Royce. I feel bad about it. I'm not so busy that I can't take an interest in his personal life.

Truthfully, I didn't realize how little I knew about him until Emma asked me about his favorite TV show. I don't even remember why she asked, but I didn't know the answer, and the look of disappointment on her face sort of made my heart sink.

"Nah. Shannon's, like, a perfectionist. She always does everything right. She was the perfect ballet dancer all through high school. She could have even gone pro if she wanted to. I fumbled through every speech and debate meet I went to. I appreciate her wanting to get involved. I'm sure it will be better than anything I could plan."

Royce frowns, then glumly takes a sip of his water.

"Well, I'm sure what you had planned would have been great, too. What did you get her?"

He throws up his hands.

"That's the thing, I haven't even gotten her anything yet. I've been so focused on trying to find the perfect gift, I haven't gotten a single gift."

"Maybe I could help? I can be a surprisingly good gift giver," I offer, stabbing a piece of cucumber with my fork.

"Really? You'd help me?" The way his face lights up is heartwarming. I'm actually starting to like the kid.

"Of course. Now tell me a little bit about your mom and the sort of stuff she likes."

"Well, she loves gardening! She has this huge flower garden in the greenhouse that she works in a lot. She loves to bake, especially pies. Oh! And she collects all these vintage brooches. She's been finding them in antique shops since she was a kid. She used to go and find them with her mom."

I smile. She sounds like a mom, that's for sure. I'm sure she and my mom would have gotten along very well.

"Okay, after we finish here, we'll go brooch shopping. And I know the perfect place to find some flowers. Does she have a favorite flower?"

"She loves begonias. Those are her favorite flowers to grow."

"Begonias it is. You finished eating?"

"Yep! I'm ready to go!"

***

After four shops, we finally found the perfect brooch, with little stones of lapis lazuli made into the shape of a flower. After ordering a bouquet of begonias to be ready for pickup on Friday before Royce leaves, we solved the gift problem faster than I thought we would.

I drop Royce back at the hotel and pick up some food before heading back to my guest room at Frances' house.

When I pull into the drive, Emma's car isn't there. It's only 4:30, so she's likely still at work.

I head into the house and sit down at the dining table. Truthfully, it's weird being here without Clark and Ginny.

The house looks completely different than it did when Ginny lived here.

Back then, it was decorated with warm earth tones, a lot of cozy furnishings and decor filling all of the rooms.

Specifically, I remember the big comfy couch in the living room, covered in plush cushions. Maybe that's where Emma gets her penchant for pillows.

Now, everything in the house seems cold. Everything is white and sterile, all sharp angles and flat surfaces where things with curves and comfort used to be. Even the couch is different, stiff and uncomfortable. Like sitting on concrete.

I frown as I open the takeout and get started on it. It was devastating when Ginny died—Clark was a mess.

It's something Emma didn't have to see, thankfully, as he tried to protect her and knew she was dealing with her own grief, but it was hard for me to watch. To see him completely fall apart like that, knowing there was nothing I could do to make it better.

I felt like a failure as a best friend, even though I tried to do my best to be there. He'd look at me with these empty, hollow eyes.

It was surprising to me when he got together with Frances.

She was the complete opposite of Ginny in every way, but maybe that was the point.

Where Ginny was a wild spirit and had an artist's soul, Frances was the embodiment of corporate. Ginny would often run around in overalls, her hair thrown up in a messy bun. I don't think I've ever seen Frances look anything less than perfect.

It's not a bad thing to look perfect all the time, I guess. It just doesn't feel human.

"Hello!" Frances' voice rings out as she steps through the front door."Jackie, are you home, dear? I have something for you."

She comes through the dining room and startles.

"Oh, goodness, Lucas. I didn't realize you were here." She pats her hair, ensuring every piece is in place. Even in her own home, she feels the need to be perfect.

"Just enjoying some dinner." I hold up the box of takeout Mexican food. "Would... you like some?"

I'm hoping beyond everything that she says no.

It's polite to offer, but I don't want to sit here with Frances alone at the table. It's enough that I have to see her practically every other waking moment of the day. I'd eat in the guest room if that wouldn't be weird and impolite.

"No, thank you. The offer is kind, but I am actually going to dinner with some friends."

"That sounds great. Where are you all heading to?"

"A little place outside of town. I'm sure you haven't heard of it." Frances waves dismissively. "Jackie's going out with a friend tonight and it will hardly do for me to eat dinner all alone."

Frances laughs and then quickly quiets. I'm not sure if she was trying to insult me or not, but I'm not going to let her get to me regardless.

"I find eating alone quite relaxing. I don't have to worry about waiting for someone else to dig in or not spilling food on my shirt. Plus I can just sort of soak in the environment while I chow down."

She gives me a sort of horrified look before nodding.

"Right, well, I'm off to get ready. Enjoy your relaxing dinner."

Frances clicks down the hallway and up the stairs. I almost find it sad; it must be hard being unable to be alone with yourself.

I wonder if she's as hyper-critical of herself as she is of Emma. Not that it's an excuse—just because you view yourself harshly doesn't mean you can treat others badly. Especially someone as kind and thoughtful as Emma.

I finish my meal and clean up before heading up to the guest room. I take pause at the room that I know to be Clark's home office before heading inside.

It looks just the same as it did when we first decorated it. Frances apparently wasn't able to get her claws on this space.

It's distinctly Clark; cozy taupe walls and classic dark wood floors. There's a substantial desk pushed up against the wall, a large and comfortable chair rolls up to it.

On the wall above the desk hang various achievements; the original floor plan we had drawn up for the hotel is now framed and on display, along with wedding pictures of his marriage to Ginny and also to Frances.

On the next wall is a collage of pictures of Emma throughout the years. A picture of her as a newborn, red-faced and screaming against a plush blanket. A couple of school pictures from elementary school.

I stop at the picture of her and Ginny at a Fourth of July parade, both donning navy blue t-shirts and waving American flags, huge smiles on their faces.

I smile and lean in, examining the similarities between the two. Emma got Ginny's gorgeous red hair, the smattering of freckles dotting their faces and her slender nose.

"Hello?" Frances' voice sounds from the hallway. I turn as she walks in, a tight smile forming on her face. "I saw the door open and knew someone was in here. I thought it might be Emma."

"No, sorry. I helped decorate Clark's office when they first bought the house. I was wondering if it was still the same or had been renovated."

She sighs and leans against the doorframe.

"He wouldn't let me touch his office. I told him he would be more productive with a lighter palette. He was always getting distracted looking at the photos or snoozing in the chair. But he insisted on leaving everything the way it was. It was something we went back and forth about."

"I rather like it. It may not be the kind of office you see in a home magazine, but it definitely has Clark's touch."

Frances' head swivels as she looks around the room, stopping at first her wedding picture, and then Clark and Ginny's.

"His touch, indeed. Well, I'm heading out for the night. Don't spend too long in here. Leaving doors open makes the place drafty."

She gives me a sour smile and then walks away. Does she hate this place because it's filled with reminders of Ginny?

When Ginny died, Clark talked about her constantly. He'd call me anytime he wanted to reminisce, or email me pictures of some event that they'd attended together, explaining the significance and back story.

They stopped coming as often after he married Frances. Was it because he stopped thinking about them as much, or because he knew it would make her insecure?

I stride over to Clark's bookshelf. It's an eclectic mix of classics, The Great Gatsby and Wuthering Heights, and horror novels, with authors like Anne Rice and James Patterson, filling the shelves. I pick up an Anne Rice novel and a slip of paper falls out. I pick it up but war with myself about opening it. Is this an invasion of privacy?

Do the dead have such a thing as privacy? After a few more seconds of contemplation, I open the paper.

Milk, eggs, green beans...

I laugh, surprise escaping me. I don't know what I was expecting, but it wasn't a grocery list from Ginny. How long has it been since these books have even been opened?

Her handwriting is curly and loopy, a mix of cursive and print that looks beautiful on the yellowed piece of paper. Emma has the same handwriting, although hers is a little more angular. The little bit of Clark that shines through her.

I plop down in the rolling chair and boot up the computer in front of me. It feels weird, almost like snooping. But I feel the incessant need to know more about my best friend's life in the years I wasn't around.

The background is a picture of him with Emma at her college graduation, both smiling brilliantly. I smile and then take notice of the email icon, blinking with a red dot. Unread emails?

Guilt courses through me as I open it- this is definitely snooping.

The inbox pops up with a variety of advertisements and order tracking, but one specific email catches my eye.

It's an email from a lawyer.

Chapter Twenty-One

Emma

"What do you even wear to a hot air balloon festival?" I mutter to myself as I throw a sundress into my suitcase. Jackson barks behind me. "I know, you're a dog and you don't have the answers. I wasn't asking you."

Jackson jumps on the bed, wagging his tail happily. Even though realistically I know he doesn't understand the concept of him having a sleepover at Lily's house for two days, I like to imagine he's excited at the idea of a change of scenery.

Lily happily agreed to watch him while Lucas and I are in Albuquerque. I definitely couldn't ask Frances, and Jackie isn't reliable enough.

I don't think Jackie hates me, but I think she is mostly invested in herself. It would almost be interesting to think about if it didn't make my life so much harder.

My phone lights up, Frances' name blinking across the screen. Speak of the devil.

"Hello?" I can't even ignore how deflated my voice sounds when answering her phone call.

"While you're in Albuquerque this weekend, please keep an eye out for stunning centerpieces we can use for the themed gala we're hosting in a few weeks."

At yesterday's meeting, Frances came up with the brilliant idea to host a roaring 20's gala in the speakeasy once all the plumbing issues were done and the hotel had dried and aired out.

It would be complete with costumes and exclusive invitations to the city's most elite—and hotel guests of course.

Lucas actually agreed that it was a good idea, stating that it could be an opportunity to showcase the hotel to potential buyers and they could see for themselves what an asset the speakeasy and prohibition theme can be.

It's been a long time since I've been to a party, but I'm honestly a little excited. The chance to drink, dance, and dress up is something I don't want to miss.

"Of course. I'll find era-appropriate pieces and grab them."

"Perfect, use the company card." There's a rustling on the other side of the phone.

"Shit."

"Frances? Everything okay?"

She lets out a grunt of frustration.

"Yes! I—ugh, I'm driving, and my stupid phone won't connect to the Bluetooth in the car. I don't know what's happening with it. I'm going to have Jackie look at it when she gets home."

She sounds far away, and then her voice gets closer. "You have the measurements for the rooms right?"

"Yes, all in my file folder."

"Good. Be sure to get the correct amount."

Frances hangs up without saying goodbye. I'm not surprised, but it does still hurt my feelings how little she seems to care. Not even a single 'be safe' or 'thanks for all the work you're putting into this.'

She treats me more like a servant than a stepdaughter.

As soon as I hang up, a text comes in from Lily, letting me know that she's on her way.

"All right, Jackson, it's go time. Let's get your stuff together and finish packing."

***

I sit up straighter as we pass a green sign that says "Albuquerque, population 560,274."

It was only an hour's drive; easily short enough for a day trip, and there is a lot more available here than in Santa Fe.

We didn't travel much growing up; the hotel kept us all busy, and our annual family vacation was usually a cruise, which required more flying than driving.

After Mom died, Dad and I would go to California instead. I'm not sure why it changed, but I always assumed that the memories of cruising with Mom made it too hard for him to continue vacationing that way.

Once Dad and Frances got married, family vacations stopped altogether. Instead, he and Frances would jet off to places like St. Lucia or Puerto Vallarta. Sometimes Jackie would go, but I was never invited. I don't think my dad intended for that to be the case; Frances probably told him I wouldn't want to go and was too busy in any event.

But I still always felt a little left out.

"Look!" Lucas points out the windshield, and I can't help but laugh at the boyish excitement on his face.

I lean forward, and then feel the awe strike me. In the air are dozens—no, hundreds—of hot air balloons. There're traditional ones, character ones, ones in vibrant colors against the bright blue New Mexico sky.

"Oh, wow. That's beautiful."

"Have you ever been in a hot air balloon?

I snort.

"Definitely not."

"I booked us a hot air balloon ride for tomorrow."

My jaw drops as I turn to him.

"You what?"

"I thought it'd be fun. There's nothing like looking down and seeing thousands of people from the sky. They almost look like ants."

"That is so... kind. Thank you for doing that."

"Of course. I wanted this to be an experience."

He smiles and squeezes my hand. "Today is all business. We'll head straight to Forest Cabinetry to check out the floors, and then head to some antique shops after lunch. I figured that would be the best way to do it. Since we're driving this moving truck anyway, it didn't seem to matter the order of events."

"Yeah, that's perfect. Oh, Frances wants us to look for things that would work as centerpieces for the gala."

"I'm not sure I'd call it a gala. That's usually used to celebrate something significant."

"That's what Frances called it. What would you call it?"

"A party."

I snort.

"Well, I guess party isn't fancy enough for the invitations."

"If she insists on calling it a gala, we should host a charity auction. Those are usually a big hit, and it would be good for the community to give back."

I light up.

"I know the perfect place. There's this community kitchen that Dad and I used to volunteer at and... "

My heart sinks a little. I haven't been back since his funeral, and it eats at me a little every Sunday when I think about that. Dad would be disappointed, I know that for sure.

"Community kitchen?"

"We make food and supply meals for people in need. Or, we used to. I haven't gone in a long while. Maybe I should start going again. I'm sure they're wondering what happened to me."

I think about the old man that I sat with every Sunday, Horace. His parents were Polish immigrants, and he would tell me stories about his mother making pierogi every Friday for dinner, or the crackers they would eat on Christmas.

"We should go," Lucas says, surprising me. I blink and then nod.

"Yeah, actually, I'd like that." I clear my throat. "Anyway, they could always use the money, and I know the coordinators would put it to good use."

"Done. I'll talk to Frances about it. I don't see why she would object. It helps the community and it makes her look good."

I smile. Frances only cares about one of those things, but looking good is definitely enough of a reason for her to be on board. Even if she doesn't care about those in need.

Lucas pulls into the parking lot of a giant warehouse. We hop out as a man comes out to meet us.

"Mr. Bennett and Ms. Stone?"

The man greets us with a warm smile and then holds out his hand, shaking each of ours. "I'm Andy. You inquired about some floors?"

Lucas and Andy get to talking as he leads us through a rolling garage door. Inside there are rows and rows of palettes holding every kind of flooring you could imagine, from thick wood to gorgeous marble tile. I know which one Frances would pick.

"This here is the wood you were inquiring about: it's a genuine replica of the maple flooring that was extremely popular in the 1920's. The roaring 20's were all about vibrant colors and maple is extremely durable."

He grins and shoves his hands in his pocket.

"I think this is almost an exact match for the floors in the rest of the hotel," I state after inspecting it.

"This is about how much we need. We're redoing the lobby as well as the second floor of the hotel. It's a lot, but if you can supply us, that would be absolutely wonderful. And it would save us a great deal of time and trouble trying to source it elsewhere."

Andy takes the file from me and whistles.

"It's cutting it close, but we should have that amount in stock. If not, you don't need to go shopping around. We can get more from our supplier in a few weeks."

Andy leaves to check the inventory. Lucas turns to me and smiles.

"Looks like we may have lucked out."

"Definitely. Thanks so much for finding this place."

Lucas shakes his head.

"Nah, that was all Royce. Kids a whiz at finding exactly what you need."

"Is that why you keep him on? He seems nice and good at what he does in some ways, but he is sort of like a 'Calamity Joe', isn't he?"

He shrugs.

"Honestly, he's a little clumsy, and he can talk your ear off if you let him. But he's a great assistant. I definitely think that once he figures out his balance issues, he'll run a very successful business."

Andy returns, a big smile on his face.

"We have enough. Will that be check or card?"

I swipe the business card, inwardly groaning at the price (hardwood floors aren't cheap) and then Lucas and Andy start loading the truck, placing soft pieces of fabric between each layer. It fills up the entire front part of the unit, stacking right up to the top. Andy straps some bungees over it all so it doesn't slide around.

"All set. Thanks for choosing Forest Cabinetry. Here's my card." Andy supplies us with a business card before we get back in the truck.

"All right, all that moving floors has me famished. What do you say we do some lunch?" Lucas asks.

"Oh yeah, I'm starving."

Lucas laughs and shakes his head.

"I don't see why you're so hungry—supervising the workers hardly racks up an appetite."

"Hey, don't dis management! Without supervision, who knows what could have gone wrong."

"All right, it's no problem. How do you feel about street tacos?"

"Love them."

"I know just the place."

***

After a filling lunch of tacos from a food truck—it almost feels like we're making up for not eating at the Farmers Market—we're browsing around an antique store called Lucy's.

"What do you think about this?" Lucas asks, running his hand along the top of an end table.

"Maybe. The wood is almost too dark, though. Also there's a chip on the back here."

"We could fix that."

"You want to pay this price for a project?" I ask, showing him the 'AS IS' price tag with a ridiculously high number. "I don't think so."

Lucas laughs and shakes his head.

I stop when I spot the wardrobe on the back wall.

"Oh, my God!" I'm practically running toward the wardrobe.

It's tall, with swirling art nouveau designs carved into the wood at the front.

"This is perfect."

Lucas opens the doors, inspecting the inside.

"There's no mark for a creator, but it seems genuine. The wood is solid."

"It would be an amazing statement piece in one of our premium suites. We absolutely need it."

Lucas eyes the wardrobe before nodding.

"You got it. Wait here and I'll get someone."

As Lucas walks away, I run my hand along the grooves in the wood. It's smooth, polished but still distinctly wood textured.

It's the sort of wardrobe Mom would have loved. I was still young when she died, but one thing she loved was antiquing.

We would spend Saturdays hitting up the antique shops. She's the one who taught me how to identify 1920's era statement pieces, and this is definitely one of them.

Lucas comes back with a salesperson.

"This has been here for a while," she nods, reaching for a tag taped to the side. "It came from an estate sale a few months ago. We're asking two thousand for it, is that okay?"

I beam.

"That's perfect."

Chapter Twenty-Two

Lucas

We get to the Airbnb rather late, around 7:00. I was hoping to arrive earlier, but Emma seemed so excited for the antique shops that I couldn't say no. Does she know the power she has over me? Sometimes I wonder.

"Wow, this is so cute!" Emma says excitedly. Despite it only being a weekend stay, Royce booked the best. Before us is a stately adobe-style mansion, all tan walls and stately windows.

"Let's head inside."

I padlocked the truck after loading the final antique piece earlier. I'm not necessarily worried about someone trying to steal a bunch of vintage furniture and wood floors, but you can never be too sure.

"Those small gold sculptures are going to look great as centerpieces, and we can reuse them for other events. Honestly, what a steal."

Emma stops, her jaw dropping as we step into the doorway.

The place is all marble flooring and crystal chandeliers, warm lighting emanating throughout the home.

"Wow, Royce really went all out for this," I murmur, cursing myself for bringing up my assistant at a moment like this.

We head further into the home and I deposit our bags onto the couch as Emma admires the huge fireplace.

She runs her hands along the stone, then finds the dial on the side. She twists it and a fire whooshes within. She claps her hands excitedly.

"This is so beautiful, wow. Thank you for coming with me."

Emma sidles up to me and loops her arms around my neck, her eyes becoming heavy.

"You know, it's only 7:00, we don't really need to get dinner yet."

"Oh, yeah? What do you think we should do to fill the time?" I ask, running my hands down her sides. Her figure shines in a pair of soft pants and the fitted t-shirt she's been wearing all day.

Emma's lips curve into a smile, a mischievous glint sparkling in her eye.

"I'm sure we can think of some things to occupy ourselves," she murmurs softly, planting her lips against my neck in a series of soft kisses. Her breath is warm against my neck, and it sends a shiver through me.

I lean in, pressing my forehead to hers.

"I've been thinking about you all day. The way you got so excited finding the wardrobe, and haggled for the console table," I confess, lowering my voice.

Emma laughs, its warmth echoing through my body.

"My bartering skills are what do it for you?"

"Everything about you turns me on, Emma."

I close the distance between us. Her lips are soft and taste like strawberry lip balm. The crackling fire behind us sets a rhythm behind us, the soft glow casting our shadows across the shiny marble floors.

Emma's fingers thread their way through my hair, tugging gently as she pushes her body against mine. I can feel the shape of her breasts against my chest, and my erection stirs at the memory of what they look like underneath her shirt.

I slide my hands beneath her shirt, tracing my fingertips against the warm skin of her back. She shivers and pulls away.

"The couch looks comfortable," she murmurs against my lips, "but I have to wonder what the bedroom looks like."

I lift her and she wraps her legs around my waist, kissing my neck as I head down the hallway and step through a door.

A king-sized bed dominates the space, covered in plush pillows and crisp white linens.

Another fireplace, less impressive but still as beautiful as the one in the living room, dominates one wall.

Emma hops down and turns the dial on it, the fire roaring to life. She bites her lip as she grabs my hand and pulls me toward the bed, stopping and looking up at me with naked desire.

I push my hands under her shirt, moving them slowly up her chest, seeking out her taut nipples. Emma sucks in a breath as my fingers graze them, her eyes not leaving mine.

When I lift her shirt over her head, her hair cascades down, tousled and messy from the action. I run my hands through it and kiss her neck.

"I love your hair."

Emma giggles and then tugs my shirt over my head, tossing it aside. She presses her body against me, warmth radiating from every inch of her.

Her lips make their way down my neck, and when she gets to my collarbone she takes a gentle nip. I can't suppress the gasp, a tremor running through me as her teeth graze my skin. I find her waist, pulling her closer to me.

The bed beckons behind her, but the moment is too precious, the feeling of her skin against mine enchanting. I reach behind her and unhook her bra in one easy motion, sliding the straps down her arms before tossing it aside.

The firelight dances across her bare skin, casting a warm glow.

"Have I told you that you're beautiful?" I ask, palming her breasts and giving each nipple a gentle squeeze.

"Only about a million times," she teases.

She guides me to the bed, pushing me down and then climbs into my lap, straddling me.

She cradles my face as our lips crash together, our tongues exploring each other's mouths. Her fingers trail down my chest until they find the button on my pants, clumsily working to unbutton and then push them to the floor.

My briefs hold my hardness against me, the fabric barely constraining my length. Emma looks down and licks her lips before kissing her way down my chest, the kisses leaving shiny spots on my chest from the strawberry lip balm.

When she reaches the waistband, she looks up at me with those eyes—eyes that could make me do anything in a heartbeat.

Her fingers hook into the elastic, pulling the briefs down so painfully slowly that it's taking everything in me not to just rip them off myself.

"You're not impatient at all," I tease. Her warm hand wraps around me, and I can't stop the groan that escapes as she moves up and down me with ease. She brushes her thumb over the sensitive tip and I suck in a breath.

"Maybe you're just overly impatient." Her words trail off as she replaces her hand with her mouth, lowering onto me.

"Fuck," I murmur, the wetness of her mouth engulfing me completely. I thread my fingers through her hair, fighting to keep my hips still. Light dances against her bare shoulders as she moves, creating a rhythm that makes me grip the sheets, pleasure building within me.

"Emma."

Her whispered name is more a warning than anything. I don't want this to be over too soon.

She pulls away with a satisfied smile, crawling on top of me.

She grinds against me and I groan, grabbing at her pants and pushing down the fabric until they're on the ground with all the other clothes. I take the opportunity to flip us over, me on top of her.

I trail kisses down her chest, licking and sucking as I make my way down to her black lace panties. A matching set; for some reason that turns me on even more.

"These are nice," I whisper, brushing my finger over her clit that lies under the fabric. It's sensitive and swollen, and her only response is to arch her back and hiss.

I kiss her through the lace and then push it aside instead of taking them off, running my tongue along the wetness.

Emma moans, her hands gripping the sheets as I work my tongue against her, each lick eliciting a sound that sends electricity shooting down my spine. She tastes intoxicating and I lose myself in the rhythm, in her reactions, and in the way her thighs start to tremble on either side of my head.

"Oh, God," Emma moans, arching her back and moving her hips to meet my mouth. "Please don't stop."

I chuckle and slide a finger into her, then another, curving them as my tongue continues its steady assault against her clit. Her breathing becomes ragged, interspersed with tiny whimpers that become more and more desperate with each passing moment.

"Lucas!" Emma cries, every part of her tensing as she cums around me. I don't stop, letting her ride out her orgasm on my fingers and mouth.

When her body finally relaxes, I climb on top of her, my face hovering above hers as I let her cunt juices drip from my mouth into hers, watching the liquid drip wetly into her waiting mouth.

Then I kiss her deeply as my erection pushes at her entrance. Emma's body responds, her hips rising to meet the tip.

I position myself and push in slowly, savoring the way her still wet pulsing pussy takes me in.

I sigh when I'm fully inside of her, not an inch of me untaken. We're still for a moment, our foreheads pressed together, and I'm enraptured by the sight of her hair glowing in the firelight and the way she licks the cunt juice from her lips.

Emma wraps her legs around me, signaling her impatience.

"You feel amazing," I murmur as I thrust into her.

Emma's unrestrained moans echo through the room, her inhibitions gone.

I begin tenderly, my hips caressing hers before increasing with intensity, fueled by desire. Emma's fingers dig into my back, clawing at me as her back arches.

I thrust into her deeper and harder as our breathing becomes more erratic, both of us getting closer to climax.

As Emma begins to tighten around me I'm careful not to change the pace, resisting the urge to go faster as my own climax is just around the corner.

"Oh, God," Emma moans. The sensation of her tightening around me, the orgasm written all over her face sends me over the edge, and I spill into her, pumping until I'm empty.

We collapse together, cuddling as our breathing returns to normal. She looks at me and giggles.

"I don't think I'll ever get tired of that."

"I hope not." I plant a kiss on her and then my stomach growls. Emma arches a brow and laughs loudly.

"Hungry?"

"Ravenous."

"Weird, we just had a three course meal."

She pokes me playfully. "Let's get some food."

***

"Oh, my God, this is amazing." A soft, hot piece of cheese stretches from the slice to Emma's lips. She yanks the slice and the cheese swings back, slapping her in the chin, and I can't help but laugh. She rolls her eyes but smiles anyway.

"Told you it was the best pizza in town."

I pull a slice from the box and savor the flavor. The perfect blend of cheese and garlic. "I'm surprised you're just a plain cheese pizza kind of person."

"Why?"

"It's just the most basic kind of pizza you can get and you seem like you'd be an adventurous eater."

"Is it basic, or is it classic?" Emma gives me a pointed look. "Besides, I like other toppings. Mushrooms and olives or whatever. But nothing beats a slice of classic cheese. It's like going back to the basics—the peak of perfection. Anything else is superfluous."

As she talks I can feel a smile form on my face. Emma frowns in response.

"Why are you looking at me like that?" she asks. Then she takes another bite.

"You're just cute when you're passionate about something." I shake my head and chuckle. "It's also amusing that cheese pizza is something you're passionate about."

Emma huffs and rolls her eyes.

"Well, you're sitting here insulting cheese pizza and..." she mutters, trailing off as she takes another bite.

Quiet music plays softly from the television in the living room as the conversation drops while we eat. I sneak glances at Emma between bites. She tossed her red hair into a bun after our pursuit in the bed, and her mascara is slightly smudged under her eyes, and I don't think I've ever seen her look more beautiful than she does in this moment, the soft kitchen lighting catching the highest points of her face.

I didn't go to Santa Fe expecting to meet a woman, yet somehow I find myself falling harder and faster for the most amazing woman I've ever met.

Chapter Twenty-Three

Emma

"Is that...a giant plate of nachos?" I ask, staring across an endless sea of hot air balloons staked to the ground in front of us.

"If it exists, there's probably a hot air balloon rendition of it somewhere in the world." Lucas shields his eyes from the sun as he takes in all the balloons.

It still feels weird to see him in casual clothing. In my mind, I associate him with Lucas Bennett, the self-made hotel mogul wearing expensive, tailored custom suits. Yet here he stands next to me, in a deep green shirt and jeans.

And he looks very good in them, if I do say so myself. I've been unable to keep my eyes off of him all morning.

Even though we were up late after pizza—we decided to watch a movie which inevitably led to another round in bed before falling asleep—we woke up at 5:00 in the morning so we would have enough time to get ready and watch the balloon launch.

Lucas threads his fingers through mine and leads me to a vendor stall. My hand tingles where his skin touches mine. It feels weird holding his hand here in public, no possibility of being seen by anyone we know.

It's not as if our relationship is a total secret—well, not that we've officially designated ourselves as being in our relationship.

Still, it's almost freeing how little there is to worry about being with him here in Albuquerque. We're here on hotel business, and there's no Frances or Jackie to be concerned about.

Lucas turns around and holds up a blanket proudly.

"Come on, let's head up that hill. They're about to start the launch," he says, leading me up the hill before unwrapping the blanket and laying it on the ground.

We sit down on the blanket, and I lean into him without a second thought. It feels so natural that it's almost terrifying, considering the only relationship I've ever been in was one where nothing ever felt the least bit natural.

Things with Andy were fine; he was nice enough, smart, and sometimes he could make me laugh. It was clear that he really cared for me, given how avidly he pursued me.

He asked me to be his girlfriend by covering the dorm common room in rose petals and giving me a big bouquet of flowers with a conversation heart topping each one. Even though I said yes, I still didn't feel anything substantial or deep from him.

"Look!" Lucas points down to a man making various signals with his arms. "The people directing the balloons are called zebras."

"'Cause of the black and white striped shirts?"

"That's exactly why. They're about to launch the first balloon."

I snuggle into Lucas' side and he wraps his arm around me. I lean my head on his shoulder as the Star-Spangled Banner rings out over the festival, a hot air balloon with the American flag rising slowly into the air, the sunrise crawling up behind it.

Shadows and crevices of light flood out across the festival, casting a soft glow over the balloons and people. I sneak a peek at Lucas from the corner of my eye and he's completely enthralled.

There's a look of almost childlike wonder, a small smile spreading across his face and lighting him up. I've never seen him look like this, all joy and amazement at the sight in front of him. I give his hand a squeeze and he looks at me, pure adoration shining from his eyes.

"How did you find out about this festival?" I ask, running my fingertips gently across his arm. His arm hairs stand on end and little goosebumps rise up underneath my hands.

"Ah, when I was little. Ten, maybe a little older. My dad and I came to Albuquerque so he could get a special gift for my mom. We didn't have a whole lot of money growing up, but it was their anniversary and he had a ring custom made for her."

"That's so sweet!"

"It was; my mother loved it. But as a cover for coming to get the ring—because my mom was very smart and she would have been suspicious if he just drove up to Albuquerque for no reason—he brought me with him and we came to the hot air balloon festival.

It was the most amazing thing I'd ever seen up to that point in my life. It felt like magic, all the balloons being lifted into the air."

I look out as more balloons follow the American flag balloon, each one distinctly patterned. There wasn't a single repeat pattern, despite there being dozens, if not hundreds, of balloons.

As they rise higher, it makes a great spectacle in the sky, the sun rising behind them. I move closer to Lucas and he runs his hand through my hair gently.

"This is magic," I whisper, and in response, Lucas plants a soft kiss on my forehead, making an already magical moment even better.

***

"All right, you ready to head back home?" Lucas asks as he padlocks the back of the truck, one final centerpiece procured from a small antique shop on a side street. It was a lucky find, a shiny brass water pitcher with carved flowers covering it.

After the festival, I took a look at a few antique shop websites—we were still missing one centerpiece, and I wanted it to be the perfect one.

Despite the fact Frances is only holding the event to attract buyers for the hotel, I want it to be a success. If Lucas ends up buying the hotel, it will mean so much more for both the community at-large and the community kitchen we're raising money for.

The shop where we found the pitcher doesn't update their website regularly—the pitcher was last listed six months ago, and honestly, it was a long shot that it would still be there.

But when we showed up, there it was, sitting proudly on a top shelf. We paid more than Lucas would have preferred—he wanted to haggle with the clerk sitting behind the front counter.

Instead, I swiped the company card and we walked out with my prize. He grumped a little at first, but then he saw the smile on my face and let it go.

I sigh.

"No, I'm not ready to go home. I wish we could stay in Albuquerque forever. Now it's back to my basement apartment and working with Frances every day."

Lucas wraps me in his arms and pulls me close, tipping his forehead to mine.

"It's not going to be like that forever. We'll buy the hotel, say bye-bye to Frances and Jackie, and live happily ever after."

I laugh and shake my head.

"Happily ever after is for fairy tales."

"Happily ever after is whatever we want it to be. I can't promise that things are always going to be perfect or easy, but you won't have to be alone. I'll be here through everything."

I arch an eyebrow.

"Yeah? That's a tall promise."

"It's one I have every intention of keeping, I can assure you that."

I stare into his brilliant blue eyes, shining brightly. Light reflects in them, like the sun sparkling off the ocean, and I believe him.

It doesn't make sense to me—I have no reason to believe him, no definitive proof that he will keep his word, but I still believe him.

He smiles, and I pull him into a deep kiss, our lips matching perfectly. His hands find my waist, digging in softly as he presses his body against mine. I wrap my hands in his hair, temptation rising in my core. Clearing my throat, I pull away and laugh.

"Okay, maybe we shouldn't be getting hot and heavy in the parking lot. I don't want to cause a scandal."

"You're right. It is a shame, though, that we don't have that Airbnb for another night. We could definitely put it to good use."

His eyes roll over me, and my body tingles under his. I shove away from him softly and walk around to the passenger side of the truck. He gets in the driver's side and smiles. "At least we get a few more hours of privacy where we can just enjoy each other."

My mind whirrs and before I can stop myself, the question is tumbling out.

"What is 'us?'"

Lucas blinks in surprise as he pulls out of the parking lot, glancing at me but not taking his eyes off the road.

"What do you mean?"

"Well, we've been doing...this. Sleeping together, romantic dates. Plotting together. But I still don't know what this is. I know we can't be open about whatever it is we've been doing together; Frances would undoubtedly find a way to use it to her benefit and definitely wouldn't sell the hotel to you. Especially since she was hoping you'd get interested in Jackie."

"Yes, that's true."

"But I'm still just...confused?"

I wave my hands, as if sorting through a muddled mess in the air in front of me. "It's clear that you feel something for me, and I know I feel something for you. I just want something more definitive. I want to know what we are."

Lucas chuckles and reaches for my hand, squeezing it gently.

"Emma, you are the most amazing, beautiful woman that I've ever known. You're so intelligent, and I think the way you tend to overthink everything is charming."

I make a face and he laughs. "That face is also adorable. The point I'm trying to make is that I'm very attracted to you, and I care about you a great deal. So I guess, what I'm saying is that I consider us a couple, although I'm not sure we can truly define what that means at this point, since it's early days yet. I know we have to hide things from Frances right now, but that won't be forever. Our relationship can continue to develop even if we have to be rather circumspect for a while yet."

My heart beats so hard that I'm sure he can hear it.

I take a deep breath and calm myself, nodding before continuing. "Yes, I care about you a lot, too, and I'm very happy you feel the same way."

Lucas nods, letting out a little chuckle at my enthusiasm. Or I assume he's chuckling at my enthusiasm. Maybe he's just very happy about me being in agreement with him on where we are right now.

"I've never really been in a serious relationship before. I mean, I've dated, but there wasn't anyone I felt was going to go the distance."

"It's been a while since I've been in a relationship myself. To be honest with you, for a long time I wasn't very good at relationships. I was always too busy, and put my business before everything else and the women in my life certainly didn't appreciate my workaholic tendencies. Don't get me wrong—my hotels, everything I've built? It's extremely important to me, and it takes up a lot of time. But this time? Things feel different with you."

"Why?"

"To start with, you understand the hotel business. You are completely aware of how time consuming it can be to own a hotel. That's huge, because a lot of the women I've dated before just didn't understand what a huge undertaking it is. But more importantly, I feel differently about you than I have about anyone else I've ever been with. It's as if we—I don't know—just fit together, I guess."

My heart swells, warmth spreading through me from head to toe. I lean over and kiss his cheek and he smiles. Sometimes a response doesn't require words.

Chapter Twenty-Four

Lucas

I stretch, sitting up in my bed in the guest room. The weekend with Emma was wonderful. When we got home, we unpacked everything into the storage unit Frances had gotten and then I dropped Emma off at Lily's.

Now that it's Monday, I'm ready for a fresh start to the week.

My phone rings, Royce's name flashing across the screen.

"Hello?" I answer.

"Mr.Bennett! I'm glad you're up—I was worried about calling this early, even though I know you wake up early, but what if you were still asleep and I woke you up? That would be—"

"What can I do for you, Royce?" I interrupt his ramblings. We have to work on building his confidence—he's good at what he does, maybe a little clumsy, but a damn good assistant, and I just need to tap into his potential and help him acquire the confidence he needs.

"I just wanted to thank you for helping me find a gift for my mom. She really loved the brooch, and I would never have found the perfect gift without you."

"I'm glad she liked it. How did the party go?"

"Oh, it was a disaster."

I blink, sitting up in surprise.

"What?"

"Yeah, it was crowded, and everyone got way too drunk too early and made a bunch of speeches that didn't make any sense. Including me," he admits, embarrassment clouding his tone.

"Plus, the caterer got the dates confused and we had to rush order a bunch of pizzas instead of having a sit-down dinner. That kind of sucked. But my mom was really happy, and loved it anyway. Which was the important part."

I laugh.

"Exactly. And I'm sure she loved your speech anyway."

"Well, she said the words were thoughtful, but she recommended that I have a few less tequila sunrises next time I have to give a speech. But yeah, it was a lot of fun."

"I'm glad you enjoyed yourself and everyone had a good time."

A thought flies through my mind. "Also, take down the name of that caterer and put them on our 'Do Not Hire' list."

Royce laughs.

"Will do, Mr.Bennett. I'm packing and I'll be headed back down to the hotel within the hour."

"When you get back, I need you to do something for me."

"Sure. Whatever you need!"

"There's a lawyer that I need to meet with—Cordell Kennedy. He's located a little outside of Santa Fe. If you could set up an appointment for us sometime this week, that would be great."

"Oh, sure." Curiosity is evident in Royce's tone, but he doesn't ask any questions. I appreciate his reticence, because I don't know how to explain the email I found on Clark's computer and the questions I have for Mr. Kennedy.

"Also, I'd like to start including you in more of the details of the hotel business. You're a great assistant, but I think you could be more."

"More?"

"I was thinking that you could help manage a lot of the day-to-day aspects of running the company, getting more involved working with the hotel GMs to troubleshoot and problem solve. Maybe do some traveling to the various properties when necessary. I don't want you to feel obligated or pressured to say yes, but I think you show a lot of promise and I can't continue to be a one-man show forever."

I realize I'm going to need more daily support working with the various properties I own, especially if I want to settle down with Emma. I know she'd willingly move and travel with me anywhere, but I want to do things right with her. I want to be involved and be present. I can't do that if I'm trying to do everything myself.

Then again, Emma will likely want to have a prominent role in the company, too, assuming things progress to that point. I'm jumping the gun a bit, but I could see Emma and I becoming partners in the business. She has remarkable untapped talent that would be a huge asset to the company.

The longer I'm here in Santa Fe, the more I feel connected to home again. I moved away from Santa Fe initially because I felt disconnected. After my parents passed, Santa Fe seemed empty to me. Even though Clark was right there, Ginny was gone by then and Frances made it impossible for us to maintain a close friendship. I was lonely.

But being back here now, and spending time with Emma, in The Signature on Main—it just feels right. The world feels more colorful now; I just wish I'd kept my parents house.

The memories were painful, and truthfully, the house wasn't in good shape by the time I sold it.

As much as I offered to help through the last few years, Dad was too proud to let me do the gutters or repaint when the house needed any kind of maintenance.

It's been fully remodeled now, with fresh coats of paint and an addition, so it doesn't much seem like the house I grew up in.

But my parents are buried here, and so is Clark, and being able to visit the cemetery now and then is appealing, too.

A knock on the door interrupts my introspection.

"Lucas?" Jackie calls softly through the door and I sigh inwardly. As much as being in Clark's house is sort of nostalgic, the present company makes it decidedly less comfortable.

"What can I do for you, Jackie?" I call through the door, climbing out of bed and throwing some clothes on.

"Can I come in?"

I look around the room, clothes strewn everywhere and my suitcase unpacked on the dresser.

"It's a little messy."

"That's okay," she says as she pushes the door open. She beams at me as she steps in. "I was wondering if you wanted to grab some breakfast."

"Oh, I actually have to be at the hotel in a little while. I've been away and there's plenty to do, especially as I'm essentially working remotely."

"Well, maybe we could pick up breakfast and bring enough for everyone on the team at the hotel? I'm sure they would appreciate that. I know Mom didn't eat before she left."

Jackie smiles, and my heart sinks to my stomach.

No matter how much of a ploy it is for Frances wanting to hook me up with Jackie, it's clear that Jackie has a very real crush on me that is not reciprocated.

Letting her down easy is going to be a delicate situation to navigate.

As much as I don't want to ride around with Jackie, grabbing breakfast for everyone is relatively harmless and will keep both Jackie and Frances happy enough that their 'plan' is working.

I sigh before nodding my head.

"We can do that. I'm sure they'd all appreciate it." I look down at my pajamas and shrug. "Let me get ready for work and I'll meet you in the foyer. Give me about 20 minutes."

Jackie looks me up and down and winks.

"I think you look amazing just as you are, but I know you love your suits. Catch you down there."

I wait until she leaves the room for the frown to spread across my face.

This is definitely going to require a gentle touch.

***

"Oh, this is so kind of you two! It's so nice to see that you're getting along," Frances' voice echoes in all corners of the room as she looks at the breakfast spread in front of us. Jackie found a place across town where we got plates of pancakes, waffles, eggs and hash browns.

Luckily, Emma is standing behind Frances, so the perturbed look on her face is only visible to the two of us.

I texted her after Jackie left my room so she wouldn't be blindsided, but Emma is unable to keep her displeasure off her face.

"We were glad to do it. Thanks for keeping me company, Lucas," Jackie singsongs as she sits down next to Frances. Emma shoots her a look before taking the seat next to me.

We all take plates of food, but before I can put a bite in my mouth, Frances slides a file folder from her bag and sets it on the table.

"This is the file for the charity auction we're having. I've managed to find some local businesses that will donate to the auction, which is wonderful. I also have a list of caterers and entertainers that are possibilities. Lucas, perhaps you and Jackie can tackle those?"

I freeze as all heads in the room swivel toward me. I clear my throat and smile but shake my head.

"While I think that's a wonderful idea, I'd actually like you to use Royce; he's good with detail and wants to know more about the hospitality business. I think it will be important for him to know how to direct event planning as he takes on more responsibility in my hotel group."

I don't want to be trapped in another situation with Jackie, and suggesting I use Emma for the work might raise some brows since Frances would likely find it unpalatable.

Emma interjects and suggests an alternative plan.

Jackie looks at her in surprise, as if she forgot Emma was even sitting at the table in the first place. "Why don't we have Royce check out the caterers, and Jackie and I can research the entertainment?"

Jackie rolls her eyes but leans back in her chair and shrugs.

"I guess that could work," she mutters.

Frances looks at Jackie and then sighs.

"Yes, I guess that's fine. The gala isn't Lucas' responsibility, anyway, and I'm happy to have Royce helping out, so thank you, Lucas, for loaning him to us for this."

She shuts the folder and gives us a tight smile. "In other news, the plumbing issues are set to be resolved by the end of this week. We'll be able to start laying down the new floors that you sourced over the weekend. How did that go, by the way?"

"Oh, it went great!" Emma says enthusiastically. Frances eyes her suspiciously, and Emma blushes. "What I mean is that the floors were perfect, and we were able to find centerpieces for every table for the gala."

"Emma picked out the centerpieces, I was mostly there for the hard labor." I shrug, and Jackie laughs a little too loud at my lame joke.

"I'm glad you both accomplished everything we needed. Certainly takes a lot off of my plate. Thank you, again, Lucas, for pitching in on this."

She cuts up a piece of the pancake on her plate, taking the first bite. "These pancakes are wonderful. Oh, I also need some invitations designed. They need to go out by tomorrow at the latest."

"Tomorrow?" Emma coughs, choking slightly on her coffee. "How are we going to manage that?"

"We're going to have to figure it out. The only other option is pushing back the date of the gala, but that is no longer an option. Quite a few buyers are going to be coming to the gala—seeing what their money will buy and whatnot. So the gala needs to be perfect."

"In two weeks?"

An annoyed crease marks Frances' forehead as she glares at Emma.

"Yes, in two weeks. I know it's short notice, but we can pull it off if we're diligent and actually put in the effort. Emma, why don't you handle the invitations? You can spend the rest of the day doing that. Roy can go check out caterers and Jackie can deal with the entertainment."

"Now that we have our day planned, I'm going to get to work. I really have a lot to do," Frances says, standing up and smoothing her skirt. She strides out the door with her phone to her ear, her food barely touched.

Chapter Twenty-Five

Emma

"Ooh, what if we got those cute little lace masks and wore those?" Lily squeals as she scrolls through outfit ideas for the gala on her phone. She pokes me in the arm and shows me a picture of a woman in a lacy black mask and matching gown.

I laugh and roll my eyes.

"It's not a masquerade, Lily. It's prohibition era themed," I respond, turning back to my laptop. "You're supposed to be helping me with these invitations."

Lily leans over to peek at my laptop, squishing Jackson in the process.

She'd come into the office close to the end of her shift, chattering about how the guy she was dating annoyed her this morning. But when she saw how stressed I was about the invitations, she offered to come to my house after work and help.

The man I spoke to on the phone assured me that if I sent him a design by 6:00, he could have a 150 invitations sent out by tomorrow afternoon. The rush order was costing us almost double the typical cost, but there wasn't much I could do about that. And I wasn't about to haggle with someone who was doing me a favor.

"Okay, I think this looks good, but there's a typo there," Lily says and points to one of the words on the screen. "Also, I think it needs some oomph."

"'Oomph?'"

"You know, some pizzazz? Make it stand out. What if—" Lily leans over and scrolls through the design options on the side bar before landing on a glitter pen.

"Perfect. Add some gold swirls to the background."

I eye her skeptically but do as she says.

"Okay, now take that slider, the opacity. Move it more to the left, but not all the way."

The glittered swirls in the background fade away as I follow her instructions.

"STOP!"

I jump at the shout, turning to her incredulously. She grins and tosses her hair.

"Sorry, that's just perfect. Make sure you ask for gold embossed letters. It costs extra but it will look amazing."

I take a second to examine the invitation on the screen before smiling with satisfaction.

"You're pretty good at this. Have you ever thought about design school?"

Lily smiles and then shrugs.

"I did go to design school for a few years, but I didn't finish. I couldn't afford it."

"Oh, gosh, I'm sorry. I didn't know."

"That's okay, how could you? Besides, I'll go back one day. For now, I like working at the hotel and I'm saving money, so that's what matters."

Jackson sighs, finally tired of being squished. Lily laughs and ruffles his fur before turning back to her phone. "Do you think they'll let the staff dress up?"

"Hmm, I'm not sure. I'll have to ask Frances."

Or rather, I'll have to have Lucas ask Frances—it just seems like that would make a positive response more likely.

I throw on some finishing touches and then send the invitations to be printed before closing my laptop with a flourish.

"Done?" Lily sits up straighter. I nod emphatically and she squeals. "Good, now we can do fun stuff. I want to hear all about your weekend with Lucas."

Lily tried to get me to spill all the details when he dropped me off at her place to get Jackson yesterday, but Frances called almost as soon as I arrived demanding I go to the hotel to fix something wrong with the spreadsheets.

Sometimes she treats me like a maid, assistant, and tech support all rolled into one.

"My weekend with Lucas—well, it was incredible." I can feel my face heating up even just thinking about everything we did. "And... we're official, I guess you could say."

I wince in preparation for her high pitched squealing, but it doesn't come. When I look over at Lily, she's staring at me with her jaw dropped. After a moment she snaps out of her trance and grins.

"Oh, my God, that's amazing. How? When? What happens now?"

I grab a pillow and hug it to my chest.

"It was on the way home. We were on the road and I started a discussion about what we were to one another at this point; you know, just trying to define the relationship, I suppose. I wasn't planning to, it just sort of happened. It had been on my mind all weekend."

I chew the side of my cheek. "The only thing is that we have to continue to be discreet because of Frances If she were to find out it might mess up the plan for Lucas to buy The Signature."

Lily scoffs and shakes her head.

"Frances is ruining your life."

"God, tell me about it."

"What about the Airbnb? What was it like?"

"So beautiful. It had these gorgeous fireplaces in the living room and the bedroom. I should have taken pictures to show you."

"That's okay, just send me the address and I can look it up later." She flashes me a bright smile. "I'm so happy for you."

Lily squeezes my arm and I giggle.

"Thanks. How was your weekend?"

"Oh, you know. I hung out with Jackson, and we went on some walks."

Lily's voice gets sugary sweet as she leans forward and kisses Jackson on the forehead. He wags his tail in response. "Seriously, anytime you need a dog sitter, I'm your girl. He's, like, the best dog I've ever met."

"Oh, I meant to ask. Assuming I got the invitations sent out, I was supposed to join Jackie to check out some entertainers for the gala. Do you want to come with me?"

Lily makes a face and I sigh. "I know, that's why I'm asking you to join. I don't know if I can handle spending so much one-on-one time with Jackie."

She sighs dramatically but grins.

"All right, fine, I'll be your buffer and offer a third opinion. It actually does sound kind of fun. What kind of entertainment?"

"Frances has a list—she sent it over to me earlier..."

I trail off and grab my phone, scrolling through my email until I find it. "Here we go. There's only six on here, but it looks like a couple singers, some bands, and a magician? I don't know what we'd do with a magician, but he must be on here for a reason."

"She can't be serious. Are we hosting a gala or a birthday party for a six year old?"

I can't stop the laugh from escaping me.

"Come on, I'm sure he's on there for a reason. Maybe it's a sophisticated close-up magician that would roam from table to table. That could be very cool."

Doubt clouds Lily's face but she shrugs anyway.

"Okay, I'm done talking about work. Let's watch a movie."

***

"That was not a sophisticated magic show, at all," Lily announces as we leave the meeting with the magician the next day.

The magician gave us a preview of his act, which included balloon animals, pulling a rabbit out of a hat, and a trick where a flower spits water into someone's face. Lily was the designated target of that trick, and the pieces of hair framing her face are still a little damp.

Jackie shakes her head in agreement.

'What was Mom thinking? It's like she pasted the first six results from Google onto a list without even looking into them."

Jackie turns around and narrows her eyes at the building, as if she can death stare the magician out of existence simply through thought.

"I'm sure she just wanted some variety," I say softly. "She couldn't have known how bad or juvenile his act was."

I don't want to say anything negative that can be relayed back to Frances, but Jackie actually hasn't been an unwelcome addition on the journey to find entertainment for the gala.

She and Lily are getting along, and she's even been friendlier to me than she ever has been before. It's weird, almost like I've stepped into an alternate universe or something.

"The bands were good."

"They were okay. Not exactly show stopping, but they could do the job, I guess," Jackie agrees, pulling out her phone and tapping loudly on the screen.

"We still have one more, right?" Lily asks, leaning in to look at the paper in my hand. I turn it toward her and she nods.

"Felicia Wilkes. Well, I guess we'll see if she makes the cut."

Lily links arms with me and Jackie trails behind slightly as we make our way down the walk to the venue where we're meeting with Felicia.

"She has good reviews!" Jackie calls out, hustling to catch up with us and linking an arm in mine. It takes all I have not to instantly pull away. "That's a good sign at least."

I let out a breath of relief and smile at her gratefully. Who knew she would turn out to be useful on this trip?

We walk in silence for a few more minutes before Jackie turns to me and gives me a shy smile.

"So, I've been wanting to ask you. Not that you'd necessarily know, but you're closer to him; him being your dad's best friend and all. Is Lucas seeing anyone?"

I blanch, whipping my head to look at her so quickly that I almost give myself whiplash.

"Why would I know that?"

Jackie throws her hands up in the air and rolls her eyes.

"Well, you just spent a whole weekend with him in Albuquerque. I'm sure you didn't just play dominoes and talk about the hotel the whole time. I figured he might have talked a bit about himself."

I'm almost worried that she's putting the pieces together, but when my eyes meet hers, they're purely full of wanting and desperation.

Oh, she has it bad for Lucas. Now it makes sense why she's been so tolerable during this excursion. Trying to butter me up to ask about Lucas.

"We were just looking at furniture and flooring. He didn't mention dating anyone, but that doesn't mean he isn't. He's a pretty private person."

It's almost amazing to me how easily the lie rolls off my tongue. I've never been much of a liar, but somehow I seem to be getting good at it.

"We're here!" Lily announces before Jackie can respond.

We step into the small jazz club and are immediately greeted by the sound of soft piano music emanating through the room. A few patrons are scattered around nursing amber colored drinks in small glasses, their eyes drawn to a petite blond woman in a glittering silver dress standing by the piano.

The piano player changes key and she starts singing. Her voice is rich and smooth, flowing through the room like thick honey. She hits an impressive low note, holding it for longer than I could even imagine doing. I glance at Lily and she's grinning from ear to ear.

"Oh, my God, is that her?" Jackie whispers, awe completely striking out any thoughts she had about Lucas.

After the song ends we make our way across the room, and I almost feel intimidated approaching her. But she smiles warmly, shaking each of our hands. Glittering rings cover her fingers, the cool metal brushing against my skin.

"You must be Emma, it is so nice to meet you. I'm Felicia Wilkes."

"It's so great to meet you. This is Lily and Jackie. You are amazing."

"No, seriously, that was incredible," Lily chimes in. Jackie nods in agreement, apparently unable to get any words out.

"Oh, that is so sweet. Thank you so much." Felicia gestures toward a table and invites us to sit. "So you're here about a gala?"

"Yes. It's in two weeks." I pull out my phone and show her the date on my calendar. "I know it's late notice, and given how incredibly talented you are, you're probably already booked, but it would sure be amazing if you could perform for us."

Felicia takes note of the date and then pulls out a little planner, flipping through the pages.

"Ah, I actually had a cancellation that night. Which hotel did you say you were from again?"

"The Signature on Main."

Felicia's eyes light up.

"The prohibition one? Oh, I've heard so many wonderful things about that place. I'd love to perform for you."

I can feel the relief rush through me.

"That is terrific news. Thank you so much."

"I'm excited." Felicia gives me a big toothy grin. "What do you say we talk price and contracts?"

Chapter Twenty-Six

Lucas

"I don't know which one to choose. They were all great!" Royce looks at the list in despair, hanging his head as if the fate of the world relies on which caterer we choose.

"Let's look at some reviews." I pull out my phone and start searching.

"Mr. Bennett?" Royce asks, his voice wavering.

I blink and look over at him. Concern fills his features, although there's more there. Maybe even doubt?

"You can call me Lucas, you know. You don't have to call me Mr. Bennett all the time."

"But you're my boss!"

"I want you to feel like an equal as we move from you being my assistant to being in a managerial position. You have a say, and I value your opinion."

He fiddles with the collar of his shirt.

"It's just... do you really think I'm good enough?"

"Good enough?" I let out a laugh that's almost too loud, filling the space of the conference room with intensity.

"Royce, you practically hold everything together. Do you know how much time you save me doing all the little things? Let me tell you, what you're doing is a lot harder than what I'm doing most of the time."

It's a small fib, but researching properties for acquisition and compiling them for me isn't an easy job, especially with all my demands and specifications. It's a far cry, though, from keeping the entire hotel portfolio of properties running smoothly. It's a necessary white lie though, because I truly believe Royce can do the job. A few weeks ago, I might have been hesitant. But he's really proven himself over the past few weeks, even if he's still somewhat of a klutz, something I will continue to work on with him.

Royce's eyes widen and his cheeks flush. He shrugs.

"It's not hard, I just make lists and read stuff online. Do what you tell me to do."

"You're good at following instructions, but you're also good at finding stuff on your own. We never would have acquired The Bradford Hotel if it wasn't for you. It wasn't even on my radar. I was so focused on The Everton, which ended up being a bust when they decided to sell to a family member anyway. It's your eye for detail, finding things that aren't easy to find, that will bring us newer and more interesting opportunities."

The tip of his ears turn red. I think I'm embarrassing him a little, but he needs the confidence boost. Confidence is the one thing I've always had in spades and with a little boost to his, I think Royce will be perfect.

"Thanks, boss," Royce gives me a bashful smile before turning back to the list. "I think Wishes Catering was the strongest. Their chicken piccata was incredible, and I loved those green beans. Plus the desserts were to die for."

I think about the chicken piccata—it was easily the best chicken piccata I've ever had, that's for sure. I lean back in the chair before shaking my head.

"Wishes Catering was great, but I actually think Erika Slim's is better for the prohibition theme. Their lobster canapes were great, and time period appropriate. As well as the deviled eggs."

"Their desserts were good."

"I think it will create a better illusion of being in the prohibition era. Hopefully, Jackie and Emma have gone in a similar direction with entertainment, but we won't know until tomorrow, I suppose."

Well, I'll likely know when I sneak into Emma's room later tonight, but I'm not telling Royce that. Not that I think he'd tell anyone, but it's none of his business and I'm not used to sharing personal details with people who work for me.

"So Slim's it is?" Royce asks, taking a note in his little notebook. He nods and scribbles some more before nodding in satisfaction. "Perfect, I'll go give them a call."

***

"I wish we didn't have to sneak around," Emma whispers, threading her fingers through mine.

"It's not forever, just until we have the hotel."

"We?" Emma gives me a teasing smile.

"Of course, we. It's more your hotel than mine at this point. I figured you'd run this one. Remember, I have a whole hotel portfolio to look after."

She sighs contentedly, snuggling closer to me. I kiss her forehead, pressing my lips gently against her forehead.

"Wow, you're hot."

"Thanks, you're not so bad yourself." Emma giggles and gives me a big wink. I roll my eyes and tickle her side.

"That's not what I meant. Your forehead is hot—are you feeling okay?"

Emma hums before shrugging.

"I don't know. I mean, I feel a little crappy, but my period is due next week so that's probably why."

"Hmm." I put my wrist to her forehead. She's warm, but not terribly so. "Just do me a favor and go to the doctor if you feel worse."

"You got it, boss."

I shudder.

"Taking lessons from Royce?"

"Yeah, he's a really good teacher."

Emma laughs, shaking the bed along with her. Emma's laugh is one of the things I love most about her—it's so rich and full. There's genuine joy in her laugh, as if whatever she's just heard is the funniest thing in the world.

"Speaking of Royce, that reminds me. Who did you go with for the entertainer?"

"We found this amazing jazz singer. Felicia Wilkes—oh gosh, I wish you could have heard her. She sounds like an angel." Emma sighs, relishing the memory. "Well, I guess you will hear her on the night of the gala. You'll love her."

"I can't wait. The caterer we chose offers a lot of prohibition themed options. Maybe not prohibition-themed specifically—they don't advertise it that way. But it fits in with what would have been served during that time."

"Do you think it matters?" Emma asks. I look at her in surprise and she shakes her head.

"No, sorry. I don't mean that the prohibition theme doesn't matter. It's important to me. I just mean, do you think people will appreciate it? That they'll know enough about prohibition era foods to care that they're eating it? Or will they be like 'oh, this couscous is good. Glad I came' and that's the end of it."

I'm unable to stop myself from laughing.

"Couscous?"

She throws her hands up.

"It's the first food that came to mind. Humor me, please."

I shift and look into her eyes. They're big and serious.

"I think that some people won't notice. Not every guest is going to be a prohibition-era interested historian. But there will definitely be some enthusiasts, and I know for a fact there will be buyers there that will have looked up every detail of the hotel's history, which means they'll appreciate the lobster canapes."

Emma sighs and frowns glumly.

"Great. The buyers will be the ones who care about the details. That's wonderful news."

"Are you okay?" I run my hands through my hair and she responds, burrowing her face in my hands.

"I think I'm just moody. And tired. Can we go to bed?" she asks, nuzzling me.

I yawn—I am tired, but I can't fall asleep down here with her. I don't let her know that, though.

"Of course."

She lays in my arms, and it takes only a few minutes until she's snoring lightly.

I shift and slowly extricate myself from her arms before sneaking out of the basement apartment and heading back to the main house.

I don't like sneaking around, but I just don't have much of a choice. If Frances were to find me creeping back in early in the morning, it could jeopardize everything and I don't want her selling to someone else just out of spite. I've been nervous about it ever since that morning I ran into her in the kitchen.

It hasn't helped my sleep problems, though. When I'm sleeping next to Emma, I fall asleep almost instantly into a dreamy state. It's like a little slice of heaven, an added benefit of finding the most incredible woman I could possibly imagine.

Away from Emma, though? That's another story. I toss and turn for hours when I'm not sleeping next to her. It's like her body next to mine is comfort incarnate, soothing my mind so soundlessly that I don't even realize it's happening.

I walk carefully up the stairs, making sure to avoid any steps that I know have creaks. It's weird how easily the memories of this house came back to me.

It looks completely different from Ginny's time, but is still inherently the same. The same stairs still creak, the same cabinets still stick when you tug them open. The first day I felt rather like a stranger, but I don't even think twice now as I move around the house instinctively.

I flop into bed, sullen as I think about how it's not quite as comfortable as Emma's. I check my phone: 2:17 am. This is definitely going to be another sleepless night.

My phone buzzes, and a text from Royce lights up the screen.

Confirmed with Slim's. They're excited for the prohibition theme. They also offer vintage glassware rentals, check email when you get a chance.

I shake my head. Even at this hour, the kid is dedicated.

Good, get some sleep. I type. Then add: Good work today.

I roll on my side and try to find a comfortable position. The bed feels too big, too empty. Not soft enough, not covered in enough pillows. I can still smell Emma's intoxicating scent on my shirt, the scent that is slowly becoming my favorite.

My mind drifts to the moment I was in my own office, just before I saw the listing for The Signature.

I felt like a whole different person back then. If someone told me back then that I would be helping to put together a gala and considering moving to Santa Fe, I would have laughed.

If someone had told me I would be falling in love with my dead best friend's daughter, I would have been suitably horrified. Yet here we are.

Now look at me. Toiling over lobster canapes while sneaking out of that woman's room.

A floorboard creaks outside my door at the same time that my phone buzzes. I reach for it and knock it off the table clumsily. It clatters to the floor and the footsteps pause outside my door. I panic and let out a loud snore.

Anyone with some kind of sense would know it wasn't a real snore— it was right out of a cartoon, too much and animated.

It's quiet for a moment, and then whoever is in the hallway passes by. I hear a door softly click shut and let out a breath.

Where'd you go? Emma's text reads.

Didn't want to raise suspicion, I send back.

Miss you already. Feel much worse, really hot and sweaty. Might skip breakfast meeting tomorrow.

I frown. I knew she was feeling warm earlier. I hope it's nothing serious.

Take care of yourself. Plenty of water. Doctor if you're not feeling better by the afternoon.

Emma likes the message so I know that she's seen it, and then presumably goes back to sleep. I put my phone back on the side table and turn on my back.

The footsteps in the hall are unnerving me. Hopefully, it's just a midnight run to the bathroom, which would undoubtedly be Jackie seeing as how Frances has an en suite bathroom.

But what if it wasn't?

What if someone suspects, and was doing the rounds to see if I'm in my room? I don't lock the door when I sleep—it just hasn't seemed necessary. But if someone had poked their head in my room around this time the past few nights, I might not have been here.

I shake my head. No, I'm just being paranoid.

I'm sure it's fine.

Chapter Twenty-Seven

Emma

I tap my foot impatiently on the linoleum floor. I've been sitting in the waiting room for thirty minutes, but I can't complain. I'm lucky they could squeeze me in at the last minute. I know I'd be waiting even longer in urgent care.

"Emma Stone?" A nurse calls out after stepping from behind a door. I follow her into the back. She takes my vitals.

"Hmm, low fever. How are you feeling?"

"Hot."

She nods and then leads me into a private room, then waves the clipboard she's holding. "You filled this out very thoroughly, thank you."

"Of course. Being thorough is my middle name," I say, mentally kicking myself. Why am I being an idiot right now? The nurse gives me a pity chuckle and then smiles.

"All righty, just the typical questions. Are you a smoker?"

I shake my head, and she turns back to the clipboard, recording my answer.

"Drinker?"

"On occasion."

"Sexually active?"

I pause. It's been so long since I've said yes to this question. I nod.

"Birth control method?"

"None."

The nurse stops and gives me a look.

"Are you trying to conceive?"

"No." I say dumbly. There's no way I could be pregnant. Right?

"When was your last period?"

"My period is scheduled to come in two days."

The nurse hmms and taps her pen on her chin.

"We'll give you a pregnancy test."

"Oh, I don't need one."

She shoots me a look.

"You're sexually active and not using protection. So unless you already know that you're pregnant?" She questions. I shake my head. "Yes, I recommend a pregnancy test."

"That's not what I'm here for."

"That's okay. Tell me why you're here."

I explain my symptoms and she nods. She swabs my nose and throat and then sends me into the bathroom.

Dread spreads through me like a dead weight. I look into the mirror and take a deep breath. It's just peeing into a cup, I can definitely do this.

My anxiety is not squashed, though. What am I going to do if I'm pregnant? Will Lucas be mad?

Of course he will be. We may be getting serious, but we haven't talked about any of the big stuff. Moving in together. Marriage. Kids.

I look in the mirror and then straighten up. I can't get ahead of myself. I just need to take the test and then go from there.

I finish what I need to and then head back to the exam room.

I can't stop looking at the clock. The minute hand seems to drag torturously slow. Every second that passes lasts forever, and thinking about it is starting to give me a headache.

After what feels like a lifetime, the doctor steps into the room and gives me a frown.

"Well, you have the flu. Unfortunately, that means a lot of fluids and bed rest, and I'm going to prescribe you some flu medicine. Don't worry; it's safe for pregnant women."

She gives me a small smile and for a moment, it feels like the entire world is spinning.

"I'm pregnant," I state. It's not really a question—the test already confirmed it, but the doctor nods anyway.

"Do you need a doctor's note for work?"

I don't think Frances would care about a doctor's note, but I nod anyway. It wouldn't hurt to have one, I suppose.

"All righty, I'll be right back."

The door clicks softly behind her and my hand moves instinctively to my stomach. It looks exactly the same as it did this morning, but now I'm aware of the tiny life growing inside me.

I stand up and pace the room, unable to sit still as I process. My heart is thundering so loud that I'm certain they can hear it from the reception desk. It's probably shaking the entire room with how hard it's beating. The fluorescent lights are suddenly overwhelming in their brightness and the room is closing in on me.

Pregnant. I'm pregnant.

The doctor comes back in and gives me an alarmed look.

"Are you okay?"

"Oh, gosh, yeah. I'm just processing." I chuckle nervously. She looks at me with uncertainty but hands me the doctor's note.

"All right, I sent your prescription over to your pharmacy. I also put in a referral to an obstetrician—she's absolutely wonderful and I can assure you you'll be in good hands. They'll give you the contact information at the front desk so you can make your first appointment, which you should do soon."

"Great. Thank you," I mutter. Then I snatch the note from her hand and rush out of the room.

***

After running to the pharmacy and grabbing my prescription, I immediately zip home and crawl into bed, but not before I snap a picture of the doctor's note and sent it to Frances, not that she's responded to it, of course.

What am I going to do? I've been browsing the internet for the past thirty minutes watching those pregnancy surprise videos that so many women have done. They're all so cute, and I definitely cannot break the news like that to Lucas. As amusing as the idea might be.

A text from Lucas lights up my phone.

How'd it go at the doctor? Need me to bring you some soup?

I sigh.

Flu. I type. Then I add a frownie face and send the text. It's not the best text I've ever sent. But what was I supposed to say? "Diagnosed with the flu, and by the way, carrying your child?"

No, that is definitely not the right thing to say.

The door swings open loudly and I scream, turning toward the door.

"Oh, God, enough of the theatrics," Frances says, rolling her eyes as she shuts the door behind her.

"Have you ever heard of knocking?" My tone is incredulous, one that I hardly ever use with Frances. The other problem I have is clouding my judgment.

Frances just shakes her head and walks toward the bed.

"So you're sick?"

"I have the flu, don't come any closer."

It's not meant to sound ominous, but somehow it does. In all the years I've known Frances, I've only seen her sick once, and it was miserable for everyone in the house.

Dramatic sighing heard down the hall, lots of calling out for water or soup. If she got sick, I'm sure I'd be the one stuck taking care of her. She'd probably have me sleep in the living room so I could be at her beck and call.

"Well, that is quite unfortunate." She makes a sympathetic face. "Did you get all the tasks done that I asked you to do?"

"Found an entertainer. She's great. The invitations have been sent out. Royce found a caterer."

"Perfect. I'm glad you were able to get everything done." She shudders dramatically. "I bet you picked up the flu at that festival you went to."

"The hot air balloon festival?" I ask. How did she know about that?

"That's the one! I've been a couple times myself. It's so much fun to see the balloons launch into the sky." Frances gives me a tight smile.

She's acting weird; being too friendly but with a dangerous undercurrent. She's up to something.

"Maybe. We were all over Albuquerque, I could have picked it up anywhere."

Frances sits on the bed and puts her wrist against my forehead, checking my temperature. It mirrors the way Lucas did it last night, but it's not the same. I want to pull away but resist.

"You definitely feel clammy, but you don't seem to have a fever." Frances studies me. "Royce told me about the lovely Airbnb that he booked for you and Lucas last weekend."

Damn that blabber-mouth assistant.

"It was very pretty. It had fireplaces." It's a lame response, I can recognize that even in my state. I just don't have a better one.

"And a hot tub. Seems quite intimate."

I shrug, trying to act casual.

"I didn't use the hot tub. It was basically just a place to sleep for the night. Although we did order pizza." I smile weakly. Frances lets out a deep sigh.

"Sounds lovely."

She rolls her eyes. "Look, I'm going to cut to the chase. However nice Lucas is being to you, it's not going to happen. He's kind to you because you're the daughter of his late best friend, nothing more. Jackie is a much more suitable match for him, and anyone with a brain knows that. So stop dilly dallying and move on."

"What?" I ask. It's almost impossible to stop the laughter from escaping me. She has no idea how wrong she is.

"I see the way you look at him. Like the moon and every star is in your eyes. He's too good for you, sweetheart." She pats my hand awkwardly. "He's wealthy, intelligent, and handsome, and way out of your league. You're lovely in your own right, but you would be much more matched with someone who… has more humble aspirations. You're my stepdaughter, so I care for you deeply. That is why I'm telling you this."

I have to stop the sigh of relief from escaping.

There's a part of me that wants to laugh in her face, tell her that Lucas is already mine and that she and Jackie are wasting their time. It sits on the tip of my tongue, but I resist the urge.

It's better for her to think I'm some lovesick schoolgirl—provides a decent cover since apparently I'm unable to keep my emotions off my face, and lets her think she's won something.

"It's kind of you to look out for me, Frances. But I have a handle on things. I'm not into Lucas that way. I don't know what it is you're seeing, but it might just be the deep admiration I have for someone so successful who was my dad's best friend."

It even sounds like lies coming out of my mouth—I guess because they are. That only sells it though. I can see the satisfaction spread across her face as I only confirm to her that I have a one-sided crush on Lucas.

"Okay, dear. Just so you're aware, if you try anything, I will know. Jackie's best interest is always at the front of my mind, and I will go to hell and back to make her happy. Keep that in mind when making decisions."

She squeezes my hand—almost too tight, as if a painful warning is needed for me to heed her message. Then she stands up, straightens her outfit and heads toward the door.

"By the way, you're welcome to take a few days off to recover from your sickness. Goodness knows you have the time off saved—you don't ever go anywhere."

She squinches her nose and then walks out the door, letting it close loudly behind her.

Jackson whines, looking up at me with his big doggy eyes. Then I can't help myself. I start laughing, quietly at first and then they turn quickly into raucous hiccups shaking my body. Nothing about any of this is funny, yet I can't seem to stop the hysterics from rising within me.

It's not long before the laughter turns to sobs, though. I'm bawling so hard that Jackson snuggles up closer, pressing his wet nose against my cheek. The tears don't stop,. All the pressure with the hotel, hiding Lucas' and my relationship, and now the pregnancy? It's all so much and I don't know how to handle it.

What if Lucas doesn't even want kids? This could be the end of us before it even begins. And then what? I'm a single mom.

Frances will definitely not let a baby live here with me. Would she fire me from the hotel? She definitely would if she knew it was Lucas'.

God knows how Lucas will react. I can't stop the vision of his face contorting with anger, even though I've never even seen it, my imagination is vivid enough to pull the expression from thin air.

This has the potential to make my whole life fall apart, and it all started because Frances wants to sell the hotel.

Oh, God, I don't know what to do.

Chapter Twenty-Eight

Lucas

"Chicken noodle, please. And extra oyster crackers." I hand some money to the girl at the counter and then walk away to wait for the soup.

I haven't talked to Emma much today, but I'm not reading into it. I'm sure she's been sleeping most of the day—I know from first-hand experience how awful having the flu is, but I think some soup will be the perfect way to make her feel at least a little better.

It feels wrong to think this, but Emma having the flu is the perfect excuse to visit her often. I won't complain about seeing Emma more, even when she's sick.

It's been a long time since I've taken care of someone. In fact, the last time I brought someone soup was when my mom had strep.

I'm determined to do something to make her feel better, though. I picked up a bouquet of sunflowers—the florist insisted that bright yellow was the perfect cure for the flu, and while I'm not sure how accurate that is, sunflowers seemed like a good choice.

"Here you go, sir," a worker says as he hands me the bag with the soup. I take it and head to Emma's. Frances is striding down the driveway as I pull up. She gives me a small wave.

"Hello, Lucas. Home for the day?" she asks as I walk past her.

"Yes. I figured I'd bring Emma some 'get better' goodies."

I wave the bag of soup and then become acutely aware of the bouquet in my arms.

"Sunflowers?" Frances looks at me quizzically, as if she's trying to figure something out.

"Oh, yeah." I shrug and force a dismissive tone. "My mom used to bring home flowers if I was sick when I was a kid. She said they purified the air or something. I don't think I believe it, but the flowers did always make me feel a little better seeing them."

It's a true story, even if I'm using it to cast off suspicion. It seems to work and Frances laughs.

"That is a nice sentiment. Although I'm sure Emma's plant collection has the air excessively pure."

I chuckle.

"That's right, I forgot about all her plants. She had me help her move them down."

"Oh goodness, she's obsessed with them. I'm sure it took you quite a while to move all those down."

I resist the urge to frown. It feels like she's starting to make fun of Emma, but instead I just shrug.

"It wasn't too bad. I was rewarded with food, that's good enough for me."

"Ever the gentleman," Frances says, smirking. "All right, I'm off to spend time with some friends. I'll probably be out late."

She opens the car door and then turns back to me.

"By the way, I meant to ask you this morning, but it slipped my mind. I heard a crash from your room very early this morning and came out to check on it."

She's lying. She was definitely out in the hallway before I knocked my phone off the table. If I call her on it, though, she'll know I was already awake. Which I'm sure she's counting on.

"Oh, I woke up to my phone on the floor. I must have knocked it off when I was sleeping. I'm sorry if it disturbed you."

She studies me for a second before making a noise. She seems satisfied enough—most of her suspicion should be gone.

Frances waves and then gets in her car. I continue on my way and then knock on Emma's door.

"Come in."

I let myself in the door as Emma sits up in bed.

"You let just anyone come in the room?"

"Frances doesn't knock. As I learned earlier."

"She came to see you?"

Emma snorts.

"Yeah, if you want to put it that way."

"What did she say?" I ask as I slip off my shoes and make my way to her bed. I hand her the flowers and she buries her face in them, lighting up instantly.

"Sunflowers?"

"Florist said they cured everything."

"I love them." She hugs them to her and then hands them back to me. "Can you put them in water?"

"As soon as you tell me what Frances said."

"Oh, it was amusing." Emma smirks. "She thinks I have a crush on you."

"What?" I can feel the alarm on my face. How is she so calm about this?

"Don't worry, she doesn't suspect anything. She thinks it's an unrequited crush and that I'm following you around like a pathetic puppy." Emma shakes her head. "She's really rooting for you and Jackie."

I groan.

"Maybe we should make her a Team Jackie shirt," she jokes, then chuckles immediately. I roll my eyes and poke her.

"Only if we make Lily a Team Emma one."

She hits me with a pillow and giggles.

"How are you feeling?" I ask. Emma sighs and then shakes her head.

"Miserable." The honesty comes through in her expression. I lean in for a hug but she moves away. "I don't want to get you sick."

"Why? We could lay in bed together all day."

Emma rolls her eyes but smiles.

"You have a problem. What's in the bag?"

I reach in and pull out the bowl of soup. Her face lights up and she licks her lips.

"Oh, my God. What is that?"

"Chicken noodle. Good for the soul, I've heard. And oyster crackers!" I pull out the small packets of soda crackers and brandish them as if they're the grand prize at the fair.

Emma squeals and grabs them from me.

"This is so sweet. I love chicken noodle soup. And I'm starving! Wait, where's yours?" She asks, staring at me quizzically.

I look down at the empty bag and sigh.

"I guess I didn't get any for me. You were at the front of my mind."

"Well, we need to order something. And I think we should rent a movie. Maybe a rom-com."

"We can watch anything you want," I murmur, burying my face in her hair and kissing it. She chuckles and scooches to the other side of the bed, farther away than normal. Probably so she doesn't get me sick.

***

Emma fell asleep halfway through the movie, so I let Jackson out for a potty break and then headed upstairs. It's not quite late enough to try to get any actual sleep, but there's not a TV in my room and Jackie is occupying the living room with one of her friends.

I scroll through my email. The one Royce sent me last night about the vintage glassware still sits unopened, but it's not the one that catches my eye.

The one that calls to me is the one from Cordell Kennedy agreeing to meet with me. A little thrill went through me when I first read it this afternoon, and I still feel the buzz of excitement on my skin when I read over it again. The possibilities are endless.

Maybe not endless, but there are a lot of ways this could go. The idea that maybe there's a will, something that leaves the hotel or at least the house to Emma, continues to play in my mind.

Although if that were the case, it must have never been finalized, otherwise the lawyer would have popped up much sooner and not in the manner of a vague appointment confirmation.

It would be easier if Cordell Kennedy didn't specialize in many areas of law; he's an estate lawyer, contract lawyer, divorce lawyer. The man truly wears a lot of hats. It's possible that Clark was just redoing some contracts, which would be disappointing but not out of character for someone who owns a hotel.

I'm not even sure he'll actually tell me anything. I know hotels and business, but I'm not a lawyer, and I'm sure there are some sort of privacy laws when it comes to people's legal affairs, even when said person is dead.

I need to prepare myself for the most realistic scenario. Getting my hopes up about there being a will can only be harmful in the long run.

I close out of the email and finally open the vintage glassware one. They're nice, and look appropriate for the era. I send back that the glassware is a go before climbing out of bed and heading downstairs. All this thought has made me thirsty. I pad softly into the kitchen and try to open the cabinet as quietly as I can, but it's not silent enough.

Jackie skips into the kitchen and beams at me.

"Oh, hey, Lucas. I haven't seen you much today."

"I was working. And I brought Emma some soup."

"Oh, is she okay?" Jackie tilts her head flirtatiously. I think she's trying to come across as concerned, but the question falls flat, revealing that she cares little about Emma's health.

"She has the flu."

"That's awful! I'll send her a get well soon text."

Jackie whips out her phone and shoots off a text at lightning speed. Then she smiles up at me.

"Are you busy? We could watch a movie in the living room. My friend Eliza is here, and we made popcorn."

Jackie steps closer and drags her fingertip across the countertop in an attempt to be seductive. I turn around, busying myself with the glass in front of me before striding to the fridge and filling it with water.

"I actually have a lot of work to do tonight. One of my hotels needs some of my attention."

"You're always working," Jackie pouts, jutting out her lower lip. A queasy feeling rises in my stomach. "Don't you ever take a break?"

I attempt an easy laugh and shrug.

"I'll rest when I'm dead. I'm going to head back upstairs. Enjoy your movie."

I turn and zip out of the kitchen as fast as I can without sprinting, but it's not fast enough to miss Jackie's heavy sigh.

Jackie is working overtime to try to grab my attention, and getting bolder with each attempt.

$$***$$

Royce and I lean over his phone, examining the email in great detail. Apparently lying about an emergency at another hotel spoke it into existence, turning it into an annoying truth.

The Bilstone has a severe case of bed bugs and needs to have all the bedding and mattresses replaced.

"Boy, this is rough," Royce states, tutting softly. I want to shake him a little; his stating the obvious is not helping the situation, but I know that is my frustration more than anything he is doing wrong.

"The Bilstone has a hundred rooms. It's my largest hotel. This is going to be costly."

"Where's this one located?"

"It's near Boston. I can't travel out there right now, not while everything here is just heating up."

Royce nods in agreement, even though we're undoubtedly talking about different things.

"Do you want me to go? I've never been to Boston." His tone is uncertain, as if he doesn't want to go but wanted to offer anyway. I shake my head.

"No, I don't know if there's anything you could do. For now, why don't you source options for replacing everything? Have them shut the place down for a week, and give most of the employees paid time off, except for those the General Manager says are necessary. I don't want them to be without pay because of a circumstance beyond their control."

Royce nods and starts tapping on his screen.

"Everything okay?" Frances asks, poking her head in. The conference room was booked today by some business retreat, which means Royce and I are relegated to having our meeting in the dining room, which isn't ideal, but it's better than having this conversation in the restaurant where some hotel guest could potentially overhear it.

"An issue with another hotel. Nothing to concern yourself about," I say, waving her off. She smiles tightly and nods.

"Of course. Whenever you get the chance, I want to talk to you about something. It's of the utmost importance."

Before I can question her more, Frances sashays out of the door.

Whatever she wants to talk about, I'm certain it's only going to add to my plate of stresses.

Chapter Twenty-Nine

Emma

"How are you feeling?" Lily asks as I walk through the hotel doors the following Monday. I beam at her.

"Much better, thank you. And thanks for leaving a fruit basket on my porch."

"Of course! I would have brought it in, but I can't get sick. Can't miss work, you know?" Lily shrugs and I laugh.

The fruit basket was really thoughtful, and honestly unexpected. I couldn't eat the pineapple—I spent the entire time I was sick Googling article after article of what I should and shouldn't eat during pregnancy. It's a very long list, but everything except the pineapple was a go. I offered the pineapple to Lucas on one of his nightly visits. No matter how much I insisted he should stay away so he didn't get sick, he came every night.

It was really sweet, as well as nerve-wracking. Every second I wondered if I would accidentally blurt out the fact that I was pregnant and ruin everything.

I keep thinking that maybe the urine sample wasn't valid. Maybe it was a false positive. But everything that I've read online has pretty much reiterated the same point: false positives are so rare they're hardly considered as an option. You're much more likely to have a false negative.

Tomorrow afternoon is my first appointment with the obstetrician. I'm so unbearably scared, but I want to get it out of the way as soon as possible. They'll do a blood test, which are so reliable that there will be no doubt in my mind that I'm pregnant, and then I'll figure out how to tell Lucas.

I'm a little less nervous after seeing how caring he's been toward me over the past week. His urge to take care of me while I've been sick has been so sweet and heartwarming, and makes me think he'll be a good father.

I hope I'll be a good mother.

It's such a weird thing to think—I've never thought about having kids before. I guess because I've never been in a serious enough relationship to consider it as an option, but I think I'll love it. I look back on the memories I have with my mom and how I'll get to continue those traditions.

"Earth to Emma?" Lily's voice interrupts my inner monologue as she waves her hand in front of my face.

"Sorry. I got a little lost in the sauce there."

She laughs and shakes her head.

"I figured. I asked if you wanted any coffee? We have a big carafe from the shop next door in the conference room. I'm guessing from that glazed over look, you actually need it."

Coffee. Another thing on the "no" list. I shake my head and smile.

"I think I'm over-caffeinated if anything. I had two cups at home this morning. I thought I'd need help adjusting to being vertical for more than five minutes at a time."

"Emma!" Frances' shrill voice echoes across the lobby.

I look to the elevator and paste a smile on my face.

"How are you feeling? Better?" She makes a face of faux sympathy but doesn't wait for an answer.

"Good. I need you in the saloon. We're working on the centerpieces, and you know how much I love designing and decorating, but I'm really needed elsewhere today."

I nod and follow her, but can't help but wonder what exactly being "needed elsewhere" means.

I've never asked her what she does all day, or thought about it much. I know she's never doing admin work. She was never involved in the hotel at all when Dad was alive, so it's curious that she seems so involved and yet is nowhere to be found unless there's something exciting going on.

We step into the saloon and I suck in a deep breath. It's been a while since I've been down here; it hardly needs my attention on a daily basis.

Although I guess I'm not a drinker at all now. Nausea swells within me, but I'm weeks away from morning sickness as a symptom according to the pregnancy website I checked.

It must be leftover nausea from the flu. According to the website, my baby is the size of a water bear. That's practically microscopic.

"This is how the tables are going to be set up for the gala. All festivities from entertainment to the actual auction itself are going to be on the stage over there. I have the bartender crafting a custom cocktail. And those gold accents over there should add to the overall appeal of the place."

Shiny streams of gold hang down behind the stage, glimmering softly in the light. I look around, raising my eyebrows in surprise. It actually looks amazing.

"Is this what you've been doing all day, every day?" I ask, unable to keep the surprise in my voice.

"Of course. You didn't think the gala was planning itself, did you?" Frances scoffs, rolling her eyes at me.

"No. It's just... it looks good."

Frances looks at me with suspicion at first, and then it turns into pride.

"Thank you. I've been working hard."

She fluffs her hair and then focuses on me.

"You picked out all the centerpieces, and I trust that you're able to decide where they go in the room. I notice a lot of them are vases or something that can hold flowers. If you could contact a florist and find something appropriate for the gala, that would be perfect. Pretty, high-end flowers. Nothing tacky looking."

She makes a face and turns on her heel, clicking away before I can ask what she considers a tacky flower.

I look at all the pieces in front of me and get busy placing them around the room, changing them out as needed. Usually I get frustrated at Frances for directing me to do things outside of my regular job description, treating me like an assistant.

Today, though, I sort of welcome the distraction since I'm able to be more creative doing this. I'm able to easily lose myself in the organizing, thoughts of pregnancy and the hotel and Lucas far away from my mind as I focus.

"Emma?" Lucas' voice rings out from behind me. I blink and look down at my phone— it's already been a couple hours. Time sure does fly when you're not thinking about all the things that are causing you stress.

"Hi," I say brightly, turning around. "These centerpieces look great, don't they?"

"They do, you've done a great job."

"And what Frances did with the stage," I gesture behind me, "also looks amazing. I think this gala is going to be a huge success."

Lucas laughs and feels my forehead. He leans in to kiss me but I pull away, looking around the room nervously. It's empty. I'm the only one in here since the bartender went to restock the liquor supply, but I'm still nervous. I know Frances doesn't watch the cameras; she might not even know they exist. We still can't be too careful.

"I glad to see you're excited about the gala. Do you have a costume yet?"

I groan.

"I knew I was forgetting something. Lily and I were supposed to get together last week to figure out our outfits, but then I got sick."

"That's okay, I have the perfect one. I even have it on rush order."

My jaw drops.

"You ordered me a dress?"

"The perfect dress. I know it will look amazing on you."

Giddiness fills me.

"I want to see!"

"It's a surprise. It will be here tomorrow afternoon."

A shadow falls over me, and judging by the look on Lucas' face, he notices right away. "Emma? Are you okay?"

"Yeah. Just nerves about my doctor's appointment tomorrow. Follow up." I brush it off casually, but concern still colors his features.

"Do you want me to go with you? I don't mind at all."

"No!" I say too quickly. He steps back, caught off guard by my hastiness. "I'm an adult and I can handle going to the doctor on my own. That's all I mean."

"Was getting the dress too much? I understand if it was. You don't have to accept it, it won't hurt my feelings."

"No, no, no, Lucas. It's perfect. I'm so excited to see it, and I'm sure I'll love it." I shake my body and laugh. "I think I still have a case of the flu grumpies."

It's a valid excuse. I was snippy and whiny the entire time I was sick. To Lucas' credit, though, he never got mad or acted like it was an inconvenience.

He smiles and squeezes my arm. I don't pull away this time; his touch is comforting and I definitely want it.

"If you say so. I wanted to ask if you want to have dinner together tonight? Frances and Jackie will apparently be busy, so I thought we could utilize the kitchen."

He wiggles his brows and I laugh.

"I'd love that." I lick my lips, taking a bold step closer. I tap my fingers on his chest and look up at him through my lashes.

"Emma," he murmurs, wrapping his arms around me. The thought that someone could walk in, is now far away from my mind. Lucas is intoxicating, and we didn't do anything while I was sick. Now I'm craving him, wanting his touch in all my most delicate places.

I take the risk, rising on my toes to touch my lips to his. They're soft and warm, perfectly matched to mine. Lucas pulls me closer as the kisses grow more urgent. I roam my hands over his body, taking note of his muscles under the clothing. His hands snake their way under my top, fluttering against the edge of my bra.

When I press closer, I can feel his hardness against my hip, pulling against the fabric of his slacks. He kisses down my neck, gently nipping at the skin. I moan, unable to contain myself. Lucas pushes me back until my butt hits the bar. His hands roam my bare legs and he chuckles, his breath tickling my neck.

"Skirt today, huh?"

"I thought it was cute."

"Cute isn't the word I'd use to describe it." His hand roams up my thigh until it's caressing the sides of my panties. I shudder and shuffle until his fingers brush over the sensitive spot through the fabric. He hisses, rubbing a small circle over it.

"Lucas," I whisper, and he kisses me in response, rubbing faster as he muffles my sounds with his mouth.

"You're going to get us in trouble," he says against my lips, slowing down the motions. I groan and tip my head back.

"I'm..." Lucas' fingers dip under the fabric, and the feeling of his skin against mine on my clit makes me let out a soft squeak, "not the one who is going to get us in trouble."

Lucas moves his fingers expertly over me, the fire building up in my core. Lucas' other hand finds my breasts, squeezing them through my shirt as his thumb moves faster over my clit and my pent up wanton feelings threaten to spill over.

I'm unable to contain myself, the flames spilling across my entire body as the orgasm flows through me. His fingers don't leave my body as I ride them through my finish. Our breathing is haggard as the door upstairs closes loudly.

We pull apart, adjusting our clothes as Lily comes bounding down the stairs. She takes one look at us and rolls her eyes.

"Really, you guys? You should know that Frances is about to head this way after she's done in the conference room, and you need to straighten yourselves up."

"Shit, shit, shit," I mutter, adjusting my skirt and smoothing my hair.

"Actually, you should probably leave. Back entrance would be best." Lily looks pointedly at Lucas.

"I do have a meeting in about an hour. I probably should go." He smiles bashfully before leaning in to hug me. Then he lowers his voice. "To be continued."

"How did you know?" I ask as soon as he's out of earshot.

"Seriously? You're down here, and then Lucas goes down. He's been down here for forty-five minutes, and if I know you at all, the centerpieces have already been figured out."

I look around the tables, acknowledging that all the centerpieces are carefully placed.

"Thanks for the warning."

"Yeah, yeah. What are friends for?"

Chapter Thirty

Lucas

I tap my fingers on my leg impatiently. The sitting area for Cordell Kennedy's law office is simply decorated, with a few water colors and his degrees covering the walls. There's an aquarium on the back wall that only has a few fish in it.

After questioning the receptionist about the lack of fish, she gave me a lengthy lecture about proper fish care. I learned a lot; most importantly, that I have no interest in owning a fish.

A door in the back opens and a man leaves looking satisfied with whatever happened in the office. It's only a few more minutes before the door opens again and an older man in a tan suit and graying hair steps out.

"Mr. Bennett?"

"That's me. You must be Mr. Kennedy."

"That's correct. Follow me." He beckons me into the office and sits behind the desk, gesturing for me to take the seat in front of him.

"Please forgive me for not shaking your hand, I have a small thing about germs."

He squirts some sanitizer into his hands as if to punctuate this. I did wash my hands three times in the bathroom at the hotel, but not shaking hands is fine by me.

"That is perfectly okay."

"What can I do for you today? I saw that you requested a meeting with regard to my estate services. Most people think that someone your age would be too young to start thinking about what to do with their estate when they pass on, but I personally think it's never too early to talk about your options."

I chuckle and shake my head.

"This is kind of odd, actually. Do you know a man named Clark Stone?"

"Ah, Mr. Stone. Yes, we met a few months ago now. It might have been longer; time sort of passes quickly when you get older."

He grins before leaning forward. "Did he recommend me to you? He never did return, so I assumed he no longer needed my services. It's always a bit rude to ghost people, but I understand that some people are too busy to send emails stating that they no longer need my services."

"No, uh. This is awkward, I assumed you knew. Clark actually passed away in a car accident."

Cordell murmurs under his breath and then shakes his head.

"I apologize for my poor etiquette, I did not realize. Did his passing make you start thinking about your own estate?"

"No. I mean, I might think about those services, but I'm here because I found out Clark had an appointment with you, but he never told me. He was my best friend, and I'm trying to... piece together, I suppose, the circumstances of what happened when he died. Or whether or not he was planning a will, I guess. His daughter, you see, she is in a bit of a predicament regarding the ownership of his estate."

He blinks, seemingly surprised.

"Well, I have to say that you're not the first person to come in here asking about a deceased person. It happens more often than you'd think.

There are many people who don't truly know what their loved ones had done with regard to their estate planning until after they pass and they're going through their documents."

"That does make sense." I nod. "So... is there a will? It would make things so much easier to know if there was something in the works. I know you said he never contacted you again, so I'm sure things weren't finalized, meaning there'd be no valid will. But I imagine that knowing that it was in the works would bring Emma, his daughter, great comfort."

Cordell clasps his hands together on the desk and leans forward.

"I'm sure it would bring her great comfort to know that; unfortunately, Mr. Stone did not come to me regarding his estate."

I can feel the shock flooding my face. I clear my throat and sit up straighter to regain my composure.

"Really? Why was he seeing you then?"

He gives me a puzzled look.

"For the divorce, of course. I've never met Mrs. Stone, but from what he told me, things were strained and he, at least, was deeply unhappy in the marriage. We had a consult session, where I explained his options to him and we discussed what a division of assets would entail, but he never returned so I assumed that he changed his mind."

"About the divorce? You didn't think he might have gone with a different lawyer?"

Cordell chuckles and leans back in the chair.

"I suppose that could have been a possibility, but no, I didn't really think that was likely. I have an excellent reputation in this area and serve a rather elite clientele. I don't think he could have found anyone more qualified within a hundred mile radius."

From anyone else, it might sound arrogant, but he states it plainly, as if it's a fact rather than his own self-inflated opinion.

"Thank you, Mr. Kennedy, for your time. I think I have all the information I need."

I stand up abruptly, bumping the chair against the desk so that everything shakes slightly. I'm not normally clumsy, but the shock of the news has pushed me off my game.

The idea that Clark was trying to divorce Frances changes things— but probably not in a legal sense. Without a will, Emma's situation remains the same, but with the information of a potential divorce? It could at least provide some sort of leverage.

"Of course. Please contact me if you have any further questions, or if you feel that you might need my services." He grabs a business card and holds it out to me. I take it and shove it into my pocket.

He escorts me into the lobby and I nod to the receptionist before exiting out the door.

Did Frances know that Clark was planning on divorcing her? I wasn't aware of his death until after the funeral, but if I had known, I could have observed her during the event. Was she upset? Or just playing the role of the grieving wife?

I can't stop my mind from going to the darkest places. What if she murdered him because he was thinking about divorcing her? Admittedly, I don't know Frances well enough to know if she is capable of such an act, but I can't discount the possibility.

The details surrounding his death; well, those that I'm aware of anyway, swirl through my mind: there was a car accident, and Frances was there. She could have sabotaged the vehicle.

I'm not sure how extensive her knowledge of cars is, but she could have paid someone to do it. There would probably be a paper trail if that was the case and, although I can't imagine her willingly getting into a car that she knows will fail, it's an avenue that I need to explore.

I know I can't tell Emma, at least not yet.

As much as I want to fill her in immediately, without more information, it will only cause more stress than she is already dealing with. I don't want to talk to her without knowing all of the facts, which is going to require some investigating on my part.

Suddenly, staying in Frances' house just became more advantageous.

She's gone with some regularity— it will be easy enough to snoop around while she's out of the house. I'll have to be careful, though. If she catches me, at best it will be an extremely awkward conversation.

I get into my car and sigh.

Everything just got so much more complicated.

***

"You're being awfully quiet tonight," Emma says. She's right, of course— thoughts stemming from my meeting with Cordell earlier are still swirling in my mind.

When I snuck down to Emma's tonight, we decided to watch a rom-com but I've been paying little attention to the plot because the soft glow of twilight filters through the sheer curtains, casting a warm amber hue over Emma's bedroom.

The air feels thick with anticipation, charged with the electric energy of desire. I stand by the edge of the bed, my shoulders relaxed yet taut, his dark eyes locked onto Emma as she moves with deliberate grace across the room.

Her bare feet whisper against the hardwood floor, her silk robe clinging to her curves like a second skin. The scent of jasmine and vanilla lingers in the air, a subtle reminder of her presence even when she's not yet close to me.

Her green eyes sparkle with mischief, her lips curved in a knowing smile. "You're staring," she teases, her voice low and husky, a velvet whisper that sends a shiver down my spine.

"Can't help it," I tell her. "You're a sight to behold."

I take a slow step forward, my shoes quiet on the floor, closing the distance between us. The room feels smaller now, the air heavier, as if the walls themselves are holding their breath.

Emma's smile softens, her playful demeanor melting into something raw and vulnerable. She lets the robe slide off her shoulders, letting it pool at her feet.

Beneath it, she wears nothing but a lace bra and matching thong, both in a deep burgundy that contrasts beautifully with her pale skin. Her body is a work of art—curves that beckon, skin that glows, and a confidence that radiates from every pore.

My breath hitches as my eyes trace the lines of her body. My hands itch to touch her, to feel the warmth of her skin beneath my fingertips. I take another step, then another, until I'm standing right in front of her. I loom over her, but there's no dominance in my stance, only reverence. "You're breathtaking," I murmur, my voice thick with emotion.

Emma's fingers curl around the hem of my shirt, pulling it up and over my head in one fluid motion. She runs her palms over my skin, feeling the heat of me, the steady rise and fall of my chest.

"You're not so bad yourself," she says, her voice laced with desire.

She steps closer, pressing her body against mine, feeling the hardness of my chest against her breasts, the warmth of my skin seeping into hers.

Her lips brush my jawline, trailing soft kisses along the stubble that scratches gently against her skin.

"Then take me," she whispers, her breath hot against his ear. "Take me now."

I groan, my hands sliding down her back to cup her ass, lifting her effortlessly until her legs wrap around my waist. She's light in my arms, but her presence feels heavy, anchoring me to the moment. I carry her to the bed, laying her down gently on the soft comforter, my eyes never leaving hers.

"You're so beautiful," I tell her again, my voice a rough whisper.

Emma arches into my touch, her nipples tightening beneath the fabric.

"Stop talking," she teases, though her voice trembles with need. "Just touch me."

I oblige, my fingers deftly unhooking her bra. The lace falls away, exposing her breasts to my hungry gaze. Her skin is flushed, her nipples pebbled and dark, begging for my attention.

I lean down, my lips brushing against the swell of her breast, my breath warm and teasing.

I take my time, kissing and nipping at her skin, my tongue swirling lazy patterns that make her squirm beneath me. My hands roam freely, cupping and squeezing, my touch both gentle and demanding.

Emma moans, her head tilting back as pleasure coils low in her belly.

"Lucas," she breathes, her fingers tangling in my hair, urging me closer. "Please."

"Please what?" I ask, my voice a challenge, a dare.

"Touch me," she demands, her voice steady despite the ache between her legs. "Touch me everywhere."

I smirk, my hands sliding down her body, tracing the curve of her waist, the dip of her navel, until my fingers hover just above the waistband of her thong.

I hook my fingers into the lace, pulling it down slowly, my eyes never leaving hers. The fabric slides over her hips, down her thighs, until it's pooled at her feet, leaving her completely bare.

Her skin is flushed, her body trembling with anticipation. My gaze is hungry, devouring her, and I know she feels exposed yet empowered, her vulnerability a strength in this moment.

I take my time, my lips brushing against her inner thigh, my tongue teasing the sensitive skin. My hands roam, my fingers tracing the curves of her hips, the hollows of her waist, as if memorizing every inch of her.

"Lucas," she whimpers, her voice desperate. "I need you."

My fingers finally drift between her legs, my touch gentle yet firm as I part her folds, my thumb brushing against her clit. Emma gasps, her hips bucking into my touch, her body already on the edge.

"So wet," I murmur, my voice a husky whisper. "You're so fucking wet for me."

My fingers dip lower, slipping inside her with ease, my touch slow and deliberate. Emma moans, her head falling back as pleasure washes over her, a tidal wave of sensation that leaves her breathless.

"Lucas," she pants, her voice a plea. "I—I can't—"

"Shh," I soothe, my lips brushing against her thigh. "Let go. Let me feel you."

My fingers move in rhythm, my touch steady and sure, as I strokes her, my thumb circling her clit in time with my fingers. Emma's body tightens, her muscles coiling as she teeters on the edge, her breath coming in short, sharp gasps.

"Lucas," she cries, her voice breaking as her orgasm crashes over her, a wave of pleasure that leaves her shaking, her body arching off the bed.

I watch her, my eyes dark with satisfaction, my lips curved in a smug smile. "That's it," I murmur, my voice a low rumble. "Feel it. Feel me."

Emma's body is still trembling, her breath ragged as she comes down from her high. She reaches for me, her hands pulling me up, her lips seeking mine in a desperate kiss.

Our mouths meet in a collision of hunger and need, our tongues tangling as we devour each other. My hands roam, my fingers tracing the lines of her body, my touch possessive yet tender.

I break the kiss, my lips trailing down her neck, my breath hot against her skin. "I want you," I growl, my voice raw with desire. "All of you."

Emma's heart races, her body thrumming with anticipation. She knows what's coming, what we both want, but the moment feels suspended, stretched thin by the weight of our desire.

My hands slide down her body, my fingers brushing against her core, still wet from her orgasm. I tease her, my touch light and delicate before slipping inside her again, my fingers curling deep.

Emma gasps, her body arching into my touch, her breath catching in her throat. "Lucas," she breathes, her voice a whisper. "Please."

I look up, my eyes locked onto hers. "Tell me what you want," I demand, my voice a challenge.

Emma's cheeks flush, her body trembling with need. "I want you," she confesses, her voice steady despite the ache between her legs. "I want you inside me. Now."

I smirk, my fingers slipping out of her, my hand reaching for the button of my jeans. The room is heavy with anticipation, the air thick with the promise of what's to come.

I undo my jeans, pushing them down my legs, my boxers following, revealing my erection, thick and hard, straining against the fabric. Emma's breath catches, her eyes widening at the sight of me, her body aching with need.

I kneel between her legs, my hands resting on her hips, my gaze burning into hers. "Ready?" I ask, my voice a rough whisper.

Emma nods, her body trembling with anticipation. "Yes," she breathes, her voice a plea. "Now."

I position myself at her entrance, my eyes locked onto hers as I push inside her, slow and steady, my thickness stretching her, filling her completely.

Emma gasps, her head falling back as I fill her, her body adjusting to my engorged size, her walls clenching around me.

"Lucas," she moans, her voice a mix of pleasure and desperation.

I hold myself still, giving her a moment to adjust, my eyes searching hers.

"You okay?"

Emma nods, her breath ragged as she meets my gaze. "More," she demands, her voice steady. "Give me more."

My hands tighten on her hips as I begin to move, my thrusts slow and deliberate, my hips snapping as I drive into her, my cock sinking deeper with each stroke.

The bed creaks beneath us, the room filled with the sounds of our bodies moving in rhythm, the wet slap of skin against skin, our moans and gasps echoing in the intimate space.

Emma's nails dig into my shoulders, her legs wrapping around my waist as she meets my thrusts, her body rising to meet mine, her hips bucking as she takes me deeper.

"Lucas," she cries, her voice breaking as pleasure coils low in her belly, a familiar ache building, threatening to consume her.

I lean down, my lips brushing against her ear, my breath hot and ragged.

"Cum for me," I growl, my voice a command. "Let me feel you fall apart."

Emma's body tightens, her muscles coiling as she teeters on the edge, her breath coming in short, sharp gasps. "Lucas," she whimpers, her voice a plea. "I—I can't—"

"Let go," I urge, my thrusts becoming harder, faster.

Emma's body shatters, her orgasm crashing over her like a wave, a tidal wave of pleasure that leaves her shaking, her body arching off the bed.

"Lucas!" she cries, her voice a mix of pleasure and desperation as she comes undone, her walls clenching around me, milking me fully, drawing me closer to the edge.

I groan, my body tensing as I follow her over the edge, my thrusts slowing, my release a rush of pleasure that leaves me breathless.

Our bodies are slick with sweat, our hearts pounding in unison as we come down from our highs.

I collapse onto her, my weight pressing her into the mattress, my breath hot against her neck.

Emma wraps her arms around me, her legs still wrapped around my waist.

I know she can still feel me, still hard inside her, my heart beating in time with hers, our bodies still connected, still joined.

The room is quiet except for the sound of our breathing, shallow and quick, as we bask in the aftermath, the air thick with satisfaction and desire.

I lift my head, my eyes searching hers.

"That was—"

Emma cuts me off with a soft kiss, her lips brushing against mine, her smile playful.

"Not done yet," she teases, her voice low and husky.

I slide my hands down her body, my fingers tracing the curves of her hips, my touch possessive yet tender.

"Oh, we're just getting started," I promise.

Chapter Thirty-One

Emma

I've gotten used to waking up to an empty bed in the mornings. At first I was caught off-guard, which sounds stupid.

Neither of us is anxious for Frances to find out about us, so it makes perfect sense that Lucas should sneak out after I've fallen asleep.

I head to the bathroom, excited to get a shower in. The warm water runs over me, and even though it's not as nice as my rainwater shower head, I can still appreciate the comfort and warmth it provides. I take the time to shampoo my long hair, even though I am faced with a mountain of work today.

Fifteen minutes pass before I step out of the shower and stand in front of the mirror.

I run the fan for a few minutes and blow the hair dryer on the mirror to de-fog it. Once it's clear, I study my reflection. My skin looks the same, my hair still long and wavy even though it hangs damp from the shower.

My eyes drift down to my stomach. It looks exactly the same as it always has, yet knowing that my body is growing a baby makes me see it in a completely different light.

I read on the pregnancy forums that sometimes first time moms show later than women do in subsequent pregnancies because their abdominal muscles are much stronger the first time the uterus stretches with pregnancy.

But I also read that sometimes they pop quickly, displaying a belly earlier than expected.

So much of the information is conflicting, and none of it seems concrete because apparently every pregnancy is different.

I have to tell Lucas sooner rather than later.

He's intelligent, and it won't take long for symptoms to start appearing.

I mentally kick myself for going off birth control— of course I was on it through college, when I was with my first boyfriend.

After we broke up, I stayed on it for a while, but I was dealing with constant nausea, headaches and was beginning to feel horribly depressed after a while.

It's something I don't like to think about often. I was so moody and irrational, constantly lashing out at Dad or friends. When I stopped hanging out with people, Dad sat me down and talked to me about seeing a doctor because I was acting so out of character.

When the doctor informed me that my birth control was causing all my issues, we decided that it was better to just take me off it than to try another method, considering I wasn't sexually active at that point. And since I haven't been socially active for years, the thought wasn't even on my mind when we started having sex.

I'm such an idiot. I should have thought it through and at least used condoms.

My phone beeps, Frances' name popping on the screen with a text message asking me to meet her in the kitchen.

I take a deep breath and try not to panic. A text doesn't mean that she knows about my relationship with Lucas or the fact that I'm pregnant. How could she know either of those things?

I put on an outfit— simple cream colored slacks, a deep green button up and low heels. Nothing fancy, but good enough for work. I feel too exhausted to put more effort into something cute. Then I trudge up to the kitchen.

"Emma, there you are," France says, flashing a smile that looks more like a grimace.

"You requested my presence, so here I am." Judging by the way she rolls her eyes, she doesn't miss the inflection of sarcasm in my tone, but she doesn't address it.

"Thank you for coming promptly." Her tone is flat. "I wanted to talk about the gala."

I can't stop my face from lighting up.

"I think it will be beautiful and a huge success." I pause for a moment and then make the conscious effort to fluff her feathers. The more I can get her to at least tolerate me, the easier everything is going to be. "You've really outdone yourself."

Frances smirks and fluffs her hair, pride swelling through her.

"I did, didn't I?"

I nod. Then she shakes her head.

"I think it will be a success, too. We need to discuss your role for the gala, though."

"My role?"

"Yes. I was thinking that you could be in charge of organizing the staff and ensuring everything goes smoothly. I'd like you to welcome guests at the door to begin with. You're the face of the hotel in many ways and can tell them about the history as you sign them in. The manager welcoming them will add a personal touch."

I blink. I expected to work, but greeting guests would keep me away from the gala.

"After all the guests have arrived, make sure the bartenders and caterers are on track. Check in with the auctioneer, ensure everything we're auctioning off is accurate. I'm sure the auctioneer will have a count, but it's better to also have our own inventory. I then want you to go table to table and check in with the guests, but don't linger. Just check in with everyone and then move... Emma, shouldn't you be writing this down?"

"Oh, I..." I scramble for my phone in my pocket, taking it out and opening my notes app. It's clear that she's making up busy tasks so that I don't have time to enjoy the gala.

Part of me is sure she hates me so much that she wants to make a very special night miserable for me, but I also have a feeling that there is another reason she wants to keep me so busy during the gala.

"Good. Actually, it might be better if I just email you all my expectations."

Frances smirks and I resist the urge to roll my eyes.

"By the way, I need you to inform the staff about the dress code for the event. All black, nice slacks and proper tops—white button ups or blouses."

"Wait, staff aren't dressing up?" I frown.

"Of course not. The purpose of staff is to fade into the background, providing effortless service with minimal presence."

"But Lucas..." I start, thoughts of the dress Lucas ordered coming to mind. It will end up being a waste.

Then my eyes meet Frances' as I take note of the curiosity in her raised eyebrow, waiting for me to finish my thought.

"Lucas said that it would feed into the magic of the experience for staff to be dressed up."

Frances shrugs.

"That might be true, but the cost of costuming the entire staff this late would be high. We can't expect the staff to pay for their own time-period relevant costumes, can we? I'm certain that would be costly, and not very fair of us to expect. Especially when they likely already have appropriate black clothing."

I nod, pushing down the sigh of disappointment that sits at the base of my lips. I know Frances well enough to know that her attempt at altruism is false, buried beneath her own motives. I can't say it aloud, though.

"Of course, Frances. I'll let them know."

Chapter Thirty-Two
Lucas

As the front door closes behind Jackie, the final one to leave the house this morning, my phone chimes.

See you at work? Emma's message lights up. I lick my lips.

As much as I want to be able to see Emma throughout the day, I need to have the house to myself to look for any evidence of wrong doing.

I don't even know where Frances would keep paperwork or documents, or how long it will take me to find them. If there's even anything to find.

There's a distinct chance that Clark didn't tell Frances he was thinking about divorce at all. There are no pictures from the funeral, not that I expected there to be, and Frances' social media is filled with posts that focus on the grieving widow.

I've considered the possibility that poking and prying into the life of a woman who is grieving her husband's death, and looking for evidence that she killed him might make me seem like a huge asshole, but the risk is worth it.

I've never cared for Frances, just like she's never cared for me, and I've spent enough time around her in the past month to know that she is nefarious and— as much as I hate to admit it— ridiculously clever.

I text Emma back, making up a lie about needing to attend to business for my other hotels. I don't want to lie to her, and a guilty feeling immediately sinks into my gut, but it's for the best.

The less she knows about my suspicions about Frances, the better.

I pad out into the hall, the quiet of the empty house making the air feel heavy around me. Or maybe it's my nerves due to the fear of getting caught.

The door to Frances' room hangs slightly ajar like a warning— the door is open but I still shouldn't enter. I shake off the thought and push open the door.

The room is light and airy, white walls surrounding the light blue linens covering the bed in the center of the room. One of the windows is open, blowing the sheer curtains softly with a light breeze.

There are two side tables with vases of flowers on either side of the bed, an enormous wardrobe, and a desk pushed into the corner with a laptop sitting on top of it. I sigh and make my way to the night stands.

I'm a little nervous about what I might find— I learned a long time ago not to go digging through bedside tables— but when I yank open the drawer on the first one, it's surprisingly empty, with nothing but a dog-eared book and a couple of pens inside.

It must have been Clark's side of the bed— he was always one to keep a neat and orderly space.

I move to the next bedside table, bracing myself for what could be inside. The drawer slides open with a soft scrape against the wood, revealing a more cluttered interior.

Inside sits a small leather journal with an engraved cover, a bottle of sleeping pills, some tissues and a few folded papers.

My heartbeat quickens when I spot the journal. I pick it up, anxiety coursing through me, but a quick thumbing through the book reveals nothing more than mundane lists and reminders for appointments. Nothing incriminating; I should have known it wouldn't be this easy.

I reach for the folded papers, careful not to tear them. I open them to find that one is Clark's obituary, and the other is a copy of a speech, presumably the one she read at the funeral.

It makes a lot of mention about how much Clark stepped in to take a fathering role for Jackie, and how much he improved their lives, but it reads more like a note of appreciation than the words of someone who is grieving a loved one.

If it weren't for the speech, the combination of the obituary, tissues and sleeping pills would be unspeakably sad.

I place everything back in the drawer exactly as it was before moving onto the wardrobe.

I pull open the doors, revealing rows of Frances' expensive clothes, organized by color in a way that makes me roll my eyes. Even her closet is trying too hard to be perfect, and she's the only one who ever sees it.

I feel around for shelves or hidden compartments, but come up empty. I'm not opening the drawers at the bottom— it's possible there's something hidden down there, but something about perusing around through a woman's underwear drawer feels especially invasive to me.

I close the doors and smooth the clothes as much as I can. Hopefully she doesn't have a photographic memory.

Finally, I turn to the desk, my eyes zeroing on the laptop. If there's any semblance of evidence to be found, I'm certain it will be on that laptop.

I carefully pull it open and sigh. I was hoping Frances would be naive enough to have no password on her device, but she's smart, so of course there is. I stare at the blinking screen— it's a pin, not an entire password, which narrows the possibilities down but not by much.

I type in Frances and Clark's wedding date, but come back with an error message. Not important enough to be her password, apparently. The tiny password hint button calls my name, and when I click it, a clue pops up on screen.

"Your pride and joy."

Jackie, of course. Do I know her birthday? Of course I don't. I scurry back to the bedside table and flip through the small journal until I find a page that is covered in exclamation points— plans for Jackie's birthday, April tenth.

I type in the numbers and the home screen pops up, a picture of Frances sitting at an office desk in a suit popping up.

I sigh and scan the icons until I find the one that contains her email. It's mostly filled with marketing emails, messages from contractors. But one specifically catches my eye. It's a message log from a therapist.

"And why does that make you feel guilty?" the message says.

I hit the "see more" button at the bottom and it takes me to an external therapy site. I say a silent prayer that she keeps her passwords saved in her computer and breathe a sigh of relief when I'm easily able to open the account.

A warning brushes through me. If snooping wasn't illegal, looking at her private therapy messages definitely is. But I can't stop myself from opening the chat log. I take a picture before reading the messages.

Kim Yuder, LPCA: And why does that make you feel guilty?

Frances Stone: I was in the car with him when we crashed. It rolled over. We were fighting.

Kim Yuder, LPCA: What was the fight about? It's important to remember that a lot of times after car accidents, victims will feel survivor's guilt when other parties don't survive. Surviving when your husband didn't doesn't mean that you are at fault.

CLAIRE KIRBY

Frances Stone: He told me he wanted a divorce. I was so blindsided. I never knew he was unhappy. I became an uncontrollable screaming mess.

Before I can continue reading the messages, the front door closes. I suck in a breath and close out of the page before shutting the laptop. Footsteps on the stairs send me into a small panic. I cannot be caught in here. Frances doesn't usually come back to the house an hour and a half after she's left.

I hurry toward the bed as the footsteps get closer. As I crawl under, I bump the side table, knocking over the vase in the process. I curse silently, sliding deeper under the bed as I watch water spill over the side of the table and onto the carpet.

"Hello?" Frances' voice echoes through the room as the door creaks open further. I watch her heels from under the bed, stepping softly around the room as she reaches the side table. She stops for a moment and then I hear the sound of the vase being adjusted on the table. She curses and then opens the door, taking out some tissues and wiping down the table.

I push deeper under the bed as she leans down and dabs at the carpet. She makes a noise of frustration and then sighs.

"I need to stop forgetting to shut that window," she mutters to herself. I hear the window close before she walks over to the desk.

I hear muffled sounds and then she leaves the room. I stay under the bed until I hear the sound of her car pulling out of the driveway and then let out a huge sigh of relief. I climb out from under the bed and peek out the window in time to see her tail lights glowing down the road. Then my eyes slide to the desk.

She forgot her laptop. It's a good thing I closed all the programs, but I don't want to spend another second in here after that close call.

Besides, I have the information I need. She knew about the divorce, and she feels guilty about Clark's death.

The therapist said people suffer from survivor's guilt, which I know is true. But what if it's not just survivors' guilt?

What if Frances has a reason to be truly guilty?

***

"What do I do with this information?" I ask Jackson as we sit on a bench at the park.

After finally dealing with the bed bug situation at The Bilstone— we were able to get emergency fumigators and the new furniture and linens delivery scheduled so that the hotel won't have to be closed for much longer— I texted Emma and asked if I could take Jackson out.

She was ecstatic about the idea of Jackson not having to be alone all day and also us bonding. Not that we need to bond— I already love the dog like my own. He's sweet and easy-going.

He noses my hand and I ruffle his fur.

"Not really an answer, bud, but I'll take it."

He lets out a doggy sigh as I stare at the blurry image on my phone. Despite the fuzziness, the messages are easy enough to read, and I've reread them probably a couple of dozen times at this point.

There's nothing I can do with this legally. All it proves is that she knew he was going to divorce her, which doesn't mean anything.

She expresses guilt but doesn't openly admit to anything, and I recognize that maybe there isn't anything to admit to. Maybe they were both emotional and Clark just lost control of the car, but I can't stop the nagging feeling that there's more to the story.

If I play things right, I might be able to talk to Frances about the events of the accident. I don't know what angle I could take to get the information I'm looking for.

She'd know instantly that something was up if I pretended that I was interested in her feelings surrounding the accident. I could potentially act like I just want to know more about what it was like in Clark's final moments, but I'm afraid that would seem simply macabre and it would definitely be out of character for me.

Jackson whines and looks up at me. If only he could talk.

"All right, let's get out of here."

I pick up his leash and he follows me. Despite being an older dog, he moves with the pep of a young, yet tired, puppy. I smile and make a split second decision to go down the walking path instead of back to the car. There's a pet store around the corner that sells specialty bakery dog treats.

As soon as we step into the store, Jackson's tail goes wild, waving from side to side with excitement. He scurries up to the bakery counter and I have to laugh. Apparently this isn't his first time here.

The woman behind their counter hands me a carob bakery cookie, then Jackson and I head home.

Chapter Thirty-Three

Emma

"It's absolutely beautiful," I whisper, rustling the paper in the box that Lucas bought for me.

The dress is a rich emerald color, shimmering threads of gold catching the light and interrupting the sea of green. Delicate gold beading adorns the neckline and cascades down in elegant strands that grace the skirt's edge. The skirt is long enough that it would fall to my knees and a gold jeweled headband and sparkly gold kitten heels accompany the outfit.

"I think it will look great on you. That color of green makes your hair stand out." Lucas tucks a strand of hair behind my ear. "Try it on."

"I want to." I frown. It's so beautiful, and it's all wasted. "I can't wear it."

"What do you mean?"

"Staff are required to wear all black for the event. No heels, either. Frances said we're 'meant to sink into the shadows.'"

Lucas lets out a laugh and shakes his head.

"You're not staff."

"Frances gave me a long list of tasks to do during the gala. I'll be welcoming guests for the first half hour. Effectively, I am staff."

"Looks like you'll have to delegate. You're coming as my date, although even if you were welcoming guests it would be more appropriate for you to wear this dress than to dress like the waitstaff."

I roll my eyes. I don't know why, but I've been so irritable all day. I even snapped at Lily earlier when she was bringing me the payroll reports. She was kind enough to take it in stride, but it bothers me that I'm so short-tempered.

I was fine yesterday— in fact, I was ecstatic. It had been a decent day at work, Lucas offered to take Jackson for an outing, and we had an even better night.

Now, he's getting under my skin and he's not even really doing anything wrong.

"Can you be realistic for a second?" The annoyance glows through my tone. "You know I can't be your date to the gala. Frances and Jackie would go ballistic if that happened."

Lucas seems taken aback that I've snapped at him, but he smiles and grabs my hand.

"It doesn't have to be romantic. I'm not going to sweep you into a kiss on the dance floor. I just want you to be happy and be able to enjoy yourself. I'm sure Frances wouldn't object to me bringing a date. I will be the one to tell her I've asked you to accompany me."

The laugh that escapes me is bitter. I drag my hand out of his and cross my arms.

"You seriously don't get it. Frances would object to you bringing any date that isn't Jackie. But it would be ten times worse if you show up with me on your arm. They are actively trying to get you together with Jackie and get me out of their way.

"Any wrong move, and I will be threatened with being thrown out of my own home— a home, by the way, that I have spent my entire life in. I understand that there is no risk involved for you. I'm sure it would be super entertaining to get under Frances' skin by bringing me to the gala, especially when the only thing you have to worry about is...is..." I give an exasperated gasp. "Do you even have to worry about anything?"

Lucas is staring at me, his eyes wide.

"Emma, I worry about you."

"Then why don't you act like it?"

My voice is rising, becoming more hysterical with every syllable. I need to calm down or I'm going to end up getting Frances' or Jackie's attention— the last thing we need at this moment.

"You say you care about me, and then you make these reckless suggestions. Frances already thinks I'm into you. The last thing we need is to give her the confirmation that we're together. Everything would be ruined."

Lucas hugs me and even though I don't want to cry, tears slip down my cheeks.

Maybe it's not really Lucas I'm angry with— maybe it's just the whole situation. Between dealing with Frances, potentially losing the hotel, having to hide our relationship and now harboring the pregnancy secret, everything feels like it's crashing down on top of me.

"Look, we won't go together. I'm sorry that I've made you feel like I don't care. I do care, and I'll be more mindful of my actions going forward and how they might impact you. I promise the last thing I'd want to do is jeopardize anything to do with your future."

He kisses my forehead and I nod, but I can't bring a smile to my face. I shake my head.

"I need to get ready for the gala. You probably should, too."

I kiss his cheek and he nods, giving my hand one last squeeze before leaving. I close the door behind him and lean against it, letting out a deep breath.

My emotions are all over the place, and I need to get a grip. Guilt threads through me; Lucas was trying to be sweet, and I practically bit his head off. Still, I can't show up as his date or Frances would have me packed and out on the street before midnight.

The dress catches my eye again, and I run my hand over the intricate beading. It truly is a beautiful gown. Maybe I'll wear it after all. Maybe I'll show Frances that I have a mind of my own and that she doesn't call all the shots.

I check my phone— it's 5:00, and the gala starts at 7:00, which means I should be there by 6:30 to be ready to welcome the guests. Time to get a move on.

I wipe my tears and head to the bathroom to splash water on my face. I glance at my reflection. My eyes are puffy and red and my cheeks are blotchy from crying. Guess I'll need a little extra concealer tonight.

Is it my imagination, or does my body already look different? I run my hand over my stomach— it's exactly the same as it was yesterday, but I still feel different. Or maybe that's just because I know what's in there— or should I say who.

"You're causing quite a stir already," I whisper as if the baby growing inside can hear me. I know from the pregnancy tracker that she doesn't even have ears yet. I can't say for sure that the baby is a girl, but I just have a feeling.

My mind races as I apply my makeup. I go a little more glam than I usually would, applying sparkly eye shadow and a sharp eyeliner.

It's bold, much bolder than I'm used to, and I have to reapply the eyeliner twice because I keep messing up, but I'm determined to enjoy the evening and I want to look my best.

Now, it's go time.

***

"Welcome to The Signature On Main. May I have your names?"

I smile at the glamorous couple in front of me. The attendees are really going all out tonight— most are showing up in gorgeous, shimmery 1920's era-esque costumes. A select few have opted for more traditional evening wear, but they still look marvelous, too, and I'm glad I opted for the green dress.

"Mr. Marshall and Alison Bridgers."

The man flashes me an easy smile. The name sounds familiar, although I'm not quite sure why. Maybe it's just from studying the guest list all morning.

"Wonderful. We are so happy to be able to host you tonight." I pick up the paper with the auction details as well as a pamphlet about the history of the hotel.

"Tonight we're raising money for the Community Kitchen off 23rd street. All the money raised will be donated to help them serve the community."

"That's wonderful," his wife says, murmuring as she looks around the hotel.

"I think so, too. The speakeasy entrance is right down the hall."

They walk away and my eyes follow them as I try to place exactly why I know his name. It doesn't come to me before the next guests step up to be greeted.

The next half hour passes in a quick blur of checking names and welcoming them to the hotel. My cheeks ache from the plastered on smile, but I don't let it drop.

As much as I dislike Frances for trying to stomp on my excitement and enjoyment of the gala, I want it to be a success. Not just for the hotel, but for the Community Kitchen and my father's memory as well.

It's been too long since I've been to the Community Kitchen. I do want to get back there at some point since it's something I used to do with Dad, and it's something I want to continue with my own child.

My child. It's almost strange how easily the thought comes to mind.

After the final guest arrives, I head downstairs.

I'm immediately in awe of how beautiful the speakeasy looks. The lighting is low and moody, illuminating the space and hitting the glitter in the evening dresses and decor at just the right spot so that everything glows spectacularly.

The flowers in the centerpieces look fresh and brighten up the space. Felicia Wilkes is on the stage, her sultry voice emanating through the room and drawing attention from the crowd. It truly is a magnificent sight.

What's drawing the majority of my attention, though, isn't the room. It's Lucas.

He's in deep conversation with an older generation, and when he lets out a laugh, his entire face lights up. He looks devastatingly handsome in his tuxedo, his hair pomaded back in a sleek 1920's style.

His eyes meet mine briefly, and he gives me a small, apologetic smile. My heart flip- flops despite my earlier irritation. I really need to apologize for snapping at him.

I sigh and head over to a display table, reviewing the historical photos of the building throughout the years. Dad had these stored away, getting them from the historical society when he first opened the hotel. Frances really has done a good job of preparing for this gala.

A shadow casts over the table as someone looms behind me.

"You know, this place really has a fascinating history. The prohibition theme is very classy— not at all cheesy as I had expected."

I turn, and Mr. Bridgers is examining a black and white photo of the hotel from 1926.

"It does," I say, turning into a tour guide. "That picture was taken when prohibition was in full swing. This entire space, which you can see is now the speakeasy, was an illegal bootlegging operation. Martin Lopez was the one running it at the time, and he owned the hotel until the 40's.

"Remarkable," he says. The tone is almost humoring, but he moves on swiftly. "You know a lot about this place."

"I grew up here. My mom and dad were the ones who opened The Signature originally."

"That's an incredible legacy. It's a shame that Frances is selling it, but I understand a hotel is an enormous undertaking. I can assure you that when I own the hotel, I will make sure to honor its history."

"'When you own the hotel?' I wasn't aware Frances had decided on a buyer yet."

"Well, I suppose it's not really official yet."

Mr. Bridgers smiles at me and raises his champagne glass. "My first offer was just to open negotiations. After seeing this place myself, though, I'm prepared to make a much better, more appropriate offer. It's beautiful, and I think it would make a wonderful addition to my hotel collection."

My stomach turns at the way he says collection. Mom and Dad's hotel deserves more than being just a part of another wealthy man's enterprise. I swallow my opinion and smile.

"I'm sure it would. If you'll excuse me, I have other duties to attend to."

If he's at all alarmed at my quick exit, he doesn't show it on his face. I can't stand and talk to him any longer, though.

I knew that there would be interest in the hotel and that the gala was a way to increase that interest. But now I can't help but wonder if Lucas and I will be able to sway Frances away from other lucrative deals that are bound to surface.

Chapter Thirty-Four

Lucas

My eyes track Emma's every move throughout the room. She looks absolutely breathtaking, a vision in shimmering green with cascading red hair.

She commands the room effortlessly. It is undeniable how beautiful she is, captivating attention and admiration as she flits across the room. Frances' attempts to dampen her presence were in vain. Nothing can extinguish her luminosity and Frances knows it and I can tell she's seething at how much Emma outshines Jackie.

After our disagreement earlier— I hesitate to call it a fight or even an argument— I've come to realize she was right.

I wasn't thinking about the possible repercussions of her being my date to the gala. The only thing I was thinking about was twirling her on the dance floor in that beautiful dress.

Emma disappears behind the stage curtain, and I turn my attention to the crowds around me.

Royce is still at The Biltstone, so there's no one to chat with to pass the time. I mosey over to the bar and order another drink; the champagne I was given as I arrived has gone flat, since I spent so much time talking to one of the guests.

He had a lot to say about the importance of prohibition history to Santa Fe, and had twice as many jokes.

"Mr. Bennett," a familiar voice says from behind me. I turn around and there stands Marshall Bridgers.

"Nice to see you again," I plaster a fake smile on my face.

Seeing him here is the opposite of nice. I wish I'd been able to see a final guest list, but unfortunately it wasn't any of my business and I didn't see a way to easily get it from Frances.

"Yes. Are you here because you have an interest in the hotel? When I heard that it was being put up for sale, I was sure that you would be my biggest competition. I know how much you love these quaint, small places." Marshall smiles, but his tone is challenging; it's clear what he thinks about these "quaint, small places."

I take a small sip of my fresh champagne, savoring the bubbles. His smug expression is making my blood boil, but I manage to keep my composure. This isn't the time or place for a confrontation. I give a small, tight smile and shake my head.

"I'm not here as a buyer. I've been helping Frances with the hotel, restoring it to its glory so that she can get a good price for it. Clark Stone was a good friend of mine, and I was very sad to hear of his passing."

"Ah, yes. I did hear about that. It truly is a shame." Marshall eyes me suspiciously. "Interesting that you're helping her turn the hotel back to the prohibition theme. I thought the updated rooms were rather beautiful."

"They were certainly updated, but they didn't conform with the identity and Prohibition era theme of the hotel. The Signature has curated a certain ambience here and offers an experience that a typical hotel can't. It's that ambience that Frances now realizes she should not have tried to obliterate, but should have instead worked to maintain.

"I know you don't have a ton of familiarity with boutique hotels, but they truly are a special piece of the industry that should be appreciated and Clark took a lot of pride in what he'd accomplished here." I chuckle. "Besides, Clark put his blood, sweat, and tears into creating a special magic in this hotel and making it an homage to its history."

Marshall shakes his head and laughs.

"Ever the sentimentalist, Bennett. I know you've built an empire, but let's be honest with each other, you certainly don't have the same profit margins as a lot of other hoteliers."

"Like yourself, you mean."

"I'm one example, yes. This speakeasy could be beautifully transformed into a spa, and you could curate an upscale experience in the heart of Santa Fe, something that isn't offered in the center of the city. That is a killer idea. There is no place for sentimentality in business. Business is about profits."

"You're wrong," I insist. "Profits are important. I am successful because I know the audience that I'm serving. This hotel attracts a certain kind of clientele, one that is looking for a special experience. Not only that, it's a part of the community at large. So much of Santa Fe's history is woven into this hotel that it would be foolish to ignore it.

"There's an upscale hotel and spa on the outskirts of the city. Sure, it's not right next to a coffee shop, or the other conveniences that downtown offers. But that hotel doesn't need those things. The last thing a small hotel like The Signature needs is to try to compete with the one uptown. They are simply two different animals."

My rant is cut off by the reappearance of Emma. She glides across the room effortlessly, leaning in to smile at guests or laugh politely at bad jokes. I let out a small sigh and Marshall laughs.

"She is a summer peach, isn't she?" he says, and my head whips to him.

"I'm sorry?"

"Clark's daughter. What's her name? Emerson? Emily?"

"Emma."

"That's it. I'm just terrible with names these days. Soon I'll have to start making myself flashcards." He winks. "But she really is something. If I wasn't married, I might offer to take her to dinner."

I make a face and he claps my shoulder.

"Don't worry, Bennett. She's all yours. Although she's a little young for you, isn't she?"

"I don't think it's appropriate for you to talk about her like this."

He holds his hands up and shrugs.

"I'm just talking. You're the one exploring her with your eyes."

Marshall picks up his drink and raises it to me. "I'm going to get back to the wife. She's positively giddy over the singer—I don't know where they found her, but she's a real hidden gem down here in Santa Fe. Truly belongs on a bigger stage."

I stare daggers at him when he walks away.

"Hello, there. Hello," Frances grins out at the audience as she taps on the microphone. "My name is Frances Stone, and I'm the current owner of The Signature on Main. I want to thank everyone for attending our little soiree tonight, and for showing your support for the Santa Fe Community Kitchen by participating in the auction..."

I tune out as the auction starts.

***

The music turns from jazz to dance music as a band joins the singer on stage and people flutter out to dance.

The auction had gone well, raising well over the amount projected, which is always a success for both the charity and the event itself. Frances seemed genuinely happy at the end of the auction, something I don't think I've ever seen before.

I turn and head to the bar, feeling a warm smile spread across my face when I spot Emma nursing a Sprite. She was busy during the entire auction, taking notes on the side of the stage. Another one of Frances' assigned tasks, I assume.

"This gala has been quite a success, if I do say so myself," I say as I sidle up next to her. She grins widely and nods.

"It really has! We raised so much money, the Kitchen folks are ecstatic! There will be so many possibilities for what they can do with this money."

Emma sighs and scooches closer. Her hand lightly brushes against mine and she smiles up at me before lowering her voice.

"I want to apologize for earlier. I've just been so irritable lately, but I shouldn't have lashed out at you."

I shake my head.

"No, I should apologize. You were completely right with everything you said, and I need to be more conscious of how my actions might affect the things you have to deal with around here."

I fight the urge to step closer and pull her into a hug. Before Emma can respond, the familiar sound of heels sound behind me.

"Emma, there you are! I need you to do an alcohol inventory."

"Now? The gala isn't even over, and I don't think— "

"Emma." Frances' mouth presses into a thin line. "Our alcohol order goes out tomorrow. We can make a pretty good prediction of how much more is going to be consumed by how much we've already gone through. Unless you want to be here at 1:00 in the morning doing alcohol inventory, I suggest you get started."

Emma sighs, hesitating for a moment before nodding.

"Yes, Frances. I will get right on that."

She's clearly annoyed, yet storms away to the supply closet behind the bar. Then Frances turns toward me and smiles.

"How are you enjoying the gala? I saw you talking to Mr. Bridgers earlier. I think he might raise his offer if we get some other interest."

I nod.

"We did chat, and I think you're right. I think he recognizes that this is indeed a gem of a boutique hotel and he doesn't want to think someone else might come in and swoop it up."

I note her spirited mood and decide to take a chance."Regardless, whatever he offers you, I'll match his amount and add another million."

Frances brows practically shoot off her forehead in surprise.

"You want the hotel for your own collection?"

"Being here and being a part of the process of returning it to its original condition, planning the gala. This hotel is beautiful and I want to be able to do Clark's memory justice. I would very much like to make it my own."

"Really? That's very thoughtful of you," Frances states, although she's treading carefully.

"Yes. I really love it and I hope you will consider my offer."

She studies me and then nods, a smug smile spreading across her face. What is she up to now?

"I absolutely will consider it." She looks around the room before settling on a spot across from us, her face lighting up. "Have you talked to Jackie tonight? She looks positively radiant."

"I'm afraid I haven't gotten the chance to talk with her yet." Frances links arms in mine and hums.

"Let's go chat with her."

Before I can object, Frances is dragging me across the dance floor. "Doesn't she look gorgeous? Her dress fits her like a glove, and I think the color just absolutely brings out her eyes."

"It is a beautiful dress. You look lovely, Jackie."

Jackie shrugs but smiles down at the frock.

I take a sip of my drink before Frances grabs it from me. I blink at her in surprise and she smiles.

"Lucas, you should dance with Jackie."

Oh. This is why she's so happy.

"You know, I'm not much of a dancer, so I'll just sit—"

"Nonsense. You can spare one dance. No one is going to be watching if you have two left feet."

She waves at the air and laughs. "Besides, it's impolite to turn down an offer for a dance."

Technically, Jackie didn't ask for a dance. When I peek at her, she's blushing hard, but there's a hopeful look on her face as she watches me. I really don't want to dance with her, but after throwing all my cards on the table with an offer on the hotel, I don't think I can refuse.

"Okay, one dance. But don't say I didn't warn you when I'm stepping on your feet." I let out an easy chuckle and Jackie holds out her hand. I take it and we step out onto the dance floor.

We sway awkwardly back and forth, her arms looped around my neck. It feels less like a dance at a gala and more like a bad prom date, but it's only until the song is over. I can survive this.

"Thanks for dancing with me," Jackie says shyly. My stomach sinks and I nod.

"Of course."

"You know, I've been hoping I'd get to talk to you all night."

"That's kind of you to say."

She steps closer and an ominous feeling flows through me.

"I want to tell you something."

"Maybe now isn't the time..." I look around the room, taking note of any onlookers. Bridgers. Frances. Lily. No sign of Emma.

"What better time than now?" She places a hand on my cheek and turns my face so that I look at her.

"I really like you Lucas. You're smart, funny, and the most handsome man I've ever seen. I think we could be a really great couple."

And then she plants a kiss on my lips.

Chapter Thirty-Five

Emma

I step out of the supply closet after doing inventory and scan the room.

On the dance floor, between the mix of people, I can catch glimpses of Lucas holding Jackie at arms' length. They look to be in a tense conversation— what's going on?

People crowd the dance floor as the music tempo gets faster, dancing around as if they don't have a care in the world. And maybe they don't.

"Emma!" Lily says my name urgently from across the bar. I turn to her and she motions for me to follow her. I look back at the dance floor, unable to find the two of them again. I shake my head and follow Lily to the corner of the room.

"What's up?" I try to be casual while I crane my neck looking for Lucas around the room. Where did they go?

"'What's up' is that Jackie just laid lip on your man." She looks at me incredulously, her eyes bugging out of her head. My brow wrinkles in confusion.

"What does laid lip mean?"

Lily rolls her eyes.

"She kissed him."

"What?!" I practically yell. Patrons gathering around us turn, murmuring while they throw the two of us dirty looks. I smile sheepishly and then drag her closer to the wall. "What do you mean she kissed him?"

"They were dancing..."

"Why were they dancing together?"

"I'm an observer, not a mind reader, Emma. But they were dancing, and she kept getting closer. And he started looking so nervous, then she whispered something to him and just planted one right on him."

"She whispered to him?"

Lily sighs.

"Okay, I don't know if she whispered. That was for dramatic effect— but she did get really close and say something before kissing him."

My stomach drops and anger flows through me. Why the hell would she kiss him? In the middle of a huge gala where there are tons of onlookers, at that.

"What did Lucas do?" I ask, my stomach dropping. I need details.

"For the record, he did not seem into it. He pushed her away so fast. I mean, they were so far apart that she might as well have been in Bermuda."

"Bermuda?" I wrinkle my nose.

"It was the furthest place I could think of on the spot!" Lily throws her hands up in the air. "You're focusing on the wrong things. He looked really upset about it."

"Did you see where Lucas went?"

"I think he went out the stage door. Jackie followed him, I'm pretty sure."

I turn to storm off, but Lily catches my arm.

"Hey, please don't do anything you're going to regret. I know things with Frances are hard, but I don't want you to make a decision in the heat of the moment that is going to make your life even more difficult than it already is."

Lily's eyes are big and sincere, a seriousness in her voice that I've never heard before. I take a deep breath and nod.

She's right. I'm seeing red, but I can't go in there guns ablaze. Jackie doesn't even know that I'm with Lucas. So even though kissing him was inappropriate, she doesn't know that she did anything wrong to me.

I need to calm down.

"You're right," I say, taking another deep breath. "I'm just going to go and find Lucas. I need to check on him and see how he's feeling."

"Good call. I'll hold down the fort here, and redirect if Frances goes looking for you." She squeezes my arm affectionately and smiles.

It's weird, because it feels like I barely knew her a month ago, but now she's practically my best friend. And it wasn't intended; she basically stormed her way into my life.

I think if it was anyone else, I would have found it off-putting how she basically butted head first into my life, but Lily has a certain charm that made me feel seen. Seen and understood.

My heart hammers against my ribs with every step closer to the door backstage. I don't even know what I'm going to say when I get there. 'Hey Jackie! Surprise! You kissed my secret boyfriend?'

I don't think so.

I step through the stage door into the dimly lit hallway. Dressing room doors hang open, the dark lights indicating their emptiness until I get to the end of the hall.

The final room's door is closed, with light flooding from underneath it. Lucas' voice floats through the door, even and serious. Jackie's voice follows, animated with a shriek-y quality.

What's my game plan? I can't walk in there and immediately launch into inquiring about the kiss. As far as either of them know, I didn't even see it. And as far as Jackie knows, I shouldn't care. I look around and grab a bottle of wine from a service cart sitting at the back entrance. Then I smooth my outfit and knock on the door, opening it before either of them could say anything.

Jackie is sitting in the vanity chair, turned around so she can look at Lucas pacing on the other side of the room. The tension in the room is palpable.

Tears glisten in Jackie's eyes, a heavy frown etching her features. Lucas looks just as distraught, although there's a glimmer of annoyance in his expression. They both look up as I come through the door. Lucas' eyes look at me with worry, while Jackie glances at me lazily.

"Emma?" Lucas asks.

"What's going on?" I swivel my head between the two of them, trying my hardest to keep a casual lilt in my tone. "I was told to bring this Bordeaux for Felicia Wilkes."

"I did something so dumb!" Jackie cries, standing up. "I read things all wrong."

I take a deep breath. In all honesty, this is the most sister-like interaction I've ever had with Jackie. Despite the years spent living together, we've never had a real argument.

"What do you mean you read things all wrong?"

Jackie sulks.

I sigh and look away.

We're all quiet for a moment, avoiding looking at each other. The tension has broken, and now there is just a general aura of awkwardness floating through the air.

"What were you guys doing in here?" I ask, trying to frame it as suspicion as opposed to jealousy.

I know Lucas didn't kiss her back. But I still feel a little green eyed monster crawling through me like a bug.

"Well, there was just a bit of an awkward situation earlier—" Lucas starts.

I know it's a lie, but the way his eyes are begging me not to call him on it tells me that he's simply trying to avoid embarrassing Jackie any further.

"I kissed Lucas!" Jackie cries, burying her face in her hands.

I throw Lucas a look and he shakes his head, looking exasperated. I hesitate before walking over to her and awkwardly patting her shoulder. I look over at Lucas.

"Why don't you leave us alone for a minute?" I ask.

Lucas nods, mouthing 'talk later' before leaving the room, closing the door softly behind him. I kneel in front of Jackie and she looks up at me, tears streaming down her face. "Why did you kiss Lucas?"

Jackie sighs and looks up at the ceiling.

"I'm such an idiot. I thought he liked me. Mom kept saying 'He would be a wonderful catch. And he's so handsome.' She kept telling me what a good match we'd make, and the more I interacted with him... He's so friendly and kind! So helpful. I clearly read the situation wrong."

Annoyance bubbles up inside me; she's talking about the father of my child here. But she doesn't know that, and I need to keep reminding myself of that fact.

"Hey, it's okay that you made a mistake. I understand why you'd like him— he is very handsome."

We both giggle. "But why did you decide to kiss him right there on the middle of the dance floor?"

"I don't know! Mom just told me to dance and flirt with him. I think I just got way too into the moment. We were so close, and I guess... I just thought it would be the perfect moment. But everyone saw him push me away and ask 'What on earth are you doing?'"

"I'm sure most people weren't paying attention. The crowd at these functions is generally very self-involved."

Jackie sits up straight and eyes me warily.

"Why are you being so nice to me?"

"What do you mean?"

"I kissed the man you like." Jackie looks at me incredulously. "I would be livid."

My jaw drops.

"You know I like him?"

Jackie snorts and rolls her eyes.

"Emma, everyone knows you like him. Even Jackson can tell."

I resist the urge to laugh. Jackson undoubtedly knows.

"Why would you kiss him knowing I like him?"

Jackie sighs and looks at her reflection in the mirror, wiping away at her smudged mascara.

"I guess I just wanted to prove that I could have something you couldn't."

"Jackie, you have my room. You're able to do whatever you want with your free time, have no responsibilities, and no worries. That's everything I want."

"Those don't count! I didn't want your room. Mom told me she was planning the renovation. Besides, I thought you'd be happier in your own space away from us."

"That's been my room my entire life. Why would I want to leave it?"

"You want to stay in your childhood room forever?" Jackie gives me a look. I sigh.

"Okay, I guess not. But my point is, that you are living the life. I'm watching my parents' work being sold in front of me and living in the basement of my own house."

"Emma, I've always been jealous of you! Your dad... he was wonderful to me. Much better than my own dad ever was. And I know he loved me, and he treated me like he did. But you were his real daughter, and he did everything to help make your dreams come true."

"He would have done anything to make yours come true, too."

"Maybe." Jackie shrugs.

"I just thought... when I figured out you liked Lucas, it was like the tip of the iceberg. You have everything— you're super pretty, super smart, have your whole life figured out. You know your purpose, and you want to run the hotel.

"I have no idea what I want to do, and I'm almost halfway through my twenties. Your parents clearly loved you a lot to leave you a legacy like this. I know your mom died, but your dad loved you so much that it's like you didn't even lose anything at all."

Okay then. That was a little rude, but she's emotional, so I'll let it slide.

"Look, my life is not perfect. I want this hotel, and I don't have it. I want my Dad, and I don't have him. Life is not easy, and you can look at me and think that I have it all, but I don't. I look at you and think the exact same thing."

I lean back and sigh. "We just need to be more understanding of and kinder to each other. That's the only way we can ever be friends."

Maybe I'm starting to like Jackie.

"Who said I wanted to be friends with you?"

I narrow my eyes at her and she laughs.

"God, I'm just kidding. Lighten up, will you? Fine. I'll be more understanding in the future. I'm going to go get a drink to wash away the embarrassment."

I watch as she leaves the room.

Scratch like. I'm starting to tolerate Jackie.

Chapter Thirty-Six

Lucas

It's much later than usual when I sneak down to Emma's room tonight. The gala ended at midnight. Frances went to sleep almost as soon as everyone came home, but Jackie was up late enough that it was almost 2:00 before I snuck down.

I barely knock on the door when she swings it open, letting me inside. She looks gorgeous, her long red hair flowing over the shoulders of her gray sweatshirt and shorts that reveal her long, freckled legs.

"You look great," I say. Emma blushes and rolls her eyes, but I see a smile slowly creeping onto her face.

She leads me to the bed and we both take a seat.

"What the hell happened tonight?" she asks.

There's no anger in her question, though. It sounds more confused than anything, as if she can't believe the events of the gala. "I feel like so much happened and I'm not even aware of half of it."

"A lot definitely happened." I suck in a breath and nod. "I told Frances I want to buy the hotel."

"What?" Emma turns to me, her eyes wide with shock. "Why did you do that?"

"I was panicking. Bridgers told me he was going to raise his offer on the hotel because he sensed there was other interest, and Frances knows he's going to. The whole point of the gala was to gain buyer interest, and well, it worked. She said he was likely going to up his offer and I panicked. Told her I'd add another million to whatever he offers."

"Oh, my God."

"I know, I know. I don't know what I was thinking. I wasn't thinking, actually. I just said it without even considering the ramifications."

Emma's quiet, and I study her. She doesn't seem mad, or even upset. Instead, it's as if the wheels in her head are turning.

"How do you think she took it? Do you think she'll accept yours over Mr. Bridgers?"

"I think I have a good shot. Or at least, I thought I did, until I flat out rejected Jackie on the dance floor. But I think Frances will go with the highest offer. Why wouldn't she?"

Emma shudders.

"Yeah, I don't know if Frances even knows about the whole dance floor fiasco," Emma says.

"I'm not sure, either. But Jackie will probably tell her."

"I don't think she will. We had a huge heart to heart in that dressing room after you left. I think we understand each other better now. Frances planted in her head the idea that you liked her."

"Of course she did. I'm glad you both came to an understanding, though. Does she know about us?"

"Oh, goodness no. I don't think I trust her to that level yet." Emma sighs. "So what do we do now? If she rejects your offer, I mean."

"I don't see why she would. I really do think she's primarily mercenary and will go where the money is."

I chew my lip. I could tell Emma about my back up plan—confronting Frances about the accident. But I don't think I should involve her just yet. Tonight was already a lot for her to handle; I don't want to make it any harder.

"Well, it was certainly an interesting night. At least the auction went well."

"Well? It was amazing."

"Yeah..." Emma turns to me, her eyes intense. "What are you doing on Sunday?"

"Nothing that can't wait."

She rolls her eyes but smiles.

"Will you come to the Community Kitchen with me? I haven't been in a long time, but I used to go every Sunday with Dad. I think I'm ready to go back."

"Of course I'll go with you."

Emma smiles and then wraps her arms around me.

"You're the best."

I pull her into my lap and kiss her forehead.

"That's definitely you."

Emma's eyes meet mine once again, and there's a sudden shift from softness to desire.

Her arms tighten around my neck as she shifts in my lap, turning to face me fully. The weight of her in my arms causes my heart to pick up speed.

"I've been thinking about you all night. Even with all the chaos at the gala, I was hardly able to take my eyes off you," she whispers, kissing my cheek softly.

I brush a strand of hair off her shoulder and then rest my fingers against her cheek.

"I wasn't able to keep mine off you either. You looked amazing tonight. That dress...fit you perfectly. Like it was made for you."

She laughs.

I stiffen in my pants at the memory of the silk resting softly against her skin. Her eyebrows rise— her pajamas are thin, which means she's able to feel everything.

"You should wear that dress as often as possible."

"I'll consider it. And I thank you again for the gift."

Our lips meet, soft and tender. My hands find their way to the hem of her sweatshirt before slipping underneath and meeting the warm skin of her stomach.

Her breath catches, and she pulls back to look at me. Her eyes reflect a mixture of desire and vulnerability. My thumb traces small circles on her hips and she leans in, kissing my neck so softly it's like her lips are barely there.

"I want you," I murmur into her hair.

In response she lifts the sweatshirt over her head, revealing a soft and sheer bra. It catches on her hair, and we both chuckle as I help her shake the top away from her strands before tossing it across the bed.

I trace her freckles first with my fingertips and then with my tongue, connecting them all together.

Emma shivers from my touch, her eyes fluttering closed for only a split second. When they open again, there's certainty in her gaze.

Her lips crash into mine in a kiss heavy with tension and wanting. Her fingers tangle in my hair, tugging as she presses herself closer. The fabric barely covering her breast rubs against my shirt, and the sudden urge to be with her, skin on skin, overcomes me.

I pull away, tugging my shirt off quickly. Then I push Emma down gently, so that she's lying on the bed in front of me.

Hard nipples push against the fabric of her bra, threatening to pierce through it.

I kneel on the edge of the bed, placing my lips just above her belly button and trailing my tongue slowly up toward her chest.

Emma sucks in a breath when I reach the edge of her bra. I take the fabric between my teeth and push it up, revealing her breasts. I cup them and they seem a little fuller than normal, but my desire overrules my curiosity, and I run my thumb over one of her nipples. She sucks in a breath, but when I put my mouth over it she jerks under me.

"You okay?"

Emma looks away, embarrassed.

"Yeah, sorry. They're just extra sensitive today."

"Gotcha." I nod. I know sensitivity can vary at different times in women's cycle. Maybe that's why they feel fuller too.

I move to her collarbone, planting small kisses up her neck and along her jaw until finally catching her lips again. Her breath hitches as I deepen the kiss, my hand sliding down to her shorts.

Her wetness seeps through the fabric, and I can't resist playing with the hem until she pushes her hips up against it.

My hand finds its way under the material, feeling the slickness between her legs as I brush against her clit.

A soft moan escapes her as I move my fingers over her clit, her hips rising to meet my hand almost involuntarily. I watch her face as I move my fingers over her sensitive spot, mesmerized by the way her face changes with each stroke, her eyes fluttering closed, cheeks flushing and lips parting.

"God, you're so beautiful," I whisper, unable to keep the thought to myself.

Emma responds by reaching for the elastic of my pants, fumbling in her eagerness. I shimmy to help her, letting them fall to the ground beneath me. Her hands find me through my briefs and my skin electrifies with her touch. She strokes me a few times as the impatience grows within me— I need to be inside her.

I drag her underwear down her legs with my hand, pulling them in one swift motion before tossing them to the floor. Emma licks her lips, her eyes meeting mine as she pushes my boxers down.

My hardness pushes out, aching and reaching for her warmth.

To my surprise, Emma sits up, taking my cock in her hand and placing her lips against the tip. I suck in a breath as she swirls her tongue around it, moving her mouth further down. I moan as she moves back and forth over the length of me, the warmth and wetness of her mouth sending shivering sensations all over my body.

I tip my head back, moaning loudly as she moves faster. As I get closer to the edge I gently pull her off, bringing her face to mine and kissing her sloppily.

Then I turn her around and get her on her knees, ass in the air. Emma looks back at me over her shoulder and licks her lips as I position myself at her entrance, admiring the shape of her body, her cunt glistening with wet juice just waiting for my cock to fuck her.

Her ass is perfectly round, just the right amount of cushion as I push slowly into her, feeling her slick wetness as I slide in and feel her walls grip me.

Emma lets out a deep sigh and moan, as if me being inside of her is the most satisfying thing she's ever felt.

I grab her hips and start to move, slowly at first, letting her adjust to the feel of me inside her from this new angle. She moans, softly at first, her fingers clutching the sheets beneath us. Her hips begin to move in time with my thrusts as she takes me deep inside herself.

She turns to look at me, her brilliant red hair falling to cascade over her shoulder.

"God, Emma, you feel so good," I moan, gripping her hips as I pick up the pace, thrusting into her faster, harder. The sound of skin against skin fills the room, accompanied only by our heavy breathing as I slam my cock into that slick pussy, so tight and so wet.

Emma pushes back against me, meeting my thrusts with an eagerness and abandon that fills me with fire.

I lean forward, pressing my chest against her back as my lips find her shoulder, kissing it softly. My hand snakes its way around our bodies, finding the spot between her legs and drawing circles over it as I slam into her, over and over.

"More," she says through ragged breaths, pushing her hips back into me as I drive deeper into her with every thrust.

I oblige her, picking up the speed with more force. Her moans grow louder, forcing me to move my fingers from her clit to cover her mouth. She takes my finger into her mouth, sucking her juices from it slowly. The sensation sends a jolt through me, making everything we're doing that much more intense.

I get closer, orgasm threatening to emerge. I slow down, moving my other hand back down to her clit. I start off with slow flicks before transitioning into making hard and fast circles over it, whimpers escaping her mouth through my hand.

"Lucas, oh!" she whispers, her body tensing. "Don't stop, please don't stop."

I keep my rhythm steady, moving my thrusts in sync with my fingers. Her breathing becomes erratic, her body trembling against mine. She lets out a long moan and I feel her inner walls clenching around me as she shudders with her most intense orgasm yet.

It's too much to handle; I follow her over the edge, my own release washing over me as I spill into her. We collapse flat onto the bed, breathing heavily until our systems calm.

My eyes grow heavy as our heartbeats sync together, and we both fall asleep.

Chapter Thirty-Seven

Emma

When I wake up in the morning, I cuddle into the warm body sleeping next to me before I realize Lucas is still with me.

I shoot up in bed and shove Lucas. He blinks and looks at me groggily. It's so cute, that for a moment I completely forget why I was panicked at all.

Then Jackson whines at the sound of a car pulling out of the driveway and I instantly remember.

"Lucas! You fell asleep down here!" I whisper urgently.

I know no one is outside the door listening in— I would have heard them coming up through the window— but for some reason I still feel the urge to keep my voice down.

"Oh, no. Do they know?"

"I haven't gotten any messages or phone calls," I say, grabbing my phone from the night stand. The screen is empty, showing nothing needing my attention. "Maybe they don't know yet. Someone just left, but I don't know who."

"I have sweats in my gym bag in the car. If you can go in the main house and distract whoever is still home, I can grab it and change really quickly. Claim I went for an early morning run."

I nod and climb out of bed, pulling on my pajama shorts and sliding my phone in the pocket. Then I throw a leash on Jackson and lead him to the door.

It's actually kind of funny, because this is eerily reminiscent of the first time we spent the night together, sneaking around Frances, trying to coordinate how to get away with being together.

"I'll text you when the coast is clear." We head out, and as Jackson does his business, I observe the cars in the driveway. Frances left, although who knows where and for how long.

I stride up to the house, bringing Jackson along with me. I'll give him a spoonful of peanut butter to justify being up here.

We waltz into the kitchen and I make my breathing extra quiet as I listen for noise upstairs. There's not even a whisper of noise from Jackie's room. I pull out my text and give Lucas the all-clear.

I pull open a cabinet and grab a jar of peanut butter. I've barely opened the drawer containing the spoons before the front door swings open. Lucas strides into the kitchen, sporting sweats and a tank top.

Desire stirs inside me— I've never seen him in workout gear, but he wears it very well. I shake my head— I cannot be thinking like this right now. Not after we risked a whole night together.

It's funny how worried I am that he spent the night in my room when just a few nights ago, I was desperately wishing he would stay.

Sneaking around with him has started to give me so many conflicting feelings. I want to be around him as often as possible, and do normal relationship things. Sleep in the same bed, go on dates, and kiss wherever we want to without worrying about who will see us.

At the same time, I know that incurring Frances' wrath will make things that much harder. We could potentially lose the hotel.

I'm caught between being with the man I love and keeping my family's dream. What a mess.

"Good morning," Lucas says, nodding at me. He looks perplexed; probably wondering why I look like I'm contemplating the answers to the universe holding a jar of peanut butter. I grab a spoon and dip it in the jar before holding it out to Jackson. He wags his tail happily before licking at the spoon. "Can dogs have peanut butter?"

"As long as it doesn't contain xylitol, they can. I buy peanut butter specifically without it for Jackson. He absolutely loves it. Most dogs do."

"I'll remember that." Lucas pulls open the fridge door and grabs a carton of orange juice when someone comes bounding down the stairs.

Jackie steps through the doorway and then blinks, seemingly surprised to see us both here. Her eyes slide to Lucas and her cheeks turn red. She's still embarrassed about last night.

"Hey, guys," Jackie says. She gives Jackson a small pet as she scoots past me and opens the fridge door, pulling out a bottle of juice.

"What kind of juice is that?" Lucas points, apparently unaware of her discomfort with his presence.

"Um, it's a special blend from the juice bar downtown. Celery, cilantro, apple juice. A few other things." Jackie shrugs.

"I didn't know there was a juice bar downtown. We should all go," Lucas says as he grabs a glass and pours himself some orange juice.

Jackie shoots me a look and I shrug. Jackson's teeth clink against the spoon as he polishes it clean and I shudder. I hate that sound.

"Sure, that sounds fun." Jackie looks down at her feet before meeting Lucas' eyes.

"Hey, I wanted to apologize again for last night. I know it wasn't appropriate for me to kiss you in the middle of the gala, and it won't happen again."

"Don't worry about it; it's already forgotten." Lucas smiles and Jackie returns an uneasy one.

"Also, Mom will be gone all day today. She's doing a spa day to de-stress, so you don't have to worry about sneaking around all day."

I gasp. Lucas and I share a look of concern.

"What are you talking about?" I ask, but I'm unable to keep the worry from my voice.

"Come on, I'm not dumb. I see the way you look at him." Jackie smirks. "Also, I saw him doing a mad dash from your room to his car through my window."

Lucas sighs, but Jackie only laughs in response.

"Don't worry, I'm not going to tell Mom. It's not her business what you both do."

I study her for a moment. That's a very mature, very surprising response from her. Much more mature than I expected.

"Plus, I'm kind of pissed at her for setting me up to embarrass myself last night."

There it is. Lucas nods.

"Thank you, Jackie. I really appreciate that. It's not that I don't think you're a fine person, but—"

Jackie holds up her hand and shakes her head.

"Look, you really don't need to say all this. It was embarrassing enough last night, but I'm a big girl. I know not every man is going to feel the same way toward me that I feel toward him and that's fine. Besides, I don't know if I had any real feelings for you or if I was just feeling amped up because Mom convinced me you had feelings for me."

She tosses her hair over her shoulder.

"Okay, I'm going upstairs to get ready. I have plans with my friends today."

Jackie smiles and then leaves the kitchen. I let out a deep sigh. At least there's one less person we have to worry about making our lives harder. Lucas looks at me and presses his lips into a thin line.

"There's something serious we need to discuss today."

"About the hotel?"

"Not necessarily. I mean, it definitely has a little to do with the hotel, but it mostly has to do with your dad."

This grabs my attention.

"You don't sound happy about it. Is it bad?"

"I don't know. It's not good." Lucas looks down at his phone, checking the time. Then he lowers his voice. "Let's get showered and ready. Then we can meet out front in an hour and go to breakfast? Discuss things in a more neutral territory."

My eyes shift toward the stairwell. Whatever he wants to tell me about my dad, it's clear that he'd rather keep it from Jackie. I nod and we part ways.

***

I pick at my omelet. After we met out front, Lucas drove me to a high-end brunch place. He tried to make small talk on the car ride, but I wasn't in the mood for it.

Anxiety is pulsing through every inch of my body, making it hard to focus on anything.

Even now, after telling me he has something to discuss concerning my dad, he's eating his eggs happily, looking out the window and making the occasional comment.

How can he be so calm and normal while I'm having an internal freakout? It's actually getting on my nerves.

"Can we just get to the point already?" I finally blurt after he cheerfully brings up the deliciousness of the fruit salad.

My patience is wearing thin. His eyes widen in surprise and he sets his silverware down. Guilt flows through me immediately.

"I'm sorry. It's just that we came here to discuss my dad and I've been a ball of anxiety since you said something this morning. I can't just sit here continuing to act like everything is normal."

Lucas nods.

"Of course. Sorry, I've just been unsure how to approach it so I keep putting it off."

Lucas takes a breath and nods. "A few weeks ago, I was in your dad's office looking for anything that could help your situation. Even if a will was unsigned, I figured if it was in the process then maybe that could help your case."

"You found a will?"

He shakes his head.

"No, but I found an email from a lawyer."

"You went through my dad's email?" I interrupt, wrinkling my nose.

Maybe my reaction isn't appropriate, judging by the way he frowns, but it still feels a little invasive. I know Dad is dead, but it doesn't seem right to be snooping through his private affairs.

"Trust me, I wasn't happy about doing it, but I was determined to help you."

I nod. As much as I dislike this, I do understand it, and appreciate that he cares enough to help.

"What did the email say?"

"It was just confirming an appointment. But I went to visit the lawyer with whom he had the appointment, hoping there would be a will. There isn't one, before you ask. Your dad wasn't in the process of creating a will at all, as far as I can tell. Not that it's surprising. He was young— I'm certainly not thinking about a will right now."

"You don't have—" I start, and then stop myself. He does have an heir, technically, even though he doesn't know it yet. "So what was the appointment about?"

"He was going to divorce Frances."

My jaw drops in surprise. This isn't what I was expecting at all.

"What?!"

Lucas nods.

"Yes, I spoke to the lawyer and that's what he told me. Although Clark passed before he could go through with the filing."

I frown.

"That's awfully suspicious."

"I thought so, too. Which is why I went looking for evidence that Frances knew about the divorce beforehand."

"When did you have time for all of this snooping?" I ask incredulously. Lucas smiles sheepishly.

"Those days I had 'other work' to do. I'm sorry for lying to you. I didn't feel good about it. I still don't, but I didn't want to tell you anything before I knew for certain there was something to tell."

"So did she know?"

"Yes." Lucas nods. "I saw a message with a therapist confirming she knew about the divorce."

"So what does that mean?"

"Truthfully, it could mean absolutely nothing."

I make a face and he shrugs. "It's important to consider all the angles. Just because she knew about the divorce doesn't mean anything nefarious happened."

"She was in the accident," I state plainly.

"I'm not sure Frances would sabotage a vehicle knowing she would be in it herself. Do you remember anything about the day of the accident?"

I shake my head.

"It was pretty normal as far as I know. They were going out for dinner, and they got in the accident on the way back home. She didn't seem particularly hesitant to get in the car, and she wasn't acting out of character."

We're quiet for a moment before my face lights up.

"I'll ask for the accident report. They offered me a copy right after the accident but I wasn't ready to read about anything. Now, though." I nod resolutely. "Now, I'm ready and I need answers."

Chapter Thirty-Eight

Lucas

I wake up early Sunday morning to get dressed.

After we got home from brunch yesterday, Emma and I headed our separate ways— her to the police station to request an accident report and me to my room so I could check up on my other hotels and see how they're doing.

The Bilstone situation has been cleared up, thank goodness. The last thing I need is a bedbug case ruining my reputation and hurting other potential hotels. Royce flew back yesterday and is spending today with his family before heading back to Santa Fe tomorrow. We have a lot of training to do to prepare him to take on more responsibility for the hotel portfolio.

Ready to go? A text from Emma pings my phone. I smile and shoot back a thumbs up before heading downstairs.

Today, we are heading to the Community Kitchen to volunteer. She hasn't spoken of it much, but from what little she has, it was important to both her and Clark.

I'm honored that she trusts me enough to do this with her, and I'm excited. It will be a good way to connect; not only with Emma, but also with Clark's memory.

I still feel a lot of guilt about not speaking to Clark for so many years. In a way, it feels like I abandoned my best friend. I know it's not my fault that he died, but I can't help but feel I perhaps could have done something— made him realize he needed a divorce sooner, or showed him Frances' true character.

I shake my head. I can't think about that now. Emma needs the best version of me to show up for her today, not the sad and sullen one. I step outside and Emma is on the doorstep. She smiles at me.

"Thanks for coming with me. It really means more than you could ever know."

"Of course. I'm here for you; whatever you need."

She looks around before squeezing my hand gently. Then we hop in the car and head out.

***

The Community Kitchen building is more underwhelming than I imagined it would be; a simple square concrete building with a couple of windows at the front.

No one waits outside— Emma informed me that their lunch service starts at 1:00, and then another shift comes in to serve dinner.

I've never volunteered before; not because I haven't wanted to, it just honestly never crossed my mind.

I smile. Being with Emma makes me a better person. I have the drive and ambition to give more, and support the community in ways I never dreamed about before becoming involved with Emma.

"Come on, we have to go in the back," Emma says, smiling as she leads the way. We step through the back door and are immediately greeted by the hustle and bustle of a busy kitchen.

People in aprons and hairnets hurry around, an older man with graying hair holding a clipboard stands off to the side. He looks up as the door opens and his face lights up when he spots Emma.

"Well, if it isn't Emma Stone! It feels like it's been a while since I've seen you."

They hug quickly and when he pulls away, his expression softens. "I was very sorry to hear about the passing of your father. He was truly a kind man. We've missed both his and your presence here every Sunday since."

Emma clears her throat and looks down at her feet.

"I know. I'm so sorry I haven't been back— it just was too hard for a long time. But I feel ready now, and I don't want to abandon the folks we serve here."

The man nods with understanding.

"You don't need to apologize. I know how it feels to lose a parent— we're just happy to have you here whenever you can offer your support."

He turns to me and offers a warm smile. "Hello. My name is Ernest Humphries, but most people call me Ernie."

I hold out my hand and he shakes it firmly.

"My name is Lucas Bennett. I'm a friend of Emma's and was also a long time friend of Clark's as well."

"Any friend of Emma's is a friend of the Kitchen! And we can always use the extra help."

"Emma has spoken very highly of this place. I know it means a lot to her and meant a lot to Clark. I'm very happy to be here."

Emma beams up at me and Ernie nods. Then he looks at his clipboard and writes something down.

"Let's get you two set up." He grabs a couple of aprons off the hooks behind him and hands them to us.

"All right, Emma, you know the drill. I'll have you on vegetable prep. Lucas, first shift for beginners is dish duty. I know it's not the most fun job, but—"

"Hey, someone needs to wash dishes, and I'm more than happy to do them," I respond, holding my hands up.

"Love the enthusiasm! That will get you far here."

He grins. "After food is prepared, everyone pitches in on plating. We're expecting about seventy-five for lunch today, although we always prepare a little more just in case. We also have about thirty box lunches being prepared for meal delivery for the sick and elderly who aren't able to attend in person."

Emma ties the apron around her waist and I do the same. She leads me through the kitchen and throws on a hairnet before handing me mine. She tucks her ponytail in it easily and I chuckle at the sight of her in a hairnet as I put mine on.

She wrinkles her nose and laughs.

"Hey, you're no runway model in a hairnet, either, you know." I laugh with her.

"I happen to think you could model in a potato sack," I shoot back. She rolls her eyes and hip bumps me.

"Good luck with the dishes," she tosses over her shoulder before heading to a station piled high with celery, carrots and onions.

The dish station is toward the back of the kitchen, a large industrial sink with sprayers that is intimidating, yet oddly satisfying. A woman with salt-and-pepper hair and a pinched face is already there, scrubbing pots dutifully.

"You the new recruit?" she asks without looking up as I approach.

"Yes, ma'am, that's me. Lucas Bennett."

"Doris. Hope you don't mind the occasional spray. Water flies everywhere over here." She gestures to a stack of prep bowls and scoots over.

"Start with those. Rinse, soap and scrub, rinse again, then sanitize. Set them on the rack after sanitizing, and don't attempt to dry them with any napkins or towels. The sanitizer shouldn't be scrubbed off."

I nod and roll up my sleeves. Most people would be put off by Doris' curtness, but I appreciate it. There's something easy about dealing with someone who is straight to the point.

I get to work, and quickly fall into a soothing rhythm— the hot water, the squeak of dishes being cleaned and the occasional chatter of people around the kitchen allows me to dive into the work.

My eyes slide to Emma every so often. She's chopping vegetables with practiced ease, chatting joyfully with the woman next to her. She looks so relaxed and at peace, as if she's right where she belongs and never left.

After an hour of washing dishes, my hands are pruned but we've made significant progress through the dish pile next to the sink. Doris eyes me and then nods approvingly.

"Nice work, fancy man."

"What makes you think I'm fancy?" I ask, eyebrows raising in surprise.

"Those hands ain't seen much dishwater before today," she explains, gesturing. I look down at my hands, my fingers wrinkled and soggy. "Emma's dad was the same way when he started."

"You knew him well?"

"Honey, everyone knew Clark. I'm not sure that man had ever met a stranger in his life."

I laugh. This is true; Clark was so people-oriented. He never left a place without having made a new friend.

"He started coming with little Emma when she was just a teen. He said he wanted her to see that giving back felt better than taking ever could."

I nod.

"Clark was a good man. He was my best friend."

Doris gives me a sympathetic look.

"I'm sorry for your loss. We were devastated to hear about the accident."

I swallow hard and nod.

"Me, too."

"Break time!" Ernie calls out across the kitchen before I can respond. "Fifteen minutes, then we start plating. Good work, people."

"Go join your girl," Doris says, shooing me away. I don't bother arguing— she's perceptive and would probably see right through any denials.

I turn and Emma smiles at me, gesturing for me to follow her. We go through a door that has a few couches, and a table shoved in the corner covered with food. A couple of people are littered around the room eating or texting.

"How'd dishes go? Did Doris scare you off?"

I shake my head.

"Nope, we just worked together in comfortable silence."

Emma smiles. Ernie walks in the room with a plastic tray of food and sets it on the table.

"Wife made blueberry muffins everyone— feel free to grab one!" he calls out.

Emma heads to the table and grabs two muffins, handing one to me.

"Ernie's wife always makes homemade treats on Sundays."

"Is that why you come on Sundays?"

She swats at me and rolls her eyes. Then she sighs.

"I didn't realize how much I missed this place until today. I think I want to start coming back every Sunday."

"We can do that."

Emma looks up at me and smiles softly.

"Yes. We can."

I take a bite of my muffin and make an audible noise. This is the best blueberry muffin I've ever had.

"Wow, this is amazing. These would kill it at a bakery."

"Don't even think about asking for a recipe. Linda's stingy with them," Doris grunts as she comes through the door.

Despite the remark, she grabs a muffin and heads back out of the room.

We enjoy the rest of our muffins before Ernie comes back in the room and announces that break time is over. Rejuvenated by the food, we all head out and start plating.

***

"That was amazing. Thank you so much for coming with me," Emma says as we get into the car.

She's absolutely glowing, but she's not the only one. It was almost mesmerizing, watching Emma interact with every single person as she served food, their faces lighting up with the interaction.

Much like Clark, she has a way of touching people that I don't think she's aware of. There's a certain glow within Emma, and it seems to transfer to everyone with whom she interacts.

The kitchen isn't the first place I've noticed this; it's the same at the hotel. Everyone from the doorman to the maintenance crew seems happier and lighter even at the simplest "hello" uttered from her mouth.

Actually, it's more than that; I know because I feel it, too. An airy happiness that comes along following every interaction I have with her.

The only person I've ever seen exhibit any dislike for her is Frances. Perhaps because Frances knows she doesn't have the gift of inner light and that she'll never touch people in the same way.

"I really enjoyed myself, too. So, thank you for asking me to come with you." I squeeze her hand and then put the car in reverse. But she puts her hand on my arm and looks at me seriously.

"Lucas, there's something that I need to tell you. It's really important, but I don't want to do it here. Maybe we could go somewhere nice? Kind of private. Not a restaurant but... I don't know. A park?"

I nod, curiosity rising within me. What could it possibly be? Maybe something she discovered about Frances, or maybe the hotel. She gives me a small smile and I nod.

"Of course. I know just the place."

Chapter Thirty-Nine

Emma

I look up at Lucas as we walk hand in hand through the park and up toward a gazebo overlooking a lake. It truly is beautiful, all white wood decorated with tulle everywhere. The perfect place for a wedding.

Not that I'm thinking about that right now. Not with the news I'm about to break to Lucas.

I don't know what it is that made me feel like today is the right time to tell him about the pregnancy. It was such a ridiculously good morning. Being back at the Kitchen was better than I could have imagined.

I thought it would be hard and that I would be overwhelmed with memories of being there with Dad. Memories did come, but they were easy to handle.

The way my dad showed me the proper way to slice and dice vegetables, how he'd tighten my apron for me. It made me happy, though, to know that I was honoring his memory. I think he'd be happy to know that I was there today and plan on returning often.

I was so happy when Lucas told me we could keep coming back. I think that's why I decided that I want to tell him about the baby today.

But now that we're here, I feel overwhelmed with the idea. What if he doesn't want the baby? What if this changes everything between us?

We arrive at the gazebo and sit down. Lucas eyes me curiously and then squeezes my hand.

"Penny for your thoughts?" His voice is soft against the afternoon breeze.

I manage a smile, but it doesn't reach my eyes.

"Just taking in the view," I say, taking time to look out.

The lake stretches out before us, sunlight dancing across the surface like a million glittering diamonds. Ducks paddle lazily by the shore, seemingly unaware of their human company.

"This is beautiful," Lucas says, putting his arm around me and pulling me in close. He closes his eyes peacefully.

I nod, my heart racing so fast that I can feel the blood pumping in every part of my body. The words feel stuck in my throat, heavy and life changing. I take a deep breath to steady myself.

"Lucas, I..." My voice catches and I clear my throat. "There's something I need to tell you."

"So you said earlier... What's up?"

He turns to look at me, his expression curious but not filled with concern. The kind eyes that helped me fall for him in the first place are now making this so much harder. Worry creeps into his voice as he studies me. "Is everything okay?"

"I think so. Well, I hope so." I take a deep breath. "Do you remember the doctor's appointment I went to a few weeks ago?"

"When you were sick?" His brows knit together. I nod. "Oh, God. Are you okay? You're not seriously ill, are you?"

I chuckle nervously and shake my head.

"No. No, I'm just—" A tear rolls down my cheek and I wipe it away. "I'm pregnant, Lucas."

The words hang between us, dry and monumental in a way that sucks all the air from the world around us. Lucas doesn't move, his expression frozen on his face. My heart pounds even harder as the seconds stretch into hours.

"You're...pregnant?" he asks cautiously as if testing the words.

I nod, unable to find my voice. It's better that I don't say anything— I'd probably tremble through every word and burst into tears.

I clasp my hands in my lap as Lucas runs a hand through his hair. He stands up suddenly and walks to the railing of the gazebo. My stomach drops— this is it.

He's going to be furious, tell me he's not ready or that this isn't what he signed up for.

Because of course it's not. Neither of us expected this to happen.

I brace myself for the worst as Lucas turns around, but his expression is one I didn't expect.

He's smiling. No, not just smiling. Beaming from ear to ear, as if he's just heard the best news of his life.

"We're having a baby?" His voice cracks, imbued with emotion. I nod and he chuckles.

"Yes, we're having a baby," I respond, allowing a small smile to creep on my face. This is more than I could have hoped for.

Lucas crosses the gazebo and takes my hands in his. He pulls me up and spins me around. I can't help but let out a loud laugh.

"We're having a baby!" he shouts excitedly. The ducks quack and start flapping their wings, flying away from the sudden noise.

"Shh! You're scaring the ducks," I chastise.

Happy tears blur my vision, turning the world into a kaleidoscope of colors around me. Lucas notices my tears and sets me down gently.

"Oh, gosh, I'm sorry. Should I not have done that? Are you feeling okay? Nausea? Do you need to sit?"

I shake my head.

"No, I'm fine. It's still early days." I look at him sheepishly. "I've just been worried sick about telling you."

"Why on earth would you be worried?"

"We haven't known each other that long. I didn't even know if you wanted kids or if you would want them now..."

"Emma." Lucas tucks a strand of hair behind my ear and kisses my forehead. "I want everything with you. Sure, this is happening sooner than I might have expected. It's a surprise for sure. But you make me happy, and I am more than happy to call you the mother of my child."

I can't help myself. I start bawling, little gasps of laughter erupting from me. All my emotions in this moment are overwhelming, yet I feel entirely elated. Lucas laughs and hugs me.

"Come on, let's get you home."

***

I blink and rub the sleep from my eyes as I sit up in bed. I look over to see Lucas sleeping next to me. I grab my phone and look at the time: 8:00. We must have fallen asleep cuddling. I shake him awake and he smiles at me.

"Enjoy your nap?" he asks.

"Very much so." I kiss him and he chuckles, then leans in for another one.

"I sleep so much better when I'm next to you."

"I wish we could sleep together all the time."

"We will be able to soon."

"Yeah?" I ask, my brows shooting up. Lucas nods.

"'Of course. We can't have you staying here being stressed all the time by your 'wicked stepmother'." He grins. "Besides, I want you all to myself."

I wrap my arms around his neck and pull him in close.

"You have me all to yourself."

Lucas' eyes darken with desire, and he pulls me flush against him. The warmth of his body sends a thrill down my spine, filling me with want. My fingers thread through his hair as our lips meet in a soft kiss. Then the kiss grows urgent as his fingers grip my sides.

His hands slide under my shirt, fingertips skimming along my ribs as they trace shapes on my skin. His touch causes me to shiver, sending little pulses of electricity through every part of my body.

I suck in a breath when Lucas' fingers reach the soft skin of my breasts, cupping them gently and giving a squeeze.

"Is that okay?" he asks.

"They're sensitive," I murmur as he brushes a thumb over my nipple, sending a jolt through my body. "But it feels amazing."

Lucas pushes up my shirt, exposing my breasts to the cool air in the room.

He places his lips on one and I can't help but moan, arching closer to him. The sensation is overwhelming, his warm mouth sending waves of pleasure through me. His tongue circles my nipple and I grip his hair harder.

"You're so beautiful, Emma," he whispers, his breath hot against my skin. Goosebumps pop up all over my skin.

I find the hem of his shirt and pull it over his head, tossing it away before running my hands over his sculpted body. His skin is warm under my touch, and when I move my hands up, feeling the steady thump of his heart beneath my palm. Lucas' lips find mine, the kisses wet and slightly sloppy.

"I want you. Right now," I whisper against his lips. I slide into his lap, straddling him as I fumble with the button on his jeans. Lucas helps me, his fingers covering mine. Our fingers tangle in clumsy urgency and Lucas laughs.

"Let me," he offers, pushing my hands aside gently. He lifts me and shimmies out of his jeans, kicking them to the floor.

His hardness presses against me through his briefs, and I rock against him. He groans, his head falling back against the headboard.

Lucas' hands find their way to my shorts, playing with the elastic before pushing them down. I shift, helping him get them off. He rolls us over so I'm lying on my back. The sight of him above me ignites warmth between my legs.

His hand snakes its way down my body, brushing lightly over my breasts and stomach until it finds the spot between my thighs. He brushes his fingers over my underwear and I make a soft noise.

"You're already soaked," he says, chuckling.

"Ugh, just get them off," I moan, pushing my body against his hand. He obliges, sliding them down slowly. It's almost torturous how long it takes, but when his fingers find my slickness, all is right with the world.

Lucas slides a finger up my wetness before finding its place at my clit, making slow circles that draw moans from me. I reach in his briefs, gripping him in my hand and brushing a thumb over the tip.

The sound he makes encourages me, and I do it again, adding more pressure. Lucas groans, moving his fingers down to dip one in me.

I gasp at the sensation as he moves his fingers in and out, picking up speed as he goes. I move my hand up and down his hardness, trying to keep up but I fall behind as he shifts and puts his thumb back on my clit, working me both in and out.

"Oh, God," I call as the pleasure builds inside me. I stop moving as it spills over, his hands not stopping until I've ridden them through my orgasm. I lick my lips as I look up at him, my body throbbing for more. I want every inch of him inside me. I push his briefs down, and his length springs out.

When Lucas removes his fingers, I almost feel empty until he positions himself at my entrance. He pushes in, slow and careful. I arch beneath him, my body welcoming him as we find our rhythm.

"You feel so amazing," he whispers. He thrusts slowly, soaking in the feeling of my body joined with his. I wrap my legs around his waist, pulling him deeper inside me.

"Don't hold back."

Lucas' eyes shift, hunger for more replacing his precise control. His pace quickens, and I match him, our bodies moving together as they have many times before.

The headboard thumps softly against the wall as we move with more urgency than we ever have before.

Lucas' hands are all over me— in my hair, cupping my breasts, gripping my hips and pulling me into every hard thrust. Each movement ignites more sparks, building the tension coiling within me.

"Lucas," I gasp, feeling myself approaching the edge. "I'm close."

He slips his hands between us, his fingers finding the exact spot on my body where they need to be. He makes fast circles, and the sensations become overwhelming. I grip his shoulders, my nails digging into the flesh.

The tension breaks like a wave crashing against the rocks and I come undone around him.

I cry out, my body shuddering beneath him as pleasure radiates every inch of my body. Lucas follows seconds later, his rhythm faltering as he buries his face in my neck, a groan vibrating my skin. I feel warmth as he spills into me, his orgasm touching both of us.

Our hearts beat together as we stay connected, breathing heavily. He lifts up and makes eye contact, caressing my chin softly as he kisses me.

"I love you, Emma."

"I love you, too."

<u>Chapter Forty</u>

Lucas

"The gala was a huge success. I already have multiple offers for the hotel. What a brilliant idea that was," Frances says as she strides into the conference room Tuesday morning.

She was suspiciously absent yesterday, and as much as I want an answer for where she's been, I doubt she'd tell me, and Jackie seemed to not have a clue either.

It occurred to me that Jackie might be playing us, but only for a split second. Truthfully, she looked completely lost without Frances around, and I doubt she's that good of an actress.

"The Community Kitchen benefited heavily, too, and they were extremely grateful."

Frances waves her hand.

"Yes, the Kitchen. But more importantly, people were able to see the value of this place. Some potential buyers had expressed initial concern that everything would have to be twenties themed all the time, but I assured them that the speakeasy can easily be transformed to fit any theme." Frances opens a folder and pulls out a paper.

"The highest bid we have so far comes from Mr. Marshall Bridgers. He has offered $20 million dollars."

I can practically see the dollar signs in her eyes. I clear my throat and smile.

"I've had my attorneys prepare my offer and I'd like to submit it at this time."

Frances blinks.

"Oh, you were serious about that?"

"Of course I was. This hotel is important to me."

She narrows her eyes, then gives a smile that doesn't meet her eyes.

"It's just interesting to me that you would come here as a 'consultant' to me, encouraging me to return the hotel to its original state, at my own expense, just to put in an offer at the last minute."

I frown at her insinuation.

"That's not what happened, Frances, and you know it. I have never hidden from you my interest in acquiring this property. If necessary, I'll add in the cost of the recent restorations, if that's what it will take." I take a breath. "I came here because Clark's death was shocking news to me, as I'm sure it was to everyone. He was my best friend, and meant a lot to me. It was important for me to check on you, Jackie and Emma. The consulting work I did with you was truly to assist you in getting the best value. If I truly wanted to screw you over, I would have bought it from you when I first got here, before any of the renovations were done, and when the value was much less than it is today."

She taps her nails on the table, apparently reassessing me. The silence is heavy, the air is tense with her suspicions. Jackie shifts uncomfortably, and then stands up, mumbling an excuse as she leaves me and Frances alone in the conference room.

"I'm offering your $25 million. That's more than enough to cover the costs of the restoration, and still gets you the best price on the table today. My attorney can send in the paperwork if you are agreeable."

Her eyebrows nearly shoot off her face in surprise, and for the first time, she seems genuinely speechless. I've never seen her caught completely off-guard, and I can't deny the satisfaction I feel. I have to hide it, though.

"Why?" She asks, her tone a mix of venom and flabbergasted. "Why do you want this place so badly?"

I lean back and fold my arms over my chest, considering her question carefully. The answer is complicated. It's tied up in memories of my best friend, my love for Emma and our coming child, and my own selfish desire to preserve something truly beautiful rather than see it turn into some soulless asset of an average hotel chain.

"Because some things are worth preserving. This hotel is worth preserving." I sit forward, clasping my hands together on the table in front of me.

"Clark saw the potential in this place when it was just a dilapidated old saloon. He transformed it into something truly incredible, a place that brings people together, a hopeful legacy for Emma. I understand why you don't see it the same way. You don't have the same connection to The Signature. You didn't pick out the furniture, paint the walls, install the floors. I don't blame you for wanting to sell off the responsibility of owning and managing a hotel; it's a lot of work. But this is what I do for a living. I love this business and I love this place, and it's exactly the kind of hotel that I prefer to work with. You may be suspicious of my reasons, and that's fine. But when we get down to brass tacks, my wanting to buy this place makes complete sense."

Frances studies me. Her expression is unreadable, the shock having worn off and now replaced with an exquisitely practiced poker face.

"You're serious, aren't you?" she finally asks.

"Dead serious." I reach for my briefcase. "I'll make a formal offer, and send you the official paperwork. We can have our lawyers meet and finalize the sale whenever you're ready. Here is his card."

I slide the small card across the table.

She doesn't reach for it immediately, which I hate to admit surprises me. For someone who's been so eager to sell, she seems much too reluctant now that an extraordinary offer is right in front of her. Maybe I miscalculated how much her love for the money outweighs her disdain for me.

"Does Emma know you're trying to buy the hotel?" she asks. My heart picks up at the mention of her name, but it's a valid question. Frances doesn't know that we're together. All she knows is that we're close and have been working together on the hotel.

"No," I lie. "This is between us for now. Please don't tell her, either. I would prefer to break the news when the paperwork is finalized."

Frances picks up the business card and studies it before sliding it in her folder.

"If the sale finalizes. I will take your offer into consideration. Thank you." Frances fluffs her hair and then stands. "If you'll excuse me. I have something important to attend to."

She clicks out of the room, leaving me sitting by myself at the conference table.

I'm offering her $25 million dollars, well over market, and she has to think about it? I'm starting to wonder if I underestimated her vindictiveness.

***

"Thanks for letting me know, Royce. I'll see you Thursday." I hang up the phone.

"Everything okay?" Emma asks, eyeing me curiously.

"His dad is having a minor surgical procedure, so he's going to hang out and take care of him after. I guess his mom and sister are on some sort of vacation."

"He seems sweet," she smiles.

"He's a good kid."

"So, I was able to get the report from Dad and Frances' car accident," Emma starts, immediately peaking my interest.

"What does it say?"

"Nothing that helps, honestly." She reaches into her bag and hands me a file of papers. I look through them, going over the details of the accident.

No inclement weather conditions that would cause the accident. The vehicle rolled, but in the final analysis it basically boils down to one thing: Clark lost control of the vehicle.

"This just doesn't make sense," I mutter. I'm grasping at straws, though.

"Maybe we're overthinking this," Emma says, sighing. "What if it really was just an accident? I struggle to think that Dad just lost control of the car, but..."

"Come on. You don't believe that anymore than I do."

"There's no evidence of tampering, no drugs or alcohol in his system. He wasn't speeding or driving recklessly. You're right; it doesn't make sense. We're at a dead end."

She looks away. "Maybe our dislike of Frances is coloring our view of things. I can't believe she would willingly get into a car that she had tampered with."

I flip through the photos of the accident. My stomach clenches tighter with each image; the mangled guard rail, crumpled hood and shattered glass covering the road.

"Was Frances hurt in the accident?" I ask. Emma nods.

"Yeah. I mean, not seriously. Not like Dad, obviously. But she had some nasty bruises and cuts all over her face. She even refused to leave the house for a while until they were healed enough to be covered well by makeup."

I pull out a photo and study the road beyond the scene of the car.

"This road is straight." I chew my cheek as I think things through. "What road is this?"

"Bell's Hollow. They were on their way home from dinner."

"It's still light outside- that's an early dinner, isn't it."

"It was 6:00 in the middle of the summer in New Mexico. That's not exactly dark hours," Emma points out.

I sigh.

"I'm sorry, I'm probably just causing you more stress than you need right now."

I wrap my arms around her and pull her close, kissing her forehead.

"It's okay. I know we're both hoping that there are more answers here somewhere, but I just don't think there are.

Sometimes things are just accidents, and shit happens." Emma looks up at me, her brown eyes wide and sad.

"That's true," I say. Then I smooth her hair and change the subject. "How are you feeling? Any new symptoms?"

Emma sits down and laughs.

"Boobs are ridiculously sore. No morning sickness yet, lucky for me. It would probably tip people off if I were suddenly throwing up all the time. I do feel more tired than usual, but I don't know if that counts." She smiles shyly. "My first ultrasound is next Wednesday. Do you want to come with me?"

My heart swells, and I sit on the bed next to her, putting the accident report down behind me.

"Are you kidding?" I take her hand in mine and give it a gentle squeeze. "I wouldn't miss it for the world."

Emma's smile brightens the entire world, and something shifts inside me. A feeling of certainty that I've never felt before. More than anything, I want this life with Emma.

"Really?" she asks, her voice soft and hopeful.

"Really." I lift her hand to my lips and kiss them. "I want to be there for everything. First heartbeat, first kick, first hiccups. I don't intend to miss a single thing.

Emma leans against me and rests her head on my shoulder.

"I'm scared, you know. What if I'm terrible at this?"

"Terrible at what?"

"Being a mom." She laughs nervously. "I keep having nightmares that I'll turn out just like Frances."

I look at her, ensuring she sees the conviction in my eyes.

"Hey, you're nothing like Frances, and every bit like your mom. She was a wonderful person, and a great mother, and you will be, too."

"How can you be so sure?"

"Because I know you, Emma. I see how you are with everyone, how much you care about the people around you. You're so kind, even to Jackie, who most people wouldn't give even an ounce of forgiveness. All the hotel employees see it, the people at the Kitchen see it, and I see it, too."

I place my hand on her stomach, still the same as it always was, yet now completely different.

"I can see how much you already care about our baby more than anything."

Emma covers her hand with mine, her eyes glistening with tears.

"We're really doing this, aren't we?"

"We are, and we're doing it together. As long as we have each other, we will do our best to make sure our baby is happy, healthy and safe."

I kiss her soft and slow. She smiles and squeezes my hand.

Then her eyes drift to the accident report behind us on the bed. I grab it and shove it in my briefcase.

"We can put that away for now. You need more rest than usual, and I have some hotel work to do."

She yawns, as if punctuating my statement. I laugh and pull the covers back, tucking her in so she's comfortable and warm.

"I am really tired. Today just felt so long."

"I know. Get some rest, and I'll see you in the morning, okay?" I kiss her on the forehead and she nods.

I shut her door behind me and then head up to the main house, acutely aware of the accident report burning a hole in my briefcase. I said we'd take a break, but I can't stop thinking about it.

How does someone lose control on a straight road when they weren't speeding, drinking, and nothing was wrong with the car?

Chapter Forty-One

Emma

"All right, I'm just going to spread this gel on your belly; it will feel a little cold," the ultrasound tech says.

I still jump when the cold gel touches my skin. Lucas squeezes my hand instantly, and I can't help but smile up at him.

The tech moves the wand over my belly, watching the screen with practiced concentration. I try not to fidget, but my heart is racing like a marathon as the foreign object glides across my skin. Lucas' thumb traces soothing circles on the back of my hand as we both stare at the monitor. I don't even know what I'm looking at. Or for.

"Let's see..." The tech adjusts something and suddenly the room fills with a rapid whooshing sound. "There's the heartbeat."

"It's so fast," I murmur, increasing my grip on Lucas' hand.

"That's normal," the tech says quickly. "There's your baby."

She turns the screen, and I study the black and white image. I was expecting something clear and easy, but instead it's just blurry. I can't see anything distinct.

"Wow," Lucas says, his face lighting up with excitement.

"Hmm." The tech leans in, searching curiously. Her brow furrows as she moves the wand, and then turns to type a few things. Then the wand is back.

"Is everything okay?" I ask, the panic rising quickly within me.

"Yes, everything is fine. I just need to get a better look at something."

Lucas and I exchange worried glances as she continues her exam, taking measurements and typing notes.

"Well, I have some interesting news for the two of you," the tech says finally, giving us a broad smile.

"What is it?" My heart skips a beat as the question leaves my mouth.

"Do you see this? This is your baby." She asks, pointing to the screen, indicating a small blob. Then she moves the wand slightly, and a second blob appears.

"And this... is also your baby." Then she adjusts once more; one more blob. "This? This is your third baby."

My jaw drops to the floor, the room filled with nothing but the sound of the ultrasound machine.

"Did you... did you say third baby?" Lucas asks, awe dripping from his voice.

"That's right." She smiles. "Congratulations. You're having triplets!"

I stare at the screen, unsure how to process the three small shapes showing in my womb. Three babies. Three.

"Are you sure? Maybe one's like... an echo or something?"

The tech chuckles and shakes her head.

"Nope, not an echo. Three separate heartbeats." The tech puts away the equipment and cleans the wand, then stands up. "I'll give you two a moment. The doctor should be in shortly."

When she leaves, Lucas and I stare at each other in silence.

"Triplets," I finally whisper.

"Three car seats," Lucas responds, holding up three fingers as if to punctuate the thought.

"Three cribs." I throw up my hands.

"Three college tuitions," Lucas finishes.

Our eyes meet, and we both burst into a laughter that almost borders on hysterical. There are tears in my eyes by the time the laughs die down. Lucas leans down and kisses me, rubbing a hand on my still gel covered belly and I begin to clean myself up a bit.

"Man, I guess when we do something, we really go all out," he murmurs against my lips.

"Overachievers," I agree, giggling through my tears. "We're going to need a big house."

"I'm not worried. We definitely have this covered."

There's a knock on the door, and we pull apart as the doctor walks in.

***

"I can't believe I have to go to an appointment every two weeks," I say, reading back over the paperwork.

"Every week once you're twenty-four weeks along." Lucas glances at me and then puts his eyes back to the road as we pull up to the hotel. "That's a lot of appointments."

"We're going to have to tell people. They're going to be suspicious if I start going for doctor's appointments every week."

"Your medical health is no one's business but yours."

"Sure, theoretically. In a perfect world that would be amazing. Unfortunately, I work for Frances."

"Maybe not for long," Lucas says, putting the car in park. "I put in an offer on the hotel."

"For how much?"

"$25 million."

My jaw drops and I turn to him.

"Oh, my God. Is the hotel worth that much?"

"You can't put a price on sentimentality." Lucas looks away for a second. "Frances hasn't officially accepted, though. I had expected an answer from her rather quickly."

"You need to talk to her again."

"I fully plan on it, I promise."

"During today's meeting," I insist. It's supposed to be the regular monthly meeting; going over numbers, looking at employee performances.

"Good idea," Lucas says, nodding. "I need to run back to the house to get some paperwork. I'll be back."

I get out of the car and glide into the hotel. Frances is nowhere to be found, but Lily is at the front desk, typing away at the computer. She looks up, and her face lights up when she sees me.

"Emma!"

"Lily!" I say. She hugs me and I can't help but laugh. "You act like you didn't just see me yesterday."

"It's the first time I've seen you by yourself. You're always with Lucas or Frances." Lily rolls her eyes but she smiles good-naturedly. She follows me into the office and then plops down in the chair across from me.

I gasp.

"Lily," I coo, smiling at her. Her brows knit together.

"What?"

"You're sitting in the chair instead of on the desk." I place my hand over my heart theatrically. "You're growing up."

Lily laughs and swats at me playfully.

"So, how are you?" she asks sincerely.

I take in a deep breath and shrug.

"I don't know. I'm okay, I guess I'm just really worried about the fate of the hotel. With bids now rolling in, the hotel can potentially be sold and I could be out of a job."

Worry mists Lily's eyes.

"I mean, what does that mean for all of us? The employees?"

I sigh and rest my chin on my hands.

"I don't know. It's not like I can talk Frances into selling to Lucas, who has made an offer, in case you were unaware. If I encouraged her to sell to him, that would only make her less inclined to do so. So we're just stuck in limbo while we wait for her decision."

I don't know much about buying and selling hotels, I admit that. But I know that if Frances sells the hotel to anyone but Lucas, it could mean great upheaval for the hotel and its staff. There are bound to be a lot of changes: new managers, new policies, and even potential layoffs and replacement of personnel.

"Lucas would keep everyone, right? He wouldn't fire anybody?" Lily asks. I can hear the uncertainty in her voice. I reach across the table and place my hand on hers.

"Of course. Lucas loves this place; he sees the value in both the hotel and the staff. He doesn't want to change a thing at this point."

"Thank goodness," she says, relief flooding her face. "Do you want to get something to eat after work? It would be so nice to just hang out and spend some time together."

Before I can respond, my phone buzzes in my purse. I reach in to grab it, but in my haste, I knock the whole thing over. The contents spill over the desk and onto the floor- lip balm, wallet, keys, and...

Oh, no.

The ultrasound pictures slides right next to Lily's feet. She doesn't realize what it is until she bends down and picks it up. Time seems to freeze as she stares at the black and white image, her mouthing forming a perfect 'o'.

"Emma," she whispers, eyes darting between the picture and my face. "Is this... are you?"

All the moisture is immediately sucked from my mouth and my heart hammers against my ribs. This isn't how I wanted anyone to find out. I'm not even ready to tell people, and I'm doubly sure Lucas isn't ready to tell people. I can't find the words to answer her, so instead I simply nod.

Lily smiles, her face a mixture of shock and excitement. She hands me back the ultrasound and I tuck it in the pocket of my purse before replacing everything else.

"How far along are you?" she asks, lowering her voice as if someone could overhear us.

"Just over six weeks," I respond weakly. Lily chuckles and then shakes her head.

"I don't know why I asked, I don't know anything about pregnancy." She throws her hands up and I can't help but laugh. "Are you excited?"

"Actually, I am. And I'm a little nervous."

"Does Lucas know?"

"Yeah, he went with me to the ultrasound appointment." I sigh. "We're having triplets."

"Oh, my God." Lily's eyes widen. "That is amazing. And also scary. I understand why you're nervous. How did Lucas take the news?"

"He's excited." I pick at my nails and then look up at her seriously. "Please don't tell anyone. You and Lucas are the only ones who know. Frances can't find out yet."

Lily scoffs and rolls her eyes.

"Um, obviously! I would never tell her anything about your private life. You're my friend and she's a total witch."

"Thanks, Lily."

My phone buzzes again. The meeting starts in ten minutes. I stand up, and Lily hugs me.

"Everything is going to be wonderful, I just know it."

I follow her out of the office and swallow. I sure hope she's right.

***

"Numbers are looking better since the gala; we've actually had a 30% increase in reservations this week compared to the same time frame last year, which really helps illustrate the value of the hotel."

Frances pats her hair and gives us a smug look.

"Yes, the gala was a roaring success. I'm very satisfied with the way it turned out."

"The media coverage of the gala was amazing, too," Royce chimes in. He blushes. "I, uh, know I'm not technically an employee here, but I wanted to see what kind of buzz the gala produced in social media, so I kept track of it online while I was gone. The reporter wrote a glowing review, and social media was abuzz with how wonderful the singer was."

"Felicia Wilkes," I state. Frances, Royce and Lucas all look at me. "That's the singer."

"She was wonderful," Lucas agrees.

I slide some papers over to Frances.

"The plumbing issues are now resolved, customers are leaving great reviews, although there have been a few complaints that the cocktails we serve aren't strong enough."

Frances rolls her eyes and shakes her head.

"Well, let's make sure the bartenders are using the correct ratios in cocktails, but I personally think they just want more alcohol for less money. I don't get it; I feel like our cocktails are reasonably priced. Anything else?"

We all look at each other, and then I shake my head. Frances gives us a tight smile and then clears her throat.

"With that business out of the way, I have some important news to share. As you three know, I've been looking to sell the hotel..."

I resist the urge to roll my eyes as she drones on. Why does she have to introduce her decision as a speech, with a ridiculous amount of fanfare? She acts as if we haven't all been here since the very beginning.

"With that being said, I've decided to sell the hotel to the Forest Elite Group."

All three of our jaws drop in shock.

"Forest Elite?" Lucas' jaw drops.

"Are you serious?" I ask.

I know a little about the Forest Elite Group; they own a large portfolio of boutique hotels around the country, but they aren't necessarily the best when it comes to management. Especially when it comes to the way they treat their employees; they have a less than stellar reputation.

"Yes, Forest Elite." Frances shoots Lucas a smug smile. "I thought about what you said when you told me sentimentality was important. Marshall Bridger's offer was generous, but at the end of the day, I truly couldn't consider someone I knew would ruin all my late husband's hard work. Forest Elite offered $5 million less, but I think they will be better stewards for the future of The Signature."

"But that means you lost $15 million by not selling to Lucas!" I cry out, unable to keep my surprise to myself.

She feigns a face of sympathy.

"I did seriously consider your offer, Lucas, but I thought it would be hard for you to keep an eye on the hotel all the way from Edgewood. Forest Elite Group will be hiring a local representative for the company to take care of day-to-day operations within the hotel."

She looks down at her watch. "Thank you all for attending. I have a very important meeting to get to."

She stands up, but I step in front of the door.

"You're not going to sign the offering papers are you?"

Frances rolls her eyes.

"No, Emma, that will happen next week. This is for something else." She shoos me to the side. "Please move along."

I don't budge.

"What's it for?"

Frances' friendly act drops, and she stares at me coldly, lowering her voice.

"Emma, I don't know what you think you're doing acting like this, but I am entitled to my privacy and I will make whatever decisions about the sale that I see fit. If you don't get out of my way, you will be finding yourself a new place to live."

We stare off for a moment, but I have to relent. I can't go toe to toe with her. Not when I have the babies to think about.

Frances passes me briskly. I turn around, Royce and Lucas both wearing grim expressions.

"That was surprising," Royce says softly. Lucas stares at me and then blinks.

"Royce, why don't you head back to Edgewood?" Lucas asks. Royce seems like he wants to protest, but simply nods and head out the door.

Then Lucas turns to me. "I think tonight is the night we need to confront Frances."

Chapter Forty-Two

Lucas

I pace around the living room as Emma and I wait for Frances to get home.

I hate to admit it, but I'm more than a little nervous to confront her about the accident. There are many ways it could go, and few will lead to good outcomes for me and Emma.

At least with regard to The Signature on Main.

Emma and I won't struggle to live a good life and raise our kids.

I am quite wealthy and have more than enough money to support us for at least a few lifetimes.

Losing the hotel, though, is unthinkable, and something that I can't bear to think about, since it's supposed to be Emma's legacy and I want so badly to preserve it for her—and now, for our children.

This entire time, I completely miscalculated Frances' interest in the profit from the sale. I feel like I failed Emma, losing her the hotel. I assured her that I would fix everything and instead I've let her down.

"Can you stop pacing? You're creating a draft," Emma says, giving me a teasing smile. She's trying her best to keep up a good face about this, but I can tell she's disappointed.

"Sorry," I say, and settle beside her on the couch. "I have to be honest with you. I'm worried about how this will go."

"You are?" she asks, looking up at me earnestly. I sigh and tuck a strand of hair behind her ear.

"Yeah, I just can't believe I misjudged her so much. I thought for sure she would go for the money over everything else. I didn't realize how she would much prefer to screw me over, and perhaps you as well. I'm really sorry, Emma."

She smiles and lays her head on my shoulder.

"It's okay. I should have known that would be the case. I've spent a lot more time around Frances than you have. It was initially shocking, but the more that I think about it, it isn't all that surprising that she'd do this. I mean, I thought she liked you since she was trying so hard to set you up with Jackie."

"Maybe she's punishing me for rejecting Jackie. Especially since it happened so publicly."

Before Emma can respond, keys jingle in the door. I shoot up from the couch, clasping my hands behind my back. The door swings open and Frances walks in, looking just the same as she did hours earlier. Does she never get tired?

"Frances," I say. Frances startles, looking at me with wide eyes and throwing a hand over her heart.

"Goodness, Lucas, don't you have any thought about frightening a woman when she walks into her own home?"

She shakes her head and lets the door close behind her. Then she looks past me. "Oh, hello, Emma."

"Frances," Emma says, standing. "We need to talk."

"Look, I know the news of the sale was upsetting, but I truly believe I am making..."

"Not about the hotel. About Dad," Emma says.

Frances eyes us suspiciously and swallows. She's definitely hiding something. She nods and joins us in the living room, but she doesn't sit.

"What questions can I answer for you about your father?" Frances asks, sounding more bored than worried. She has no idea what this discussion is going to be about.

I gesture to Emma before stepping forward.

"Frances, I recently met with a lawyer named Cordell Kennedy. Does that name ring a bell to you?" I study her for a hint of recognition, but she just shrugs and rolls her eyes, staring off to the other side of the living room.

"No? Should it?"

"I was simply curious, since he's the divorce lawyer Clark was speaking to."

Frances' head snaps to me, her eyes widening.

"I'm sorry?"

"Cordell Kennedy. I discovered Clark had made an appointment with him shortly before his death." I don't mention how I came by this information. It seems better to not admit that I went snooping around her home.

"So I decided to go see him myself."

"But why?" Frances sounds incredulous.

"I thought perhaps Clark was working on a will. Kennedy does estate work as well as family law. When I went to see him, the idea that Clark was looking for a divorce was pretty baffling to me."

"Of course it was! Clark wanting to divorce is preposterous."

"If it's so preposterous, why aren't you surprised?" Emma asks, her voice soft but firm.

"Excuse me?"

"You aren't the least bit surprised by the news that Dad wanted to divorce you. The only thing that seemed to shock you is the fact that Lucas and I know."

"Well," Frances sniffs, sitting up straight.

She's blinking too much, the way people do when they know they've been caught in a lie and they're trying to think of excuses to get out of it.

"It did catch me off guard that you and Lucas seem to be sharing so much information with each other."

I roll my eyes.

"Don't deflect. You knew about the divorce beforehand," I say.

"Fine, I did. So what?"

Emma balks.

"So you know the hotel isn't rightfully yours. This house isn't yours, at least not entirely. You've been continuously threatening to kick me out of a house that you don't even have a moral right to."

Emma's eyes are lit up with fire. I've never seen her this angry. "What the hell is wrong with you?"

Frances stands up indignantly.

"This is my house. Your father may have been thinking about divorce, but when he died he was still my husband. So whatever you think you're owed, you are wrong."

"That's ridiculous! You..." Emma starts, but I cut her off.

"Frances, what really happened the night of the accident?"

Both of their heads whip to me. Emma looks more annoyed that I cut her off than anything, but Frances' eyes are wide with worry.

"What?" Frances asks, her voice small.

"I've seen the accident report, and something about it doesn't sit right with me. Clark losing control of the vehicle doesn't make any sense. He wasn't a distracted driver, the road conditions weren't bad, there was nothing wrong with the car and he hadn't been drinking. So what happened?"

"That's just not even relevant to this—"

"Don't you ever get sick of being a snake about everything?" Emma shouts, her temper broiling over.

"Everything you do is so disgustingly calculated. You were awful before Dad died, but you've been absolutely unbearable since he's been gone. I don't even understand why he was with you, since you clearly didn't love him!"

"Of course I loved him!" Frances insists. "I loved him so much. The accident was just that: an accident."

"Oh, please!" Emma throws her hands up.

"But it was my fault!" Frances drops her face in her hands, and her shoulders start to shake.

Emma looks at me, her eyes confused. I just shrug and kneel across from Frances. Emma keeps her distance, though.

"How was it your fault, Frances?" I ask.

"God," Frances looks up, and it's the first time I've seen her look imperfect, with mascara running down her face and a large frown.

"It was so stupid. We went out to dinner like we usually did. It was a lovely time, we talked just like we always did. Nothing seemed out of the ordinary. On the way home, he looked at me and told me he wanted a divorce."

Emma and I are both quiet.

"So, then we got into an argument. I kept insisting he didn't know what he was talking about and he kept telling me he had put a lot of thought into it. I got so angry that I grabbed the wheel. I wasn't thinking, I just wanted to stop the car so we could have a real conversation about it. But Clark pulled it back his way, and we spun out of control. When we hit the guard rail, we started rolling and he couldn't stop it."

Frances sniffs and wipes her eyes. "I still don't even know why he wanted a divorce. I never found out."

I don't even know what to say. It's not the answer I expected, but I get the feeling that it's the truth.

"I believe you," Emma says. Her face is stony and impossible for me to read. "But it doesn't excuse your behavior. You know Dad would have wanted me to have the hotel."

Frances runs a hand through her hair and sighs.

"God, Emma, sometimes it's just impossible for you to see past yourself, isn't it?"

She rolls her eyes. "It wasn't about you. I've been so angry with your father. I loved him, but that news hurt. Compounded with how guilty I've been feeling... I know it's not fair that I've been taking those feelings out on you, but you remind me so much of him that it's been difficult for me not to."

"You've never been nice to me," Emma scoffs. Frances laughs.

"Yeah, well, you've always been an insufferable brat. You did everything you could to make life difficult from the day your dad married me."

Frances sighs and then looks up at us with pleading eyes. "Please, don't tell Jackie. I love her so much, and I just know that she loved Clark like he was her own father. She'd be devastated. She would hate me."

I swallow and my eyes slide to Emma. This is no longer my fight to have. She's quiet for what feels like a long time before she speaks.

"I won't say anything, but I think you should tell Jackie. It will be hard, and she will definitely be angry with you, but she will eventually forgive you," Emma says. "I, on the other hand, will not."

Emma turns to leave, but Frances stops her, catching her arm.

"That's it? You're not going to insist I give you the house for your silence or anything?"

Emma shoves Frances' hand off and looks her square in the eyes.

"I'm not like you, Frances. I'm not going to blackmail you to get what I want. I do think that the right thing to do for everyone would be to sell to Lucas. You will get more money, you and Jackie will never have to worry about money, you can decide where you want to go from here, and the hotel will be in the best possible hands."

Frances sucks in a breath and nods. Emma leaves, the front door slamming behind her. Frances looks up at me, sniffling.

"You won't tell Jackie?"

"I don't think I have a place in this conversation, so I won't say anything. I think Emma covered it pretty well." I give her a grim smile.

"I'll sell you the hotel," Frances stares at me. "I don't want to think about the hotel anymore. I don't think I even want to stay in Santa Fe anymore. There are too many painful memories here."

I pat her shoulder awkwardly.

"I'll gladly buy the hotel from you for the same bid I offered before." I clear my throat. "You should go rest. I'm going to check on Emma."

***

When I step through Emma's door, she's lying in bed just staring at the ceiling. I climb in bed next to her, pulling her into my arms.

"I hate her," she whispers.

"I know."

"I can't live here anymore. I don't care where I go, but I don't want to spend one more day under this roof."

"We can start looking for places," I murmur, stroking her hair gently.

"She killed him and took everything." Emma shakes her head. "Vile. I can't believe Dad ever married a woman like her."

"I don't know what he saw in her, but the great thing about your dad is that he saw the potential in things and in people that hadn't yet been realized. He spent a lot of time improving things instead of giving up on them. Maybe that's what he tried to do with Frances."

Emma sighs.

"Maybe. What do we do now?"

I kiss her cheek.

"Well, we have the hotel. Frances just told me she'd sell to me. Which means it's ours."

Emma turns to me.

"You're serious?" She asks. I nod, and she gives me a small smile. "That's great news."

"It's amazing news. The first step to making things right. I think she might leave, too. We can probably buy the house, too."

Emma shakes her head.

"I don't want the house. I thought I did at first. But this isn't the home I grew up in anymore. Every wall, every surface feels tainted by her touch. I want to move forward with a new house. Create a home for our children that feels like the love my parents had for each other."

I squeeze her tightly.

"That's exactly what we'll do."

Chapter Forty-Three
Emma

Two years later...

I admire my reflection in the mirror, turning to look at the dress from the side. The train is a little longer than I thought it would be, since I went with shorter heels, but the tiny flecks of glitter woven into the lace make it sparkle in the light shining through the window.

"You look amazing," Lily says from behind me, smiling. I pull her in for a hug. It's amusing to me how she bulldozed her way from front desk girl to my very best friend and Maid of Honor.

After Frances had finalized the paperwork for the sale of the hotel to Lucas, I decided to start training Lily as a manager. I knew I'd want to take a maternity leave to spend a few months with the babies and Lucas would have his hands full with a brand new hotel as well as running his entire hotel empire.

"Okay, look, there's Mama!" A voice rings out before throwing open the door to the bridal suite. Jackie strides in with the triplets in a stroller.

After the big confrontation with Frances, it took her a while to come clean to Jackie. Jackie was, understandably, destroyed.

But she picked herself up, went to school to get a real estate license, and has been pretty successful in her work. In her free time, she loves to come hang out with the babies and gossip about what's happening around town.

It's weird to think about how close we've become, especially considering how distant we were for so long, but we've developed a great relationship, and I'm grateful for it and my children have a wonderful aunt in Jackie.

Memories of my dad — and our mutual love for him — connect us more than I would have thought possible.

"Hi, my sweet ones!" I coo, leaning in to kiss each of their foreheads. Annie reaches out her pudgy hands and I laugh, picking her up to hold her for a second.

"You look beautiful, Emma," Jackie says, smiling at me.

"I wanted to come check on you. The wedding planner is fixing the florals— I guess the arrangements were the wrong shape— but she wanted me to tell you that the ceremony starts in thirty minutes."

"Thank you. I can't believe I'm getting married today," I say giddily. Lucas proposed to me in the same beautiful gazebo where I told him I was pregnant.

We wanted to get married there, but they tore it down two months after we got engaged. I was devastated at first, but we decided that the perfect place to marry would be the gardens at The Signature, and the venue is beautiful.

"It's going to be perfect." Jackie's phone beeps and she looks down. "All right, I have to go and get the babies prepped to join the wedding party. See you soon."

I set Annie back in the stroller and gently tap the other two on the nose. When we were discussing names, we had a tough time choosing. Coming up with one would have been overwhelming enough, but three?

We went back and forth for a long time, only making our final decisions on the day they were born.

But eventually we settled on the perfect ones. Clark Alexander, for my father. Kara Ginnifer, for my mom. And Anna Carleen, for Lucas' mother.

Clark is the spitting image of Lucas, but Kara and Anna are a combination of us both in the opposite way. Anna has red hair and blue eyes, while Kara has dark hair and brown eyes. It's like the universe gave us every possible combination it could think of.

"You okay?" Lily asks, pushing a flyaway hair back into my long braid. I sigh.

"I just wish my parents could be here for this. I was never the kind of girl who dreamed about my wedding day, but I still wish they were here."

Lily squeezes my hand. "Of course you do. It would be very strange if you felt any other way. I can't imagine how hard it is. I bet, though, that they're here in spirit."

Lily smiles at me through the mirror, and I smile back. I'm sure she's right. Mom and Dad wouldn't miss my wedding for the world.

"Ready to walk down the aisle?"

"Absolutely."

Music starts up as I come from behind the partition and start down the garden's stone pathway.

It's a simple melody, played by a string quartet tucked discreetly back beside the fern garden in the shade and they fill the small garden with magic.

I clutch my bouquet, glancing down at the cascading lilies, lilacs, and white roses. The exact same flowers Dad brought Mom for their first date and the same flowers we can see now in bloom throughout The Signature's garden.

Mom used to love telling me about how he showed up with this outrageously enormous bouquet. It felt natural for this for me to carry this down the aisle in her memory.

I look up, and my eyes immediately land on Lucas.

He stands to the side of the beautifully decorated arch, tears in his eyes as he watches me make my way down the aisle.

His dark hair is neatly combed, though one rebellious strand has popped out and curls on his forehead. His bright blue eyes find mine, and the smile that spreads across his face makes my heart tumble over itself.

He almost looks surprised, as if he can't believe this moment is finally here.

Honestly, I can't quite believe it either. Everything felt against us, but we managed to get through it all together.

"You look beautiful," Lucas mouths as I approach. I smile, tears threatening to prick at my eyes. I've never loved anyone the way that I love Lucas.

The officiant starts speaking, but I honestly barely hear the words.

I stare into Lucas' eyes, rehearsing my vows in my head.

It was important to us to write our own, and I'm hoping that mine are good enough to let Lucas know how I really feel. Not that we necessarily need vows to do that— we both show each other how much we love each other every single day.

Still, there is something beautiful about stepping up in front of all the most important people in our lives, and declaring to each other just how much we believe in our love.

"The couple has chosen to read their own vows. Emma, would you like to start?" the officiant asks, turning to me. I smile and nod as I begin.

"Lucas," I start.

My voice cracks, so I clear it and start again. "Lucas, I never thought much about perfect timing before I met you. But you came into my life when I least expected it, and right when I needed you the most. I don't know if you even realize how much you have changed my life. I promise to be your partner in every aspect of life— to wipe your tears when you're sad, kiss your cheeks when you're happy, and to be the good cop to your bad cop whenever the kids get up to any sort of trouble."

Laughter ripples through the small crowd.

"I love you so much more than you could ever know. Thank you so much for finding me and becoming mine."

Lucas' smile wobbles and he blinks away tears. He reaches out, his fingers brushing mine before he takes a deep breath and pulls a piece of paper out of his pocket. He turns to the crowd.

"Emma apparently has a far superior memory, since she was able to remember her vows, but I am not as talented."

He turns back to me. "I rehearsed this a thousand times, but now that you're standing here in front of me, looking more beautiful than I could have ever imagined, I've forgotten every single line."

More laughter escapes our guests, and I can't help but roll my eyes.

"Emma, I promise to be the person who makes your coffee just the way you like it every morning, even when I'm exhausted. I promise to hold your hand in every storm, to dance with you at every gala, and to always, always show up for you, and for our children, every single day."

He swallows, his voice shaky. "Before I met you, I was going through the motions. You've taught me what it means to live fully in every moment and to love without hesitation. You are my best friend, my favorite person, and now, through some miracle, my wife."

He folds the paper up and shoves it back in his pocket.

"I don't need a paper to tell you that I will spend every second of every day making sure you never regret choosing me."

The tears are streaming down my cheeks now, and I'm so grateful the makeup artist used a waterproof mascara. The officiant makes a mention of the rings and Lily steps up, handing Lucas and me our rings. Lucas slides the beautiful platinum diamond ring over my finger and I slide a plain platinum band on his.

"By the power vested in me by the state of New Mexico," the officiant announces, "I now pronounce you husband and wife. Lucas, you may now kiss the bride."

True to his vows, Lucas doesn't hesitate. He pulls me close, a hand cradling my face as his lips meet mine. He pulls me closer, deepening the kiss. The garden erupts in applause, but all I can focus on is the feelings of his arms around me, the taste of his lips on mine, and how the sun feels just a little bit brighter than it usually does, as if the heavens, and my mother and father, are celebrating along with us.

***

"And now the beautiful couple will have their first dance," the emcee announces before pressing a button. As the first notes of Etta James' "At Last" play over the speakers, Lucas leads me to the dance floor.

He spins me and leans in close.

"What did you think of the wedding?" he asks, nuzzling my neck.

This is the first time we've really had a moment to talk to each other, given the chaos of the day.

"It was absolutely perfect. Your vows were amazing."

Lucas chuckles.

"It was your vows that were amazing. I can't believe you memorized them."

"Well, my dress doesn't have pockets. I wasn't about to pull my vows from my cleavage," I joke.

He smiles as we rock back and forth to the rhythm of the music. "I'm so excited about the honeymoon. A week in St. Lucia. It's like a dream."

We haven't traveled much since the triplets were born. In fact, the farthest we've been able to travel was to Albuquerque for the hot air balloon festival. We've made it an annual tradition and we stay in the original Airbnb we found that first year.

"St. Lucia will be beautiful," Lucas nods. "But anywhere we go will be a dream as long as you're there with me."

"Cheesy," I tease, kissing him on the nose. I frown.

"Do you really think Lily and Jackie can handle the triplets? I worry they're in over their heads."

"They'll be fine. The nanny will be doing most of the work, and Lily and Jackie are great with the kids."

I sigh, and Lucas lifts my chin.

"Hey, what's on your mind?"

"I don't know, I guess... Life is so much harder without either of our parents around. And I guess I just wish they could be with us, especially today. I wish Dad could have walked me down the aisle and Mom could have fluffed my dress and cried during our vows."

Lucas smiles sympathetically.

"I know it's hard, but I really do think they're here with us. I felt your dad's love and your mom's calmness surrounding us the entire day."

I look up at Lucas and consider his words. And then I nod. Lily said something similar, but most of all, I agree.

"That was a beautiful first dance, let's give it up for the bride and groom, Mr. and Mrs. Lucas Bennett!"

Our wedding crowd erupts in applause, and then the energy shifts as people crowd onto the dance floor with the thumping beat of the music. Lily shimmies up to me, and I laugh at the goofy disco dance she attempts.

"Come on, you know you want to do the Q-tip!" she shouts over the music. Lucas follows suit, throwing it away until I'm laughing uncontrollably.

Lucas is definitely right. Whether they know it or not, my parents' infectious positive energy is ever present at our wedding.

Chapter Forty-Four
Lucas

Emma and I lay side by side, looking up at the stars above us. The beach behind our cabana is secluded enough that we've spent at least a few hours every day out here, although this is the first time we've been out here at night. The night swim was her idea, and drying out on the picnic blanket afterward was mine.

"I can't believe it's our last night here," Emma says, sighing heavily. "This whole honeymoon has been like a dream."

"It truly has. I've enjoyed this time with you more than you know." I turn to face her. Emma smiles, running her fingers along my bare chest. I catch her hand and kiss it. "Your fingers are cold."

"Drying off after a swim makes me a little chilly."

"Here, I'll help," I murmur, bringing her hands up and kissing them against the warmth of my lips.

A heat ignites behind her eyes and she smiles shyly.

"I can think of another way you can warm me up," she says, looking directly into my eyes.

She bites her lip, a teasing habit I've come to adore.

"Is that so?" I whisper, kissing her cheek and moving slowly down her neck. She shivers, inching closer until our bodies are touching, the thin fabric of our swimsuits leaving little to the imagination.

Her skin is cool, but somehow her body feels warm against mine, sending little zings of excitement through my entire body.

"Absolutely," she whispers back.

I slowly run my hand down her back and around the curve of her hip, bringing my palm to rest gently on her thigh. My fingers graze against the inside silky skin, and I savor the way she shudders in response.

I lean in, pressing my lips against hers with urgency. Gentleness has been out of the question for the entirety of our honeymoon, with passion replacing the sweetness that usually takes precedence when we have sex, especially during the time she was pregnant with the triplets.

Emma's mouth opens to mine, our tongues tangling together and darting around each other. My fingers find the strings on her bikini, and I untie it deftly before moving onto the other one.

Then I move my hand to caress between her legs, finding that her soft folds are slick with desire.

A moan escapes Emma's lips as I carefully slip a finger inside her, feeling her warmth and wetness. I add another finger, pushing in and out of her with increasing speed. Emma's moans echo in the night as if playing a symphony for which she and I are the only audience.

When her breath begins getting heavy, I slow down slightly. Emma grunts in frustration, but I only chuckle.

"Be patient," I murmur, licking down her body with my tongue flat against her. Her skin tastes salty and tantalizing from our time swimming, and I savor the taste until my mouth meets where my fingers are inside her.

I lick at her clit and her back arches. I grin devilishly before picking the speed back up, both inside and out.

"Oh, Lucas," Emma calls out, her hips bucking down to meet my fingers with every thrust. I feel her warmth tighten around them as she moans, orgasm overtaking her. I don't stop moving until she's done. Her eyes flutter open and she looks at me with raw desire.

"Your turn."

Emma pushes me down against the towel, her hands drifting down my body as she looks down at me. She reaches my hips and quickly gets rid of my swim trunks. Then she grasps my hips before the excruciating graze of a single finger circles the base of my erection.

I suck in a breath as I quiver with need, desperate to feel her entire hand around my length.

Instead, she winks at me and sinks her mouth over the head, swirling her tongue so expertly that I let out a noise. I wrap my fingers in her hair and grip it softly so I can watch as

Emma's mouth sinks further down on my length, engulfing me completely in her warmth.

My head tips back against the soft sand as she bobs up and down on my hardness, swirling her tongue along the tip with each ascension.

After all our time together, she knows exactly what turns me on.

Just when I think I can't take anymore of her delicious torture, Emma releases me, breaking the suction with an audible noise.

Her eyes, dark with desire, don't leave mine as she crawls up my body. I didn't know it was possible to become harder than I already was, but watching her do that definitely did it. The moonlight bathes her skin in silver rays, making her look ethereal in the soft glow.

"I want to feel you," she whispers, leaning down close to my ear.

She positions herself above me, her thighs on either side of my hips. Heat radiates from her core, so close to where my body aches for her to be. Emma reaches between us, wrapping her delicate fingers around my pulsing hardness and guides me to her entrance.

The anticipation is almost unbearable as she teases herself with the tip, sliding it through her wet folds.

"Emma," I groan, my hands gripping her hips.

With deliberate slowness, she starts to sink down onto me. The sensation is almost overwhelming— her exquisite heat engulfing me inch by inch.

I watch, mesmerized, as her body accepts mine, joining us in the most intimate way possible. Her lips part in a gasp as she takes me completely, her eyes closing with pleasure.

"I love the way you feel around me," I say.

I can't take my eyes off her body. Emma leans forward and places her palms against my chest, using it as leverage as she begins to move. She rises up until just the tip remains inside, then slides back down in one fluid moment that leaves us both gasping. The rhythm she sets at first is unhurried— a tantalizing rise and fall that allows us to savor every sensation.

Her flaming red hair falls around her face as she moves above me, catching the moonlight in its waves. I brush it back, wanting to see every expression she makes as she moves so magically above me. Her eyes are half-lidded, her cheeks flushed from pleasure.

I love watching her like this. My hands roam her body from her thighs up to her breasts, cupping her breast over the swim top and admiring their perfect weight in my hands.

Emma moans, her pace quickening in response. She rolls her hips and I'm seeing stars, an involuntary moan leaving me as she grinds against me with each downward stroke. The sound of our breathing synchronizes with the crash of the waves behind us.

I thrust upward to meet her and she cries out.

Our bodies move together in perfect harmony as we find a rhythm that builds the pressure inside us both. Emma's thighs start to tremble, a sure sign that she's close, and I work my hand between us until my thumb finds the sensitive bundle of nerves there.

"Yes!" Emma's inner walls flutter around me as I circle the spot with increasing pressure.

Her movements become erratic, almost desperate. She throws her head back, exposing her throat as she rides me with reckless abandon.

The sight of her, wild and inhibited above me, combined with the incredible sensation of her tight heat pulsating around me, is enough to push me dangerously close to the edge.

"Emma," I groan, digging my fingers into her hips. "I'm not going to last much longer if you keep going like this."

She leans down to kiss me, rocking her hips as she whispers against my lips.

"Then don't," she responds.

It's all the permission I need. I wrap my arms around her, holding her tight against me as I thrust upward with renewed vigor. The angle changes, hitting a spot inside her that makes her gasp and clutch at my shoulders. "Oh, God, Lucas, right there!"

Her body tenses, her inner muscles clenching around me as she reaches her peak. Her moans of pleasure echo around the empty beach as she shudders in my arms.

The sight of her, coming undone in her orgasm tips me past the edge. With one final thrust, I bury myself deep within her and release my own waves of pleasure.

We remain locked together for several moments, trembling from aftershocks. Then Emma collapses against my chest, her skin dewy with sweat. I wrap my arms around her and pull her close, our hearts gradually slowing as we relax into each other.

A comfortable silence hangs over us as we lay together, collecting ourselves while also drawing out our time together. I run my fingers through her hair as I stare up at the stars.

"Are you sad we have to leave tomorrow?" I murmur.

"Hmmm," Emma says, tapping her fingers against my chest thoughtfully. "I wouldn't say I'm sad. I love it here, and this is the best honeymoon we could have hoped for. But I'm excited to get home and get back to the kids."

I smile, thinking about what the little rascals might be getting up to right now.

"Me, too. I miss them."

Emma nods and then looks up at me, gazing deeply into my eyes.

"I've loved our honeymoon so much. But the life I live with you every single day is my very best life."

I smile back, and then our lips collide in a kiss that is filled with every shared moment of sadness, hope, and love we've ever experienced.

THE END

Thank you for reading! Care to make my day?
An honest review would be the cherry on top of this author's sundae and most appreciated!
Your thoughts can help other readers decide on their own next great read.

If you enjoyed the story of Lucas and Emma, you can find your next book boyfriend in
another Claire Kirby steamy romance!
Don't miss "Once Upon A One Night Stand"
a steamy, age gap, secret pregnancy, unputdownable romance with a great HEA!
Available now and FREE on Kindle Unlimited!

His command was absolute, both in the courtroom and the bedroom.
Now I have a blue-eyed three-year-old secret he's about to discover.

I knew taking a job at Lambert & Associates meant serving New York's most formidable legal tyrant.

What I never calculated was surrendering my innocent body
on his leather couch—
or fleeing Manhattan with his heir growing inside me.

Then three years of carefully constructed distance is
shattered by one merger announcement.

When Trevor's penetrating gaze lands on my daughter's
photo,
recognition blazes across his face like summer lightning.

As he navigates fatherhood with the same intensity he
commands his empire,
our chemistry ignites hotter than before—
a dangerous flame neither of us can extinguish, nor fully
embrace.

Now Trevor battles for us both against his calculating father,
a man who sees Charlotte as a dynasty continuation,
not the granddaughter who giggles at butterfly kisses.

The ruthless billionaire who once seduced me now stands at
a crossroads between the cold legacy
he was bred for and the messy, beautiful family that has
blindsided his heart.

As he shields us from his father's poisonous influence, I
witness the wounded child beneath the power suit—
and realize our one-night mistake is actually destiny's most
perfect beginning...

Made in United States
North Haven, CT
18 July 2025

70808505R00267